DIG MY GRAVE DEEP

Daniel Port works for Stoker as his number two man, the brains behind
all the crooked deals that's kept Stoker's gang going for years. But
there's a new set-up in town, a supposed reform party led by Bellamy.
Trouble is, Bellamy's worse than Stoker and Port wants out of the whole
rotten mess. But Stoker needs him and won't let him go, and Bellamy is
putting a lot of pressure on Port to force him to join his side. All Port
wants is a ticket out of town, with Shelly by his side. What he's got to
do to make it happen is put together one more deal for Stoker. First
though, he's got to get around George and Kirby, Bellamy's bully boys;
and Fries, Stoker's fiercely loyal heir apparent. Then there's Calvin,
Shelly's kid brother, who wants to be a big shot. Port's got a lot riding
on this deal—it could just be the deal of his life.

THE OUT IS DEATH

Abe Dalton has been in the joint too long. Now that he's out, the aging
safecracker wants to stay out. But Dicky Corday has other plans.
Holding an old job over his head, Corday forces Dalton to help him
plan a robbery at the Newton plant. Dalton is desperate, and calls on
his old friend, Dan Port, to help him get out of the deal. Port comes to
town and sets up a meeting with Corday. But Corday's obsessed and
this job is going to happen no matter what. Corday won't be stopped—
not by Port, meddling in Corday's business; not Dalton, trying to work
his way out of his promise; and not his woman, Letty, who finds a
certain sympathy with Port, who treats her better than Corday ever has.
Port soon gets more than he bargained for with Corday—behind his
bullying lurks the promise of madness.

IT'S MY FUNERAL

Turning his back on his past, Port heads to Los Angeles where no one
knows him. Or so he thinks. An unpleasant face from his past appears,
and it's Joko Mulnik, part of that past he thought he'd left behind.
What luck for Mulnik finding Port—he's perfect for a deal he's setting
up. Mulnik is promoting new talent but when he shows Port his new
set-up, along with it comes a nice little blackmail job as well. Mulnik's
got some compromising pictures of a studio's biggest star, and he wants
Port to broker the deal. Port wants nothing to do with Mulnik or his
seedy schemes, but he gets pulled into the scheme anyway. f.
fall guy, then as the actress's white knig]
you can never escape your past.

PETER RABE BIBLIOGRAPHY

From Here to Maternity (1955)
Stop This Man! (1955)
Benny Muscles In (1955)
A Shroud for Jesso (1955)
A House in Naples (1956)
Kill the Boss Good-by (1956)
Dig My Grave Deep (1956) *
The Out is Death (1957) *
Agreement to Kill (1957)
It's My Funeral (1957) *
Journey Into Terror (1957)
Mission for Vengeance (1958)
Blood on the Desert (1958)
The Cut of the Whip (1958) *
Bring Me Another
    Corpse (1959) *
Time Enough to Die (1959) *
Anatomy of a Killer (1960)
My Lovely Executioner (1960)
Murder Me for Nickels (1960)
The Box (1962)
His Neighbor's Wife (1962)
Girl in a Big Brass Bed (1965) **
The Spy Who Was
    Three Feet Tall (1966) **

Code Name Gadget (1967) **
Tobruk (1967)
War of the Dons (1972)
Black Mafia (1974)
The Silent Wall (2011)
The Return of
    Marvin Palaver (2011)

*Daniel Port series
**Manny DeWitt series

As by "Marco Malaponte"
New Man in the House (1963)
Her High-School Lover (1963)

As by "J. T. MacCargo"
Mannix #2: A Fine Day for Dying
    (1975)
Mannix #4: Round Trip to
    Nowhere (1975)

Short Stories
"Hard Case Redhead"
    (*Mystery Tales*, 1959)
"A Matter of Balance"
    (*Story*, 1961)

DANIEL PORT OMNIBUS 1

Dig My Grave Deep
The Out is Death
It's My Funeral

Three Novels by
Peter Rabe

STARK
HOUSE

Stark House Press • Eureka California

DANIEL PORT OMINBUS 1: DIG MY GRAVE DEEP /
THE OUT IS DEATH / IT'S MY FUNERAL

Published by Stark House Press
1315 H Street
Eureka, CA 95501
griffinskye3@sbcglobal.net
www.starkhousepress.com

ISBN: 1-933586-65-6
ISBN-13: 978-1-933586-65-6

Cover design and layout by Mark Shepard, www.shepgraphics.com
Proofreading by Rick Ollerman

First Stark House Press Edition: November 2014

Contents

Danny and Manny: The Series Characters of Peter Rabe
by Rick Ollerman

Peter Rabe was anything but a formula writer. He didn't follow any sort of rules from book to book: he didn't re-use or recycle the same structure or foundation for events, and his characters were always different, even if they were in the same profession. When he wrote about mobsters or killers or other sorts of bad men, they weren't the same mobsters, killers or bad men. They were unique characters placed in settings particular to them.

To one degree or another his characters tended to have a moral ambiguity to them, conflicted and torn on the inside, not knowing what it took to get what they wanted. There were always others standing in their own way, unintentionally or not. Bad guys were clearly more interesting to Rabe, though it may be more accurate to say his protagonists were always a combination of good and bad traits. No on was wholly good and no one was wholly bad. In any case, no two of them were alike.

Rabe focused on writing the books and the characters that he himself found so fascinating. Free from the walls of a self-imposed and repeating structure, he gave himself the ability to explore new stories with new characters in each succeeding book. Rabe was a writer's writer who wasn't trying to lock in on *the* narrative formula that would bring him a certain success. This allowed him to explore and express whatever it was that a particular book needed to say. And to do it in the specific voice of each character.

Widespread success or bestsellerdom may have eluded him—the genre lists of today are filled with more or less copycat books that follow or repeat the same formula—but the integrity and skill to pull it off so well is precisely the reason his work is as well-regarded and influential as it is today. The twenty-sixth entry in the *x* series may follow previous numbers to the NYT top ten, but it is likely a cookie cutter version of the books preceding it. Series like this are successful because readers know what to expect, they're comfortable with the set pieces. For a writer like Rabe, giving comfort was not in his mind. Writing provocative and engaging stories—and characters—that haven't been seen before, was.

When Rabe published his sixth novel, *Dig My Grave Deep* (1956), it featured a man he called Daniel Port, a political "fixer" or ward heeler for an organization headed by an old and unwell man. Rabe had planned on writing a series at some point but he hadn't intended Port to be the featured character. As he told George Tuttle in a 1989 interview, "it was an arbitrary decision." Indeed, as the series of six books played out, Port carried on a much different role in each successive book. He was always the same man, he had the same strengths and weaknesses, but what was interesting was how he used those skills in some very different situations.

Like Wade Miller's character of Steve Beck from 1949's *Devil on Two Sticks*, Port works for a crooked organization and is thus by definition a crook himself, but both men are actually much more than that. They are smarter than their respective bosses and without them it would be highly unlikely their employers would last or be as successful as they otherwise would. Beck and Port know where the bodies are buried, though in most cases they didn't put them there themselves. Even if they had, no one else in the organization would know about it. They are the keepers of others' secrets; no one keeps theirs.

Each of them could probably very easily have taken over the top spot if they wanted, realizing their bosses' biggest fears, but this wouldn't serve their purposes. In fact, probably the biggest differences between these men, these fixers, and their wholly corrupted bosses, is that to them, what they do is just a job. A job that only they can do. They get paid all they want (or usually enough), they have at least the grudging respect of every man in their organizations, but above all they fool themselves in two very important ways: they think they're not as bad as everybody else in the mob, and they think that they can walk away whenever they want. They don't see themselves as the same *kind* of criminal as those around them.

Without their egos they couldn't do what they do, but those egos often lead to significant blind spots. They keep hidden the resentment from the rank and file mobsters, the ones who feel they're tougher and dirtier than these pretty boys who are the bosses' favorites. It's easy for the influential fixer to find someone to push a gun for them; much harder to conceive of someone who won't push one back at them.

A delicate balance is struck. The boss gives a man like Beck or Port respect, money, and not insignificantly, freedom to act independently in the boss's interest, and he gets what he wants in return: the votes, the influence, the other men in line, support where he needs it. These men make things happen, they keep the boss on top. On the other side, though, is that these fixers can never be fully trusted. It's against the criminals' nature. The boss knows his man could outsmart him if he wanted, possibly even take over, but he has to believe that his man is acting in ways that he himself can't understand. After all, the boss likely got to be the boss because he pushed someone else out. He finds it difficult to believe that someone else, someone actually more capable, wouldn't want to do the same to him.

In Beck's case, his boss's suspicions cause him trouble, but ultimately he undoes himself because of a woman. Rabe's Daniel Port wants out but he doesn't want to betray his friend and boss, Stoker, a man who gave him a break when he was coming up. But Stoker's a man who is now very sick and he doesn't want to let Port go because he sees how much the organization will need him when Stoker's gone.

It's not just Port's boss that's the problem, though. Fries is next in line for Stoker's top job, or so he thinks, but he knows he can't stick without Port's help. While Port agrees to one last task for Stoker, Fries refuses to accept this and is willing to use the full force of the organization to get his way.

But the fixer's main attribute is his resourcefulness, his ability to see things and make connections where others don't, and this extends to his own situation as well. Fries can try his best but his strongarm methods are exactly the tactics a man like Port finds easiest to maneuver around. His is the world of brains, not brawn.

Dig My Grave Deep follows Rabe's own *Kill the Boss Good-by* (1956), a book Donald E. Westlake called "one of the most purely *interesting* crime novels ever written," another mob-centered story about succession though told in an entirely different manner. Both are among Rabe's best books, but that list would include so many of his more than thirty that it makes that label almost meaningless.

In *Kill the Boss*, it's the situation of the character that matters—a boss suffering a mental breakdown while trying to hold tight the reins of his organization—but in *Dig My Grave* the book is more about Port himself and the omnipresent question of 'will he or won't he?' or perhaps 'can he or can't he?' And the story is told in the way that only Rabe, as unique a stylist as we have from the paperback original world, can tell.

In no way does *Dig My Grave Deep* read like the opening book in a series. There is an unresolved situation at the very end that would have worked very well as an open or ambiguous question, almost a trifling thing, that could have led to a "next" book. If the "arbitrary decision" to make Port the star of a series was made here, the reader could point to the paragraph where it was made. There's almost a tacked on feeling to the last few hundred words that seem to exist only to give Port a reason to go on in another book. That next book, though, turns out to be *The Out is Death* (1957) and no mention is made of the final question in *Dig My Grave Deep*. It's as though we've all moved on, which is fine—the unpredictability, another hallmark of Rabe's novels, comes off much better this way.

With the second book in this almost anti-series of Daniel Port stories, Port seems to have achieved the mythical, unheard of status among the underworld of the man who got out, the man who left an organization where, like the title of the second book implies, the only way out is death. Once you're in the organization, your ability to make that choice is forfeit. But Port has succeeded, again outsmarting the mob and forcing them to allow him to walk away.

Port is a traveler throughout the rest of the series, never going back to his original stomping grounds in Chicago but instead moving from place to place, doing different things but, most importantly, always being Daniel Port. Which doesn't always work out so well for him. No longer the untouchable criminal, his ego is still far larger than the average man's.

This is another way of saying that Rabe does not allow the changing of Port's situation to change the character of Port himself. This is significant as each book in the series offers something new; none of the books is a repeat of any of the others. Only Port remains the same, and that is what makes this series different from most others: each plot is its own, each could very nearly be a standalone book. This is not the same character doing the same thing only in a different locale or setting. Far from it. If the first book gives us the story of how Dan Port became Dan Port, *The Out is Death* shows us what it's like for him to discover how to attempt to exist outside of his old life. Later, the third book shows us something different again, an episode where he is much more at ease with his new situation but happy to draw on his past as needed.

Despite his fame or his infamy in the underworld, not everyone respects or admires what he's been able to do. These are career criminals, men who would kill to have achieved a fraction of what Port has chosen to give up, and some fear him for it while others look down on him—they don't understand—and try to use him.

Abe Dalton is an old man, not long out of prison, who wants nothing more than to go home and spend his failing years in peace. Dicky Corday is a man who wants something only Dalton can give him, no matter that Dalton may be too weak to actually deliver. Corday intends to have the man's help even if it means Dalton won't survive. And Corday has the leverage to make it happen.

As his last and only resort, Dalton contacts Port, who shows up just in time, bringing with him that supreme confidence in his own abilities, and he tells

Dalton not to worry. Corday is a punk, a nobody, and for a while at least, Dalton is relieved. If a man like Port says a small-timer like Corday is nothing.... But a punk is still a punk, and can be mean and vicious, a man who in his own way has just as much confidence in himself as does Dan Port. Port may be able to play the long game, to see three or four moves ahead, but that doesn't mean he's always right, or that he can't underestimate the sheer unwillingness of his foe to admit defeat. What Port thinks might be a simple task may be just that, but that doesn't make it easy when his opponents may not see the wisdom in playing by Port's rules.

If there's a higher-tone feel to *Dig My Grave Deep*, there is a much grittier texture to *The Out is Death*. Port's job is an ugly one, trying to save an old man from the sins of his past amidst the clutches of a true lowlife. It's a book that seems like it's always deep in the night, always raining, and always taking place on unclean streets in a working class town. It's a sort of good vs. evil battle taking place in the dirt under our feet.

If *Dig My Grave Deep* is most similar to a David Goodis novel, then the third book in the series, *It's My Funeral* (1957), reads like Rabe doing a fine Harry Whittington impersonation, with plot turn after plot turn coming at an almost breakneck pace. There's a new town, another rubbing up against former associates, and more having to prove himself in a situation that he initially thinks will be an easy thing to wrap up. Perhaps because he'd spent his criminal career mostly above the ranks of the violently sociopathic he tends to overlook what these criminal opponents are capable of and who they truly are. Port believes he's a giant. His penny ante opponents think he's vulnerable—after all, why else would he have walked away when he could have reached the absolute top? In a way, neither one ever fully understands the other.

In *It's My Funeral* Rabe takes Port to Hollywood and his original mission, one that is constantly interrupted throughout the book, is merely to get closer romantically to a singer named Tess Dolphin. This shows Rabe's offbeat humor as time and again Port's assignations are thwarted by one party or another, and a common theme throughout the book is whether Port can finally buck this trend and finally get the girl. Mostly though, the book is a continual change of scenery amid a series of plot twists and is a much sunnier, much more optimistic book than the previous entry. Ironically, Rabe himself said he was sick much of the time during the writing and says he found the writing of the book "oddly difficult." This isn't easy to see, however, especially since it was in the previous book, *Dig My Grave Deep,* that death, fatalism and lingering illness were so prevalent.

As a character, Daniel Port is very different from Rabe's other series hero, Manny DeWitt, star of *Girl in a Big Brass Bed* (1965), *The Spy Who Was Three Feet Tall* 1966) and *Code Name Gadget* (1967). Where Port charges ahead either in response to a call for help or because his own code of ethics demands it, DeWitt is a lawyer and troubleshooter for a Dutch industrialist named Hans Lobbe. Where Port is the master of his own destiny, DeWitt is at the mercy of Lobbe, sent all over the world ostensibly to take care of one matter that quite often turns into something else entirely. Port makes his own way; DeWitt has to grope for his, often without the complete information or confidence of his boss. He knows, or at least suspects, that he never quite has the whole story. Port is a free agent, his own man, and Manny DeWitt functions more or less as a James Bond sort of industrial spy. He just may not know all the rules.

Rabe told Tuttle that he had "no particular feeling for spy fiction" although I think he had very much disproved that with the earlier novel *Blood on the Desert* (1958), featuring spy-extraordinaire Anthony Wheeler, a character straight out of the mold of Len Deighton. A wonderful story of a rumored shipment of contraband, Wheeler, a white man in the deserts of Tunisia, is charged with discovering exactly who is involved, how to stop it, and ultimately how to prevent a war. Not knowing who he can trust, he's very much on his own, similar to Daniel Port and Manny DeWitt, but he's much more competent in his chosen field, and he's playing ahead in a game that even his bosses don't fully understand.

More than spy fiction, the DeWitt series shows off a really bizarre aspect of Rabe's sense of humor, which is spread throughout each of the three books. Rabe told Tuttle that the books had "a very self-conscious humor" and I take that to mean that at the time of their writing, Rabe appreciated the sort of wry commentary he was portraying in the books, but later came to see that as some sort of flaw with the narratives, as evidenced by the fact that he told Tuttle that in his view the books actually "fall short."

The DeWitt books are somewhat less successful than the Daniel Port series. For one thing, they are not nearly as varied in plot and tone. They have much more in common to what we usually think of as a series than do the Port books. DeWitt's purpose is to facilitate Lobbe's objectives, though he may not always be fully aware of what they are. He fully belongs to Lobbe though we often wonder why. But as a series of similar adventures, the "series" aspect of these books is much more defined. As a sequence their cohesion is more evident than in the Port stories.

Daniel Port becomes sort of an underworld Richard Kimball, moving from place to place, not to stay ahead of the law or look for a one-armed man, but because what he wanted from the mob was his freedom; once he achieved it he became his own man, able to roam. And often, he helps people, though the methods learned from his previous career are the tools he uses to do so. Port is beholden to no one. DeWitt, on the other hand, belongs to Hans Lobbe.

In 1960—after the Port books but before the DeWitt series—Rabe wrote another of what should be counted among his finest works: *Murder Me for Nickels*. There is humor in that book also but not the strange, hard to fathom sort that later appears in the DeWitt stories. And there's also another "fixer" type character, this time a man named Jack St. Louis.

St. Louis works for a man who controls the jukebox business in town, the kind where an establishment is told just how many machines they're going to place in their business and just how much they're going to make from them—and how much they're going to pay. The jukes were big business back then, serving as a sort of protection racket, and when another mob tries to muscle in on St. Louis's territory, he's the one charged with keeping them out and his boss's racket on top. All this is complicated by St. Louis's relationship with the boss himself—not as strong as the Port/Stoker relationship—and not incidentally with the boss's wife, an ambitious though light on talent lounge singer. At least as far as her music is concerned.

In Port's first book, he stays around longer than he'd like out of respect for his boss and the fact that he'd made him a promise. St. Louis has a rockier relationship with his own boss, Walter Lippitt. There's not the same sort of friendship that binds the two men and when things get tough in the business, they get messier for St. Louis. Though there is danger for both, Port works on disengaging while St. Louis is focused on staying alive.

In significant ways, though, they are similar characters. Port's a bit tougher, more ruthless, perhaps too much the romantic, and St. Louis is the lover, still tough but maybe just a bit too easily distracted. Port comes from a larger mob; St. Louis is more of a local operator. Rabe has shown us what he could do with series about Port and DeWitt, but one can't help but wonder how he would have seen Jack St. Louis in a series: as a more accessible Port-like character? Was he a conscious refinement or modification of Daniel Port? It's something we'll never know.

Comparing the character of Manny DeWitt to Anthony Wheeler may be easier. Where Wheeler is a highly competent super-spy, DeWitt is a reluctant one, though no less resourceful for that. Neither man fully relies on the word of his superiors, but where Lobbe is never entirely sure how to pro-

ceed, Wheeler seems quite capable of forging his own path with some degree of confidence. Less a James Bond and more of a George Smiley, Wheeler
would have been an excellent candidate for another series. Based on *Blood
on the Desert,* one could easily imagine how that series could have brought
fame enough in that genre to perhaps rival someone like John LeCarre.

It is difficult to see which others of Rabe's creations could have stood up
to starring in multiple books. Rabe wrote about far too many anti-heroes or
bad guys, characters who rose to their level of incompetence and had fallen
so much that by the end of their books there may not have been much left
to write about later. Perhaps the most intriguing candidate would be the
mob-ousted lawyer Quinn, stranded in the African port city of Okar and left
for dead. By the end of his story in perhaps Rabe's very best book, 1962's
The Box, Rabe gives us that rare ambiguous ending—we don't know where
Quinn is or where he might turn up next. That's assuming he's even still
alive. The ending is so enigmatic that Rabe left anything possible.

In the end, over the length of his career, what we can say is that Rabe did
manage to give us two distinct series. One contains at least one of his best
books and several very good ones, and the other is arguably less successful
as the offbeat humor, the strange struggle between boss Lobbe and his trou-
bleshooter/spy DeWitt may leave readers scratching their heads maybe just
a bit too much wondering exactly as to the nature of DeWitt and his activities. In this case, the exceptional Rabe may have been playing a bit too clever
for his readers' comfort.

Still, though, it's the characters that Rabe gives us that are so memorable.
It's the trademarked Rabe ability to go where only he can go, to deliver that
unpredicted yet perfect note where another author might present the
telegraphed and expected every time. This is why Rabe is not easy, not in
the way of endless entries in faceless series: each of his books are different.
Every book in the Port series can stand alone, not because all the information from previous books is encapsulated in each text, but because the setting, the goal—what the character wants—is different in each book. The
plots are not the same.

The DeWitt series, on the other hand, is something different. It works as
almost three facets of the same experiment, Rabe playing the scientist
who's not quite willing to give up on a hypothesis even when it doesn't quite
seem to prove out.

When you read the Daniel Port series, see if you agree. If you have a mind
to compare, read about Jack St. Louis in *Murder Me for Nickels* and follow it

up with Steve Beck's story in Wade Miller's *Devil on Two Sticks*. I would love to identify more books about these fixer types, the men who could be king but for reasons of their own, devote their loyalties to lesser men.

But then get back to reading the Port series. Every book is different, every book is its own adventure. That's what we get with Port over characters like St. Louis and Wheeler: more stories, more different adventures. And with a writer like Peter Rabe, it's never enough....

—June, 2014
Littleton, NH

Sources:
Tuttle, George, "A Too Brief Conversation with Peter Rabe," *The Big Book of Noir,* ed. by Ed Gorman, Lee Server, Martin H. Greenberg, Carroll & Graf, 1998

Dig My Grave Deep
by Peter Rabe

Chapter 1

At seven in the morning he turned over in bed and woke up. There was a cup of cold coffee on the night-stand next to his bed. He swung his legs to the floor, drank the coffee, and looked across the room with no show of interest. He could have lived there a week or a year—the room didn't tell—or maybe he didn't spend time there. He put the empty cup down and went to take a shower, after which he got dressed. At seven-thirty, when he opened the door to go out, the phone started ringing. It rang three times while he looked at it and moved his mouth to whistle. He walked out of the room and closed the door. The phone was still ringing when he went downstairs.

After a two-block walk he stopped at the glass and tile front with the big sign that said *United* and went in. There was a well-groomed girl behind the counter who smiled at him happily, because that's how she'd been trained.

"Daniel Port," he said to the girl. "Reservation on your noon flight to New York."

She got it ready and said, "Are you paying for it now?" and then she took his two large bills and gave him a little bit of change. When he walked out, the girl smiled at him the way she had been trained, but Port wasn't paying attention. He wondered what he should do between now and noon, and whether it wouldn't have been better to leave town some other way. It was eight in the morning and he felt hungry. When he found that there wasn't enough change in his pocket he decided to go back to his room for some money.

His door wasn't locked, but that wasn't unusual.

He closed the door and said, "Why don't you give up, Stoker?"

Stoker was short, and big around the middle. There was much loose skin in his face, like when a fat man goes on a sudden diet. The skin had the flush that comes from a bad heart. Stoker was sitting, and the other man stood next to his chair. He was the same size as Daniel Port, but very stringy, with no show of muscle. He kept his face in a tight scowl, except when it broke because of the tic under one eye.

"If it were up to Fries," said Stoker, and he gave the man next to him a look that was tired, "I wouldn't have come."

"Why did you?" said Port.

"You didn't answer," and Stoker looked at the phone.

"You got my answer. The last time you got my answer was yesterday."

"I remember."

They looked at each other for a moment, and then Daniel Port went to the closet and pulled out a suitcase. The rest of the closet was empty. He put the suitcase on the bed, opened it up, and took out some money. He closed the suitcase and looked back at Stoker, who had been watching without a word.

"You want to hear it again?" said Port.

"Better I didn't hear you the first time, Danny."

Daniel Port sat down on the bed and pulled out a cigarette and lit it. He couldn't say anything new because he had told Stoker all there was to be said several times before.

"Nobody walks out," said Fries. "Not even the fair-haired boy of the old man himself."

"Don't say that," said Stoker.

Fries reacted as if he had been insulted. It was a habit with him. He controlled himself and said, "Look at the closet, empty, and the suitcase there—"

"Don't call me old man," said Stoker. Then he turned to Daniel Port and looked him straight in the face. "About the rest, he's right, Danny. You don't walk out."

"I'm not walking out. I'm leaving."

"Nobody leaves," said Fries. "Did you ever hear of somebody leaving?"

"No—not before me." The way Port said it, without trying for any effect, Stoker and Fries both knew that he meant it. Stoker made his face go tired because he had to stay calm all the time. Only the flush in his skin started to waver.

Fries said, "You're so special? You any different from me? Don't forget it, Port, you're just a hood!"

"Was," said Port. "I was a hood."

Fries leaned forward a little, stretching his mouth to show how disgusted he was. "If I had my way, you sure as hell would be."

Daniel Port blew out smoke. He kept his mouth that way to give a tuneless whistle. He mashed out the cigarette in the tray next to the bed and when he was through and got up he was still whistling. The sound was mostly a hiss and he wasn't looking at anybody.

"I don't want it this way," said Stoker. "Don't listen to Fries right now. Danny, listen to me."

Port stopped the whistling noise and looked at Stoker, who looked pink in the face, but exhausted. Then he smiled at Port. "We still friends, Danny?"

"Sure," said Port. "You know that, Max."

"So listen to a friend, Danny. I don't want it the way Fries was saying."

"I know. But there it is. Either your way, or Fries's way. Right?"

"Right."

"How about my way?"

Then Stoker got up and went to the door. Fries opened it for him, but Stoker didn't go out yet.

"Don't leave, Daniel." He stepped out into the hall, then turned back. "I'm at the office all day. I'll be waiting. Come visit, like a friend." He walked down the hall, not wanting to talk any more.

Daniel Port closed the door behind them and went to the window. Stoker's car was in front. It was long and specially built, with a back door that was cut partway into the roof so that a man didn't have to stoop when he got in or out of the car. Stoker got into the back and Fries sat next to the driver. After they drove off, the street was empty. There wouldn't be anyone waiting for Port because Stoker didn't want it that way. He had said so. They had been friends and Stoker would wait for him, because that's the way Stoker wanted to run it. Fries was something else, but Fries wouldn't go against the old man.

Port remembered that he hadn't eaten. He left his room without bothering to lock it and went to the diner at the end of the street, where he ordered breakfast. He ordered the coffee first and let it get almost cold before he drank it. Then he walked back to his apartment. There were a few cars on the street, and a cruising taxi came toward Port, who could see the hackie's face, smiling and expectant. Port shook his head when the taxi stopped, but the hackie had the rear door open already. Then somebody stepped out of a doorway close by and came up fast. Port had never seen the man before, but when he was close Port hit the man under the heart. He could just see the man gag when Port suddenly felt that his head was coming off.

Chapter 2

The sore spot was on the back of his head and because he was lying against the car seat the movement gave him a lot of pain. He must have made a sound, because they were all looking at him when he opened his eyes.

They were all suntanned; the one who had played the cabby, the wiry man next to the cabby, and the tall one in gray who sat with Port. The cabby turned around again to watch his driving, but the wiry one kept looking at Port over the back of the seat. He was chewing his lip, and there was a glim-

mery light in his eyes, hard and mean. Port remembered the man from the
street.

The tall one next to Port said, "Sit still, Daniel." He didn't hold a gun in
his hand, but Port sat back anyway and tried to relax. There was no point
trying anything else.

The cab had left the residential streets, cut through midtown traffic, and
headed out through the factory section. If this was a ride to the country, they
weren't doing it right. If they wanted the river, or the warehouses, that was
the other way. And they weren't going to any of Stoker's places, but perhaps
that didn't make sense. It wouldn't make sense for Stoker to pick him up for
another talk. The cab turned into the slums. They were getting close to Ward
Nine, Stoker's own hot potato, but that wasn't going to help any now. Port
knew the place well, all the streets and a lot of the people, but on this ride
that wouldn't mean a thing. The man in front had his gun out now and the
big one next to Port started to shift. When the cab stopped by the curb they
were ready.

"Now you go out easy, Daniel," said the big one, "and mind you step where
we say to step."

Port did as he was told, because the one with the gun was on the sidewalk
already and his gun, back in the pocket now, was waiting for Port. The man
stood with a crouch, a careful bend of the back, as if he were holding a bas-
ket of eggs in front and afraid something might happen to them. The man
was still hurting. Port stood on the sidewalk and watched the cabby and the
tall one get out. They didn't hurry, but the one with the gun looked eager.

They had picked their place well. They could have shot him right there by
the curb and not caused enough of a stir to worry about. The cabby was lock-
ing the car, because of the neighborhood, and Port waited, the gun spiking
his back. There was cardboard on broken windows, and in some places there
were scrawls making ugly figures on the sidewalk. Port thought that Ward
Nine hadn't looked so ugly before; all the colors were lead-gray, as if the sky
had a permanent overcast.

"In here," said the tall one, and the one with the gun took it up, poking
the barrel into the soft flesh next to Port's spine. Port turned and walked to
the basement door. There was a girl walking across the street now, watching the men go into the basement but not wondering about it. Port stumbled going down the steps. He waited while the cabby opened the door, and
then he walked through. He thought he would like to see the street again,
even the way it was, and, once more, the girl across the way.

The door banged and the cabby leaned against it. Port saw that much. And
he made out a chair but nothing else. The room smelled wet.

"Sit." The tall one waved at the chair.

"Let him stand," said the one with the gun, and the gun came out of his pocket, butt end up. But the tall one reached out for the gun and pulled it free with hardly an effort. He dropped it into his pocket.

"We only talk, Kirby," and when Kirby made a quick move for his gun the tall one reached over and gave a push. Kirby stumbled across the room and slammed into the wall.

If Kirby hadn't been without the gun he wouldn't have stood there, but the tall one kept the gun in his pocket and turned to Port.

"He's sore on account of that poke you give him. We just came to talk."

Port felt the back of his head and said nothing.

"That's because you hit Kirby," said the tall one. "Else I wouldn't have clipped you."

Kirby came away from the wall and stood by the chair where Port was sitting. Port felt jumpy and it showed.

"Later," said the tall one. "Maybe later, Kirby. First we talk."

Kirby stepped away from the chair again, but just far enough not to rile the tall one. Port didn't relax. They were so slow about it, making no sense, that Port couldn't think straight. He had to look around the room to shake off the feeling of nowhere, but there was nothing to look at. Just the walls, one high window, and the door where the cabby was leaning. He was unwrapping a stick of gum.

Port had to say something.

"What's your name?" he said to the tall one.

"I'm George," said the tall one. "I'm here to tell you, Daniel, we want you shouldn't leave town."

"You working for Fries?"

"I don't know any Fries." George treated it like an interruption, very patient about it, and then got back to the subject. "Because you're leaving Stoker...."

"He sent you himself?"

George made an annoyed face, but he was still patient. "I never seen Stoker," he said.

It meant nothing.

"You left him, didn't you?" and George stood in front of the chair, waiting for an answer.

Port said, "Why?"

"Because otherwise I got nothing to talk about."

Port said, "Yes, I left him." That's what he had wanted to do and if he hadn't said yes, George might have stopped talking too early.

"It's about the setup you got here in town," said George. "Stoker's bunch, where you come from, and Bellamy, the one that heads up the Reform party. You know who I mean."

Port knew what was coming. The relief he had felt hadn't lasted long, and he almost wished that George had been sent by Stoker. But that wouldn't have made any sense, Stoker pulling an act like this. Instead, he would wait in his office, just as he had said, and wait for Port to come back, because Stoker couldn't believe anything else.

But Bellamy would. He knew Port less and had more the temperament for a primitive stunt like this.

"Bellamy wants you," said George.

Stoker's loss would be Bellamy's gain. He would think like that. If you don't like Stoker, you got to like Bellamy. What else was there?

Port started to whistle and sat back in his chair. He waited till he felt that he wasn't going to lose his temper, that he could push it out of the way for a while. He said, "Tell me, George, then why any of this? Why this basement stunt?"

"Bellamy thought you'd be used to it."

"Or if you ain't," said Kirby, "then Bellamy figured it's time you knew what it's like."

"I'm surprised. Shocked and surprised," said Port. "After all, the Reform party in this town...."

"She's reforming," said Kirby.

"And then you had to come along and spoil it," said Port. He put his hands in his pockets to hunt for a cigarette, when Kirby swung with his fist. Port went blind with the water that shot into his eyes, because the punch had caught the bridge of his nose. A slow pain started to grow, leaving Port awake but feeling weak and alone. He even had room to think of the man who had hit him, what kind of man he must be, and real amazement went through Port's mind. Then the second punch knocked him out.

There was the bare wall again, then the high window, next to Kirby. This time Kirby was on the chair. And this time he had his gun. The tail end of a conversation went on with George saying something about wasting time and Kirby laughing that it was worth it, that there was nothing to worry about because it had only been the butt end of the gun, not the real McCoy.

"He's up," said the cabby at the door. He had a newspaper in his hand, looking over it.

Kirby stood up and gave Port a kick. Then George was there too. He reached down, took Port by one hand, and pulled him off the floor. It felt worse than the kick. Port leaned against the wall and heard them talking at him.

"You're making a mistake, Daniel—"

"Make it again. Come on, sport, make it again—"

"He wants you to listen to sense. Bellamy says—"

"One way or the other, sport, have it any way you want—"

"Not the same deal like this Stoker. Bellamy wants you—"

"But the works, sport, whichever way—"

"Kirby," said Port, "which way is up?"

They both stopped. They watched Port straighten up, pushing away from the wall.

"Up? Up what?" said Kirby.

"Up yours," and Port swung from low down, catching Kirby under the nose so his head flipped back and then the whole man went over backward.

George caught him in his arms, because he was standing that way, and tossed the limp Kirby right back at Port. George would do something like that. Port had stepped clear and saw Kirby crash into the wall.

"About our talk," said Port. He hadn't moved again, watching George, and George didn't come any closer. As long as Port didn't make a wrong move, George wouldn't. That's where Kirby had been different, but now Kirby was out.

"Bellamy wants you to come over," said George, "and I'm here to give you the message,"

"I left Stoker," said Port, "because I want out. I've had mine and now I want out."

"You can't leave."

"That's what Stoker said."

"Forget about Stoker. It's Bellamy now."

"I wouldn't do him any good."

"He wants you to come over. There's all kinds of dirt on Stoker, and you're the one who would know about it. Bellamy...."

"I told you, George, I'm through with the local dirt."

"You selling elsewhere?"

"No."

"You protecting Stoker?"

"You don't listen, do you?"

George shrugged, gave a short look at Kirby out on the floor, then turned back to Port.

"Bellamy wants the dirt."

"He can make his own."

George gave a short grin, which surprised Port, and said, "He mentioned that. To start with, he can make his own."

"Fine. That leaves me out."

"But you're in it." George laughed again. Then he changed back and was sober. "Think it over, boy. And don't try to leave town. Won't work."

George went over where Kirby was on the floor and picked him up. He carried him to the door and gave him to the cabby. Then he came back.

"And keep your hands off Kirby," he said to Port. He hit under the heart and didn't wait to see Port sink to the floor. Then the door opened, and when Port looked again the door was still open but the men were gone.

Chapter 3

When he left the building it was getting dark and the same overcast lay everywhere. Port gave himself time to rest and to look at the street. Then he saw the girl again. She was coming the other way, on his side of the street, and she was wearing a different outfit of white nylon, buttoned down the front and very antiseptic-looking, like a nurse's uniform. But he was sure she wasn't a nurse. Her legs were bare and over one breast she wore a red carnation. Her skin was dark and her thick hair shiny black, making the red flower more vivid and the nylon more white. As she came closer she looked at him standing by the steps, but without special interest. She still didn't look away when she came past.

Port said, "Pardon me. You got the time?"

She said, "Close to six," and walked by without breaking her pace.

"Wait."

She stopped and looked back at him.

"I— You know, I saw you before, across the street."

"I know," she said. "I saw you go in here."

He walked up to her, smiling, but didn't know of anything else to say. He looked at her. He looked at her feet, then up, and stopped at her face. He didn't care what she thought. He smiled again and she must have misunderstood.

"No," she said, turned around and walked down the street without looking back.

After a moment Port turned the other way and walked steadily for a while, careful not to jar the aches in his body. By the time he had left the slums he was going faster. His mouth looked thinner, and hardly moved when he started to whistle.

The Lee building was closed when Port got there, but he rapped on the glass door and waited for the night man to show up. He came across the wide lobby, squinting to see the entrance. When he saw it was Port he got out his keys and unlocked the door.

"Evening, Mr. Port." He held the door open. "You lose your key, Mr. Port?"

"Is Stoker still in?"

"He's there. He said he wouldn't be leaving till nine or so, he and Mr. Fries. I think they...."

"Take me up, will you?"

"Sure, Mr. Port."

All the way up the night man wanted to say more but Port didn't encourage him. Port left the elevator on the tenth floor.

Stoker's door said *Civic Services, Inc.* The frosted glass showed a light. Port walked into the reception room, then through the big one with the desks and typewriters, and down the corridor with the doors to the private offices. One of them opened and Fries came out. He stopped short and stared.

"Where's Stoker?" said Port.

Fries didn't answer, but the frown came back to his face, and he turned and ran down the length of the corridor. He opened a door and before Port could get there he heard Fries talking to Stoker.

Port walked in. Stoker got up from behind his desk and Fries stood by, one hand working the back of a chair.

"What's the matter?" Port looked from one to the other.

For a moment nobody answered. The only change was the flushing color in Stoker's face. He leaned over his desk, looking straight at Port, and his breath was noisy.

"You son of a bitch!" he said.

Port stood for a moment and then took a step toward the desk.

"Sit down," said Fries. He hit the back legs of the chair on the floor and stood by, waiting for Port. "I said, sit."

Port saw Fries's hand come out of the pocket, holding a blackjack, and he walked up to the chair. He kicked it hard, making it fly into Fries's shins. Fries doubled over, sweating, and Port went up to the desk.

"Everybody nuts in this place? Since when does that creep go around telling me things?" he demanded.

Stoker sat down without answering. He looked over at Fries, who was straightening up painfully, and when Fries started for the desk Stoker said, "Go outside. Call Abe and his sidekick up here. They're down in the garage. And then wait outside."

"But if Port..." Fries started.

"He won't," said Stoker.

Fries left and Stoker waved at the chair.

"Go ahead, Port. Sit down."

Port sat down.

"I'm really interested," said Stoker. "So help me, I don't know why you came here."

"How could you. That's why I...."

"Shut up."

Port frowned but didn't say anything.

"Now, I admit I've been wrong before, like thinking you were a friend when you're nothing but a son of a bitch—"

"Stop calling me that," said Port.

"Wait till I'm through, Port. Just wait till I'm through."

Port let it go and sat back to listen. He knew that Stoker had to run himself out. He didn't get this way very often. He was long-winded only when he was too excited and wanted to calm down before finishing up.

"Come to think of it, now, I do know why you're back. What you did was just the beginning, and of course you and I know you got plenty more. So here you're back to let your old pal know...."

"Stoker, I don't know what you're talking about."

Stoker stared across the desk. He frowned and rubbed the loose skin under his face. "So help me," he said. "So help me if you don't sound like you meant it." Stoker put his right hand on top of the desk and put down his gun. Then he reached into a drawer, drew out a paper, and threw it on top of the desk. It came open, front up.

"Read it," said Stoker. "Unless you already know all about it."

Port picked it up.

STOKER MOB BLOCK SLUM CLEARANCE

The slum clearance project, long on the docket of our City Planning Board without receiving the urgent attention which it deserves, has long been stalled by machinations of the Stoker machine. Stoker controls Ward Nine, comprising the major area of substandard housing, and slum clearance and relocation of the Stoker machine vote victims would wipe out Ward Nine as a political tool. Is it therefore any wonder—and we give you proof positive, with names, dates, and reasons—why Boss Hoodlum Stoker and his Grand Vizier Port have tried at any price, and to the detriment of the unfortunates forced to dwell in the slums, and to the total detriment of our city, have threatened and bribed slum clearance into an all but dead stall. Planning Board members Erzberg, Cummins, Utescu, threatened by Daniel Port. Members Toms, and Vancoon, bribed with one hundred dollars in cash plus personal gifts and one hundred and fifteen dollars in cash and personal gifts. The bribes were arranged by Daniel Port and executed at his direction. And all this in our city! Now it has long been the aim of your Reform Party, etc., etc.

Port tossed the paper back on the desk and lit himself a cigarette. When he looked up again Stoker sat waiting. Port exhaled.

"This is news?"

"News! Now it's the truth, you jackass. It's been printed!"

"Don't yell, Stoker. You can't afford...."

"If I drop dead I'm going to lay this thing out for you. You walk out, you walk off with three guys we don't know, you get lost all afternoon, next this mess of an Extra with names, dates, and prices, and on top of that—and on top of that you got the gall to come in here and...."

"Who saw me? Fries?"

"Somebody he sent."

"Did your bird dog...."

"Fries had the idea. Until now I didn't think it was necessary to have a friend of mine shadowed."

"Did the bird dog also report that I got slugged?"

"That you made a good show of it."

"I could show you my wound," said Port. He mashed his cigarette into an ashtray, which kept him from seeing how Stoker meant to react. When Port looked up again Stoker was leaning back in his chair, rigid with pain. He tried to breathe carefully, and his face was suffused with blood. Port jumped up, got the pills out of Stoker's vest pocket, and dropped them on the man's tongue. They were still lying there when Port put the glass of water up to the mouth and poured.

After a while Stoker came around. He didn't look at Port, but wiped the cold sweat off his face.

"That was a bad one," said Port.

"Closer." Stoker's voice was strained. "Each time closer and closer."

Port frowned, then turned away. He went to the window and lit himself another cigarette.

"Danny," said Stoker.

Port turned.

"Danny. What can I believe?"

"You could believe me," said Port.

"You were walking out."

"I told you that months ago. I don't lie."

Stoker just nodded.

"And I'm still leaving."

"Then why did you come here?"

Port shrugged, getting impatient.

"I thought I had news for you."

"What was it?"

"It isn't news any more." He flipped one finger at the paper on top of the desk. "I got picked up and they told me they were going to spring something like this."

"Bellamy?"

"Not himself. He's too reformed for that."

"What did he want?"

"Me."

Stoker sat without talking, rubbing his chin with the back of his hand. Then he said, "You know why, don't you, Danny?"

"Because I was leaving."

"And you know why he sprang this dirt in the papers."

"There's nothing in that sheet that Bellamy didn't know months ago."

"True," said Stoker. He put both hands on the desk and leaned forward. "He timed it, Danny. He sprang it when it would hurt most—when you were leaving."

Port didn't answer. Instead he started to whistle. He sat down in the chair and got up again, and then Stoker went on.

"You still think you can walk out and nothing will happen?" Stoker sounded really tired now, and he kept plopping his hands together in a listless manner. "If I say, Danny, go ahead and pack up, you think that's enough? You know that isn't enough. You're taking too much with you. Sit down, Danny."

Port sat down. He wished he had left earlier, some other way, maybe, and he wished he had never told anyone about it. But it was too late now. And Stoker being his friend couldn't make any difference.

"Listen, Danny, how long we been together?"

"What do you want, Max?"

"Didn't I treat you right, Danny? You weren't so much, you know, when I picked you up after the war."

"I know. Lots of stuff but no application."

"But you learned. And now what are you doing? You're throwing it all down the drain. You don't make enough, maybe? Or you think this setup is too local or something?"

"I make enough, Max."

"So what is it?"

Port held his breath and looked out the window. It was dark outside. He thought that if Stoker didn't know by now, there was no use going into it again.

"Tell me again, Danny."

"I want out, that's all." Port tried to hold his temper, but it didn't work. "I want out because I learned all there was: there's a deal, and a deal to match that one, and the next day the same thing and the same faces and you spit at one guy and tip your hat to another, because one belongs here and the other one over there, and, hell, don't upset the organization whatever you do, because we all got to stick together so we don't get the shaft from some unexpected source. Right, Max? Hang together because it's too scary to hang alone. Well? Did I say something new? Something I didn't tell you before?"

"Nothing new." Stoker ran one hand over his face. "I knew this before you came along." He looked at the window and said, "That's why I'm here till I kick off."

The only sound was Stoker's careful breathing and Port's careful shifting of his feet. Then Port said, "Not for me."

It changed the mood in the room, as if Port didn't want to talk any more and had said all there was. Only Stoker didn't leave it that way.

"What else, Danny?"

"Nothing."

"It happened too sudden, your losing interest."

They both knew what Stoker was talking about, but Port didn't want to go into it. He was suddenly angry. He didn't say anything.

"When your kid brother got it is when you lost interest, isn't it?"

Port got up and went to the window, then back to the desk. He tried to talk very quietly.

"Bob got killed working for you. You sent him out to fix up that policy trouble with Welman. For a talk—just to talk with Welman. Maybe that's all you thought it was going to be, but you also knew that there might be trouble. You knew Welman for a nut with a gun, and that my brother had more temper than brains. And you sent him out there."

"Blaming me—" Stoker started, but Port wasn't listening.

"I didn't want him to go! I didn't even want that kid hanging around you!"

Port took a breath and stared at the dark window.

"Blame you?" he said. "I don't know. I don't know whom to blame."

"Now you listen to me." Stoker put his elbows on the desk and rubbed both hands over his face. When he looked up again he nodded at Port. "You don't know whom to blame, but I know whom you're blaming. I'm going to...."

Port made an impatient gesture but Stoker didn't let him talk.

"I'm not done. I know you're going to ask what this has to do with your staying or leaving, so I'm telling you. Listen. I picked you up broke in New York, broke because you were wet-nursing that brother you had. The kid gets out of the army and falls in with bad companions and you to the rescue. He loses his roll. He gambles himself red, white and blue in the face and you stake him to a comeback." Stoker sat back and laughed. "All through the war, did you see him, did you nurse him along? No. He's in the Pacific and you in the ETO. Does he get along without you all that time? Sure he does; never a scratch. But you meet up in New York, you take care of him, and you both end up in the gutter. Right? Answer me!"

"Yeah. So what?"

"So I make a long story short and tell you I pick you up, I take you in, and from then on you started sailing. You and me, Danny, we got along fine because you got respect for a man who shows you what you don't know and you got it in you to learn."

"What's that got to do...."

"I said wait." Stoker lowered his voice. "And all this time you keep wet-nursing the kid brother along. Maybe you thought he was too dumb or maybe you thought I'd take advantage of him, but it comes out the same way: Dan Port, his brother's keeper."

"You're damn right I was my brother's keeper!"

"You don't have to yell, Dan. I know. Except for this." Stoker paused to look up at Port's face. "Now I'll tell you why you're quitting. Your kid brother's dead and it's your fault."

Port didn't say anything because he knew Stoker was right. He didn't say anything because he thought Stoker was through.

"All through the war the kid gets along with no help from you. Then you take him in hand and he dies."

"You said that!"

"To let you hear it. To let you hear that it sounds too good to be true. So now here is the real stinger, why you want to quit."

They stared at each other and then Stoker didn't let Port wait any longer.

"The work you've been doing for me went along fine and you never batted an eye. You could take it because you were your brother's keeper. It made all the rest all right, just like having a built-in excuse. Then Bob got killed. You not only failed, Dan; you lost your excuse for sticking around!"

Port was at the window and at the last words he turned around fast, but when he saw Stoker he didn't talk right away. After a while he talked very evenly.

"Now we both know. Now I leave," and he got up without looking at Stoker.

"Dan."

Port stopped, turned around.

"Your brother is dead and you walk out." Stoker looked up. "But I'm not dead—yet."

"It's got nothing to do with you, Max," Port said to the wall.

"You're leaving when it's going to hurt most."

"You took care of your own before I came along."

"I wasn't this sick." He said it before he could stop himself, and then he went on fast. "You're walking out with that Reform thing riding the crest. After this dirt in the paper, how long do you think I'm going to hold on to Ward Nine? You know I need that ward, don't you? You know if they tear down those slums, and spread the voters all over the precincts the way it's been planned, you know what'll happen to me, don't you, Dan?"

"I know."

"I lose the machine, I lose territory, I lose out with the setup from out of town. And you know what comes then?"

"You're a sick man, Max. They wouldn't drop you."

"That's why they would. Hard."

Neither of them said anything for a while and when Stoker talked again he was mumbling.

"If I tell you I need you, Dan—"

"I'm leaving, Max. I'm going to fix up that ward for you, and then I'm leaving."

Stoker looked down in his lap. "Better I didn't hear you, Dan. Just fix up that ward and don't talk."

Port walked to the door. He nodded his head without looking at Stoker and said, "All right, Max," and walked out.

Chapter 4

At eight in the morning Port was ready to go. When he went to the door he looked at the telephone but it didn't ring this time. Instead there was a knock on the door. Port stood back and said, "Come in."

He said, "Hi, Simon," and waved at the bald man to come in. Simon shook his head and grinned. "I brought something over, for a present. You going downstairs?"

Port said yes and they went down in the elevator.

"It's from the boss. He says I should bring it over with his compliments."

"Stoker must have had a good night."

"He arranged it yesterday. Called me up late and told me to bring it over by eight."

They got out of the elevator and walked through the lobby.

"You staying after all, huh?"

"Sure. So where's this present?"

"Right outside," said Simon, and when they got to the street, there was Fries.

Port stopped and gave Simon a disgusted look.

"What's the matter?" said Simon.

"You just ruined my day." Port turned to Fries, who came away from the curb where he had been waiting.

"Not him," said Simon. "He just come along for the...."

"Just one word with you, Port," Fries blinked the eye with the tic.

"Honest, Dan, I wouldn't play you a trick like that," said Simon. "I brought you the car. Stoker's present."

They all looked at the car by the curb, and Fries had to wait while Port went close to admire it. The car was a long convertible with a black nylon top and metallic gray body.

"It's a rare one, all right. No two-tone," said Port.

"And did you see the antennas?" Simon went to the rear. "One on each fender."

"For tuna fishing," said Port. "Fries, did you ever go tuna fishing?"

Fries wasn't in the mood. "Just one word," he said.

"Say it."

"I see you talked around the old man and you're back."

"That's right."

"Beat it, Simon," and Fries waited till Simon had walked out of earshot.

"And you want to tell me to take a powder."

"No. Nobody leaves," said Fries.

"I'm back. What more do you want?"

"Stay in your place. Just do your job and quit shining up to the old man."

"I should shine up to you. Right?"

But Fries didn't treat it as a joke.

"You can do that, if you think you know how. Might as well learn sooner than later."

Port stuck his hands in his pockets and grinned at Fries. "Am I mistaken, or am I talking to the heir apparent?"

"I don't care what you call it...."

"But I might as well face the facts."

"That's right."

"So when the time comes, Fries, when Stoker doesn't make it with an attack, that's going to be my time?"

"That's going to be my time," said Fries. "That's when I take over."

"That's what I meant when I said...."

"I know what you meant. I'm correcting you."

"You sound like you're giving me a sentence. Am I gonna get killed?"

Fries made an impatient noise. "What's good for the organization is good enough for me. Just work like you have been and we're fine."

"And we might even be friends."

"I don't know what you're talking about," said Fries, and waved at Simon to come back.

They all nodded at each other and Simon nodded at the car too, and then Port got in behind the wheel. On his way down the street he passed Fries and Simon, who was walking a few steps behind, and the sight made the ward business that much more urgent to Port.

Most of the slum houses were frame, but a few were brownstone, and the one in the best repair had a clean, sandblasted front with a small sign that said *Social Club*. The inside was mostly new. There was an addition which held a gym, a foyer with a cloakroom, and past some columns varnished dark brown was a bar, the room with the easy chairs, and a bare place with a stage and some folding chairs stacked by the walls. Upstairs there were more rooms.

The whole place had been paid for and built for Boss Stoker. He had never been there, which made little difference as long as the place was for Stoker.

Daniel Port left his car in the front by the No Parking sign and headed for the stairs. Before he got to them he turned back, locked both doors of the car, and then went into the club.

Downstairs looked empty. In the room with the easy chairs Port found two men sitting by the fireplace. They had a small volley ball and kept tossing it back and forth. Port said, "Is Lantek in?" and the men looked around at him.

"Should be," said one of them. They kept tossing the ball. Port went upstairs without seeing anyone else, until he came to the back corridor. The man at one of the doors paid no attention to Port.

"You seen Lantek?" said Port.

The man looked up and nodded. Then he leaned back against the wall and looked at his magazine. Port tried again.

"Where is he?"

"Who wants to know?"

Port had never seen the man before. He was slight and dark, and Port guessed what the man lacked in strength he might well make up in speed.

"You new here?" said Port.

"Yes. Perhaps a month."

With Lantek at the club, things could mostly be run by phone, and Port hadn't been there in over a month.

"All right. Where's Lantek?"

"He's busy. Come back in half an hour."

"You're new here," said Port. "You don't know who I am. Just tell me where Lantek is."

"Who are you?"

"Dan Port."

The man closed his magazine quickly and looked attentive. "I'm sorry," he said. "I didn't know who you were. If I can do anything...."

"You can tell me where Lantek is."

The man was uncomfortable. He wanted to please, but he couldn't.

"He told me—he said not before half an hour. I'm new here, and maybe you better...."

"He's in there?" and Port looked at the door, because the new man had edged himself in front of it.

"He is, Mr. Port, but he said nobody, or nothing, for half an hour."

"You're eager," said Port. "I bet Lantek likes that."

"I hope so," said the man.

"Don't be so eager it makes you scared. Open that door."

The new man stepped aside and let Port go in.

The room had a table, some chairs, and a couch. They were all by the couch, backs to the door, and they didn't notice Port right away. Only the girl did, because she was facing his way. She got off the couch and looked sullen. She said, "He's extra. He's not part of the deal."

She wore shoes and a blouse—and nothing else.

Port closed the door and they all looked at him. There were Lantek and several others.

"Jeez," said Port. "It's only ten in the morning!"

The girl walked up to Port and stopped with her hands on her hips. She said, "Don't act like I asked you to take a drink before noon. All I said was...."

"Put your clothes on," said Port.

Lantek stepped up, a big man with his hair cut down to a stiff stubble and a jaw like a trap. He smiled at Port and shrugged one shoulder.

"Hell, Danny—you want in on it?"

"Not if you don't raise the ante," said the girl. One of the seven others was trying to shush her but she pushed him aside and got louder. "When I make a deal—" she started, but Port interrupted.

"Lady, there's no deal. Put your clothes on and go."

They all started talking together and they all had the same thing in mind. Lantek couldn't keep them quiet and Port didn't try. He waited a while longer till they were all looking at him.

"Put your clothes on," he said to the girl.

She put on the skirt and a jacket and buttoned up, not looking happy about it. "I didn't get paid yet," she said.

"For what?" said one of the men, and another voice, "Nothing happened. Why should...."

"I come up here!" said the girl, angry now. "What about wasting my time and—the indignity!"

"Get out," said Lantek.

His voice made her jump and she started for the door.

"She gets paid half," said Port. "For her time—and the indignity."

He lit a cigarette and waited while the girl collected the half-fee and then left the room. Then the men stood in the room, without talking, waiting for Port.

"Which one of you guys handles the phone in this place?"

One man raised his hand, but didn't say anything. Then Port wanted to know who did the soliciting, who made the rounds on the charity cases, which one ran the errands, and who kept the books. He nodded each time a man raised his hand, and when he was finished he left a moment of silence, making them all hope he was through. Then he dismissed them.

They were out of the room in short order, leaving only Port and Lantek, who was rubbing one hand through his hair and looking back and forth between Port and the window. Port looked at him briefly. He mumbled, "Jeez. At ten in the morning," and opened the door. The new man was still standing there. "Bring him along," said Port. He went into a room fixed like an office, sat down at the desk, and waited for Lantek and the new one to come in. Lantek sat down by the desk, but the new man stood.

"I never asked you your name," said Port.

"I'm Ramon. Calvin Ramon."

"You say Calvin?"

"He's Mexican," said Lantek, as if that explained it.

"Or Spanish."

"My parents were," said Ramon. "I was born here. I mean in Los Angeles. And my parents had it in their minds—they always said, 'A new country, a new name. Make a break with the past.' You know what I mean."

Port said, "Oh," and crossed his legs. He turned to Lantek. "I need a man to head up a team collecting signatures. Can you spare him?" He nodded at the new man.

"Sure," said Lantek. "But he's new. I can get you Cholly—or how about Tim, if it's really important. I been keeping my eye on Tim for a while now, and the way I see it...."

"Look," Port sounded resigned. "We fix men up with jobs all the time. We do it all over the city and with some of the county jobs." Then Port sat up, talking more clearly, "But we don't horse around like that with jobs in the organization! Try to remember that." He looked back at the new man.

"Here's what it is, Ramon." He handed Ramon a typed sheet of paper. "It's a questionnaire. Have that mimeographed and then get twenty men from Lantek to make the rounds. It says yes and no, behind the answers. They should all be marked. On the bottom I want signatures. Real, original signatures. Okay with you, Lantek?"

"Sure, Danny, sure."

"Hand them out tonight, starting at six, and have them ready for me here at nine in the morning. Okay, Ramon?"

"Sure thing, Danny. I'll start now."

"Have the mimeograph done by Schuster, on Lane Street and Scranton. Know where that is?"

Ramon was so anxious to say yes, he started to stutter. He didn't know where the place was.

"I'm driving by there," said Port. "Come along."

Port told Lantek to line up twenty men for six sharp, and left with Ramon. When they got to Port's car Ramon hadn't stopped talking once. He apologized for being new, he was grateful for being given the chance, he would do all he could, and when they got to the car he started admiring that. "And back here," he said, walking around to the trunk, "what lines, what antennas! You know something, Dan? I've lived in California. Did you ever see those boats they have, those boats they rig up for tuna fishing? These antennas here...."

"Is that so?" said Port. Then he offered Ramon a cigarette. "Come on across the street. I'll buy you a coffee."

They went into the short-order place with the grocery counter in front and sat down near the grill. Then they waited for someone to show.

"You know why I picked you?" said Port.

Ramon shook his head.

"Because you're eager."

"I am, Dan. I think this town has opportunities. What I mean is, I can really do something for this—in this club, because when I have half a chance...."

"I know," said Port. "I know what you got in mind."

"With half a chance...."

"Sure, Ramon. I use you and you try the same with me and we both win. That what you mean?"

"I don't really mean...."

"Ramon, listen. I'm in a hurry, and you're eager. That's why I picked you, and you like it for your own reasons. Okay? Don't bring it up again."

Ramon didn't answer, just nodded his head.

"Now listen close," said Port. "Here's the rest of the deal."

"About the mimeographing?"

"After the mimeographing. This is something else."

Ramon got very attentive but Port didn't say anything else. He watched the waitress come in from the back, seeing the red carnation before he had seen her face. She put a soup pot on the grill. When she recognized Port her face stayed as bland as he remembered it from the street. Then she smiled, and it was an easy smile which changed her face in a beautiful way. "Nino," she said. "You didn't come home last night." Then she got two cups of coffee without asking.

"I'm five years older than she is," said Ramon, "and she still calls me Nino."

"Yeah," said Port. He picked up his coffee, burned his mouth, because he wasn't used to drinking it hot.

"Meet my sister," said Ramon, and to her, "this is Daniel Port."

She smiled again, but less than before, and said, "How are you? You look better today."

"Thank you," said Port. "You look the same. It's hard improving on you."

She raised her eyebrows at him, giving a half-smile, and went to the grill to set the soup into the steam table.

"You know each other?" asked Ramon.

"No," she said. "We just met on the street."

"I asked her the time," said Port.

Ramon nodded and drank his coffee. He watched his sister and he tried watching Port, but he couldn't tell a thing. If they knew each other they didn't show a thing. It might be nice if they did. There would be no harm done, if Port would show interest.

"Finish up and we'll go," said Port. He put thirty cents on the counter and got up.

"You were going to tell me something else," said Ramon. "Some other deal you had in mind."

Port waved at Ramon's sister and said, "See you again." She smiled and nodded. You could make of it what you wanted.

Outside, Port crossed the street to his car and got behind the wheel. Ramon sat next to him. Port started the car.

"You never told me her name," he said. "I'm sure it can't be anything like Dolores or Carmen."

"Her name is Shelly." Ramon looked out the window. "You like Shelly?"

"It's better than Calvin," said Port.

Chapter 5

Ramon came back to the club at eight the next morning. He pushed the front door open with one shoulder, because he was carrying the questionnaires with both hands. In the front hall he put the stack on the counter of the cloak room and took a deep breath. He felt like sitting down; he wanted a cup of hot coffee and afterwards some sleep. The job had been more work than he'd figured. It had taken all night. There were only three questions with only a "yes" or "no" answer, but it had taken all night to tally them up. Shelly had come into the kitchen twice and offered to help him. He had told her to go back to bed, the job was too important.

Ramon stood behind the counter and stacked the sheets. Then he went to the bar and found a carton with empty whisky bottles. He put the bottles on the floor, took the carton and put the stacked sheets inside it.

At eight-thirty Lantek came in. He nodded at Ramon and came over to look into the box. The top sheet had the totals on it.

"What you got here?"

"The questionnaires. You remember, Dan told me...."

"This here," and Lantek took up the sheet with the totals.

"I added the whole thing up. I was sure we'd need the whole thing tallied, so I did it last night. Don't you think...."

Lantek looked ill-humored and put the sheet back.

"You're wasting your time," he said. "Dan don't impress."

"We need the tallies, don't we?"

Lantek looked up at the tone but didn't say anything. The whole thing was done, anyway. "You're done," he said, and picked up the box.

"Leave it. I'll give it to him. I'm supposed to wait for him anyway."

Lantek put down the box. "You're done, I said."

They looked at each other for a moment.

"Out, Ramon. And don't come back."

Ramon felt suddenly weak, with a filminess getting into his vision. His effort to get back his strength made the sweat come out on his forehead. But then he couldn't talk.

"Don't look at me," said Lantek. "I get my orders, same as you, straight from Port."

He picked up the box with the stack of papers inside and went to the stairs. Before going up he turned and called back. "You waiting for me to throw you out?" He stood at the bottom step, watching, till Ramon had gone out of the door.

At first he was not going anywhere, just walking away, but when he got down to the street he had to stop because the tension would not let him walk any further. To leave now would make the break physically final. From one day to the next—and all night, working to get it done for the next big day—Shelly sleeping in the next room, plans and thoughts about what he would do with—for—Shelly. He was going to throw her at him. His own sister. He was going to get her messed up with that Port bastard who had it in his hands to make or to break him.

Ramon sat down on the steps of the club and scraped his nails over his scalp. His throat pained, as if he had been screaming. He raked his nails through his hair, made two fists and held on. Whom would he kill first? Port? Of course Port, and then that swinehead back in the club. And there were a few more that might get in his way and the thing would be.... But first back to Port.

Ramon heard footsteps on the pavement and sat up immediately. He coughed hard, distorting his face. He did this without thought, but it served to blank out what he had been doing, as if it was necessary to blank it out or else it might show. Whoever was walking on the street would see Ramon on the steps, coughing.

Across the street a boy was walking by and he looked at Ramon only because he was coughing.

Now that Ramon was not thinking about the murder any more he felt lost and aimless. Ramon did not feel that he wanted to see anyone he might know, because his feelings were out of hand, confused and painful. Of course with Port it would be different—there would be the sharp, clear, incisive thing. When Ramon turned to cross the street the car slid up and cut off his view. The two antennas dipped and weaved over the massive hulk of the car. If heraldic standards had flown from the antennas it would not have surprised Ramon.

Port looked at Ramon over the top of the car while he slammed the door shut.

"Morning. You been inside?"

Ramon stared at Port, waiting for his rage to come to him.

"Hey—Calvin!"

Ramon started chewing his lip, but no rage came to his aid, not even insults. Port came around the car, one hand in his pocket. He stopped with one foot on the curb, and looked at Ramon. Port was so casual, Ramon thought for a moment he could hit the man now.

"Come along," said Port. "I'll buy you some coffee."

Then Ramon ran after him and started to talk before he even caught up. "Why? Why did you do it? You threw me out without even a chance for me to make good, to do anything. I'm a member for two weeks, after it took me maybe three months—ever since we moved into the neighborhood. And you don't even—"

He stopped when Port turned to look at him at the door to the shop. Ramon burst out, finally angry.

"Did you tell that swinehead to throw me out? Did you?"

"Sure I did," said Port, and held the door open for Ramon.

Ramon looked inside and remembered that Shelly would not be there, not until later. He went in and sat down at the counter.

"Two coffees," said Port to the man at the grill. Then he looked at Ramon. "Now shut up and listen."

Ramon sat still, his mouth open.

"You wormed your way into the club. You're in for two weeks, and you get thrown out. We don t want you. That's what Lantek knows, that's what anybody knows who cares to ask about it." Port stopped to blow on his coffee. "I got a job for you and for that job you got to be thrown out of the club."

Ramon burned his mouth on the coffee.

"Now here's the deal. Let me know if you want it."

Ramon had a sensation of quivering and was afraid it might show. He sucked in his breath, he smiled with mouth wide and stiff.

"Sure, Dan. Anything. But why didn't you tell me? Why send Lantek— and me not knowing a thing, Dan. I thought I was going nuts!"

Port looked at his coffee and blew on it.

"Don't get so eager it makes you scared, Ramon. I told you once."

"You can talk. You're on top, and nothing can...."

"You had a bad morning?" Port paused. "When you're in, Ramon, this happens all the time."

Port drank coffee and didn't say any more for a while. He poured water into the coffee and drank it that way. Ramon sat and waited. He thought about what he had heard, and didn't believe a word of it. After a while he said, "You have a job for me?"

"As a gardener."

"You mean—in a garden?"

"Go to the Apex Employment Bureau. They know you're coming. They got a request for a gardener and I want you to apply for the job. You'll be the only applicant, so you shouldn't have any trouble. Sam White at the agency will show you a sheet with dates and references. Learn it by heart, because that's your background. You've been a gardener most of your life." Ramon listened for more.

"After you try for the job go home and wait for me there. Where do you live?"

Ramon told him.

"I'll be over late. If you have the job, I'll tell you the rest." Port got up, paid for the coffee. "And keep away from the club. You're out, and you don't like it."

Ramon nodded and watched Port walk out the door. Ramon felt he should be elated, now that everything was again well in hand; except, as he found it, nothing seemed to be in his own hands.

Chapter 6

Port pulled the car into a space marked *Reserved for Officials,* and walked into the Municipal Building carrying the whisky carton with the questionnaires under his arm. Inside he said hello to the guard at the information desk and walked to the elevator. The old man who ran it said, "Nice seeing you, Danny," and tried to carry the box into the elevator for him. Port thanked him and held on to it himself. He said, "Is McFarlane in?"

"He's always in," said the old man.

"That figures," said Port. "It takes double time, playing both ends against the middle."

"Why you keep dealing with him, Danny, knowing he isn't straight?"

"If he were straight, Pop, you think he'd be dealing with me?"

The old man pulled his head into his shoulders and didn't answer. He let Port out on the third floor and watched him go through the door where it said *City Solicitor.*

The city solicitor wasn't in until Port told the girl who he was. "Mr. McFarlane will see you," she said. "Since you told me so." Port predicted for her a fine future with the fine attitude she was displaying, but advised that it would be better if she got married instead. She said that was her plan, except she was right now beholden to Mr. McFarlane, who would be unable to keep his composure if ten times a day he couldn't watch the way her back curved when she sits on her typist's chair. She swiveled toward the half-open door of the inner office and said, "Did you want me, Mr. McFarlane?"

There was a severe *harrump* and the door opened all the way. McFarlane came out with strides that were meant to suggest how busy he was.

"Hello, Port. All right, Miss Trent, are you finished with—"

"Yes, Mr. McFarlane." She handed a folder to him.

McFarlane had twitchy eyebrows which detracted from the fact that he rarely looked a person straight in the face. Miss Trent turned her back, curved it beautifully, and started to type. McFarlane's eyebrows stopped jumping, but then he remembered Port. "Come along, Dan," he said, and took hasty steps into his office.

Port stood by the window and watched McFarlane settle down behind his desk. After a while Port said, "About that slum deal, McFarlane. What's your thought?"

"Hardly my problem." He looked at his fingernails and then up at Port. "Why this visit? Come to the point."

Port folded his arms and sat down on the window sill.

"Where is the recommendation to raze the slum district?"

"It's left City Planning. You know that."

Port smiled. "It left the commission a year ago. What I mean is, how hard is Bellamy pushing to get it before City Council?"

"You read the paper, didn't you? Then you know how hard he's pushing." McFarlane made a nervous squint while he lit a cigarette. "You're wasting time, Port. My time, at any rate."

Port's smile got wider, and then he laughed. "It's a fact you aren't wasting any time, McFarlane. A day hasn't passed since Bellamy's move, and already you hate to be seen with me. You sure Stoker will lose his ward?"

McFarlane puffed hard on his cigarette. He almost looked at Port, but his eyes wandered off again.

"So far, the slum clearance thing is only a resolution," said Port. "It's before the council, or will be, but it hasn't been passed upon yet. They haven't even debated."

"You're whistling in the dark," said McFarlane.

"I'm just trying to give you courage, Counsellor."

McFarlane got up to reach for papers.

"I'm busy, Port. I'm very busy. I'm due at a hearing in half an hour, and I've got to...."

"Then you got half an hour. Tell me, McFarlane, did you make a ruling on that recommendation? City codes, and so forth?"

"There was no need for a ruling. You know that this slum clearance thing is clean all the way through."

Port came away from the window and sat down by the desk.

"The council can't vote the recommendation for clearing the area into special ordinance unless your office gives a legal ruling."

"Look, Port. That thing has come through my office maybe a dozen times, and you know it. It's routine when a resolution is as pure-white as this."

"Let's say you were asked, McFarlane. Let's say you were asked if that slum clearance project didn't violate city statutes. Would you know?"

"Of course I'd know! Who do you think is responsible for the legality...."

"You are. And I'm asking."

"It's clean! All the way through!"

"Don't act like it frightens you, McFarlane."

McFarlane controlled himself and hunched over the desk. His eyebrows stopped jumping, stayed way up on his forehead, and he talked with theatrical patience.

"The old lodgings don't meet architectural codes; the proposed new ones do. The old lodgings don't meet health department ordinances; the new ones do. The old lodgings don't meet zoning laws; the new ones do. The old lodgings...."

"So you have no thoughts on the subject, is that right?"

McFarlane sat up again. "What do you mean?" he asked.

"Here's what I want you to do," said Port. "Make a ruling on the assessment for utilities."

McFarlane waited.

"You and I know, McFarlane, that the utility companies aren't willing to pay more than fifty per cent of the cost for new installations in the homes for resettlement."

"Whatever you have in mind, you and I know that the city will pay the difference."

"By special assessment. And you, Counsellor, are the one who decides whether the special assessment is allowable under existing city ordinances."

"It is. And now, Port, if you will excuse...."

"It isn't."

McFarlane sat down again.

"The assessed money comes from taxes. Taxes are paid by the people. This assessment to pay for utilities benefits only some of the people. Under its statutes this city—any city, McFarlane—is not authorized to apply tax funds for the benefit of a special group." Port looked inquisitive. "How's it sound, Counsellor?"

This time McFarlane looked straight *at* Port, but he didn't say anything.

"They can't tear down the slums," said Port, "because the slum dwellers have no place to move. They got no place to move because the projected settlements won't have any utilities. They won't have any utilities, because the companies only pay fifty percent of the new installations—and the city won't pay the rest. The city can't. Violation of statutes."

"That's my ruling?" said McFarlane.

"That's your ruling."

"What if I don't?"

"I'll tell Councilman Epp to bring it up at debate. Then the question will be why in hell you didn't look into that point. Neglect of office, McFarlane." Port shook his head.

McFarlane got up, stacked some folders together, and put them under his arm. He put out the cigarette that was smoking itself in the ashtray, and went out the door, Port following him.

"How do you want me to submit it, at debate?"

"Leave the grandstand plays to Reform. Just submit it in writing to the council committee that'll bring up the debate. A quiet demise."

"Whatever you like," said McFarlane. He watched Port pick up his whisky carton. "I don't know how quiet it will be. Sump is chairman of that committee. You know Sump."

"I didn't mean to keep this thing buried. Just dignified."

"Sump will take care of that, too," said McFarlane.

Port laughed. "He after you now?"

"I told you I have this hearing." McFarlane looked at his watch. "And I'm late."

Port laughed and opened the door. "I'll go with you. Then you can blame it on me."

When they went through the office in front Port stopped where Miss Trent was typing and put his carton on top of the desk.

"May I leave this with you?"

She looked up and smiled straight in his face. "Anything," and then she smiled at McFarlane too. He turned and went hastily out of the door.

One floor below they went through the double doors where Probate Court used to be. The room was pretty much the same, except for the bannister, which was gone, and the witness stand. However, the judge's bench had been kept in place, and that's where Councilman Sump was sitting. He was in the middle of a sentence, finishing it with the plaintive drone he affected, while he watched Port and McFarlane walk into the room. They walked past the seats for the public—Sump had always thought it was bad politics to have sessions in private—and McFarlane went to the witness table while Port sat down at the side, in one of the press seats. The press wasn't represented that day.

"... and as soon as the city solicitor can spare us his time we need no longer hold up the committee's proceedings," said Sump. Meaning no offense, the plaintive note had taken strong hold now, but the drone had remained the same.

"I'm ready, Councilman." McFarlane looked up at the bench. But Sump wasn't looking at his witness. He was eying Port, who nodded back with an angelic smile. Sump didn't acknowledge it.

"If our city solicitor can now spare us...."

"I'm ready. I said I was ready."

Sump looked pained, with just the right hint that he would bear up under it all. "The committee apologizes, not having heard the witness the first time. Please speak up, Mr. McFarlane. Speak up so the public can hear you, because it is the public, Mr. McFarlane, the public whose interests are vitally involved. The function of this committee," and Councilman Sump sat up straight, there being no other members of the committee present, "as servants of our good citizens, is to act as the detergent quality, as the acid bath which removes the filth of disuse from truth. What we want, Mr. McFarlane, is truth scrubbed clean!"

Port looked at the audience and saw they were having a fairly good time. There were some housewives with shopping bags, and one of the women was massaging her shoeless foot. One or two bums sat in the back, a man in a frayed overcoat taking constant notes, high-school kids, and a farmer from out of town who thought this was still the Probate Court.

"This committee has submitted the question to you, Mr. Counsellor: whether relocation of tenement dwellers has taken into account the will of the public. I am referring to our list of particulars—a copy is here in my hand—which your office has had under advisement for the past two months. Have you, Mr. McFarlane, seen the list of particulars?"

"I have."

"Then why, why has this committee received no answer?"

McFarlane played it straight. He opened a folder and referred to notes. "On May twenty-seventh, last year, my office passed ruling on a resolution dealing with eviction and reimbursement of parties residing in the Highland area where, at the time, our new throughway was being built. Our ruling was posited on the spirit of eminent domain. When your list of particulars was submitted we referred you to that earlier ruling—our reply was filed on a Wednesday, which was two days after your submission—since in our opinion...."

"In your *opinion?*"

"That's what you asked for, wasn't it?"

Sump lowered his eyes, sad now, and spoke like a father confessor. "Mac, you and I know, don't we, that opinion can never replace hard, crystal-clear facts?"

"I fail to see the relevance—"

"You fail to see?" Sump was roaring a full, righteous roar. "You fail, Counsellor—you fail in your office of trust, is my answer! Now then, let's get at the facts as we find them. On that Monday, when the committee submitted to you the list of particulars—this list of particulars—" Sump held his copy high—"on that Monday—just where were you?"

"I beg your pardon?"

"Not *my* pardon, Mr. McFarlane!" After allowing it to reverberate Sump lowered his voice, off-handed now. "You're an elected official of the city government?"

"No, sir. My office is filled by appointment."

"Oh. Appointment. And when you were appointed, I'm merely guessing now, but when you were appointed, were you not appraised of the various duties contingent...."

"I have been city solicitor for the past twelve years, Mr. Councilman. During the entire time of my tenure...."

"You're interrupting."

"Mr. Sump!"

"I hear you talking, Mac, but you haven't said a thing."

There was a silence, noticed by all, and then Sump got down to the part that made him famous.

"Without the flim-flam, now, McFarlane, don't you think it funny that a man in your position should display a guilty conscience as easily as you just did?"

"I didn't display anything of the sort!"

"You weren't shouting? You sit there in the eyes of the public gathered behind you, and have the gall to say, in the face of the facts...."

"I mean to say...."

"You mean! Just what do you mean?"

"Your assumption of guilt is ridiculous," McFarlane said very quietly.

"Facts are ridiculous?" Sump swelled, and then he started declaiming. Port had had enough and got up. He walked down the length of the room, to the door in back, and when he was halfway there he turned and looked at Sump on the judge's bench. Sump saw him but didn't interrupt the crescendo he was building to when Port jerked his head. Sump went on for a moment, and then got up. "This session will not be terminated until the facts have been shown! I'll be back in a minute." He walked out the door which once had led to the judge's chambers.

Port met him in the hall. Sump was shorter than Port, and had a way of looking up as if he expected to be slapped. "What do you want?" he said.

"I want the crystal-clear truth, Mr. Chairman."

"Why don't you shut up?" said Sump.

Port said, "I want you to come up to the third floor with me. I got something for you. For the committee."

They walked up the stairs and down the hall.

"Make it snappy," said Sump. "I have a hearing downstairs."

"I know," said Port.

They went into the office where Miss Trent was sitting. She looked up with a smile and Sump straightened his tie.

"Why, Mr. Sump," she said. "What are you doing in the enemy's camp?"

Sump straightened his tie.

Port picked the box with the papers off the desk and said, "Thanks for keeping it for me."

She said, "Anything," and watched Port walk out of the office.

When Sump had closed the door Port gave him the carton. He took a questionnaire off the top and said, "I hold here in my hand...."

"Why don't you shut up?" said Sump again.

"It's a questionnaire. They all are. Answered and signed by the voters in Ward Nine. Since your committee will introduce debate on the slum clearance thing, you'll want to know all about this. The voice of the public, you know. Is that crystal-clear?"

Sump put the box on the floor, because it was getting heavy.

"There are three questions," said Port. "One: Would you allow the city to increase your expenses? Two: Would you move to better housing if it cost you one third more than you are paying now? Three: Would you be willing to pay up to twice as much more for your utilities? The answers are *no* to all questions, in ninety-nine per cent of the cases."

"What is this?" said Sump.

"Slum clearance cannot take place unless the city pays fifty per cent of the cost for installing utilities, and the city won't do it."

"I haven't heard anything about...."

"You will. That leaves the move up to the slum dwellers themselves. If they want to foot the bill, fine. But they won't. Here's their answer."

Sump stared at Port, then picked up the whisky carton. "You've got it sewed up, haven't you?"

"That's the truth, scrubbed clean," said Port and walked to the stairs.

Chapter 7

When Port came out of Municipal Building he saw the man standing at the bottom of the stairs with one elbow on the front foot of the marble lion. The man had a lined face and simple eyes. He was waiting for Port.

"Landis," said Port. "I thought you went back to legitimate law."

"May I see you, Daniel?"

They went across the street to the restaurant where judges and bondsmen hung out. "You drink coffee, don't you?" said Landis. They took a booth and ordered coffee for Port and a small beer for Landis.

"How's the Reform movement?" said Port.

"I'm sure you know better than I do," said Landis.

"I just asked, seeing you started it."

"Yes. Not that it shows any more."

"That's Bellamy for you. One great fixer, Bellamy. Why'd you ever take him in, Landis?"

"Inexperience. However, it won't happen again."

Port looked over the rim of his cup. "You still in the game?"

Landis had a trim gray mustache, and he rubbed it with his finger. "First of all, Port, this is not a game. It is not, I think, even a game for you. And second, I wouldn't have started the movement if I didn't think it had the strength to achieve eventually what its name suggests."

"Have it your way," said Port.

"I will."

Landis sipped cold beer and Port drank some cold coffee. Then he said, "I'm sure you wanted something, Landis."

"I saw you inside," said Landis, "at the Sump performance."

"Funny, wasn't it?"

"Hardly. I was surprised to see you, Port, because I had heard you were leaving."

"I didn't."

"Why? Pressure, or misguided loyalty?"

"What's the difference?"

"Yes. Anyway, I wondered if you would tell me this, Port. Are you back for good, or is this just temporary?"

"Why do you ask, Landis?"

"Your presence in town makes a difference. I told you quite frankly that I wasn't through, and I tell you just as frankly that my plans for the Reform party would differ, depending on whether or not you are here."

"You'll never make a politician, Landis."

"Wouldn't you figure out what I told you yourself?"

"On second thought, you might make a good one."

"Would you answer my question?"

"Why should I?"

"I thought you might, as long as it doesn't do damage to you or to your loyalties."

"You flatter me, Landis."

"No. I appreciate you."

"Then please appreciate that I won't give you an answer."

Landis nodded his head, but he wasn't through. "Would you tell me this much, Port. Do you intend staying indefinitely?"

Port lit a cigarette and blew the smoke into the aisle. "You know something, Landis, you're taking a lot of liberties. What makes you think I'd give you information that you could use?"

"Because I know as well as you do that basically you don't give a damn what goes on in this town." Landis put out a hand and said, "May I have one of your cigarettes?" They didn't talk while Landis lit up. Then he said, "Or maybe you do. Maybe that's why you were leaving."

Port didn't answer.

"Well?" and Landis put his head to one side.

Port sat back, felt around in an inside pocket. He put some envelopes on the table, a travel folder, and two membership cards. He put everything back in his pocket except for one of the envelopes. He opened it and took out his airplane ticket.

"I bought this. You see? One way out. Take it, Landis," and when Landis held it in his hand Port got up.

Landis said, "All right," and tapped the ticket against one nail. He watched Port pull down his jacket and turn to go.

"If I ask you for it—then you know," said Port and walked away.

"I'll hold on to it," said Landis, but Port was too far away to hear.

Ramon fixed his tie in front of the mirror and looked at it to see if it was quiet enough. It wouldn't do to wear the wrong color, or too much of it, or even to indicate that he had given it thought. He looked sideways at Shelly. She was wearing an apron over her dress, and she was humming.

"How about it," he said. "You almost done with that sink?"

She gave him a smile and stopped the humming. "You worry too much, Nino. I'll be done long before your Mr. Port comes in. You look very nice," she added.

He didn't appreciate the remark and waited till she had turned back to the sink. Then he spat in his palm and smoothed it along one side of his hair.

"And you gotta change yet," he said after a moment.

Shelly wiped her hands dry and went to the stove.

"I'll be out before he gets here," she said, but that wasn't what Ramon had meant.

"You stay here." There was more force behind his voice than he had expected, but Shelly didn't seem to notice. She picked up the percolator with the hot coffee and poured some of it into a little pot.

"You'll be all right," she said. "You're too eager, Nino." She had her back turned to him, so she didn't see his angry frown.

After a while he said, "I wish you'd stay, Shelly. You know, just to be polite."

"But it's business," she said.

"You can always leave later."

She went to the door of her room and said, "What do you want me to wear?"

He shrugged and looked at the oilcloth on the kitchen table. "You know better than I. Just look right, you know?"

She wasn't sure that she knew what he meant, but she knew how anxious he was. She closed the door to her room and started to change into something else. Nino had always been anxious, but then it hadn't mattered. Nino had never done anything. Now it was different. He was doing something, or perhaps someone else was doing something to Nino. She didn't know which.

She heard the knock at the door outside, and when her dress had stopped
rustling around her ears she heard chairs scraping at the kitchen table, and
Nino laughing. It didn't sound as if there had been a joke, but Nino laughed,
said something, laughed again. The other one hadn't said a thing. Shelly buttoned up, shook her hair back, and went to the kitchen.

The first thing Port saw was that she wasn't wearing a red carnation. He
said hello to her and he said he hoped she didn't mind his taking up her quarters, but what he was really thinking had to do with the flower. I must bring
her a flower, he thought. He frowned and looked at Ramon.

"Shelly," said Ramon, "pour us some coffee, will you?"

Shelly went to the stove. "If you'd like to be alone, Mr. Port, I can...."

"Just for a while. Do you mind?"

"You can go in the other room," said Ramon.

"I'll tell you," Port took his cup from her and put it down on the table.
"We'll finish this and then your brother and I can go someplace else. I did-
n't mean to...."

"Oh, no!" Ramon laughed. "You go out, Shelly, and come back in half an
hour. Okay? Okay, Dan?"

Port said, "Fine," and picked up his cup.

Shelly took a handbag off a hook in the wall and went toward the door.
When she passed her brother's chair she touched his shoulder, and when
he looked up she smiled at him and said, "I'll see you later." She nodded at
Port and opened the door.

"Thanks for the coffee," said Port. He smiled at her and she stood in the
door for a moment, smiling back at him. "That was nice of you," he said. She
nodded and went out.

Ramon had the feeling they had made quite a lot of that coffee bit. He
wished that she could have stayed. Maybe they knew each other better than
he thought? Maybe, that thing about having met on the street— He put his
cup down.

"What happened with the job?" Port asked.

"I went to the agency, as you said to, and before they sent me out there I
memorized those references that were on the card they had ready...."

"The job, Ramon."

"I got it."

Port sat back and took a breath and said, "Good."

"It's from eight to five, and they want me to room out there. A room they
got in the basement. Their name is Bellamy."

"I know that."

"Oh." Then Ramon waited.

"You know who Bellamy is?"

"I didn't know it was *the* Bellamy. The way you said it…."

"It's him."

Ramon felt suspended, even a little shaky, and he didn't know whether it was from eagerness or from fear. But he knew for sure that he was now very important.

Port was drawing a square on the paper and pointed at it.

"Here's your room. Your bed stands over here, and there is a washstand, so, and a table."

"How—how did you know?"

"The electrician that worked at the house yesterday told me." Port took a sip from his cup, then looked up. "You starting tomorrow?"

"Yes. They want me to start tomorrow."

Port drew again.

"Next time you go there lie down on your bed, reach down where the floor board is, here, and pull it away from the wall. It'll pull away easy. Reach in by the corner and there is an earphone."

"Earphone?"

"Yeah. The cord's long enough so you can lie on the pillow and listen with the earphone next to your ear."

"I'll be damned."

"Yeah. Now I don't care about any calls but the ones Bellamy makes, or gets. He's got a daughter, but she isn't likely to use the phone we rigged. She has her own. Now, Bellamy doesn't get in till around nine. I want you to get your sleep between five, when you get off, and nine when he gets in. Tapping is a tiresome job. Watch it you don't fall asleep while you lie there listening. Sometimes nothing happens at all."

Ramon nodded. His mouth was open.

"Bellamy does business on the phone till late at night. He always has. Most of the stuff I don't care about. He's got deals in construction, he talks to New York about fighter contracts, boxing and wrestling; forget it. What I want is local. Whom does he talk to about the Reform party, what does he say, what about Stoker, plans, meetings, what is said about the new tie-up with slum clearance…."

"It's—you tied it up again?"

"He'll be talking about that. Some, anyway. But whatever it is, in this connection, listen hard. Write it down if you can't remember, but don't write it down if you can help it. Get names, names of outfits, anything that can tie down the place he is calling, like a club or an office. You got this clear, Ramon?"

Ramon nodded seriously and repeated what Port had said. Port balled up the paper and threw it into a trash carton under the sink. Then he told Ramon how to get in touch with him. Unless it sounded hot he should not use the phone booth that stood at the intersection a short walk from the house, never to use any phone inside the house, but he should talk to the mailman that came to Bellamy's at around nine in the morning. "He's an old one. If he says to you tomorrow, 'Been digging up any worms?' that's him."

"Been digging up any worms," said Ramon. He nodded to himself and looked nervous.

"When's your day off?"

"Uh—Thursday. But not this Thursday."

"He's always been a cheapskate," said Port. He smiled at Ramon. "How much you making?"

"Thirty-five, with room and board."

"That's why he keeps changing the help. He won't pay a real professional."

"His daughter hired me."

"How much does a real gardener make?"

"I don't know. I don't know nothing from gardening. It worries me, you know? You ever think of that?"

"You won't be there long enough."

"Oh."

"Do a good job, Ramon, and you're in."

Ramon lit up, but the real relief didn't show in his face until a few moments later, when a key turned in the door and Shelly came in. She said, "If I'm too early...."

"No, this is fine," said Port, and noticed that Ramon relaxed. "I'm just going. I apologize," he started when Ramon got up and said he wouldn't have it, that Port should stay. His sister would want him to stay and she should slice up some of the cake she had made.

"I don't know if Mr. Port...."

"I like cake," said Port.

He stayed in his chair and watched Shelly slice cake. He saw her from the back and the curve of her back made him think of the girl in McFarlane's office, but he liked this girl better. Or her looks, anyway, since he didn't know Shelly at all.

Ramon was running around, looking in drawers and on shelves and then he said, "I'll be right back. I can't find the cigarettes."

"Use mine," said Port, but Ramon was at the door, explaining that he only smoked one kind and Port's wasn't it. He closed the door and was gone.

They both looked at the door and then Shelly came to the table.

"You still want the cake?"

Port looked up at her and saw what she meant. "I don't think he'll be back so soon," he said.

Shelly sat down at the table and pushed the cake out of the way. The movement showed the inside of her arm and she moved so slowly that Port thought he was looking at it a very long time. He didn't care if she noticed. She folded her arms on the table and he didn't notice how she looked at him. When she talked he looked up quickly.

"He is trying very hard."

"Ramon? Yes, he is."

"He won't be back for a while, so there's time for me to ask you something."

Port went to the stove and poured himself another cup of coffee.

"What do you want from my brother?"

"It's mutual," said Port. "I need talent, and he wants to give it."

"He has no talent. All he has is big dreams of how to be an operator."

"I won't strain his talents."

"How about his self-respect?"

Suddenly Port didn't like her. He thought her eyes were too large, her fingers too long, and her face had the toneless color of a dark complexion without enough sun.

"He can take it or leave it. So can you."

She poked at the cake with the long knife she was holding, but she kept looking at him.

"You've harmed him already," she said. "He's never done this before."

"What's that?"

"Pimp his sister."

Port put out his cigarette.

"I didn't take him up on it," he said.

Her eyes got narrow and she put down the knife. But her voice was as even as ever.

"You stayed, didn't you?"

Port sat still, letting the tension turn to a physical sting on his skin.

"I would have stayed anyway," he said.

"That's how you planned it?"

"No," he felt irritable with her suspicion. "I just decided. I took one look at that cake of yours...."

She jumped up so fast he thought she had in mind leaping at him. He watched how her breasts moved with her breathing and then the color that darkened her face.

"Get out," she said.

He pushed back his chair and got up. Her emotion surprised him.

"And now what, you scream?"

She didn't answer. She picked up the knife and held the point into the oil-cloth. Port went to the door, opened it, and turned back to the girl.

"I'll see you," he said.

She punched the knife into the oilcloth again, but didn't move otherwise. Only her face was full of life. "You know," she said, "I don't know how to throw this. If I knew how to throw a knife, I would."

"I'm glad you can't," he said and walked away without closing the door. Shelly could hear him whistling.

Chapter 8

When Port got to the Lee building the nightman opened the door for him. "Mr. Stoker ain't in," he said, "if that's who you want."

"Where did he go?" Port said.

"He never came in today. Fries was here, but he's gone by now."

Port went back to his car. He leaned against the rear fender and jiggled the antenna that stuck out at an angle. He hoped Stoker hadn't left town for some reason, but he didn't think Stoker would, not at this time. He got into his car.

When he got to the apartment, Mrs. Stoker opened the door. She gave him a hostile look and told him which door to take.

Port knocked at the door and waited till it was opened by Fries, who stepped aside to let Port come in. Stoker was in bed.

There was a knee desk in front of him, a phone by his elbow, and his color was fresh, which—in a case like Stoker's—didn't mean health.

"If it's good, tell him," said Fries. "If it isn't, don't hang around here till you've fixed it."

Port said hello and sat down near the bed. "You've got a good man here," he said to Stoker. "It proves we all got a good side, no matter how bad the first impression is." Then he smiled at Fries.

"One day, horse around like that," said Fries, "and you're gonna be...."

"Fries, there's no such thing as a spontaneous ulcer, but you're working on it," Port said.

"All right," said Stoker, "all right, all right—"

"What if a real catastrophe should happen to you," Port went on, "then what could you do? Burst into flame?"

Fries had a lot of control. It killed his appetite, made him gassy, gave him shooting pains in the back—but none of this showed, which was the point. He said, "You and I must have a talk some day."

"Another one?"

"Another kind."

"If you're both through performing," said Stoker, "before I die from a couple of things that've got nothing to do with my heart—"

"Okay," said Port. "All right if I smoke?"

"Makes no difference," said Stoker.

Port lit up. "I think we've got the ward for a while longer, maybe."

Nobody expected it, not even Fries. He got out of his chair and started to bellow.

"Maybe!" A vein jumped out on his forehead, thick blue, and he was hoarse. "A while longer, maybe! You got an idea that's enough? You got an idea you do us a favor sticking around while you feel like it and swing a little deal on the side so maybe it works and maybe it don't? Now get this straight, Port, and you listen too, Max! There's been a lot of horsing around here doing some greasing now and then, or a pep talk now and then, when it looked like business might get out of hand. That's not good enough now! We got the machine in this town, and we can make it hum. But you gotta first throw the right lever, and believe me, Port, that takes muscle!"

Fries stopped with a hard breath in his throat, and then he sat down. He looked away for a moment, rubbing his mouth, as if he were afraid it might start screaming again. Stoker sat still in his bed and Port looked at him.

"What was that?" he said, and the surprise in his face was real.

Fries was back to normal when he said to Port, "If you're going to start making jokes again...."

"He won't." Stoker might have felt sick, but he didn't sound it. Fries closed his mouth and Port listened. "Three of his men got into a brawl."

"Got jumped," said Fries.

"Three of his men got jumped. That's why he's talking that way."

"If Bellamy thinks...."

"I think they're imports," said Port. "The three I was talking to were suntanned, and who do you know in this town, this time of year, who've got suntans."

"Very clever," said Fries. "I'm really impressed. Most of all by the way you figured that out. They had suntans!" To Fries it didn't sound funny. The tic came back into one of his eyes and he said, "That Reform Party started to roll when Bellamy took it over. Next thing you know he bulldozed right over everything our brain-truster here ever set up. And next thing you know, he imports hoods. The difference between...."

"I'll tell you the difference," said Stoker. "Some places it's muscle, other places that doesn't work. That's the difference, but Bellamy doesn't know it. He starts heaving muscle in this game and maybe starts thinking that's all he needs...."

"What makes you think he's got no brains?"

"The first real move he made," said Port. "That's what makes me think so."

"Listen." Fries showed how little he liked being contradicted. "If you mean that newspaper release, it pretty near wrecked us. For all you've said around here, it's still got us running."

"If you'll listen a minute, Fries." Port pulled out his cigarettes. "His first big move is a dumb move. He throws it around to the public that we bribed the Planning Board. So we did. So what. To make hay on that, there's got to be two things. One, we have to give him an argument so the public can get involved; two, he's got to be ready with something to follow it up, some concrete thing that shows him to be better than us. He didn't have it. All he had was a lot of political hogwash hung on to his revelations. So there's Bellamy yelling robbers, but he isn't making a move to chase 'em himself." Port looked at Fries. "That makes him dumb. Remember that, Fries."

Stoker rolled over in bed and closed his eyes as if he were tired. "I want to hear what you did about it."

Port told him. He explained what he did with McFarlane and with Councilman Sump. There wasn't a chance for the city to tear down the slums and ruin Boss Stoker's Ward Nine. It sounded complete and final.

"You satisfied?" said Stoker from the bed.

"You'll have to watch it to see what they do next."

"Who do you mean by 'you'?" said Stoker.

Port didn't answer, so Stoker went on.

"Let's say I ask Fries to watch it. What should he be watching for?"

"He's an old hand," said Port.

"Let's say Fries keeps watching Bellamy's hoods, so his monkeys don't get clobbered when they drink beer some place."

"That would be bad," said Port.

"What should I be watching?" asked Fries.

Port ignored the tone and answered him.

"Stalling the slum clearance can work for years, but it's never better than stalling. After a while there won't be any slums."

"You sound like Landis," said Fries.

"He's got brains."

"Let's stick to the point," said Stoker. "What happens now?"

"We stalled them on a legal gimmick. An interpretation. So the next move from Reform should be a re-interpretation."

"State Capitol?" Stoker asked.

"I don't know. Maybe they can do it locally."

"I can handle that. But I'm not good enough to handle the Capitol."

"They haven't gotten that far yet. Maybe they never will."

"But what if they do? We gotta have the next step all laid out. We can't...."

"Leave me out of it, Max." Port got up.

Stoker turned on his back.

"Danny."

"What do you want from me?" The other two men looked up. "You want a thirty-year contract or something? Or an oath? I told you before what you're going to get from me. I'm through explaining. I don't run out, and I don't leave you a mess. There won't be any loose ends when I'm through, and I'm going to be through when they vote down the clearance project. And meantime don't keep pushing at me or dreaming up extra work to take home nights." He went to the door and said, "I'm going to bed."

Boss Stoker stopped him.

"There's a new arrangement," he said, "because of Bellamy and his new methods."

Port waited, keeping his hand on the door knob. "Beginning tomorrow you don't go out except with protection. You got a gun?" Stoker continued.

"I always sleep with a gun under my pillow."

Stoker ignored it.

"Fries will send over a man in the morning. He goes with you."

Port said, "Go to hell," and slammed the door shut.

Chapter 9

When Port got out of the shower he heard the telephone in the next room. It was barely past eight in the morning. He stopped toweling himself and picked up the phone. The voice started right in, "Hello, hello? That you, Dan?"

"Yeah."

"Dan, this is Ramon."

"Where you calling from, damn it?"

"The booth down at the corner from Bellamy's place—"

"All right, what is it?"

"This morning, maybe five, ten minutes ago, I just happened to pick up the receiver—I don't go to work till nine, you know—and there's Bellamy talking."

"About what?"

"I didn't listen long enough, Dan, I thought you ought to know who the other guy was."

"All right, who?"

"McFarlane!... Did you hear me?"

"You said McFarlane."

There was a pause from Ramon, and then he said, "Well, that's it. Isn't he supposed to be in with us? What's he doing having talks with Bellamy?"

Port rubbed his hair with the towel. Then he said, "McFarlane plays both sides of the fence. I thought you knew."

"He does? And you do business with him?"

"Why not? He never gets told anything the other side isn't supposed to know, and meanwhile he delivers."

Ramon was glad that Port couldn't see him.

"Christ, I thought—I'm sorry I called for nothing."

"Don't worry about it."

"Really, Dan, if I had known...."

"As long as you didn't know, you did right."

"If you say so."

"Now get back there and dig in the garden."

Ramon said good-by and hung up, but the thing stayed with him for quite a while longer.

Port forgot about it and got dressed. When he got downstairs and walked out on the street a man pushed away from the wall of the building and said, "Bang." Then he grinned.

For a minute Port thought he'd murder the guy, but then he took a deep breath and rubbed his hands so they would stop shaking.

Simon laughed. "You see, Danny, Max was right. You do need protection."

Port came up with a long string of profanity, repeating himself several times and inventing some new things. Simon waited. When Port was through Simon said, "That was beautiful. Are you through?"

"You're through. Now beat it!"

But Stoker had picked the right man, because Simon could not be impressed. He could be told what to do; after that it was hard to get to him, and when it was contradictory there was no use talking to him at all. "I could beat the stuffing out of you and leave you on the street," said Port.

"No, you couldn't."

Port knew this was true.

"Look, Simon, you're too slow. I can't use you. What if something comes up all of a sudden, I get jumped, for instance...."

"I'm good from close in."

This was true too. Simon had the nervous system of a slow worm. It made him sluggish, but it also made him immune to pain. With Simon the other man always got off the first punch. After that—when the other man slowed down in surprise—is when Simon paid off. He could hit, and he could last, like granite.

"All right, come on," said Port. "But keep out of my way."

"What you say, Danny?" Port didn't bother to answer and kept still all the way to the club, where he went into a room with a desk and a typewriter. A club member was sleeping in the swivel chair and Port told Simon to throw him out. Simon did this. Then Port told Simon to leave the room and to let nobody in. Port wasn't bothered for the next five hours. He put typing paper and carbon into the machine and typed almost continuously. Sometimes he stopped, closed his eyes while he got things straight, and then he would write again. Part of the time Simon could hear Port whistling.

When Port finished he addressed an envelope and called Simon. "Run down to the office in front and get Phil up here. He should bring his notary public thing. And if you see Lantek tell him to come up, too. If you don't see him, bring anyone."

Simon came back with Lantek and Phil, who had brought his notary public stamp.

"All you guys stand over there by the wall. Can you see me writing?" Port took a desk pen and made passes at the sheets in front of him, as if he were writing.

"You're making passes at the paper there," said Simon. Lantek nodded and so did Phil. They couldn't read the typing, but they could see where Port started to sign each page in the margin. The last page he signed on the bottom. He turned the pile over, blank side up, and had Phil sign his notary spiel and apply his stamp. Under that he got the two others to witness the notarizing. He did this with each sheet. When it was done he sent them all out again. Port sealed the original into the envelope and fastened the carbon together with a paper clip. He put those two things, and the carbon paper, into his pocket. When Port went downstairs, Simon followed him.

"What did you write, Danny?"

"Last will and testament, seeing you're here to protect me."

Simon laughed at that. He was still laughing when Port stopped at the curb outside.

"Take my car," said Port, "and run down to Tucker Street. I'll wait for you here while you pick...."

"That means you're staying here alone!"

There was a short pause by both of them, but after a moment Port started to walk to his car. Simon followed. When they turned into Tucker Street Simon couldn't wait any longer. "I know you don't want to talk to me, Danny, but I'm getting hungry. For me it's way past lunchtime right now. I'm wondering...."

"I noticed you got kind of lively," said Port. "We'll eat right now."

Simon was pleased until he saw where Port stopped and where he went in, because a flower shop wasn't what Simon expected. Port came back with a short-stemmed red carnation and Simon didn't say a word. They drove back to Ward Nine, parked near the club, and Port led the way to the beanery with the grocery counter in front. The special was corned beef hash patties with a fried egg, and a tomato salad. They ordered that and sat at a table. Simon sat facing the door, since he took his job seriously, and Port sat facing the back. Shelly wasn't there. The fat grocer served them. Port ate with one hand, holding the flower in the other.

"Danny, I don't mean to be personal," said Simon, "but the flower—"

"You like it?"

"Just don't hold it the way you do, Danny. I'm eating corned beef and smelling carnation."

Port moved the flower and they finished eating. Shelly still hadn't showed up.

The door opened and a girl came in. Port couldn't see her because he was facing the other way, but he guessed that it was a girl from Simon's expression. They both watched her pass to the counter where she sat on a stool. They had a good view. Port missed seeing Shelly come in from the back, and he missed what she did. Shelly stopped in the back door when she saw Port and took off the red carnation she had on her lapel. She put it behind the counter.

Then the girl on the stool turned around and got up. She came to the table and said, "You're Danny Port, ain't you?"

"Sit down, sit down," said Simon and pulled out a chair for her. She sat without looking at Simon, and then Port remembered. She had worn only a blouse and shoes, and eight men had been with her.

"You don't remember? I was up in the club, with eight of 'em."

"Sure, I remember. How's it been—"

"Kate."

"How's it been, Kate?"

"What you mean, eight of 'em?" Simon wanted to know.

"I'm a hooker," said Kate and turned back to Port.

He twirled the stem of the flower between two fingers, and tried to catch Shelly's eye. When she looked at him he smiled, but she didn't give it back. "Three coffees," he called, and then looked back at Kate.

"You working?" he asked her.

Shelly came over with three cups of coffee and put them down without saying a word. Port kept twirling the red carnation, kept trying to look at her, but Shelly looked elsewhere. When she was gone and Port picked up his cup it seemed to him he'd never had coffee that hot before.

"I'm not working," said Kate. She had a careless face and a careless body, and when she leaned back in her chair Simon spilled coffee down his chin.

"I come to thank you," said Kate, "for the way you treated me."

"Sure, Kate."

"They coulda throwed me out without paying, except you told them to."

"You're welcome, honey."

She looked at Port for a moment, as if she were waiting for more. Then she said, "I come to thank you."

Port smiled at her and said, "Good," because he thought she had said thank you often enough.

Simon leaned over the table and sounded as if he had a raw throat. "She means in trade, for God's sakes. She wants to pay you back in trade."

"Kate, you don't owe me a thing."

"I think so."

"Dan," said Simon, "*she* thinks so. What in hell is the matter with you?"

Kate said, "Ain't that Shelly's flower? Shelly always...."

"Not yet," said Port, and stopped twirling the carnation between his fingers. "I haven't given it to her yet."

"Is she watching?" said Kate.

"No."

"So why don't you go out and wait at the car. Where's your car?"

"Honey, I said no."

Kate looked from one to the other, not knowing what to do next. "So how am I gonna return the favor?"

Port didn't know what to say, and Simon couldn't talk. He was grinning, biting his lip, and his eyes looked wet.

"He a friend of yours?" and Kate nodded at Simon.

"Quite a while now."

"Maybe you owe him a favor."

Simon, at special times, could be very fast. He said, "Does he! He owes me favors from way back. Danny, don't you remember from way back the favors you…."

"Okay then," said Kate. She got up and waited for Simon, who almost knocked over the table.

Port said, "Jeesis," and watched them go out of the door.

After a while he called to Shelly that he wanted another coffee and when she came the first thing he saw was that she was wearing a red carnation. She put his fresh cup down and picked up the three old ones.

"I brought you this," said Port and held up the flower. "I thought…."

"I got one."

"Yours is wilted, Shelly."

"I don't think so. I think the one I have is fine."

"Then wear two. One here, and one there."

She didn't answer, and took the used cups back to the counter. Port got up and went to sit on a stool. Shelly turned to look down at him.

"Would you like something else?" She could look mean as hell.

"Sure."

"No," she said. "Like the first time, on the street."

Port grinned and smelled the flower.

Shelly turned away to clean up the grill, which was already clean. It made her feel silly after a while, and there was a place on her back that started to itch.

"Look," she said, "just because you got my brother to take jumps and make cartwheels for you, don't think…."

"I'm not thinking of your brother. I'm sitting here looking at you, and it's got nothing to do with your brother."

She glared at him, because he was looking at her and there wasn't a thing she could do. She drew herself a coke and started to sip it. She leaned against the ice cream tank behind her, crossed her legs, and folded her arms.

"When you get real impatient," she said, "why don't you go out and find Kate. She'll take anything."

"Don't slam Kate. At least she knows what she's got."

Shelly felt like hiding. She recrossed her legs and her thoughts made her furious.

"You know," said Port, "right now I'm just sitting here, waiting for Simon to get back. I thought at first you and me could have a visit while I was waiting. But right now I'm just waiting for them to get back."

She was working her teeth into her lower lip, which made her look like an animal. Port massaged the palms of his hands. "When I first came in, I just wanted to give you this flower."

"All right, give it to me," and she stepped up to the counter. She took her flower off and dropped it into the sink, but didn't reach for the new one. She had her arms by her side, leaned forward a little, and nodded down at herself. "Go ahead. You put it on."

Port got up, smiled at her, and said he was glad to do that.

"No, not the lapel. Where the pocket is."

She said it with her eyes narrowed, and Port did the job with the flower carefully. Then he sat down. "You should appreciate this," he said. "I've never done that before."

"I could tell." She leaned back against the ice cream tank and took off the flower. She moved it up to pin it where it belonged. "But you learn fast. Just don't forget what you learn."

Port got up and paid his check.

"The next lesson, I give," and he walked out.

Chapter 10

Port stood on the street for a while and looked across to the club. His car wasn't there any more so he walked down the block a short way to look into the empty lot. His car and a few others were there. He smoked a cigarette, and walked around for fifteen minutes. Simon didn't show. Port went into the lot. He figured by this time his bodyguard needed some saving.

Simon was in the back. He was on his stomach, sprawled out limp, and the lump on the back of his head showed plainly. Kate wasn't there.

Port got Simon into a sitting position, but Simon was still out. Port started to snap his finger under the limp man's nose, which woke Simon after a while.

"You look exhausted, Simon. Let me tell you."

Simon groaned and took the cigarette Port handed to him.

"As a matter of fact, Simon, I'm going to ask Fries to assign a man to you, somebody that'll follow you no matter what. Then, maybe...."

"Danny, please. Don't yell so loud."

Port slid behind the wheel, then turned back again. "I'm going to start the motor. You think the vibration will be too much for you?"

"Danny, what am I gonna say? What are you gonna tell Fries about this?"

"Nothing. But you tell me something. How did she do it? How did that little bitty girl...."

"Oh, Christ—" moaned Simon.

"At least tell me this, Simon."

"I don't know. So help me I can't remember!"

Simon looked down at his knees. "I know I was doing all right there. Just for a while."

"Then what did she do?"

"I don't know. I thought that she was doing all right too."

"Anyway," and Port turned to start the car, "at least she doesn't owe me anything any more."

"I don't know, Danny. I think she still does."

The rest of the day Port spent in different places. He dropped in on McFarlane, checked progress with Councilman Sump, spent some time at the club in Ward Nine when a local matter came up there, and he mailed the envelope with the sheets he had typed in the morning. He sent it, registered, to an address in New York, requesting a return receipt. When he got home at night he put the carbon copy into his trunk. He sat smoking for a while in the dark, because that way he could see out the window. He imagined he wouldn't see this view for much longer, because when the council voted down the slum resolution that would be that. Just a few days, maybe. He went to bed and was asleep in a very short time....

He didn't think he had slept very long. He sat up, in the dark, and heard the knock on the door again. When he got out of bed the voice said, "It's me," and it knocked again. Port switched on the lamp by his bed and put on a bathrobe. Then he opened the door.

"You alone?" said Kate.

"That's real delicate of you," said Port. He stepped aside to let her in. "Where's your blackjack?"

"I don't carry no blackjack." She walked in and put her purse down on a chair. She put her hands on her hips and waited for Port to close the door. "What would I need a blackjack for?"

Port looked at her in the light that was coming at her from one side and said, "Yeah. What for is right." Then he sat down on the bed and fixed himself a cigarette.

"Did Simon tell you?" she asked. There was an easy chair near the bed where she sat down.

"No, but he showed me. He showed me the lump on the back of his head and to this moment I can't figure out just how you did it." Port saw she was pushing one shoe off her foot with the other. "You going to show me how it's done?"

"I didn't do it," she said.

Port didn't see her push off the other shoe because he was surprised and looked at her face.

"I thought you were an honest whore, Kate. Dames that play badger games like this I don't like."

"I didn't know the guys did it to him."

Port frowned, and then he saw Kate unbutton her jacket.

He said, "Hey—" but then he watched when she slipped it off. She paused after that and frowned back at him.

"Katie, look. I know it's hard as hell for a woman to just take it when I say no to her. So pull yourself together and...."

"Whatsa matter with you? Didn't Simon tell you?"

"He got conked. What could he tell me?"

"I still owe you. At least he shoulda knowed what he didn't get."

"No," said Port. He closed his eyes when he said it so Kate was half done by the time he looked back. She had her blouse open and was flapping it back. She did all this with no ado, without doing any more than removing her clothes.

Port got up and took a few steps. Kate looked after him.

"I also come to tell you about them two guys. Something you might have a use for."

"What in hell you going to do? Sit there naked?"

"You don't wear nothing under that robe." She used his tone of voice.

He controlled himself. "What was that, an argument?"

"Who's arguing?" and she unhooked her brassiere in the back.

He stopped arguing and watched what she did. Then he remembered about Simon.

"You were going to tell me something about those two guys."

"Well, they tore open the door and Simon and me were in the back. Simon is kind of slow anyway, so before he got adjusted one of the guys, the short one, gave him a belt."

"On the back of the head?"

"I thought it was coming off."

"Simon wasn't out cold right then?"

"You arguing or listening? Simon tries getting up when the short guy says, 'Just a sample, lamebrain, of what we think of Port and his bodyguard.' Then he slams Simon on the head again. They shut the door and I try getting up from underneath Simon."

She stood up and undid the zipper on the side of her skirt.

"That's it?" said Port.

"Then they came back. 'Might as well,' says one of them and tells me to get out of the car. And they take me to this place." She dropped the skirt and stepped out of it. "You know the apartment house on Birch. Twelve hundred Birch?"

"I know where it is."

"Well, they take me up on the second floor and they got a layout there. What I mean is, not like an apartment, but with phones and bunks and a messy kitchen like there hasn't been a woman in the house—I mean a housewife in the house—for ages."

"So they live there like pigs."

"No. It's like your club. Like some rooms in your club, you know?"

"Who were they, you know?"

"They were none of your ward men. And these had suntans."

Port remembered, and perhaps Kate had told him something. They lived in the ward, and the way Kate had told it, these two weren't the only ones. Not a bad notion for Bellamy to put his hoods down close to the center of things. If he was going to use his new crew, the likeliest place would be Ward Nine. Trouble in Stoker's notorious Ward Nine. Gangsterism and Crime, etc.

"Did you get their names?"

"One was Kirby, the short mean one."

"And George?"

"Maybe. I didn't call them by name."

It made Port smile. Then he said, "Did they pay you?"

She shook her head.

"How much are you?"

"Nothing, to you."

"I mean them."

"On my own, I wouldn't have anything to do with them for fifty bucks."

He saw she meant it. He also saw she was kicking her panties off and stood there naked. She stood there as if she didn't know about clothes and no clothes, as if it were all the same. That wasn't the way Port felt when she stepped closer and put her head to one side.

Port tried to speak, but nothing much came of it. Kate noticed and put her hands up to reach for his neck when she suddenly found there was no more distance between them. He didn't have time to turn off the light.

Chapter 11

Ten-thirty a.m. Simon was still waiting in front of the building. He figured three hours' waiting would be long enough; he would wait till eleven and then go upstairs. He looked down the length of the block to the diner, because he hadn't eaten that day. Then he looked back at the building entrance because that's what he was supposed to do. When he saw Kate come out, it confused him and failed to connect with his mission. She said, "Hi, Simon," and it immediately brought back the past to him. He ran up to her and grabbed her arm. "How did you do it?" he wanted to know. "I can't figure out, and Port can't either."

"Do what?"

"Yesterday. In the car."

"I didn't do anything," she said. "And you didn't either."

Simon held on to her arm and started to think. It made his face sullen. "You know, that makes me mad."

Kate pulled her arm out of his hand. "All right. You had a good time. Now you feel better?"

He kept looking at her, then took her arm again. "There's something here ain't kosher. I had such a good time I got a bump on the back of my head?"

"That wasn't me. I was in front of you."

It connected Simon with the past, and when Kate tried to pull away again Simon held on. His thumb started to rub the soft of her arm.

"No," she said. "I'm tired."

"Hell, it's ten in the morning."

"That's why. Ten in the morning isn't nice," and she pulled her arm out of his hand.

He felt like going after her when Port came out of the door and tapped Simon on the back. "Had your breakfast yet?"

"Where were you?" said Simon. "I been standing here without breakfast or anything."

"I thought you might, and that's why I got up to take you to breakfast." Port took Simon by the arm and they went to the diner. After they ate they had to sit for a while longer because Port's coffee was still too hot.

"You know something?" said Simon. "That hooker, she come outa your building."

"You mean that, Simon?"

"Sure enough. You know, she still owes you that thank you, and I'm going to see to it she pays up."

"Don't bother, Simon. I made an arrangement with her so she won't have to pay."

"What you do that for?"

Port gave a soothing pat to Simon's arm and handed him a cigarette. Then they went for the car and drove toward Ward Nine.

Less than halfway there Simon spotted the girl on the street. "Kate!" he said, and when Port pulled up next to her Simon had the door already open.

"I'm going your way," said Port. "You want a lift?" She said yes and Simon flipped the back rest forward so she could get in the rear.

"Simon," said Port. "You sit in front."

Simon obeyed but made clear how sore he was by looking out of the window and not talking to anybody.

When Port started the car again Kate caught his eye in the rear-view mirror. She grinned at him and said, "Thank you, Port."

Port stopped the car. He turned around to the back and said, "That's perfectly all right, Kate. It's a common courtesy, and please don't think that you now owe me anything."

She grinned at him again and Port started driving.

When they got to the old streets of Ward Nine, Kate told them where she lived. When they reached her house Simon got out of the car and waited for Kate to pass.

"Now you know where I live," she said to Simon, "come over some time." She was gone into the house before Simon could answer.

They drove down to the club and Simon went to the room with the easy chairs to toss the volley ball with the two guys that were sitting there. Port went upstairs. At twelve-fifteen he got a call from a gray-haired mailman who for ten minutes repeated for Port all that Ramon had told him that morning. Then he waited while Port didn't say a thing. After a while Port said, "You sure you got all of it?"

"I'm sure, Dan. Anything in it?"

"I don't know yet."

"In case you're interested, Dan, I got some Special Delivery for that street. You want me to drop in on the boy again?"

Port thought for a moment and then, "It might help. Tell him to come to his house tonight."

"After work?"

"After his real job. I figure there won't be anything so I'll expect him around two. At his house."

"I'll tell him," said the mailman and hung up.

There hadn't been much to put your finger on, but Port wrote it all down, because his memory wasn't as good as some. The main thing that struck him was an address, and he would have to ask Ramon how it was mentioned, just what the connection was. The address was 1200 Birch.

This time Port was glad to have Simon along. They walked the few blocks to the apartment building, and in the entrance hall Port checked the names of the tenants. The place was valuable. Three floors with two apartments, each apartment divided in half and half the apartments rented per room. And rent went per person. The place was built of brick, so the upkeep hadn't been very much. The plumbing was galvanized iron or lead, very old, and the upkeep on that was charged to the tenants. With the rents, they didn't have much to complain about.

"I can't find the super," said Port.

They went through the list of twenty-nine people again. This time Port found the name with the gold star behind it. "We'll try her," said Port, and at the end of the ground-floor hall found the door with another gold star pasted on the wood. A sign said: HOURS FROM 11 TO 12 A.M. AND 2 TO 3 P.M.

"She don't leave much room for business," said Simon.

"Her tenants don't have much to complain about." Then Port checked his watch. He was in luck, the time being just after two, and knocked on the door.

A buzzer sounded which made the door spring open a crack. They walked in.

"Pick up your form as you pass that table," said the voice. Port couldn't tell whether it was a hoarse woman or a cantankerous man, but it turned out to be a woman, a large one, half hidden by the chintz wing chair by the window in back. Port and Simon each picked up a printed form, reading Tenant Application Form and Waiver of Liability.

"Step around," said the woman, and they did.

There was a strong odor of roses in the air, the kind that came in cakes of crystal, sold at the five and dime. Port was sure that the use of the perfume was no affectation; it masked plumbing odors.

"Fill out both sides of each page and sign in my presence," said the woman.

"Are you Mrs. Fragonard?" Port asked her.

"I am. And the super."

Simon said, "Gee." Her face looked ageless under rose powder, and her hair was blue except for the white roots. But what added the real excitement was the orange robe. Port saw no lapdog, no parrot, not even a cat. Fish, then, he thought, but the basin on the window sill at her side was a terrarium, and the pet inside was a large bullfrog. He seemed asleep, breathing quickly in and out a few times and then not at all for several minutes.

"Before we fill this thing out," Port started.

"You better hurry it up. I don't see nobody after three."

"I understand. But...."

"I get just overrun with chores and demands if I don't stick to a regular working day."

"Of course—"

"No time to myself at all, elsewise."

She sat with hands folded in her lap and looked at her bullfrog.

"You got a room for the two of us?"

"No."

"That's a shame," said Port.

"Fill that out anyways. Come vacancy time you'll be all set to move in."

"What about this waiver thing, Mrs. Fragonard. Who...."

"That means I don't owe you nothing. I can't be bothered all day long and have my time taken up with chores."

"About paying in cash, Mrs. Fragonard, the fact is, when I move in I want to pay you by check. The reason...."

"Can't do it."

"I don't want to mess with your routine, Mrs. Fragonard, but isn't it dangerous taking that much cash out of here to the bank every week?"

"No trouble to me. They pick it up and...."

"Who picks it up?"

She looked away from the bullfrog and gave Port a cold look. It didn't go with the rose powder. "If you think you're casing yourself a caper, young man, let me tell you I work for a big outfit. They don't...."

"That's what I wanted to know. Who they are, I mean."

"Why?"

"I won't be here part of the time, to pay rent, but I can send my check to the owners and save you the trouble."

"Now you listen to me...."

"Please, Mrs. Fragonard. Of course I'll pay you your deposit. And any surcharges that might accrue."

"In cash."

"Of course."

"The name is Sun Property Management. They have offices...."

"I know where," said Port and got up. He put the application form down and then Simon got up and put his down, too. "I'll just look around the premises, Mrs. Fragonard, and come back to sign, later."

"I don't see how," she said. "It's near two-thirty, and I'm closing at three. I can't have chores and demands...."

"I'll make it in time. Tomorrow."

"Put the forms back on the table," she called after them. They did, and said good-by. She was looking at her bullfrog.

"We moving in here?" said Simon when they were back in the hall.

"She doesn't seem very anxious."

"I don't like her either," said Simon. "A dame's got no business with lizards."

"Bullfrog."

"I mean."

"What did you want her to do, look at you all the time?"

"And why not?"

Port was reading the tenant list and didn't answer. Then he went up the stairs. They stopped in front of a door with the number 22, and Port pulled Simon close. "It's a longish story but I'll tell you all of it, all at once. You remember Kate?"

"What are you talking about, do I remember Kate?"

"In the car yesterday, she didn't do a thing to you. I mean she had nothing to do with that bump on the head.'

"I got the bump, don't I?"

"There's two guys in here, Simon, and they hit you. They opened the car door and slammed you on the back of the head."

"Is that so? Why?"

"They saw what you were doing and wanted to stop you."

"They prudes or something?"

"They wanted Katie themselves."

"They did?" Simon started to breathe hard.

"And they did."

"Open up that double damn door," said Simon. Port knocked on the door.

"Who wants in?" said a voice. Port thought it must be Kirby.

"Mrs. Fragonard," said Port, not worrying that his voice was too low.

"Huh?" And then, "I don't believe it."

Footsteps came to the door and Kirby opened it. He took one look, a smirk came over his face, and he stepped back ceremoniously. "Walk in! While you can walk," he added, and started to laugh.

Simon stepped to one side so Port could go in first, and then he followed without haste. He walked slowly up to Kirby and moved his arm toward Kirby so that it looked like nothing. Kirby collapsed on the floor and Simon shut the door quietly.

"Where's that other bastard?" said Simon.

George was on a couch in back, up on one elbow, and it seemed he had been asleep. He looked at Kirby lying on the floor and blinked. Port had stopped, but Simon was coming across the room. Then George jumped up very quickly. He reached for his jacket hanging on a chair when Port said, "Don't, George." Port had both hands in his pockets and George stopped still.

"What about him!" he said, and watched Simon coming.

"Not yet, Simon. I first gotta ask him something."

Simon stopped, but he was very agitated. He reached for George's coat and tore it straight down the back. Then he tore off the sleeves.

"Don't waste it," said Port.

Simon said, "Ha! You wanner see what I got left? You want me…."

"Later, Simon."

George took a deep breath and sat down on the couch again.

"I've come to ask," said Port, "why Bellamy put you here."

Simon had a trick of opening and closing his hands so the knuckles cracked. He did this, and George said, "To make a mess here. In the ward."

"When?"

"After the council vote."

"And now I want to ask something else. You know this girl Katie?"

"I don't know no girl Katie."

"Yesterday. The one you took away from my friend Simon."

"Oh," said George and looked at Simon.

"She says you didn't pay her."

George didn't answer because he was watching Simon.

"You owe her," said Port.

"All right. Lemme put my hands in my pocket."

"Fifty bucks," said Port.

"Fifty!"

He meant to say more, but Simon had thrown the chair at him. They gave him a little time and then Simon helped him pull money out of his pocket. There were eighty dollars in bills and Simon took fifty of that and handed it over to Port.

"Now Kirby," said Port.

Simon went over to Kirby, who was out on the floor, and came back with fifty dollars.

"We are leaving now," said Port, "and once your buddy wakes up we want you to do the same. Who else lives here?"

"Five of us. There's five of us Bellamy put here."

"Tell them to leave, too. I'm sending Simon over tomorrow to help you move in case you're still here."

"You gonna be here?" Simon asked.

"No," said George.

"Let's go," said Port and went to the door.

"But what about him?"

"Leave him be, Simon."

"But I ain't through!"

"Kick a chair or something."

Port went out and stood in the hall while Simon made a racket inside. When he came out Port could see the pile of wrecked furniture in the middle of the room.

At ten that night Port went home, because that was the only way he could get rid of Simon. He parked his car and Simon walked as far as the door. Port said, "You going to see Katie tonight?"

Simon nodded.

"Then take her this," and Port handed over the hundred dollars.

He watched Simon take it and fold it with some other bills out of his pocket.

"Where'd you get that pile?" Port asked him.

"After you left. When I was cleaning their room."

"Simon, I never thought of you as a crook."

"It's only fifty, Dan."

"Still—"

"I needed it, Dan. I just told you I'm gonna see Katie."

Port looked at Simon and said, "Oh." He nodded his head and went quickly into the building.

Chapter 12

At twelve that night Port reached Ramon's apartment. There was a light in the kitchen which showed under the door, but when he knocked nobody answered. He knocked a few more times and then he tried the door. It opened, but nobody was in.

Port sat down at the kitchen table and waited. There was a coffee pot on the stove, so Port went and poured himself a cup. Then he saw Shelly. He saw her through the half-open door in the next room, where she was lying on a bed, eyes closed. She was on her stomach, breathing regularly, and only her shoes were off. Port put the rest of the coffee back on the stove and lit a flame under the pot. Before he sat down at the table again he went to the room and opened the door enough so he could see her from his chair.

He sat watching her, watching how her bare arm hung over the side of the bed, how the black hair was sprawling all over, and how the curve of her back moved with her breathing.

After a while she frowned, rubbed her face into the pillow, and woke. Port saw there had been a book under her, and when she sat up she rubbed her belly.

"Good evening," said Port.

She looked around, wide-eyed, but if there had been fear it was gone much too soon to tell. She jumped up and came running into the kitchen. She was so mad she couldn't talk. Just when Port was sure she was going to claw him she frowned again and ran to the stove. Port suddenly noticed that the coffee odor was heavy, and when Shelly took the pot off the flame there was nothing left inside the pot but black charcoal. She threw the pot into the sink and came to the table. Her hair was wild, her blouse was half out, the skirt made oblique wrinkles from hips over the belly—and he thought she was magnificent. Then she put her arms akimbo and yelled.

"Now, get out!"

"I just came."

"I don't want you!"

He shrugged, said, "But I want you."

She glared at him, but the wind was gone out of her. She bit her lip and tucked in the blouse. It made one of the buttons pop open in front. She looked down at it and stamped her foot while Port enjoyed how it bounced her. Then she ran out of the room.

Port thought he would put on another pot of coffee while she was gone, but Shelly came back almost immediately. She wore the same things, only this time there was a big blanket robe over everything.

"I see you're still here," she said.

"I came to see your brother."

"You are lying."

"True. I came courtin'. After that, your brother."

"What?" she said.

"Courting. An old-fashioned term we sometimes use when we have it in mind."

"I know what you want, but I don't want it."

"I didn't mean now. Besides, your brother will be here soon. Would you make us another pot of that coffee?"

"When is my brother coming?"

"Around two, I think."

She looked at the clock on a shelf, then back at Port. "It's not even one yet!"

"Honey, I told you I came courtin."

She took a deep breath that spread open the robe, and let the air come out of her throat like a growl. She closed her eyes for a moment, then looked at Port.

"Now, you listen to me." She stepped up to Port and he saw that her face was all relaxed, except for the eyes. It made her look so completely evil that Port had to blink. "I want one thing from you, to go away and not to come back. And I know what you want. All right, I'll go to bed with you and after you're through, don't come back. Right now," she said, eying him.

He sat down at the table and lit a cigarette. When he blew smoke it came out a whistle.

"Not now," he said. "I don't like your attitude."

She just stared at him.

"You knew that, didn't you?" he said.

Shelly sat down and looked at the table for a moment. "Yes. But that does not matter."

"You mean for Nino...."

"I sleep with whom I like."

"Shelly. You just told me you don't like me."

She leaned toward him, over the table, and Port saw how angry she was. "You can talk, try to confuse me; it doesn't matter. I can sleep with you and not even know it, and that's how...."

"That's what I meant. I don't like that attitude." He hadn't expected it, not knowing her well, but he saw her sit back, and she was suddenly no longer angry. She looked tired.

"You are very good, trying to confuse me," she said. "Why are you trying?"

"I'm not. I'm just trying to talk to you. Not Ramon's sister. You."

She gave a short laugh, but said nothing.

"I even know why," he said.

"Tell me."

"Perhaps you've been living the way Kate does," he said, "but not the way Kate can do it. To Kate nothing much matters."

"I have not lived the way Kate does," she said.

"Then why did you offer?"

She shrugged and looked away.

"Ramon doesn't matter here," said Port. "I told you that."

"I raised him." She gave her short laugh again and said, "He is three years younger than I, but I raised him."

"No parents?"

"Oh yes. But they always worked. When they came to this country," she said, "all they ever did was work."

"He's grown up now," said Port. "You don't have to be your brother's keeper—"

Now she was angry again. She got up, stepped away from the table, and said, "How would you know?"

Port didn't answer, for his own reasons, and Shelly thought that it meant Port couldn't understand. For one moment it even felt as if she herself didn't understand any longer and it made her feel even more angry. She would let Port sit and she would have nothing further to do with him. It was suddenly easy to dislike him.

She went back to her room and slammed the door. Port sat alone in the kitchen, and nothing felt right. He sat waiting for Ramon, impatient but without real interest.

When Ramon came in Port felt some relief. It would at least change the atmosphere.

"Sit down," he said. "You sure took your time getting here."

Shelly came out of her room. She was wearing the blanket robe, nodded at her brother, and crossed the kitchen to go into the bathroom. Ramon noticed that Shelly's legs were bare.

"All right," said Port, "tell me again about the calls yesterday. It's important."

Ramon turned around and tried to concentrate.

"Everything," said Port.

Ramon closed his eyes and recited. "First a call from McFarlane. In the evening—not the morning call. Bellamy asked why in hell he couldn't render a different interpretation of that special-group statute." Ramon looked up. "I'm sure he said special group, but I...."

"That's all right. I know what he meant."

Ramon closed his eyes again. "Next Bellamy called somebody called Pump on the phone. Pump or Sump. He only said the name once."

"He said Sump. Go on."

"This one he gave holy hell. He said it's an affront to the sensitivity...."

"Sensibility."

"All right, sensibility. He says it's an affront to that, the way the committee was handling the slum clearance thing, and then this Sump gives it back to Bellamy. Like a revival meeting, let me tell you."

"Just in brief, what did he say?"

"He said for Bellamy to go to hell. That's the way I figure it, anyway."

"What next?"

"Next, Bellamy makes a business call about some fine point about property. After that he talks to a man called Landis. This was very short, and...."

"What about that business call. Any details you remember?"

"Wait a minute. This Landis call, now, Bellamy tells the man to stay out of politics or else, and Landis says, I am out. Out of your kind, anyway. Then Landis hangs up."

Ramon looked at Port, pleased with himself, but Port's reaction offended him.

"What about that business call?"

Ramon drummed his fingers a few times.

"You know, Dan, if you'd tell me what you're after, maybe I could listen better. I'd know what to listen for. You know what I mean?"

"You're doing fine."

At that moment Shelly came in. She went to the sink to do something or other, but most of all she interrupted. Before either of the men could say anything she went back to her room.

"All right, Ramon, what about that property? You remember the address?"

"I told you already. I told that mailman character. Twelve hundred Birch."

"That's right. What did Bellamy say?"

"Nothing. Just a question about escrow. I think he said, 'Is it in escrow,' or something like that."

"Whom did he talk to?"

"He called the man Jack. And Jack, all he said was 'Yes sir' and 'No sir.'"

Port frowned and said, "Maybe there's something."

"How would I know? But if you'd tell me what this is all about—"

"Did he say, 'Yes, it's in escrow'?"

"Look, I don't know what escrow is and when they talked about it, it's just double talk to me."

"Double talk about what?"

"How in hell do I know!"

"Don't yell. You'll wake up your sister."

But Shelly opened her door right then and came back into the kitchen. "Are you all right, Nino?" she asked.

"Stop calling me Nino, will you? And don't keep busting in here like that when I'm talking business."

"I live here, Nino." She said it to Ramon, with a gentle voice, as if she thought he might have forgotten. She closed a cupboard door and went back to her room.

"Don't mind her, Ramon. She...."

"What do you mean, don't mind her? When I'm trying to do a job, especially something like this...."

"You're doing fine."

"I could do better, if I knew what in hell you're after."

"Let's get back to that call, Ramon." Port was patient. He would have to make the best of the situation, and he would have to remember not to come here again. Not to talk business, to mix business and pleasure— He almost laughed when he thought of the pleasure he'd had with Shelly.

"The Jack guy mentioned the Realty Improvement Company."

"Realty Improvement?"

"That's what I said."

"Did anyone mention Sun Property Management?"

"No. I'm sure nobody did."

Port leaned back, rubbing one hand through his hair.

Ramon sat for a while, waiting, and then he asked, "Did I tell you something?"

"It sounds like they're selling. Sun Property owns the building and Realty Improvement is a broker. They handle sales."

"Maybe something crooked, seeing that Bellamy is in it."

Port shook his head. "Bellamy owns Realty Improvement, but that doesn't make it crooked. And if you want to sell property in this town, Realty Improvement is the best outfit to go to."

"So why the questions, if it's just one of Bellamy's legitimate business deals?"

"I don't know. Mostly because Bellamy's hoods turned up at that address. But that doesn't mean anything either, come to think of it."

"Would anyone like more coffee?" said Shelly. She came back into the kitchen and both men looked at her. She hadn't interrupted anything this time, so they just nodded and watched her pour from the pot.

She smiled at Port and said, "You want more, too, Danny?"

It surprised Port and it made Ramon frown.

"I only ask," she went on, "because you've been drinking the stuff over two hours." She had finished pouring and went back to the stove.

"Two hours?" said Ramon. "When did you get here?"

"He got here about twelve," said Shelly. She turned to walk back into her room and Ramon saw her bare knee where the robe came apart.

Ramon suddenly found that he couldn't look at Port. Two hours; so what? And besides, Ramon then remembered how he had thought that it might be a good thing if he brought Port and his sister together. But the thought gave him such pain now he felt the sweat come out of his palms like tiny

needles and next only sharp rage could make it all good. Ramon looked up
at Port, whose face was bland, who was blowing the steam off his coffee, who
sat relaxed in his strength—and Ramon got depressed. He sank into a safe,
heavy torpor, wishing only that he were asleep.

"What calls did you get tonight?" Port asked him. And then, "Hey, Ramon."

"Tonight?"

"Yeah. Anything tonight?"

It was important to be impersonal now. It would be easy. There was nothing quite so impersonal as talking about business—only it wasn't true. This,
Ramon's job, was his life, could be the start for everything he'd never had.

"You get spells like that often?" said Port.

The light tone of voice helped, a tone that implied that Port didn't know
what went on.

"Yes, several calls," said Ramon. "One call about a boxing contract, a long-
distance call, and the man wanted to know if Bellamy meant to sell. Bellamy
said he didn't know for sure, but...."

"Give me the next call."

"Next call. A man calls up to say Kirby was in the hospital, and they had
to move out, and where should they go. He says a bastard by the name of
Simon did it, and the big shot with him. He didn't say who this big shot is,
but Bellamy seemed to know, from the way he started cursing."

Port started to laugh and then he asked, "Bellamy give any instructions to
the man?"

"To go to hell, he told him. And to show up in his office in the morning."

"Okay, what next."

"A cultured guy calls up, long distance, and Bellamy is now doing the yes
sir, no sir. I didn't catch the name, but he says 'Judge' to him. The judge gives
a speech about ethics—no, about ethics of his office making the sale necessary, so that speed of sale rather than profit are essential."

"This is a business call?"

"Strictly. Because this judge apologized that he couldn't reach Bellamy at
the office...."

"What office?"

"That's right! Realty Improvement! Bellamy is selling a piece of property
for this guy, this judge, and the judge wants to know how it's going. And
he wants no delays because of price quibbling."

"Did they sound like they knew each other?"

"No. They don't talk very long, anyway. After that call Bellamy talks to this
Jack, you remember this Jack. He's a bookkeeper, it turns out, and Bellamy
tells him to put the closing charges on the bill for Swinburn."

"What Swinburn, did he say?"

"Something about a motel. I think Swinburn owns it."

"That's right. South of town." Port got up, stretched his legs. "Any others?"

"That's all. Did you get something out of it?"

"I don't know yet, Ramon."

"What about this judge and Swinburn and all that?"

"Whatever it is, it sounds like legitimate business of Bellamy's real estate company."

Port paced back and forth, and Ramon gathered his courage.

"Dan, I would like to ask you something."

"Let me think for a minute."

But Ramon couldn't wait. "Dan, look, you gave me a job and I'm trying my best. Are you listening?"

Port nodded, looked at Ramon, and listened.

"But I think my best right now isn't good enough."

"You're doing...."

"No, let me finish. Would you say it's pretty important?"

"Yes, I'd say that."

"Then I think you should tell me what it's all about. If I'm going to do this thing right...."

"You know all you need to know."

"I don't think so. Unless I'm going to tap wire at Bellamy's for the rest of my life, and tell you about it like a parrot, it's not good enough."

"And," said Port, "you're not going to do that all your life. That's what you mean?"

"I figure I can grow in the organization. I figure with the way I'm working out, doing this job the way I am—" Ramon's courage failed him, and he stopped. He fought to find his way back, but for a moment nothing came.

"Go on, Ramon."

"I want in!" He bit his lip, but then it was too late. "I want in, I want to grow, and you're holding me up. I don't want to end up nowhere when this job ends up nowhere, because I got plans for myself! I don't think you're doing right by the job I'm doing, and you aren't doing right by me, if— After all, you picked me because I got something."

Port waited a moment, to give Ramon a fair chance to hear.

"You got something, and that's why I picked you. You're eager. And right from the start, Ramon, I told you not to get so eager that you get scared. You're scared of losing out. So you push. Don't push that hard, Ramon."

"Why not? You got one good reason why not?"

Port gave it up. He raised his arms, dropped them, and said, "You wouldn't believe me, Ramon."

"Just try me."

"All right: because it isn't worth it."

They looked at each other, and Port saw he had been right. He had said too much and Ramon couldn't understand.

"Worth it! Just look where it got you! You trying to tell me that it's worth staying a hick? You...."

"No. Not a hick. I didn't say that."

"You telling me you don't like what you're doing? Well, try me! I'll know what to do with it. I'd like to see those jerks snap to when I walk into the club, break up their daisy chain, tell them to run me an errand. What's more, I'd be good at it. I got the organization in mind just as much as myself. I can...."

"Right now you can shut up."

Ramon hadn't heard Port speak sharply before, and it startled him. But then he gave it the wrong label.

"Hold me back, will you? I'm not scared now, let me tell you, and while I'm at it, why don't you tell me the works, what I'm doing in Bellamy's basement? Maybe you're scared! Maybe if I know too much...."

"You almost got it, Ramon." Port's voice was just as sharp, but much lower. It gave the feel of a muscle tensing, but it hadn't moved yet. "If they catch you, Ramon, with the wire down in your room, what'll they do? They'll twist your arm till you talk. Not so you can tell them how much it hurts, but to tell them all you know. How long do you think you'd last, not spilling, if you knew what I know and they're twisting your arm? Tell me! How long?"

Ramon sat down in his chair and his mouth came open.

"Simple enough?"

Ramon still didn't talk.

"Or didn't you know that kind of thing is part of the big position you're after?"

Ramon breathed hard, to kill his confusion.

"And following orders without knowing why, and getting the pants scared off you, like right now, that's part of the big career you got in mind. You got that clear now?"

Shelly had come back into the kitchen, and she stood by the door, not moving. Then Ramon thought he had the clincher.

"The way you talk, Dan, how come you stick around?"

"He likes it," said Shelly.

Port gave her a look that made her catch her breath. Then Port talked to Ramon.

"I'll tell you this much. After the Bellamy job you can stay in or bow out."
Just by chance, Port thought, Ramon might understand. But Shelly answered.

"He will," she said. "He'll bow out!"

Ramon whirled around as if stung, but didn't look at his sister for long. When he turned back to Port his face was livid.

"I'm in, and I stick! Nobody pushes me out!"

Port looked from one to the other, then he went to the door. "You know the score," he said. "Report to the mailman, like before."

After he had closed the door nobody spoke in the kitchen.

Chapter 13

That morning the sun was very bright and the air fresh, making Port think of taking a walk. He took a few deep breaths and wondered why the town was so big, getting bigger all the time, but nobody minding the weather the way it was most of the time. A day like this happened only a few times a year. Then he noticed that Simon hadn't shown up. He grinned to himself and got his car.

After a short ride downtown, Port pulled up to the clothing store. The right side sold suits and ties and the left sold dresses and things for women. Port said, "Hello, Marv," to the man in the store and asked him if he might use the phone. "There's nobody in back," said Marv, and Port would be welcome.

Port sat in back where the small window looked out on a row of cans in the yard. He used the phone; nobody bothered him and he stayed there several hours. His calls had to do with 1200 Birch, with Swinburn's motel, with Realty Improvement Company, and with Sun Property Management. He didn't call Realty Improvement itself because he had no connections in Bellamy's office. His calls were to some local finance companies, to the recorder's office, and to the file room of the Real Estate Board.

It all turned out to make sense. Stoker could make of it what he wanted.

When he got to the Lee building office Stoker wasn't there, but Fries was. He took Port into Stoker's office, sat behind Stoker's desk, and said, "What have you got?"

"How come I'm talking to you?" said Port. "Where's Stoker?"

"Home in bed. While he's gone...."

"Something worse?"

"A few days in bed and he'll be back. In the meantime I handle the details."

Port sat down on the couch and put up one leg. Fries had to shift to see Port, and it spoiled his pose. He had an idea Port had done this intentionally, but he kept it to himself and started to play with a pencil. He let it slide through his fingers so the point hit the loop of a paper clip on the desk. He kept doing that.

"I think you can take it from here," said Port. "I'll give you the details."

"You sound like you're leaving," said Fries.

Port looked at his fingernails and then up at the ceiling. "You can stop clowning, Fries. You know the same thing Stoker knows. I'm leaving when it's set up so Ward Nine stays together."

"I've heard you say it, but I don't know any such thing."

"So don't worry about it, Fries."

"I'm only worried about the important part. What did you set up?"

"The council will vote on the thing on Friday, next week. As far as I'm concerned it's in the bag. We should know what the vote will be a few days before. Like always."

"I don't know any such thing."

"Hell, Fries, you're supposed to take Stoker's place. Don't you know when the vote will be certain?"

"Stoker keeps track of that part."

"I thought you said...."

"He's got a phone, doesn't he? And besides, how come you don't know?"

"I've been doing other things."

"Any better than fixing McFarlane? Like you said yourself, his slum ruling will stand up just so long. If you're thinking of leaving when the council votes...."

"Fries, when somebody offers you a cigarette, I bet you say, 'Let's have the whole pack.'"

"I don't smoke."

The fine click when Fries dropped his pencil was getting on Port's nerves, but if Fries hadn't been doing that, something else would have gotten on Port's nerves. The thought made his irritation worse. He thought he was acting like Ramon, fishing for praise, and that didn't help. Then he made the mistake of trying to make Fries stop playing with the pencil. He said, "If you'll stop playing with your pencil a minute, Fries...."

"Why don't you come to the point," said Fries.

Port got up and came over to the desk. He kept his lips shut tight because he didn't want to start whistling, and he didn't look at Fries, because he didn't want to lose his temper. He looked out the window and thought how nice the weather was, and how in a short while he wouldn't look at it any more, in this town.

"Here's what I found out, and then you can figure on how to use it. I think it's good enough to keep the ward almost indefinitely."

"Not counting the unforeseen," said Fries and dropped his pencil.

"Don't bother me."

"You might as well learn, Dan...."

Port reached over and grabbed the pencil out of Fries's hand and threw it down on the desk. "You want a clean deal on that ward job, or don't you? If you don't, I'll blow now and you can sew it up your way."

"I don't sew."

Port shut his eyes and groaned.

"Besides," said Fries, "you promised Stoker...."

"I got only one weakness," said Port; "one great self-destroying weakness. I let you get under my skin."

"I have hardly said a word, Port, and all you've said doesn't add up to a hell of a lot either." Fries had started to scratch at an inkspot, scratching at it with one long, horny nail.

"Here," and Port handed the pencil over. "Take your pencil, please. Just take it, click it, point it, and let me get out of here."

Fries colored, but kept still. Other people's irritations meant nothing to him, but a sharp voice made him apprehensive.

"Once more," said Port. He sat down, and went through the whole thing. "Like I told you and Stoker, they can't clear the slums, now that McFarlane ruled that it violates statutes. That can last a while, but not forever. What would hurt most is if they take it to the Capitol, and if I know Bellamy it'll be only a matter of time and he will."

"How do you know?"

"Fries, don't bother me, will you?" Then he went on while Fries sat and listened, though for a long time Fries didn't get the connection.

"The Supreme Court judge with the weight in this matter is Paternik. Paternik comes from this town, he's got the seniority, he's a figure. Did you know Paternik owns real estate here?" Fries waited. "There's an outfit in town, Sun Property Management. They don't just manage property, they also own some. It's a stock company, but the stock is family-owned. The name of the family is Evoy, but that doesn't mean a thing. It turns out they own the stock in the name of a relative, all very legal, and for no reasons of concealment. When you're rich, that's how you do it. Judge Paternik owns Sun Property Management, and that's how he owns Twelve hundred Birch."

"I see."

"You will. Right now the judge is trying to sell the property on Birch, because it is a blotch on his name. It's a substandard tenement in Ward Nine, and what with the stink about the slums, if it should come out that the judge owned property there—well, it's a stink."

"Paternik isn't in with Stoker," said Fries.

"So what? It doesn't look good. So here's your setup, Fries. Step in and put Paternik over a barrel."

There was silence for a while, because Fries didn't know what Port meant. Then he said, "I'll tell Stoker about it."

"You mean you don't know what I'm talking about."

Fries accidentally broke the point of his pencil, which meant he was much too busy to answer right away.

"Here's what you do, Fries. Buy the building from Paternik."

"Stoker has made it a policy—" Fries started, and was glad when Port interrupted.

"Stoker buys the building through a dummy, and he pays higher than valuation, way higher. Then if it's ever important to push the judge, you put it this way: Paternik sold something to Stoker—that's bad in itself. Paternik sold for more than the building's value. Is Stoker a jerk who pays more than something is worth? Not Stoker. Then what did the judge get the extra dough for? For services rendered. Judge Paternik in the pay of the Stoker mob!"

"I'll be damned!"

"You tell that to the judge once the sale has been made, and the judge jumps."

"He can show that the whole thing...."

"Don't use it till you need it. That's when you can ruin the man."

Port lit a cigarette and watched Fries get up. Fries took several steps, back and forth, and then he stopped in front of Port's chair. "Very nice. If it works. Get going on it."

"Run your own errands," said Port. He killed the cigarette without having smoked it. He got up and pushed Fries out of the way. When he got to the door he told Fries, "I sent Simon home. I won't need him any more."

Chapter 14

Port made a phone call from the lobby and talked to Stoker. "I just gave Fries all there was. He'll take it from there."

"What is it, Dan?"

"You got two setups now. The McFarlane ruling, to keep Council from voting against you. And if that doesn't hold there's a setup to keep the Supreme Court in line. Fries will give you the details."

Stoker smiled into the phone, thinking how glad he was that Port hadn't left.

"That ties up the bargain, Max. I'm through."

Stoker kept as calm as he could. He breathed deeply and let the first impulse go by. Then he said, "The vote isn't in, Danny. You promised...."

"What's the difference? How can they vote, except...."

"Danny. I'm in bed. I'll be up after the weekend. I won't have word on that vote till after next week's committee meeting. At least you can do me the courtesy to not take off at a time like this. Over the phone, me in bed—"

"When, next week?"

"The vote should be certain the day before council meets. That's next Thursday. Dan, you can make it easier for me and wait just those few days."

"I don't see what good it'll do, except to give you more time figuring out some new angle."

"Thursday night Bellamy's got an affair in his house. Political good-will meeting, he calls it. I want you to come with me."

"For display? So it looks like one happy family?"

"Do me the favor, Dan. All of downtown will be there, both parties. And some of the Capitol men."

"How come I didn't know about this?"

"Bellamy called me himself."

"Arranged from the top down. And plenty of press coverage at the last minute."

"How would I look, Danny, if you aren't along?"

A few days, so Stoker could look good in public, so Bellamy wouldn't smell the rift. It made sense, and Port thought of the delay as the last installment on paying a sick man.

"I'll be there," he said, and hung up before Stoker could thank him.

His impatience didn't catch up with him until he got out of the booth. The few days' delay suddenly became like a sentence. Port lit a cigarette, dragged too hard, felt the smoke tear a raw scratch down his throat. He coughed, making it worse. Nothing had shown while he had been busy. He had done his work with practiced speed, doing it well because Stoker needed it. He had taken Stoker's machine and for a few days of concentrated maneuvering had made it turn tricks. For Stoker, and for himself. For Stoker so he could keep his machine, for himself so he could get rid of it.

And now he was out. Nobody else might think so, but Port wanted to—

except for a few, loose-end days in a town he didn't like, with faces he didn't want to see, and with a past riding his shoulder as long as he stayed. Maybe longer, except that once he was out it wouldn't be staring at him from quite so close.

Port walked to the parking lot and felt worse than he had in a long time. It upset him to find himself at the end but without the feel of conclusiveness. Stoker's damn party; Fries's damn threats; Shelly's damn attitude—Port got into his car, overtipped the attendant, and drove off too fast.

What if he were leaving today—what about Shelly? It occurred to him that he had never really thought of it, either because he had been too busy, or because— He yanked the car through a curve and then noticed where he was heading. A ten-minute drive and he'd be there. Then a few days with nothing to do but to concentrate. Shelly took concentration. With anyone else he might have thought of it like a sport, but not this time. This was a necessity.

He pulled up near the club, because most likely Shelly would be working the counter in the corner store.

She wasn't there. The grocer was working the counter himself and he didn't know where Shelly might be. Shelly had quit.

When Port got to the apartment nobody was there. He knocked, he tried the door, but nothing happened. He went downstairs again, reminding himself that there were, after all, several days left.

He walked half a block to the club, more out of habit than purpose, and stood in the archway to the room with the easy chairs. He watched the two guys tossing their ball back and forth and then Lantek dropped by. "There was a call for you. Maybe an hour ago."

"Who was it?"

"I don't know. Said she'd call again." Lantek looked at the clock in the hall. "At two. Ten minutes from now."

"You don't know who it was?"

"She didn't say. Sounded like a secretary."

Port couldn't place it, but then Lantek wouldn't know what a secretary sounded like.

"And the mailman was here," said Lantek. "He wrote something down and left it in the office."

Port frowned, because he had forgotten about the mailman. He didn't need him any more, but he shouldn't have forgotten.

They stood watching the ball go back and forth a few times and then Lantek said, "You seen Katie around?"

"No," said Port.

"We been kinda looking for her. She mostly don't stay away this long."

"Maybe she hit the jackpost someplace."

Lantek said, "Ha," and Port laughed too, but for a different reason.

He went to the office off the hall and got his letter out of the box. The mail-man had listed three calls. One by Bellamy to McFarlane, urging the city so-licitor to reverse his slum ruling. The answer was no, what was done was done. To that Bellamy had answered he'd take the matter as far as the Capi-tol—to the Supreme Court, if need be. McFarlane had answered that was perfectly proper and if Bellamy needed legal advice McFarlane's personal ef-forts' would be at his disposal.

The next call had been to Stoker, inviting him to the good-will dinner next week. Port knew about that one. And the last call had been to Landis, with the same request, except Landis's answer had been that he would not be part of any more political farces.

Bellamy hadn't been very active that night. Only three calls. He had started at nine and had finished at nine-thirty.

When Port tore up the paper to throw it into the wastebasket the phone rang. He didn't get there till the man assigned to the office had lifted the re-ceiver and said, "Neighborhoodsocialclubwardnine." He listened for a mo-ment and handed the phone to Port. "A very nice voice," he said and started to grin, but stopped it abruptly. Port nodded at him to blow and put the phone to his ear. "Port, speaking."

"One moment, Mr. Port. I have Mr. Bellamy on the line for you."

She was a secretary.

"Is that you, Dan?"

Port held the phone away from his ear.

"Yes, I can hear you."

"Look, boy, if you got a minute or so would you mind running out to my place? Just a talk, you and me. What do you say, boy?"

"You think you'll get any further than George and Kirby did?"

Bellamy roared with laughter and then said, "They didn't half try!"

"Bellamy, let me...."

"No, seriously, boy. Just you and me, for good all around. The good of the community, if you know what I mean. Now I'm at the office and could pick you up on my way out, except I don't think it would look right, me stopping over at your club. What do you say, boy? Half an hour?"

Port was quite certain Shelly wouldn't show up until evening. Job-hunt-ing, probably, or working someplace else....

"I'll be there," said Port.

The place was as expansive as Bellamy himself. Port stopped on the rotunda in front of the house and tried to decide whether to go in at the Tudor entrance, the French Provincial one, or the screen door with the aluminum bird. A butler decided for him, showing up on the Italian terrace. Port followed him. Before leaving the terrace he saw Ramon in the distance. Ramon was raking a gravel walk that wound far across the side of a hill.

Bellamy was waiting beside a small frame to which a hooked rug was pinned. It was only half finished and Bellamy was fingering the needle. In his other hand he was holding a snifter half full of whisky, with a piece of ice in it.

"Sit down, boy, sit down!" He came across the Persian rug. Port and Bellamy shook hands, and Port wondered why some people insisted on trying to crush a man's hand, as if that proved something or other.

"Bollwick, bring Mr. Port—what'll you have, Port?"

"Rye."

"Bring him rye, Bollwick. Port, I see you are looking at my daughter's hooked rug. Amazing, isn't it?"

Port nodded and wondered why Bellamy put out all the energy; there was enough noise from the bright pepper and salt suit, the green tartan vest, and—of course—argyle socks. Bellamy was big and whatever he wore showed a lot.

"Here's the rye," said Bellamy. He watched Port take a sip and stroked the thin yellow hairs over his scalp.

Port said, "What do you want?"

First Bellamy had to give a big laugh again, and then he leaned forward. "What are your plans, Danny?"

"I'm right now planning to hear you out. Very good rye."

"I thought you were leaving Stoker," said Bellamy.

"That's hearsay."

"Not that you're acting like it." Bellamy took a large swig and swallowed noisily. "What with all the snooping and swooping you been doing the last couple days."

Port grinned. "Pretty clever of me, huh?"

Bellamy closed his eyes and said with a voice that sounded oratorial, "I have only the greatest admiration for you, Daniel."

"You said that beautifully."

"I mean it. You're hot stuff."

Port nodded and sipped his drink.

"So how come you're hanging around a broken-down outfit like Stoker's?" Bellamy wanted to know.

"Because Stoker is a friend of mine."

"Oh, brother!" said Bellamy and took a big drink. Then he said, "Don't you like me, Daniel?"

"I think you stink."

Port was sorry he had said that because now came the laugh again. It lasted until Port thought Bellamy had an affliction. It turned into a terrible cough which made Bellamy's scalp red.

"Oh, brother!" said Bellamy again, and then he got up. "Come along, Danny. I want to show you something."

Port followed Bellamy through several rooms, through a hall, down some stairs, and after passing a Ping-pong table they walked around the furnace. Bellamy went through a door and waited for Port by the bed in the room.

"You know where it is?" said Bellamy.

"Huh?"

"Maybe you don't." Bellamy pushed the bed out of the way, kicked at the floorboard, and watched the earphone fall out. The wire attached to it was just long enough to reach up to a man lying on the bed.

"Oh, that," said Port. "I know about that."

"So do I."

"Since when?"

"Ever since you sent your bogus electrician to put it in."

Port leaned against the wall of the room and put his hands in his pockets. "You're lying, Bellamy. You didn't know till last night."

Bellamy sat down on the bed and made the ice cube spin in his glass. "How do you figure I'm lying?"

"Because of what you said on the phone during the last few days. And because yesterday you suddenly stopped."

"You're right. I'm lying."

"Now tell me something, Bellamy. How did you find out?"

Bellamy laughed and got up. "It's a funny story. Let's go back upstairs." They went back upstairs and Bellamy kept chuckling and talking, because it was the kind of story he would tell at the club. For many years he intended to tell that story at the club.

He'd been up there phoning, in his study, when he decided he might as well have some coffee. So he rang the house phone to the kitchen and told the girl there to bring it up. The maid came in after a while and when she put down the tray on his desk Bellamy thought, What the hell, this is for me. Direct type that he is, he makes a grab for the girl, and she wouldn't stand for it. She knocked his hand out of the way and tried to walk out. Not to be put upon, Bellamy jumped up fast as he could, and all in clean fun, you understand, tried a new tackle. She held still just long enough to grab for the phone, gave him the knee, and then threw the instrument at him. "Believe me," said Bellamy, "I let her go."

They sat down in the room where the half-finished rug was on the frame and Bellamy went on. "So I figure, the hell with her, or at least, the hell with her right now, and pick up the phone. There's nothing wrong with it, except the wire is torn out of the wall box. And there was that other one, that thin little wire that went right down to the basement. Some story, huh?"

"Some maid," said Port. "How come she sticks around here?"

"She's my daughter's maid, mostly, and she hasn't been here too long."

"She won't be much longer, the way you described it."

Bellamy laughed himself out of the easy chair and went to the door. He opened it and yelled, "Bollwick, send in that new one!" He came back with a bottle from the small liquor cabinet and poured some into Port's glass. "Wait till you see her, Danny. Some girl."

The door opened and Shelly came in.

Port thought his collar was going to strangle him, and it seemed that the moment was never going to pass. She stood in the door, unable to move, because she didn't know what to do. Then Port got up, slowly, and solved it for her.

"How in hell did you get here?" he yelled.

"I don't have to tell you a thing!" She sounded just as loud as Port did.

After that came a silence. Bellamy clinked his ice back and forth. Then he said, "You two know each other?"

They both looked at him as if he didn't belong there, and Port stopped close to him on his way toward Shelly. "You son of a bitch," he said, but didn't wait for an answer. He took Shelly's arm and gave her a shake.

"Don't you know enough to...."

"Let go of my arm."

"And you get that damn uniform off and wait for me out in front."

"You'd like that, wouldn't you!"

"A damn sight better than that operetta outfit you're busting out of!"

"Daniel," said Bellamy. "You're talking to my help." It distracted him. Port turned around, hoping that Bellamy would say just one more wrong thing.

"This isn't slave labor, you know. And my daughter did the hiring."

"She's unhired." He saw Shelly make a small move and snapped at her, "You shut up."

"The fact is," said Bellamy, "you better take her. I didn't know about her brother being your man, when she got hired."

"She's not in on this," said Port.

"How do I know? Her brother recommended the girl when we needed a maid."

"Why in hell did you come here?" Port looked at Shelly. But she was too mad to answer.

"I'm sure," said Bellamy, "her brother had reasons, what with the neighborhood where she's been living. And not too far from that Neighborhood Frolic Club you run in that ward."

"Are you going to get out of that uniform, Shelly, or do I…."

"You better," said Bellamy, and because it hadn't been Port who had told her she walked out of the room without any more ado.

As soon as she was gone things were different. Port got his bearings back, he picked up his glass, and drank what was left there. Then he nodded at Bellamy and went to the door.

"Wait a minute, Daniel. We're not through yet."

Port waited.

"You didn't answer me, Daniel. I want you to switch over."

"You shoulda laughed right after that one," said Port, and opened the door.

"You come over and I won't touch your man," said Bellamy. "The gardener. Or did you think I was going to keep him on?"

"Go ahead and fire him."

"How do you think it's going to be between you and the girl friend, Daniel, when it turns out he doesn't show up any more. You make me mad enough, Port, and I sink him. She's going to like you for that?"

"What does he mean?" Shelly came running across the hall. She dropped her suitcase on the way and again said, "What does he mean?"

Port stopped her at the door and then looked at Bellamy. "He said he'd kill your brother, didn't you, Bellamy?"

The girl gasped and Bellamy's face got dark red with anger.

"She heard you, Bellamy. One witness too many."

Shelly yanked her arm to get free of Port. "You stand here and say that? You stand here and calmly discuss…."

"Yes!" Port was shouting. "He says it the same way you've learned to do it, the way you talked, that night in the kitchen. Remember? Like talking about some kind of merchandise," and he started walking across the hall, holding her arm.

"I can't leave," she tried to say, but Port cut her short. He kept pulling her.

"And he wouldn't do it any more than you would have, in the kitchen. Come on!"

On the way out he grabbed up her suitcase.

Chapter 15

He got her into the car by force and slammed the door shut behind her. She sat there, not moving. Port thought she might try to get out again, but she didn't move. He got in at his side and drove off with a fast jolt. She said nothing till they shot out through Bellamy's gate. Then she turned on him.

"You swine, stop this car!"

"And pick up Nino?"

"Yes, and pick up Nino!"

"Because you've raised him and he needs you all the time? That's how good a job of raising you've done? That what you mean?"

The car gathered speed and went down the highway, away from the city. The wind made a furious racket along the shut windows. It matched the mood inside the car.

"Your clever mind," she hissed at him. "I hate it!" And then, "Where are you going?"

"I'm driving."

"Not with me!" and her hand shot out for the keys on the dashboard.

He slapped it out of the way.

"Sit still."

"I want Nino!"

"Aha! That's a different sound altogether. Now you've said it loud and clear. You'd feel better with Nino around, wouldn't you?"

"I said...."

"Safe and prim as hell, right? What is it, Shelly, afraid I'm going to rape you?"

"You know you can't! You know...."

"No. As long as there's you and Nino I wouldn't think of it. You're not even here! And all you ever feel is sisterly love, isn't it?"

She sat still, and Port started to think she was going to let it pass, when she suddenly swung out her arm and cracked the back of her hand into his face.

He jammed on the brake. At first he thought he was going to laugh but then felt himself getting furious.

"Stop the car," she said. She sat crouched in the seat, and she had one of her shoes in her hand, holding it so the heel made a hammer. Then she said again, "Stop the car and let me out!"

Port made a fast turn into a dirt lane and stopped the car. He was out before Shelly had found her balance.

The air was rainy and cool, with a strong leaf odor out of the woods next to the road, and while Port stood there, breathing it, he wondered whether she'd ever come out. Her teeth showed like an animal's, and when she stood in the road she stopped to kick off the other shoe and then didn't wait any longer. She didn't wait for him to move, but came at him.

He hadn't figured she was very strong or as determined as she turned out to be, but before he got the shoe out of her hand she had clipped him hard over the ear, had tried to knee him, and then bit his neck. He had to let go of her to get a good grip, and that's when he stopped fighting her off. He got a hold on her that changed the whole thing, except that Shelly wouldn't give in.

The next time she tried to knee him Port lost his temper. He picked her up, tossed her over the ditch, and was next to her when she jumped up. There was one heated look between them and then the front of her dress came apart in one loud rip. She froze, but Port wasn't through. He reached out and tore the rest she had on, and when she tried to free her arm to claw him, he yanked it all down.

He was holding her as if she might get away long after Shelly had no such thought.

He had taken his jacket off and Shelly was wearing it, and when she had reached for the cigarette he had lit for her she left the jacket the way it had fallen because they were still far out of town. Port was surprised to see how far they had come.

She said, "Your place or mine, Daniel?"

"Mine's more private."

"But mine is closer."

"And I got better accommodations."

"Except my clothes are at home."

He shook his head sadly and kept on driving....

"Mind you," she said, "it's no problem right now, but with no clothes how will I ever get out of here?"

Port said, "Huh?"

She rolled on her stomach and pulled the pillow out from under his head. "I said, with no clothes, Daniel...."

"Yes. It's been on my mind something terrific."

She smiled down at him and then reached across to turn on the radio that stood by the side of the bed.

"It's a fact," he said. "You'll never get out of here...."

The radio was still playing the next morning. Of course, there was nothing in the refrigerator. They held out till the afternoon, and then Port went shopping. He bought coffee, and steak, and lettuce, and eggs for breakfast. He forgot a number of things, including the bread, but they didn't notice that till the next day.

Port woke up from the sound of the shower and jumped up very quickly, but when he got to the bathroom Shelly was through already and wrapped in a towel.

She said, "Why, don't you always take your showers alone?" and laughed when he tried to grab her.

His shower was a disappointment to him, but he took it so fast Shelly was still wet when he came out again....

She couldn't see him because it was dark in the room, but she knew he was looking at her.

"Are you awake?" he asked.

"For hours."

"Then why didn't you answer me before?"

"Did I have to?"

"Yes."

She came closer and put her arms around him. "Ask me again."

"Will you come with me?"

He noticed that she was holding her breath, and when she exhaled she didn't say anything.

"Will you answer me?"

"I don't have to, Daniel. You know that."

Chapter 16

He bought her some clothes which she wore just long enough to go out and buy herself something that fit. She took much longer than she had ever done in the past, because Port had told her to spend all he had given her. He waited for her in a hushed room with hushed salesladies and the clothes displayed ornamentally. There were no ashtrays, and Port felt uncomfortable.

After that they went out and had their first full meal in several days and finished with coffee. Port offered her a cigarette but she didn't want one.

"You look sleepy," he said.

"So would you be," she said. "You don't know what it's like, shopping."

He said, "Of course," and then they sat a while longer.

"I have to go now," said Port. "There's still some business."

It changed her mood. It showed even though she tried hiding it.

"A few days, Shelly, and it'll be over."

"Why not now, Daniel. What's a few days?"

"A promise."

"And then we leave?"

"For good, Shelly. Both of us."

She smiled at him and nodded. She took a mirror out of her bag and looked at her lipstick. Then she straightened her hair.

"I'm ready, Daniel. Drop me off at home."

"Look, Shelly," he started.

"I want to see Nino, to tell him that I'm leaving."

Port drove past the club on his way to her house and thought how often he had been in this street and how soon he wouldn't see it any more. And Shelly thought how she would never look at these streets again because she would pick up a few things, explain to her brother, and then leave for good.

After she had opened the door to the kitchen she and Port stood there a moment because they hadn't recognized Ramon.

He sat more bent than usual and when he turned he did it slowly. One side of his face was puffed and discolored, a white piece of tape covered part of his eye, and he carried one arm as if his shoulder was sore.

"Nino!" She ran to the table and stopped only when she saw how he was afraid she might touch him. "Nino! Can you talk? Will you tell me what...."

"I can talk," he said.

His voice was normal, and looking at him from a certain angle, even his face looked the same. But he had changed.

"You don't look surprised," he said to Port.

Port closed the door and came over.

"Like maybe you knew it all along," Ramon went on.

Port sat down and said, "Don't be an ass."

"Nino, will you please look at me. Nino, what happened?"

"You don't see Danny Port asking questions, do you, Shelly? He knows already."

Shelly looked at Port, and for a moment he was reminded of the way she used to look at him, here in the kitchen, not too many days ago.

"He got beat up," said Port. "By the Reform Party."

Shelly didn't act as if she had heard, as if it weren't important. She took off her coat, put it over a chair, and went to her brother. "Get up, Nino." She took him under the arms. "Nino. Can you get up?"

"Leave me be."

"You are going to lie down and sleep, if you can. Come to your room."

He came with her and lay down on the bed and Shelly took off his shoes.

"Sleep now. I'll take care of you."

"Sure," he said. "Between you and him, over there...."

"Be quiet, Nino."

"And close my eyes? And turn the other way while you and that bastard...."

"Shut up, Ramon," Port said from the doorway.

"Shut up? I should keep quiet when nobody else does? You know what they said, what they asked me? They called me a pimp!" Ramon screamed. "Whether I pimped for her and what is Port paying! That's what they asked me, you stinking bastard."

Ramon stopped, coughing badly, and when he turned on his side to hide his face Shelly put out her hand and stroked his hair. Port said nothing because he saw how Ramon felt.

"Nino, don't," she said. She said it several times, soothingly, and kept stroking his head.

After a while he turned around and sat up. He had changed again, back to the cold, suspicious man they had found in the kitchen.

"They were riding you," said Port. "You know what they said isn't true."

"Do I? Where were you all this time?"

"I was with Daniel," said Shelly.

"You don't mean it!"

"I sleep with whom I like."

"Did you sleep good?"

Shelly drew back her hand and stood up, but didn't say anything.

"Don't take it out on her," said Port. "I don't care how bad you're hurt, Ramon, but don't take it out on her."

"You don't scare me any more, Port. I've had mine."

"I'm not trying to scare you, but don't talk like a pimp. You're her brother."

Ramon didn't like it. "That's why I'm telling you, Port. Get the hell out of here."

"What happened?" Port made a pause. "Did you talk?"

The whole thing came back to Ramon, the two men and Bellamy waiting in the room in the basement. They had started to beat him without explanation, and then Bellamy had said to lay off for a minute. He had asked, "What did you hear on the phone, what did you tell Port, what was he after, what's he going to do, what'll he spring, what, what, what," and each time they had hit him, in the same place, each time in the same place till he thought his face would burst open. He hadn't told them a thing.

He didn't know whether it was because he hadn't known anything or because he was strong. The doubt made a sore knot in his chest.

"What did you tell them, Ramon?"

"Nothing!"

"Would you have, if you had known anything?"

"Get out! Scram the hell outa here!"

Port sat down on the bed and took out his cigarettes. Then he asked Shelly to leave. She went to the kitchen and they could hear her at the stove.

"Something's eating you, and maybe I ought to know."

"Beat it."

"We're through?"

"I told you, Port, you don't scare me one bit."

Port took a deep breath, put a cigarette in his mouth, and offered one to Ramon. Ramon didn't take it.

"Maybe you don't remember, Nino...."

"Don't call me that."

"You're too mean not to be scared. But not of me. I never gave you cause, did I, Ramon?"

Ramon looked away.

"I even warned you not to get that way."

"So what? You warned me about getting beat up, too. That doesn't make me any less sore."

Port took a drag of his cigarette and watched the smoke disappear.

"I give you one more piece of advice. Get out of it, Ramon. You're not built for it."

Ramon laughed hard, even though it hurt his face. "The boot? I did the job, and now I get the boot?"

"I think you're out already. Except not the way I meant."

"You know so much."

"I think you switched. You got in real deep this time, and switched to Bellamy."

"I did?"

"You'll find out, Ramon. It's no joke, if you stay."

"You buying me back?"

"There's a difference between you and me, kid—at least I know a mistake."

"You've had more experience."

"That's true, and a good reason why you should listen to me."

"Why don't you leave?" said Ramon. The good side of his face looked cocky, but the bad one looked soft and tired.

"I brought you some tea," said Shelly and put the tray next to the bed. She turned to look at. Port. "Is he leaving with us?" And to Ramon, "You're coming with us?"

Ramon saw how Port's face got very still.

"I shouldn't have told him?" said Shelly.

"I don't know. He's in deep."

"Nino, what did you do?"

"Nothing. It's the same as before, except he's trying to make something of it. That Reform crowd is any worse than your outfit? Don't make me laugh, Port!"

"I wouldn't. They're both the same. Except you were working for me, not the Stoker outfit."

Ramon laughed good and hard this time, screwing his face around so it wouldn't hurt so much.

"Nino, answer me!"

"He joined up with Bellamy."

"Because he made sense! When I didn't crack he sat up, and then he made sense. About old man Stoker half dead, about you never giving a damn, about Fries who's a jerk from way back, and what Bellamy had to offer on the other side. I look out for myself, and that's all I go by."

"But Nino, it's no good. Daniel told me. And he asked you to come."

"I didn't hear any such thing," said Ramon. "All I know is he's got hold of you and he's lamming out."

"I said you made a mistake, Ramon, and maybe you can make it good. I don't want you along, but if you want out I'll give you a hand."

All Ramon heard was the part about Shelly. All he could think of was Shelly and Port and how it had all worked out for them, just as if he had planned it himself the way he had once wanted to plan it himself. And Bellamy had called him a pimp.

"It's not only that I'm staying," he said, "but so is Shelly."

Port got up and looked for a place to drop his cigarette. He dropped it out the window and came back to the bed. He took Shelly's arm and said, "Come along."

"I'm staying, Daniel. He's sick." When Port frowned she went on. "I'm not staying because of the way he talked, but because he needs me. You go home alone. Call for me when it's time."

Port smiled and hated himself. She hadn't meant what he had thought.

"Wear something nice," he said. "We got a party tonight."

He went to the door, but Ramon called him back.

"So you don't get it wrong, you bastard." He waited till Port turned around. "Shelly stays here. Or maybe you don't get a chance to leave town at all."

If Shelly hadn't been there in the room Port would have marked up the other side of Ramon's face. He hunched his shoulders and tried to control his voice. "Bellamy told you that I never give a damn. You start fooling with me, Nino, and you'll learn different."

Nobody talked as he went out.

Port drove out of town because he felt like driving fast. He was preoccupied enough not to notice the car that was following him.

Chapter 17

When he did, Port was out on the empty highway. Once a hay truck came driving the other way, but that didn't slow Port or the car behind. Port couldn't shake it. He felt in a bad enough temper without finding himself being chased down a highway, and when the next bend showed a roadhouse further down he stepped on the gas as if he were going past. At the last safe minute he swerved and skidded a black, ragged gutter into the gravel and watched the other car shoot by on the highway. It came to a stop when Port was out of his car and running through the door of the roadhouse.

There was just the bartender, doubling as fry cook, and a farmer who was drinking beer with his tuna fish sandwich. Port came around the bar before anyone realized what he was doing and looked in the shelf space under the cash register. There was nothing. There was no stick, no billy, no nothing. The bartender came up, more surprised than angry when Port slapped a bill down on the counter. "Take it! Take it and move," he said and had the cash drawer open just when the car outside made a long squeal and stopped.

The gun was in the back of the drawer and Port skinned his knuckles yanking it out. He made the other side of the bar when the car doors slammed, and he sat down as if waiting for a drink.

That's what it looked like to Bellamy, who pushed his two hoods in ahead of him. He grinned at Port from the door and watched one of the hoods go to sit on Port's right and the other one on Port's left. When he saw Port whip out, make a fat sound that snapped back his man's head and his man flat on the floor with the well of red blood covering the bad shape of the face. Port couldn't have watched all that because when Bellamy looked back at him, Port was sitting still, obscured by the other hood, and that one was dropping his gun to the floor.

"Pick it up, Bellamy."

Bellamy didn't see the gun Port was holding till he came around and stooped to the floor. The gun followed him down and then up again.

"Put it on the bar."

Bellamy did. He smiled at the bartender and then at the farmer in back. Neither of them had moved, and the farmer's sandwich was trembling in his hand.

"I'm going to ask these good people here," said Bellamy, "to back me up when I prefer charges. I'm sure that...."

"They don't want to be bothered," said Port. "The thing about bystanders, they much rather stay that way. Don't you, guys?" They didn't answer. "Especially when the fight's between hoods?"

This time the bartender nodded and the farmer pushed the sandwich into his mouth.

"With hoods," said Port, "a talking bystander gets it in the neck no matter which way he talks. You guys know that, don't you?"

They both nodded.

Bellamy shrugged and grinned to show what a good sport he was. "All right," he said. "I just want to talk to you, Danny."

"I'm not interested."

"You got a back room, bartender?"

The bartender nodded and went to the rear. Bellamy followed him, and after Port had told the hood with his arms up to pick up his buddy they all followed toward the back.

They stood around while the bartender was there. Then Port said, "You ought to order some drinks, Bellamy. Make it worth his while."

"Bring something," said Bellamy, who had lost his good humor. "Beer."

"Make mine rye. And a glass of water," said Port.

They waited around without talking while Port kept the gun in sight. The bartender came back with three beers and the whisky, and everybody took his off the tray. One beer was left because the man with the bloody face was still on the floor, breathing badly.

"You drink it," said Port. "Mr. Bellamy will pay you."

Bellamy did, and the bartender rushed out of the room, forgetting his tray and the extra beer.

"Before you start laughing and cutting up," said Port, "I want you to know what a filthy mood I'm in. I also got a date for nine tonight and have to change yet. All right?"

"My party?" said Bellamy.

"That's right."

"I don't want to see you there. I want you to lay low for a while, for your own good."

"What's in it for you?"

Bellamy hadn't tried joking once, and the sight of Port's gun nettled him. It made him very direct, without the usual mannerisms. "I'm taking this town sooner or later, and I want you to switch."

"I knew the last part."

"I know how you feel about it. You told me. Now I'm telling you. There's a little thing comes out in the afternoon paper about Daniel Port, Stoker's right-hand man, defecting in the interest of civic advancement and the Reform. It means you don't show up at the party tonight to make a display of yourself with Stoker, and it means you better lie low while the Stoker bunch cools off after reading the news. That's why I'm here. I got a place all set up for you…."

"When's that paper come out, Bellamy?"

"Don't worry about that part. I'm through horsing around with you, because once I decide…."

"Who's the animal?" said Port, and pointed at the hood who was sipping his beer.

"Now you listen to me, Port…."

"What's his name?"

"My name's Sherman," said the hood.

"All right, Sherman, finish your beer."

The hood finished his beer and then looked from one to the other.

"Now turn around, Sherman."

"Don't listen to him!" yelled Bellamy. "I'll see to it that…."

"It's my skin," said Sherman, and turned around.

He closed his eyes, waiting for Port to hit him, which Port did. Sherman fell down. Bellamy had to jump out of the way.

"You'll regret this! I'm going to make it my business…" when Port raked the gun barrel down Bellamy's front, making all the buttons on the tattersall vest bust open.

"Get on the phone," said Port.

"If you think strong-arming me is going…."

"I know it will," said Port, and hit Bellamy under the heart.

"You got a gun—you wouldn't dare act like this—"

Bellamy went to the phone on the desk in the corner, walking crouched over because of the pain in his middle.

"Now call up that paper."

"It's too late. They printed hours ago."

"But they don't hit the streets till six. Call up and cancel the thing."

Bellamy laughed, for real this time, and called up the paper. He asked for the editor-in-chief, whom he called by his first name, and started out, "Look, Billy, this is stupid, but I'm supposed to tell you to keep your edition off the streets. It's too late, isn't it, Billy?"

Port held the gun in Bellamy's back and took the phone out of his hand. When he had the receiver at his ear he heard the editor's laughter.

"This is Port speaking. Daniel Port."

The laughing stopped.

"You know whom you're listening to?"

"I do. Yes, sir, I do."

"And now I want you to listen to Bellamy."

Port held the phone to Bellamy's face and then did a painful thing with the gun barrel in Bellamy's back. The raw sound which Bellamy made into the phone was impressive.

"That was Bellamy," said Port. "He's now going to...."

"Duress!" Bellamy yelled into the phone. "I'm under duress!"

Port listened for something from the other end, but the editor had nothing to say. Only his breathing was audible.

"Bellamy is right," said Port after a while. "And it's not the kind of duress you would want on your conscience. Here's your buddy again."

Port gave the phone back to Bellamy, who could hardly talk.

"Do like he says, Billy. I don't care what it costs, do what he says!"

"And tell him I'm going to cripple you if he doesn't," said Port.

"Yes, you heard right, Billy. Do just what he said."

"And tell him you're a vindictive man, especially from a wheel chair."

"Billy, promise!"

Billy promised, and Bellamy hung up. He was bathed in sweat and when Port stepped back, Bellamy sank into the chair that stood by the desk. He groaned and didn't know whether to sit up straight or double over. Port sat down too and smoked a cigarette to give the man time to recover.

"I didn't know you were vicious," said Bellamy after a while.

"Push me hard enough and I'm all manner of things."

"I can use you," said Bellamy.

"No you couldn't."

"I pay. I can pay you...."

"I don't do it for pay, only for necessity."

"Give it any name you want, Port."

"And I can also go without sleep for seventy-two hours, but not if I can help it."

Port went over to the two hoods on the floor, and saw that they were good the way they were for a while longer. He told Bellamy to get up, they were leaving, and followed him out to the room with the bar. Bellamy waited at the door while Port stopped to give the gun back to the bartender. "And there's two in the back room," he said. "On the floor."

The bartender stared, reached for the gun automatically. "I—I don't get it. I got nothing but blanks in this thing!"

Port held on to the bar for a minute, to feel the pressure under his palms and to think of nothing else.

"I was afraid to tell you before, but the gun...."

"Will you keep your voice down, for God's sake!"

The bartender swallowed what he had meant to say, but his expression didn't change.

"About those two in the back—how did you, what did you—"

"I scared them to death," said Port. "The way you just did me."

He followed Bellamy out of the door.

Chapter 18

It was getting dark when they got to Port's apartment. He shaved and changed but didn't take a shower because Bellamy was no longer wrapped up enough to be left alone for that long. He sat in a chair watching Port. Bellamy thought he could kill him—which would be a mess for sure; or he could force Stoker to break with him, which might even the balance. And in each case he would lose Port. How valuable is one man? If he let the man go, it would be like never having tried; if he just made him bleed, Port would come back to him; if he had him killed—Bellamy found himself back at the beginning and not one step closer to the right solution. He knew only that he hadn't solved it, and the thought wouldn't leave him alone.

Port took Bellamy to Ward Nine and when he picked up Shelly he even took him upstairs. Shelly's smile dropped off fast when she saw him, making Bellamy take a short step back.

"He came to drive us," said Port, "so me and you can sit in the back." They grinned at each other and Bellamy went down the stairs ahead of them. Ramon didn't show up. He had stayed in bed, smoking.

Bellamy's driveway had two entrances and there were two policemen at each. They had nothing to do but stand there, tip their hats regardless of which party affiliation drove through, and at the end of the evening there was an envelope waiting for them in the kitchen. The two at the entrance

gate were kept busy saluting and waving the cars through to avoid a traffic problem, while the two at
the exit gate just stood around, bored with each other. Every so often one of them took off for the kitchen, the old one for beer and little caviar canapés, the younger one to drink coffee and watch the maids. At the house another uniform waited. This one had been hired from one of the clubs, epauletted and braided like a South American general. He opened car doors and helped riders get to the curb safely, and then he blew his whistle to make the chauffeur drive on. Port and Shelly stood by the curb and waited for the general to blow his whistle, except this time he didn't know what to do.

"Tell Mr. Bellamy to park the car," said Port. "And tell him we'll wait for him here."

The general did that. After the car had torn off to the parking area the general came back to the curb. "He says not to wait for him. He says he'll meet you inside."

Port and Shelly went up the stairs, laughing, but they would have been sorry had they known what they missed. When Bellamy tried to sneak into a side entrance he got stopped by one of the exit cops who was just on his way back from the kitchen. Bellamy's evil mood, his torn vest, and his haste in general meant a long delay while the cop decided to check with some guests whether it was all right to let Bellamy in. It made a spectacle which left the main hall deserted, except for Bellamy's daughter, who was doing the hostessing. Even the butler had left.

Janice Bellamy had her father's light hair and reddish complexion, but where he was heavy she was dry and thin. She looked up when Port and Shelly came in and said, "Mr. Port!"

"Miss Bellamy. May I present Miss Ramon."

Miss Bellamy stared, being short-sighted but without glasses on gala occasions, and when she recognized Shelly she just managed to say, "How unusual—"

Shelly smiled at her and made the mistake of slipping her cape off her shoulders. It showed the long evening dress which was designed to make broad lights over the hips and to reveal the bareness on top.

"Well," said Miss Bellamy. "It looks positively new."

"It is."

"Did Mr. Port buy it for you?"

"I gave her the money," said Port.

"I couldn't have swung it, on a maid's salary," said Shelly.

"I know that," said Miss Bellamy. "But I'm sure you know how to make out in spite of having lost your legitimate job."

Port took the cape from Shelly. "We'll join the guests," he said. "Will we see you after you're through here?" and he handed the cape to Miss Bellamy. Port and Shelly walked into the room with the guests.

Because of the commotion that Bellamy had caused, almost everyone was at one end of the room. Port recognized several people but didn't see Stoker. He saw Fries, though, who was standing at this end of the room, fingering the half-finished hooked rug on the frame. He looked up and came over.

"Where've you been anyway? I thought you told Stoker to...."

"I couldn't make it in time. Besides, I had to pick up Shelly. Mr. Fries," he introduced, "Miss Ramon."

But Fries didn't unbend.

"Isn't she the sister of that Ramon who got thrown out of the club?"

"It's worse than that, Fries. He's a Bellamy man."

Fries wasn't going to be party-spirited, so Port and Shelly left him to the hooked rug. Then Port saw Stoker.

"Shelly, I'll leave you here. You want me to bring you a drink?"

"Just tell the man with the tray. I'll wait for you here." She sat down on a couch.

Port waved at the waiter and left Shelly.

Stoker looked old. He seemed to have lost more weight and his face was pale. He acted animated enough but the tiredness showed. When he saw Port he stopped talking. A low-key color came into his face.

"Hi, Stoker. Ready to make the rounds?"

"Where in hell you been?"

"I wouldn't run out on you, Max. Come on, let's circulate."

They walked, said hello here and there, looking casual. "After the way you been acting, and no word from you for the past few days...."

"I didn't feel like answering the telephone."

Stoker looked up.

"How'd you know I called? You been home?"

"Most of the time." Port noded and said, "Hello, McFarlane."

"Don't overdo it," said Stoker.

"Hello, Sump."

Stoker said hello too, but kept on walking. Port held Stoker's arm.

"Aren't you talking to him?"

"What for?"

"What for? Listen, Max, I came here for one reason only."

"He doesn't know a thing, if you mean the vote."

"He heads the committee. He ought to know what...."

"I won't know till ten. They're having a meeting and after that Ekstain will call here."

Port looked at his watch and saw it would be another half an hour.

"Half an hour isn't going to kill you," said Stoker.

"Just don't be so offhand about it."

"I know why you're here. We'll talk about it after ten."

Port didn't answer. He didn't feel like talking about it now, or half an hour later. He would sit out his promised duty, he would stick close to Stoker, for the show, but he had said his good-bys. Port looked for Shelly, and saw she wasn't alone any more. Two old men were on either side of her, acting like billy goats, and three middle-aged ones stood close by, each telling a joke but all at the same time. Shelly smiled and nodded, and tried to lean out of the way.

"I see Paternik," said Port. "Did you say hello to him yet?"

"We shook hands."

"How'd that real estate thing go? Did you try it?"

"I told Fries to handle it. I haven't asked him since."

"You want to keep track of him, Max. Not like you been handling me."

Stoker gave Port a sour look. He nodded a few hellos, shook his head at a waiter who was carrying a tray, and kept walking. It wasn't a very festive mood, thought Port, not the way Stoker acted.

"Did you see our host?" he asked.

"I saw him come in."

"Max, you're not laughing and smiling. I'm here so we'll look friendly together, and when it comes to Bellamy that should really amuse you."

"I barely caught a glimpse," said Stoker. "There was something about the policeman not wanting to let him in."

"And his clothes all mussed. Wasn't that funny?"

"How do you know? You just got in."

"I brought him."

Port thought it would give Stoker a laugh and told him how the day had gone, about Bellamy, his two apes, and the paper. Port didn't like Stoker's mood and tried to put things in a funny way, tried to make light of an evening which he meant to be his and Stoker's last together.

"I don't think it's funny," said Stoker. "When a guy like Bellamy gets that anxious...."

"He's bluffing," said Port, not believing it.

"Watch him, no matter what you do."

"You sound like a speech, Max. Come, I'll show you something nice," and Port took Stoker to the couch where Shelly was sitting.

She got up when she saw Port and so did the two old men sitting next to her.

"I'd like you to meet Mr. Stoker," said Port. "The old man himself, and my guardian angel."

They all laughed and then Shelly said, "And this is Judge Paternik and his clerk, Mr.—"

"Auburn," said the clerk. He was as old and impressive looking as Judge Paternik, but Paternik had something special. Nobody looked at the clerk any more while Judge Paternik started to crackle with magnetism.

"Mr. Stoker," he said, "and Mr. Port. I know both of you by reputation and welcome this chance, this non-partisan chance, to meet both of you man to man."

"We're delighted," said Port. "And I hope your presence, your non-partisan presence, will serve to temper...."

The judge couldn't have been listening because he interrupted to say, "Why, when it comes down to it, gentlemen, we all are, are we not, of the same...."

"You put it well, Judge, and I'm glad you did. Shelly, has the judge...."

"I have that, I indeed have that," said the judge, and under the guise of paternal affection he patted Shelly's bare arm.

"While I introduce Miss Ramon to our host, I'll leave you and Mr. Stoker together," said Port. He saw Stoker unbend and get affable, because the party was, after all, business.

"Why do we have to meet Bellamy again?" said Shelly. She held on to Port's arm and pushed herself close.

"Just to make it polite," said Port. "After all, he got dressed for us."

His tuxedo jacket—it went without saying—was Scotch plaid, and so was the cummerbund. In his haste he had grabbed a pair of pants with a plaid stripe down the side that didn't quite match the jacket. When they reached Bellamy, Shelly was happy to see there wasn't going to be much conversation. They passed each other, nodded with smiles, and Bellamy was gone. Port had not seen Bellamy being short before, not in public.

"I see the terrace," said Shelly and steered Port by the arm.

They went outside and leaned against the stone railing. They smoked and were glad to be together.

"It's over soon?" said Shelly.

"Tonight."

"And nobody knows?"

"Stoker does, but he won't believe it."

"I believe you. I believe you without your explaining it, just seeing how different you are from those—" She nodded towards the house.

"They're not that different from anyone else."

"But they think so."

"Let them. It makes them easier to spot."

Port looked into the lighted room and saw the rat race in operation. The false smile, the innuendo, the threat by omission, and the dirty jokes and the club-house bravado, all making a hail-fellow-well-met gesturing out of the knife in the back.

Port saw Paternik standing alone, looking for the waiter who went around with the tray. Stoker had left him. Stoker was not in the room.

"Okay, honey—"

"You're leaving?"

"Once more. Have a chat with Mr. Auburn, to be completely safe."

She gave him a smile and they went inside. Shelly went one way and Port went toward the half-finished hooked rug where Fries was standing.

"Stoker get his phone call?" asked Port.

"Sure. You anxious?"

"Is he still on the phone?"

"He hasn't come back yet," said Fries.

They stood by the hooked rug and Port caught himself counting stitches.

When Stoker came in he looked subdued and had a flush on his face. He saw Port and Fries and came toward them casually.

"Well? What did you hear?" Port asked.

"You don't sound like you got much confidence in your setups no more," said Fries.

Port ignored it and waited for Stoker to speak.

"The Ward stays," said Stoker. "They're voting it our way."

Port found that his excitement had been artificial. He heard the words—meaning it's now all over—but there was no relief. Or the excitement was genuine but it had nothing to do with the news on the vote. He knew what the vote was going to be; he had known it for days. He thought he had known that with the vote in the bag it was over, and now he knew that it wasn't. Stoker put it into words for him.

"Danny, now comes the serious part. Come along."

He followed Stoker out of the room, and decided to make the break final. For the moment he didn't remember that he used to think he had done so before.

Chapter 19

"All right," said Port. "Don't act like a wake."

But Stoker didn't say anything, and Fries just closed the door. The room was long, with a sunken effect, and a sandstone fireplace designed for a bigger room. Stoker walked back and forth for a while, looking out the window, looking into the fireplace. Port didn't press him. This time, for the last time, let Stoker pour his heart out, tell of the old times and how far they had come, and the big things in the future as long as the team held together. Port wouldn't pay any attention to Fries, because Fries and his two cents' worth of wise comments weren't going to get in the way at a time like this. Port would concentrate on the appeal in Stoker's voice, his paternal pleading, and having heard it all before would let it come and go like a recital.

"Danny," said Stoker, "maybe you've made up your mind. If you have, maybe it'll kill you."

Port didn't talk, didn't even whistle. He watched Stoker stand by the fireplace, one foot on the sandstone apron, and the way Stoker looked it didn't fit the old image at all.

"I'm not arguing any more," said Stoker. "Pardon the phrase, but it's now bigger than you and me."

Maybe a joke right now. Maybe a little chuckle right here where the silence was thickest, and Port wouldn't feel so pushed any more. He couldn't make up his mind fast enough, because Stoker went on.

"You're a hood, Port. What's worse, you're a hood in the know."

Port narrowed his eyes, and this time he did start to whistle. It was as tuneless as ever, as offhand as all the times when he'd heard himself do it, except he was thinking how false it rang. If he were alone, he'd be screaming right now.

Stoker kept watching him.

"Why don't I trust you? You don't have to ask. I trust you, but that's neither here nor there. One day I'm going to be dead. Before you, most likely."

Now maybe he'd revert to type and start with the old-times'-sake sermon. Port sat down in a leather chair, closed his eyes, and listened to the pillow sigh.

"Maybe even Fries trusts you." Stoker paused for a moment. "You know more than Fries does, did you know that?"

Port looked up at the ceiling.

"About our hookup," Stoker went on, "about the ins and outs of all kinds of traffic, how our little setup—our vote insurance setup—is just one of the cogs in the whole scheme, the whole balanced scheme."

Port chewed his lip and wondered how he might feel five minutes from now.

"That's how smart you are. In fact, sometimes I wonder, Danny, why you haven't moved up out of this setup." Suddenly Stoker changed his voice. "But you're not smart enough to walk out!"

The five minutes hadn't passed, but Port felt the change, the clarity come back into his feeling, and if he didn't quite know what he ought to do, at least the dullness was gone, the cottony vagueness which hangs, waiting, just before the fright sets in.

"You listening, Port?"

Port looked at Fries and then at Stoker. Either of them could have said it, and neither of them would understand his answer.

"I make sense," Stoker said. "Don't I?"

"Sure. Your kind of sense."

"What's that supposed to mean?" Fries wanted to know. Port got out of the chair. Not too much later he'd be walking out.

"It means that you and I don't think the same way."

"How come? You're maybe some kind of superior species?" Fries said.

Port turned away from Fries so the impulse to answer him would go away. "Max, tell him to leave, will you?"

"Wait in the other room," said Stoker.

"By the hooked rug," said Port.

Fries was at the door with not enough time to think of a comeback. He closed the door behind him and the silence in the room started to grow again.

Abruptly Port said, "It all adds up to the same thing. I'm leaving."

He said it calmly, clearly, but Stoker did not want to listen. He talked as if he had not been interrupted.

"Here's your choice. It's either you or Fries."

"What?"

"Face the facts, Danny. I won't be here much longer. Which way do you want it: With Fries under you, or you under Fries?"

Port felt the rage grow, and he couldn't stop it this time. "To me, that's not even a choice."

"There's another one. The one I told you at first."

Stoker saw the color come into Port's face, a thing he had never seen, and like an infection he felt his own face become glutted with blood, the heart-pound loud in his ears, and he shouted, "Take it or leave it! I'm through begging you! Take it or leave it, and I don't give one stinking damn!"

Port's voice came out hoarse. He controlled its strength but no longer anything else.

"You go to hell!"

"Wha—"

"If I can't get rid of you and the air you breathe, you and the Frieses and Bellamys and the big shots with small heads and the small shots with big heads, then I'd sooner crap out!"

"I'll see you will!"

"Try it, Stoker. Try stopping me now!"

Port saw Stoker stare, breathing hard, his face ugly with great drops of sweat, and then he swiveled fast because of the sound.

But the door was closing already. When Paternik saw that Port was looking at him he went back half a step, smiled softly, and said, "I apologize. I heard voices. You will forgive an old man's curiosity...."

"Sure. That's all right—"

Port saw Paternik stand there, and then he came closer.

"Forget it," said Port, but Paternik didn't hear. Port could tell by his face. He wasn't even looking at Port. He was cocking his white-haired head, frowning, and seemed to be on the point of clearing his throat. He made a smooth movement closing the door, and when he spoke it came suddenly.

"For heaven's sake!"

Then Port heard what the judge was seeing, a thin, sick groan that cut off as if choked. A choke which was pain itself, pain freezing all motion to death.

It was a miracle that Stoker still stood. He did not even weave. His arms were out, a pathetic gesture of a hug interrupted, and the worn face was full of struggle. But nothing moved.

He collapsed suddenly, one leg still on the stone apron, and if it hadn't been for the sound on the stone, Stoker's falling to lie stretched out would have been a relief. The face was past tiredness and the arms were through trying to reach.

Chapter 20

The party broke up very quickly. Port didn't see anyone leave, but he heard the murmuring and the awed tones through the door, as if Stoker were suddenly somebody else and all the old relationships had died with him.

Before everyone left, and right after the cops from the gates had come into the house, Port had paid one of them to take Shelly home. Once Shelly was out of the house, Port went back to the room.

In the room with the dead man there were Port and Judge Paternik; Bellamy, who was the host, and Fries, who now had position. Fries left after a while because he had a lot to do elsewhere. They sat in the room with dead Stoker, one of the cops from the gate guarding the door.

"Not to distract from the tragedy," said Judge Paternik, "but it was fortunate that I came in."

Port smoked silently and Bellamy, who had his arms on his knees, looked up with a wrinkled forehead. He licked his lower lip once, then looked down again. His forehead stayed creased.

"I speak from the legal point of view. My entrance made me a witness."

"Not that it needed one," said Bellamy.

Port sat without thinking, waiting for the police, for the routine, but he was waiting for more. He hadn't reacted yet. He wondered whether it might have been easier to know how he felt if Stoker and he had finished their argument. Then, perhaps, it would all be clear now.

"Of course, when you say he had a heart condition," the judge was saying, "that makes the matter nothing but routine. Including the skull fracture."

"Is it fractured?" asked Bellamy.

"The sound was quite awful," said the judge.

Port remembered the sound. It had been like something mechanical, nothing alive. Port looked at Stoker as if he hadn't known until now that Stoker was dead.

It seemed to Port they had to wait quite a while. Off and on Bellamy and the judge exchanged a few words, and then Bellamy urged the judge to go home. There was no reason for him to stay, and a person in his position was certainly not required to go through the routine of police questioning. The judge thought the same.

"I can be reached at my home here in town," he told Port and Bellamy.

"I'll tell them," said Bellamy. "Maybe just a written statement, in case they bring it up."

"Of course," said the judge.

"I'll drop around," said Bellamy. "Just to see how you are and to give my respects to your wife."

"Mrs. Paternik stayed in the Capitol," said the judge. "Her activities rarely permit her...."

"That's wonderful," said Bellamy. "I admire that."

They all nodded at each other and the policeman at the door let the judge through.

When the detectives and the medical examiner came it turned out to be open-and-shut, and the inquest would be of the briefest kind. The detectives did all their duties, the lab men had just come along for the ride, and there would be a few more formalities later, nothing time-consuming, just the sort of thing requiring legal presence. It could even be done by mail.

It made a peculiar after-the-party feeling in the empty house, leaving no tensions and causing no stir.

"Want a drink before leaving?" said Bellamy.

"No thanks. I'll be going."

"Take your time," said Bellamy. "When it happens, it's always a surprise."

"Yeah. That's true."

"You don't know where to put your feelings."

Port didn't like to hear it from Bellamy, but it was true.

"Take your time. If you want a drink, you know where to find it," and Bellamy walked out of the room, leaving the door open.

Port got up too, but when he got to the hall it was empty. He had a hat somewhere. He found it on the hall table, only one hat left on the table, and then he went back to the room with the bar. He reached for a bottle to pour a drink, but then he stopped, wondering why he needed a drink because he suddenly found that his ties were gone.

He walked out of the house, closed the big door behind him, and stood on the dim terrace. There was another light further away, at the curve of the driveway, and it showed the wet night fog hanging in the air. Port breathed deeply.

This was the time! He had thought his planning had made him ready, his schemes, and then in the end, if nothing else, his decision. But Stoker had been alive, and the sick man's invisible hold, stronger than threats, had worked better than arguments, because leaving then had still been a walking out. But not any more.

He ran down the stairs three at a time and kept running till he got to his car. It wasn't a need to hurry, just the feel in his muscles, in his lungs, of moving freely. He was whistling when he drove off, loud and strong.

He wasn't going to wait till morning. He would pick up Shelly in the middle of the night and they'd drive out of town before the light came up. And if she were in bed, that would only delay them long enough for her to get dressed. But he was sorry—on the way to her house—that all the florists were closed.

Shelly wasn't in.

There was a light in the kitchen, the door wasn't locked, and Ramon was lying in bed. One side of his face was dark purple, with a white, professional bandage higher up.

"Where's Shelly?"

Ramon was smoking and didn't answer. He took long, steady drags and lay on the bed, dressed, without moving.

"You got a fever?"

"I'm all right."

"I asked you where Shelly is!"

Ramon dropped ashes into the cup by his bed and said, "She's out."

Port sat down on the bed and didn't look at Ramon. "Did she get home?"

Ramon was very casual—except for the strong hostile streak under his voice.

"She got home. Then she went out."

"For medicine or something?"

"Yeah."

Port looked at his watch, then took out a cigarette. When he had lit it he blew the smoke up in the air so it wouldn't drift toward the sick man. Then he looked at Ramon.

"Why don't you lay off me. You'd make it that much easier all around," Port asked.

"What makes you think I want to make it easier for you?"

"I don't know what, but I'm not in your way."

"I'm seeing to that," Ramon snapped.

"What more do you want? I'm leaving, and you're all set with Bellamy."

"I'm remembering that."

"And with the upset in the Stoker outfit right now, you made a good thing of it."

"That's what I'm working on."

"Do that. And leave me alone."

"I'll do that. When you stay away from my sister."

Port got up. "You're going to be a real big wheel. I can see that. You not only get excited about things you got nothing to do with, but you keep bucking the wrong people."

"You don't scare me," said Ramon.

Port gave him a tired look and walked toward the kitchen. He said, "I'll blame it on the fever," and sat down.

Port sat and waited. He could hear his own breathing and now and then the creaking of Ramon's bed, small sounds but heavy. The sound of someone moving in bed was always a heavy sound, as if the bed wouldn't let go. Then the feel of it spread to the kitchen and Port sat very still, feeling the weight grow in the room, and he didn't move because he was balancing lt.

He had imagined this differently, his coming in, the first words, and then

what Shelly would do. He was going to say, "Now, Shelly," and that's all he
would have to say for her to know what came next—she would just go with
him, and that would be their beginning.

Port wiped his hand across his mouth and went back into the room
where Ramon was.

"I'm going home to get my bags," said Port. "When Shelly comes in tell her
I'll pick her up."

"Like hell."

Port controlled himself, remembering that the man was sick.

"Just tell her."

"I'll tell *you* something," said Ramon. "I don't pimp for my sister."

Port could make out Ramon's face by the light from the kitchen, but with
Ramon's face disfigured it was hard to tell what he felt at the moment. He
hadn't sounded just tough, the way he must have meant it. Perhaps it was
the pain and the fever. Mostly fever.

It was long after midnight, and Port made good time. When he got to the
building he took the stairs up because it felt faster, and when he saw the light
under his door he started to run. It explained Ramon's answers; he hadn't
known where Shelly was. Port opened the door.

Chapter 21

"Now that you're here, close the door," said Bellamy.

Port closed the door.

Kirby was there with a gun in his hand, and Judge Paternik was sitting
on the bed.

"You can put the gun away, Kirby. He doesn't carry one," said Bellamy.

Kirby did, and then Port started to tremble.

"You might as well hear all of it, Port." Bellamy turned to the judge. "You
want to tell him?"

"Perhaps you should ask him first," said the judge.

Bellamy shrugged. "Port, I've asked you often, I've asked you nice. You're
staying in town, working for me."

There was a tight knot of hate inside Port's chest, and he held it there,
sweating, till he could use it.

"No answer, Daniel?"

"Why don't you take a flying...."

"Shut up, you crazy hood!"

It felt very much like the mood in Ramon's kitchen, with the growing weight pressing down hard. There was something here, something very big, like the foreboding before a dream turns into a nightmare.

"I've got you dead to rights this time."

"What?" said Port, and he sounded hoarse.

"Judge?" and Bellamy raised his eyebrows.

"It was murder," said the judge.

Port felt his limp arms and very heavy hands. As a rational man he would not have believed this; he might even have laughed. But he wasn't that. He heard what the judge had said.

"I saw you do it, Port. I witnessed the crime, which I will detail to the police."

"Unless you join up," said Bellamy, but Port didn't hear him.

The judge said, "Why haven't I done so yet? Very simple, Mr. Port. I too have a heart condition, and as a consequence of the murder I witnessed I could have stayed only upon jeopardy of my health."

"You're sewed up."

"Now, in detail," said the judge. "I walked in at the end of a quarrel—it was the shouting which had attracted my attention—and saw you deliver a powerful blow to the back of Stoker's head. I will say that having witnessed this, it is my opinion, no matter what the immediate cause of death, I feel that if this isn't murder, the law is a farce!"

Kirby half sat on the windowsill, arms folded, grinning. Bellamy sat hunched forward now, with his shoulders more massive because of his pose; and the judge sat upright and gave Port a clear glance. The white hair was as imposing as ever, the full eyebrows gave depth to his eyes, and the old mouth was in a settled line, not severe, but contained.

"Why—" said Port. He was looking at the judge. "Why you?"

"Didn't you know?" said Bellamy. "The judge heads up the Reform Party."

They gave it a chance to sink in. They watched Port open his mouth without making a sound, and when he closed it they felt he was done. Nothing showed in his face, nothing moved, only his hands started to rub up and down the sides of his pants.

"You see it now?" asked Bellamy.

Port saw nothing. He only felt that they could do anything, that they had everything, but he saw nothing. They had the powerful, big Bellamy, the name and brain of Paternik, gun-happy Kirby, big-dreaming Ramon—everything.

"Where is Shelly?" Port said.

Port didn't notice the way they frowned, not knowing what he wanted, but Port didn't follow it up. The tight knot of hate had started to loosen and grow, and the size of it grew over his head. It got so big for him that he couldn't stand it and it turned into panic. When he moved it was panic that pushed him.

He was out of the room fast and then out of the building. He didn't think of the men in the room and what they might do, about the distance to go, how long it might take him. He was back in the slums, with no knowledge of time and no change in pace. Only one thing had suddenly changed—his drive was no longer a crazy splatter of fear but a very sharp, pointed force. If he hadn't been out of breath he would have whistled now, but when he stood in Ramon's room he was very still.

"Where is she, Ramon?"

Ramon laughed.

Port stepped closer and the man in the bed was out of the shadow now, back in the dim light from the kitchen. Ramon was on his back, as before, and the gun in his hand was pointing at Port.

Port saw it, but it had no effect. His thinking was clear, his movements decisive, and he could hold them forever, to get his advantage.

"Bellamy's going to tear off your skin, Calvin, if you shoot me."

Ramon laughed again.

"He's the one that called you were coming, and said I should be expecting you."

"And to bring me back."

"Alive—if I can," Ramon said softly.

"Can you?"

"Any gun's bigger than you," said Ramon, and sat up in bed.

"That's why," said Port and before Ramon was properly settled the gun flew out of his hand with Port's sudden slap.

He didn't hit Ramon. He watched him get up, and then he spoke once more.

"Where is Shelly?"

Ramon stood stiff and afraid, with a fast spasm inside his stomach. When Port took a step forward Ramon said, "She is safe," and then he stopped.

Port wondered about Ramon's fear for his life and the stubborn answer. It was a part of Ramon he had never seen, and Port frowned.

"I tell you this because I'm afraid," said Ramon, "but I am not so afraid that I'd tell you more."

"Then I believe that she's safe."

For a very brief moment they were not enemies, but then Ramon cast down his eyes, as if the feeling shamed him, and Port stepped back to the wall to pick up the gun. Shelly was safe. There was time now for unfinished business.

"We're going to do like Bellamy wants it. Where's he waiting?"

"At your place."

When they got into the car, Port put the gun in his pocket and drove back the way he had come. He drove back just as fast but he knew why he was doing it now, and the wild excitement inside him was bright and hot.

They stopped at a building unfamiliar to Ramon, and when Port pressed the button downstairs there was only a number next to it. The buzzer sounded, and Port pushed Ramon ahead. The apartment door opened as soon as Port reached for the bell.

Fries had been in bed, but his thin hair was combed, he wore trousers, and the silk coat and ascot looked very correct.

"Let me in," said Port.

Fries wouldn't step aside.

"What do you want?"

"I'll tell you inside," said Port and pushed Fries out of the way. Ramon came in too.

Fries said, "What's he doing here? Isn't he the guy that got thrown out of the club? If you think for a minute...."

"Close the door, Fries." Port was going to the lighted room with the desk, and Ramon was following him.

Then Fries came in. "You're not starting out very well," he said, "now that Stoker is dead. From now on this free-wheeling stuff is out. I'm setting up regular hours...."

"This couldn't wait, Fries. Listen to me. Did you buy the Paternik building?"

Fries didn't seem to hear. He sat down at his desk and picked up one of the sharp pencils he kept there.

"Now then," he said.

"Twelve hundred Birch—did you buy it?"

Fries tapped the pencil on the desk and said, "What's it to you?"

"I need it! I need that frame for a trade, or Paternik will push me into a murder indictment. He was there when Stoker died."

"You murdered Stoker?"

"For Christ's sake, Fries!"

It would have been easy to grab Fries and choke the ascot around his neck. Port swallowed and lowered his voice.

"Yes or no, Fries. Did you set up the frame?"

The voice made Fries look up, and he saw the murder in Port's face, close to the surface.

"Yes," he said. "I did."

Port relaxed and started to smile. From now on it would just be one step after another to the end.

"Fries, you're a doll. Let me have the papers."

"What papers?"

"How much did Stoker pay extra for that property?"

"Twenty thousand."

"Receipted separately?"

"Of course."

"That's what I want. That receipt."

Fries pursed his lips and looked at his pencil.

"Or I'll break you."

Fries looked up, because his first thought was that Port meant it now. He couldn't tell what Port's exact meaning had been, and he had a thousand vague speculations. But the thing about Fries was his stiff, well-armored shell.

"You don't have to do that," he said. His insides were twisting, but all that showed was his remark. It carried him over the moment, and Port relaxed too.

"All right, I'm waiting."

Then Fries went on hastily. "What would you do afterwards—leave? You take the receipts and the organization can't use them any more. And on top of that, you blow."

Port felt something near boredom. He said, "If you don't give it to me I'm out of the organization just the same. He's framing a murder, I told you."

"It wouldn't stick. At best they can make it manslaughter. And with the weight we carry around here...."

"Give me the paper."

"And you stay."

Port looked away to reach for a chair and when Fries saw his face again, Port wore a small, vicious smile.

"I stay," said Port.

That made Fries sit up, his face very still, all the tics gone out of it. Then he heard Port go on, smiling.

"And when I stay, Fries, do you think you'll be the top man? Even Stoker told you, don't you remember, he even told you I know more than you do."

"Just a minute, Port...."

"I don't like you, Fries, and when I'm in, you're going to feel it. You understand that sort of thing, don't you, Fries?"

"If you think for a minute...." Fries stopped.

Port said, "Your kind of gutless creep never knows why you can't make the top, with all your filthy scheming. I'll tell you why not, Fries: because all you ever know and all you can ever do is to kick up the dust so your tracks don't, show, so your scared insides don't give you away, and the scream for help doesn't bust out of you! I know that better than you, and that's why you can't win, not with me around, not as long as I run my business my way. I stay, Fries, and I'm going to ruin you! It wouldn't kill you, but you'd look a mess. Tell the truth, Fries, that's worse than anything, isn't it? That's worse than death to you."

Fries covered one side of his face, because his tic was now driving him crazy. He thought one eye might jump out or spit would drip out of his mouth.

"Give me the paper, Fries, and I'll blow."

There wasn't any more argument.

They drove to the Lee building and went up to the office where Stoker used to be. Fries went to the safe in the corner, and when he came back he had what Port wanted. Port took the paper. But for Fries there had now been enough time to collect himself; not that the words would matter too much, but he had to say it.

"You can't get away with it. If I want to...."

"But you won't, will you?" Port was smiling, which in a way was worse to Fries than shouting would have been.

Port took a sheaf of papers out of his pocket, folded typing paper which Fries saw was a carbon copy. Port laid it all down on the desk.

"Read it, Fries. And when you're through, you'll know as much as I do. About dirty politics, about our hookup, about payments to whom, and what law violations didn't get on the docket. With a lot of details about you and—more important—about men higher up. A criminal investigator's dream, big shot—and insurance for me."

"Where—where is the original?"

"Where will it be if I die?"

Fries waited.

"It'll be all over. So here's what you do with it, Fries. Pass it on to the top when you make your report about Daniel Port leaving the fold, and point out that it's safer that I stay alive."

Fries put the papers down. He would read them later.

"There are ways, Port. There are experts who make a death look like...."

"It says right at the bottom, Fries, this thing comes out when I die. No matter how. That trick ought to impress you." Port started to laugh.

Fries tried to think of something else he could say now. "You can't—you can't—" he managed.

"Can't what?" Port was still smiling.

"Can't take the car! It's company property, if you come right down to it. Stoker just...."

Port's laughter was like a volley of slaps in the face, and when he threw some keys on the desk Fries grabbed them up as if they were his salvation.

"You'll like that, won't you, Fries? Those two big antennae in back, they really got to you, huh?"

Port waved at Ramon, who ran to open the door, and then they walked through the outer office. Port stopped at the switchboard and made three calls. One was for a taxi and with the other two Port used first names. Ramon didn't know what the calls meant.

Since losing his gun Ramon hadn't said a word, and Port hadn't tried talking to him. If he would talk, Ramon thought, maybe it would be like a sting which could arouse him again, make him find his old role, the one he had lost when they left the kitchen. The one he had lost when Port didn't beat an answer out of him. But they sat in the taxi and nobody talked.

Chapter 22

When the taxi pulled up at Port's place, the prowl car was waiting. Ramon saw it first. He felt like crouching into the seat, hiding himself, and he was afraid Port might notice. But Port wasn't paying any attention.

One cop was on the sidewalk, the other one sat in the car.

"You better both come," said Port and ran into the building. He heard one of them say, "Yes, Mr. Port," and then Port tapped his foot nervously, waiting for the elevator to open. He pushed Ramon in first, then let the policemen pass by. On the way up he said, "You wait in the hall. When I'm ready for witnesses, I'll call you in."

"How many are there?" asked one of the cops.

"There's Bellamy. You know Bellamy."

The cops looked at each other and then Port went on, "And Judge Paternik. You've heard of him."

The elevator doors opened, so the cops didn't have a chance to look at each other.

They stopped in the corridor and Port said, "You can tell it's important. When you come in I want you to make an impression. Have your guns out."

They nodded without understanding and watched Port and Ramon walk to the door.

They were all there: Paternik at one end of the bed, Bellamy at the other, like balances on a scale. Kirby was on a chair, his gun looking at Port.

"What happened?" said Bellamy. His voice was loud, irritated, and he looked from Port to Ramon.

"Just stay by the door," said Port to Ramon, and stepped into the middle of the room.

"And you drop it," said Kirby.

Port shrugged, reached for the bulge in his pocket, and tossed Ramon's gun on the floor.

"I'll get to you later," Bellamy yelled at Ramon. "When I give an order...."

"He brought me, didn't he?" Port smiled.

"All right. Now you, Port. You've taken all the sweet time you're going to get...."

"Why don't you tell your dog to put down the gun. You know I don't carry any."

"He stays as he is!" roared Bellamy, and Kirby did.

If Port was impressed it didn't show. He went to the couch where his suitcase was. He did it so easily, without sudden movements, Kirby let him do it. Port opened the suitcase, took out a handkerchief, and blew his nose. They waited, with the tension thick in the air.

Port put the handkerchief back in the suitcase and when he straightened up he shot Kirby.

The man fell smoothly out of the chair. After a moment he slowly pulled up his legs and made low sounds. Port said to Ramon, "Stick your head out the door and tell them it's nothing. They should wait."

Ramon did it. Port tossed his gun up and down, waiting, and they all waited for Port. When the door was closed again he smiled at the judge.

"I'm back."

The judge frowned, cleared his throat, gave one quick look at Bellamy. But Bellamy wasn't helping.

"I'm here to trade murders," said Port.

There was a pause while Port let them catch up with the words. Then he said, "Paternik, did you ever sell that building?"

"I fail to see— The serious matter—" said the judge, not understanding.

"Paternik, listen to me. Twelve hundred Birch—you sold that, remember? And at what a price!"

"If you think stalling around with that gun in your hand...."

"Shut up, Bellamy."

Bellamy's face got mottled but he didn't move.

"You sold it to Stoker," said Port. "You know what that means, Paternik?"

"Port, what are you saying?"

"That alone looks like collusion with gangsters. And now this!" and Port held out the receipt. "You got a price that has nothing to do with the property's value. You got paid extra. You know what that extra was for, Paternik?"

"You must be insane!"

Port smiled and waved the receipt back and forth.

"That's not how it's going to look after I get through making mud out of you. It's going to look like political murder!" Port smiled. "You and me, Paternik, are going to trade murders."

"For heaven's sake—"

Port went over to Kirby and looked down at the man. A wet stain was spreading high up on one leg.

"Tell them, Kirby. How's it feel?"

Kirby started to make little sounds, and they all heard.

"And this one," said Port to the judge; "he's going to be as good as new in a month or so. What'll you be doing, Judge Paternik, in a month or so?"

The old man got up, then sat down again. He looked at Bellamy, who hadn't said a word.

"I'm through waiting," said Port. "Call them in," and he nodded at Ramon.

The judge got up fast, talking urgently. "Mr. Port, you asked me to consider. You offered a bargain to which I—" That's when Bellamy moved. While the judge held Port's arm, talking to him, Bellamy charged to the end of the room where the guns were lying. It wasn't clear what he meant to accomplish, because had he tried shooting Port the judge would have been in the way, but it never came to that. The two cops came in, with guns, and one of them said, "You're under arrest. Assault with a deadly weapon."

The gun fell out of Bellamy's hand.

"And this one," said Port, "is Judge Paternik. He is...."

"Please! Mr. Port!"

"He is here to give us a statement. A straight witness statement, because he hasn't had a chance to tell the police about Stoker's death."

"Yes," said Paternik. "A mere formality. I was present when Stoker suffered his heart attack, and then fell on the stone apron at the fireplace. This young man and I saw it happen, and though I was present, witnessed the natural death, I have not had an opportunity to submit my statement. I welcome this chance...."

"That's enough," said Port. "Now get this one for breaking and entering."

"Okay," said one of the cops, and took Paternik by the arm. When he had him up to the door, he told Paternik to wait while he picked Kirby up from the floor.

"This will never stand up!" yelled Bellamy, and the cop who was holding him said, "You should tell it to the judge."

The judge and Bellamy looked at each other like strangers. Port said, "It's good enough till tomorrow, right, officer?"

"Okay, Mr. Port." They started to leave.

"Wait a minute." Port came after them. He tapped the judge on the shoulder, smiled at him. "This is yours," he said, and gave him the twenty-thousand-dollar receipt. When they had gone Port and Ramon left too. Ramon carried the two suitcases.

Landis opened the door himself. He had been waiting for over an hour but the hair standing up in back of his head and the shadows under his eyes made him look as if he had just come out of bed.

"I thought you were alone," Landis said.

"Ramon will wait in another room," Port answered, and Ramon left.

Landis took Port into the kitchen and asked him if he wanted coffee. Port said no, and Landis picked up his cup, leading the way to the study.

"I'm not used to being up at this hour, Port, so if you'll come to the point—"

Port waited till Landis sat down.

"You still got my airplane ticket?"

Landis put down his cup very carefully.

"I thought you were joking, the last time I saw you."

Port shrugged.

"The fact is," said Landis, "I do have it."

"You can give it to me now."

Landis went to the desk and found the ticket. He gave it to Port. "And have a good trip," he said.

"Thank you, Landis."

Landis went back to his cup but did not sit down.

"You wouldn't consider staying?"

"No."

"You are simply leaving the mess."

Port gave a short laugh. "Yeah, it's that simple."

"I had thought, when you called me...."

"I called to leave you the mess."

Landis raised his eyebrows.

"You want it?" said Port.

Landis went to the desk, sat down, took a pencil and moved a long pad into position. Port walked back and forth in the room and while he talked Landis wrote it all down.

When Landis got up he drank what was left of his coffee, never noticing that it was cold. Then he said, "You realize this implicates your organization as much as the Bellamy group."

"I'm through here."

"Yes. I see that. May I ask how you expect to survive this kind of exposure?"

"What I gave you is local. Nothing else."

"Yes. I see that."

Port went to the door.

"If you want to start," he said, "two of them are in the jug right now. Eighteenth precinct."

"Really?"

"Bellamy and Paternik. The charge on them won't hold unless you get down there before morning."

"What!" His robe flapped when he rushed to the phone.

Port said, "Thanks for the ticket," but Landis didn't hear him.

Port had let the taxi go. He walked down the street carrying one suitcase, and Ramon had the other one. With the dawn almost there, a clammy coldness had come into the streets. It made the pavement look harder and the light from the posts seemed more distant. They listened to their footsteps and the air felt empty.

Port stopped at a corner. He put down the suitcase and waited till Ramon had done the same.

"Where is Shelly, Ramon?"

The question didn't sound the same to Ramon as it had before. It did not stiffen his back and make the blood pound in his head.

"I sent her away."

If Port would hit him now, in order to force him, it would mean little to Ramon, and the little it meant would not have to do with Port, but with Shelly.

"How could you do it, Ramon?"

How? He thought of several answers, all true, then told one.

"I told her you had been killed in a fight, trying to leave."

Port sucked the cold air into his lungs, then let it come out. "Why did she leave?"

"Why stay?"

Now he would ask the next one, the one about Ramon. He would want to know why Ramon had done it. Then maybe Port would swing at him or do something like that. Ramon touched the side of his face and felt the pain. He had no more fever, just pain.

"Where is she, Ramon?"

"You are going there?"

"After you tell me."

Ramon nodded. Then he said, "Will you tell her I want to—I send my regards?"

"Yes."

Ramon turned so the street light fell on his hands, and with a small pencil he wrote an address on a matchbook cover. "She went to the West Coast. Near the Border." He gave Port the matchbook.

Port put it into his pocket. When he looked up again he saw Ramon walking down the dark street.

Port, picked up his suitcases and went the other way. By the time it was full dawn he had exchanged his New York ticket for one that went the other way.

THE END

The Out is Death
by Peter Rabe

Chapter 1

The tight overcoat gave him the long shape of a tube and he walked bent forward to keep the rain out of his face. He walked fast and it showed his age. Once he stopped to take a deep breath, and then moved on again. He crossed the street without looking up.

There was a place near the corner with gold letters on grimy glass which said *Sport Parlor*. Through the glass a room showed dimly, a room with a jukebox that made silent flashes, and two men at the edge of a pool table. The men smoked and made gestures which seemed meaningless unaccompanied by the sounds of their voices. They both looked out to the street, and one man pursed his mouth to let his cigarette drop to the floor. He stepped on it with a quick twist of his heel and he laughed in pantomime. Then he walked out onto the street.

He zipped up his jacket, hunched his shoulders when the drizzle hit him, and ran to his car. The car glittered with rain and chrome and leaped away from the curb almost as soon as the door flew shut.

The old man stopped at the bus sign and stood near the curb. His hand was on the post of the sign and he looked tired. He was standing like that when the car shot close. The car squealed and stopped spectacularly, splashing the old man from the waist down.

"Hey, Dalton! You get wet?"

The man in the car put his head out of the window. He looked at the old man and laughed. The sound was unfriendly.

"Hey Dalton—"

The old man had not moved and his hand was still clasped tightly around the post. Then he let go of it and wiped his face.

"What?" he said. "What now?"

The man in the car opened the door and got out in a single quick movement.

"Hey, Dalton," he said again. "You going someplace? You're not going far, are you, Dalton?"

The old man stepped back a little, because the other man had stepped very close. The other man was holding onto the old man's coat and Dalton could not step back very far.

"I'm taking the bus," he said. "I'm just taking the bus downtown." Then he pushed the other man's hand away from his coat.

"You look sick, Dalton," said the other man. "All this running around out-doors after ten years indoors." He laughed. "That ain't healthy." He took the old man's coat again and smiled. "You wouldn't do anything unhealthy, would you, Dalton?"

Dalton pushed the hand away again and watched his bus splash down the street.

"Dicky," he said, "it's noon and you gave me until evening. I said this evening."

"You look awful tricky to me, Dalton. I don't know if I can afford to let you wait till evening."

Dalton watched the bus come nearer. He tried to step to the curb but Dicky got in his way.

The old man wasn't afraid, but he felt weak. He only wanted to avoid friction, and to get his bus.

"I said tonight, Dicky. You ever know me to cross anyone up?"

"You been in stir so long, Dalton, I think maybe you changed. I don't know any more what goes on in your head."

"Lemme go," said Dalton, and tried to wave at the bus. Dicky held down the old man's arm.

The bus was very close now and both men could see the driver. The driver did not know whether or not the men at the stop were fares.

"Damn it, I can't miss it," Dalton began, but Dicky laughed and shook his head at the bus.

The old man cursed softly, and watched the bus go on past down the street. The fat tires squished through a puddle and then started to sing against the wet asphalt.

Dicky got back into his car and cupped his hands to light a cigarette. He watched the old man over his hands and his eyes crinkled. Then he laughed through a big billow of smoke.

"I trust you, Dalton. I was just kidding around."

Dalton said nothing.

"Remember how you and me used to kid around, Dalton? You don't kid much no more, do you? That last stretch really rocked you, huh?" Dicky gunned the motor a couple of times, but he did not seem to be in a hurry to leave.

"Dalton," he called from the car.

The old man ignored him.

Dicky backed up the car with a sudden bounce and stopped it in front of the old man.

"Kidding time is over, huh, Dalton?" Dicky shifted, held the clutch. "Just don't you forget it," he said. The way the car shot off, it seemed angry.

The old man did not watch the car out of sight. He closed his eyes and ran both hands over his face. The gesture smoothed his face for a moment, making him look the way he might have looked ten or fifteen years before.

He dropped his hands to his side and his face was old again. By the time the next bus came along he was shivering with the wet, and with nervousness.

He got off the bus in the center of town, crossed a small park, and went toward a restaurant which had a red and white canopy over the entrance. There was a potted plant on either side of the grilled door and a doorman in front of it with an umbrella. He saw Dalton but did not think he was a customer. He looked across the street to the park.

The door closed behind Dalton with a pneumatic swish. He stood in the foyer for a moment and then approached the wide steps that went down into the dining room. The hatcheck girl saw the old man but did not think he was a customer. She put down her nail file and leaned over the counter to see what the maitre d'hotel would do.

Dalton was stopped before he reached the steps. The maitre was sure that he was not a customer.

"Good afternoon," the maitre d'hotel said. He went no further, waiting for Dalton to explain himself.

"Good afternoon," Dalton said. He nodded with a vague smile and tried to look into the dining room.

"Have you a reservation?" asked the man.

"I'm meeting someone. Could I just take a look, and...."

"Does your party have a reservation?"

Dalton had to step back because the man had not moved out of the way.

"I don't know. I don't think so." Dalton tried smiling again to cover his nervousness, but it did not help. "Could I just— Would you let me look? It's important I meet him. I have to meet him—"

The maitre d'hotel stepped aside unexpectedly. He even smiled, very briefly, and nodded. "Of course, sir. Follow me." Dalton followed him into the dining room.

"Do you see your party?"

Dalton looked carefully, and then shook his head. He was holding his lower lip in his teeth to keep himself from making a sound.

"Perhaps your party has left? Perhaps you had in mind a similar restaurant, further down the street?"

"No. No, it was here. I'm late. I knew I'd be late." Dalton sounded as if he were talking to himself.

The maitre d'hotel stood there for a moment, and then shrugged.

"I'm sorry. Did you wish to order, in the meantime?"

"Look," said Dalton. He had not been listening. "He must have been here. Or maybe he'll come back, because...."

"What is the name of your party? Can you describe him?"

Dalton looked around again and unbuttoned his overcoat. He felt damp and warm. He saw haw the maitre d'hotel looked at the overcoat, and then turned to the stairs. Dalton had to follow or the maitre d'hotel would not have heard him.

"A young man—hard to describe. He wears dark clothes, a dark suit most of the time. His face, his eyes are light, but he has black hair—" Dalton ran into the maitre d'hotel who had stopped at the top of the stairs. "I'm sorry— I was saying—"

"I don't seem to recall such a party. Your description—" The maitre d'hotel did not finish. He was looking elsewhere.

"He might have been here," Dalton insisted. "He would have drunk coffee. He lets it sit till it gets cold and then he drinks it."

"I'm sorry."

The maitre d'hotel stepped aside. He did not offer the old man one of the seats in the foyer. He watched briefly as the old man went back to the door.

It was still raining outside, but it was only a fine mist now. Slowly, Dalton walked back the way he had come, and when he entered the park he sat down on a bench. His coat was still open. He sat and looked at his feet.

Across the street a taxi stopped at the awning. The attendant with the umbrella rushed to the cab, but he wasn't in time. And he wasn't in time to hold open the grilled door to the restaurant.

By that time the man was in the foyer. He asked the maitre d'hotel for a table and ordered coffee. He wore a dark suit and did not touch his cup until the coffee had gotten quite cold.

Chapter 2

Daniel Port sat there for a while longer. Now and then he tapped the rim of his empty cup, looked at the foyer, and looked away again. Then he started to whistle, hardly audibly. Finally he put a bill on the table and went back to the foyer.

"I was expecting an elderly man," he said to the maitre d'hotel. "Tall, sort of, and thin. Has he been here?"

"An elderly man?"

"His name is Dalton. I was to meet...."

"He did not give his name. Someone like that was here about ten or fifteen minutes ago. I'm afraid he...."

"If he comes back, ask him to wait, will you?" Port left.

He didn't have to ask the doorman about Dalton because he saw the old man on the other side of the street, sitting in the park. Dalton was hunched over on the bench, watching the restaurant, but without the purpose which would have enabled him to make out Port.

Port ran across the street and started waving.

"Hey, Abe! Here I am! Abe!"

Then Dalton was up, smiling tremulously, and the two men shook hands.

"Abe, am I glad to see you! Jesus I'm sorry I almost missed you. Why didn't you wait inside? Come on, man, you look like hell out here in the rain—"

Dalton looked at Port and smiled at him again. "You came," he said. "You got my note. Danny, you're looking good, very good." Then he let Port take him by the arm and guide him across the street.

"Why didn't you wait inside?" Port asked again. "Sitting there like a wet cat—" He made Dalton laugh. Dalton was very glad to see Port.

"You know," he said. "The kind of a place it is, and me, the way I am—"

"Jesus, you picked the place. Why did you pick that kind of a place?"

They were at the door and the doorman sprang to open it for them. Port looked at the maitre d'hotel and held up two fingers. "Why this place?" he said again.

"Because—well, meeting you," Dalton said, almost whispering, "I figured maybe this is the kind of place you always go to. I been hearing how you done well and all that, and maybe this is the only kind you go to any more. You know—"

"Christ!" said Port.

They sat down, and then Dalton got up again to take off his overcoat. The waiter took it back to the checkroom.

"Whatever you got to say, I'm not listening, Abe," Port said. "Not till you eat." Dalton ordered some soup and a pudding and he ate while Port sat over a fresh cup of coffee and smoked.

"How long you been out, Abe?" he asked after a while.

"Almost a month," said Dalton. He put down his spoon and said, "Look, Danny. The reason...."

"Eat." Dalton ate and Port said, "Didn't you get fifteen?"

Dalton nodded and said, "Good behavior." The waiter came back to ask if there'd be anything else.

"Something to drink," said Port. "Coffee, Abe?"

Dalton shook his head and ordered milk. When the waiter had gone he said, "And for health. They let me out, considering my health." The milk came and he started to sip it. "I was costing too much."

"You lost a lot of weight," said Port. "You couldn't have cost much on the food bill."

Dalton put his hand on the table and looked at the bony knuckles.

"No stomach," he said. "They took out seven eighths of the stomach." Dalton put down his glass with a sudden clunk. He looked at Port and smiled. "So tell me, Danny. Is it true what I hear? About you and the Stoker outfit?"

"I don't know what you heard," said Port, "but Stoker died and I quit the racket."

"That's what I heard," said Dalton. He kept looking at Port and started shaking his head. "Imagine," he said. "Imagine. Ten years ago, just a kid, almost...."

"I was no kid," said Port.

"No." Dalton laughed shortly. "Not the way you were starting to climb. You and Stoker sure got along, didn't you?"

"He tried to teach me, yes."

Dalton leaned over the table and said, "So how come you quit, Danny?"

"Stoker died."

"You could have taken over. How come?"

Port gestured to the waiter to bring him more coffee.

"I hear you left clean, Danny. Why?"

Port moved his mouth as if he meant to whistle, and then he said, "I had mine. There're some people I wouldn't work with."

"But last time I saw you...."

"I was ten years younger."

Port watched the waiter put down the coffee and then he said, "You and me had quite a time there, for a while, huh, Abe?" He smiled at the old man.

"I remember. When I asked Stoker about pulling that job in his territory, you told him he shouldn't let me."

"Stoker never was a jug heavy. He ran a political territory, and for you to knock over a bank in a hot ward like his meant nothing but trouble."

"Yes," said Dalton. He sipped his milk again. "I got caught. I was getting old." They were both silent for a moment. "Anyway, Danny, you were real good to me afterwards. Trying to help with the law, and in prison."

Port said, "I got respect for a man with a craft." He gave Dalton's old hand a pat. "Pure art, the way you used to set up some of your jobs. As a matter of fact, Abe, I can't think of a single jug heavy today...."

"That's over," said Dalton. His voice was suddenly very cold with control, and Port heard the change in tone.

"How did you know I was in town?" he said.

"I asked around. I wanted to see you, Danny."

"Yes," said Port. "That's why I came."

They looked at each other and then Dalton said, "Could we go someplace else, Dan?"

Port paid the bill, and asked the doorman to call a taxi.

"My place?" he asked Dalton.

"I don't know, Dan. Maybe someplace else, maybe...."

"Go up ten blocks," Port told, the cabby.

They got out in front of the museum and went up the stone steps. The wetness blew into their faces and the feeling of dankness did not leave them when they went inside. The hall was gray marble and the ceiling was very high. A guard looked at them and then looked away. They went into a room that recreated an early New England kitchen, with beams on the ceiling, chinked walls, a black pot hanging inside a hearth, and a wooden table covered with pewter dishes. Dalton sat down on a bench and unbuttoned his coat. He looked up at Port, then back down at his coat again. Port was at the table, touching the pewter ware. The plates had been nailed to the table boards and the utensils had been wired down. Port sat down next to Dalton.

"Did you know I'm from New England?" said Dalton.

Port shook his head.

"I'm out the last time," said Dalton. "The next time is for good."

"I know," said Port.

"I need your help."

"Of course, Abe. You need money?"

"No." Dalton's old hands started stroking each other, making drying motions.

"All right," said Port. He tried to think of something to say that would change the mood of tiredness that showed in Dalton. "Sure," he said. "You used to pick well. The Baintree job, fifteen thousand; the National job, sixty-five thousand; and all those...."

"I have five hundred and twenty-one dollars," said Dalton, "and I want to go home. I have a ticket for the train going east and once I get home I won't need much. A room, a small job— I have a nephew there. He once promised—" Dalton's voice trailed off. He spoke again, his voice was suddenly raw now. "I am very sick. I am not going to die in prison."

Port said nothing.

"I can't lose again," said Dalton.

"Tell me, Abe. Somebody won't let you quit?"

Dalton nodded.

"How hard is he squeezing you?"

"If I don't handle his heist, I go back to prison. He can put me there."

"How sure are you?"

"Very." Dalton laughed harshly. "I trained that kid. I used to show him the plans of jobs I did alone. I showed him so he'd learn. Jobs they never pinned on me."

"Who is he?"

"Dicky."

"I don't think I know him."

"He's changed a lot." Dalton seemed to be talking to himself. "He acts crazy—"

"He's in town?"

"Yes. Dicky Corday."

Chapter 3

Dicky Corday lived in a hotel on the south side of town. The plaster was peeling in great strips and the wallpaper in all the rooms had large, faded flowers. None of this bothered Corday because he wasn't going to stay there much longer. First came a small burg called Newton, then Palm Springs or Hot Springs or some place like that. He whistled at himself in the mirror and pulled up his tie so that his silk collar would drape like two leaves on each side.

"You still in that shower?" he yelled suddenly, but the girl in the shower couldn't hear him because of the water.

"Letty!"

She heard him that time. She turned off the water and in her haste got a cold spray down her back that made her gasp.

"What now?"

"Nothing," she said. "Nothing, Dicky."

"Don't gimme that nothing! I just heard you say something in there and I wanna know what it was!"

"Dicky, please. All it was I got cold water down over my back and all I did was make a sound."

He started cursing her for being a lamebrain and more stupid than anyone ought to be. His voice frightened her and she wrapped a towel around her and then rubbed her head so she couldn't hear what he said. But she heard him yelling again.

"—coming outa there pretty soon?"

"I'm drying myself, Dicky. Please, don't be yelling at me all the time."

"Drying yourself? Come outa there and dry yourself in here."

She sighed, held the towel so it wouldn't drag on the floor, and came out of the bathroom.

Dicky sat in the green chair with the doilies and one leg was dipping up and down over the arm rest. The girl watched his leg dipping and worried about his mood.

"Let's go," he said. "Let's see you dry yourself."

She started on her head again, holding the towel so that it wouldn't slip.

"The body, for Chrissakes! Who cares about the head!"

"But my hair...."

"Just drop it," he said. "Drop the towel."

She dropped the towel and stood there while he looked. She lowered her head to see her feet, trying to keep herself from feeling embarrassed, but then she saw her breasts.

"You're blushing," said Dicky and he roared with laughter. "An old pro like you, and blushing."

She wasn't old and she was no pro, and the situation she found herself in now wasn't anything new. It was his look, she thought, his look would make her blush even with clothes on.

"Okay," he said. "Start drying."

She dried herself and Dicky watched. He sat sprawled in the chair and he laughed when she looked awkward.

She was shaped beautifully. Her skin was very white and her slight plumpness gave her soft shadows. She looked all soft. The same quality, in her face, gave her a look of something unfinished. She seemed to have just awakened.

"Come here," he said. "Drop that damn towel and come here."

"But I'm not dry yet, Dicky. I got to...."

"Why don't you shut up that mouth?" he said and started cursing again. He yanked her down by one arm, and when she had fallen across the chair he grabbed her hard around her back, dug his face into her neck, and bit her. She struggled, afraid to struggle too much, and gasped, afraid to scream. When he let her go she sat up. She looked at him and made herself smile because he was grinning at her.

"Like that, huh?" He gave her a slap.

She got up and said, "I want to get dressed now, Dicky, so we can...."

"You liked that, huh?"

"Yes, Dicky."

"What are you lying for, you stupid dame! Huh? Answer me!"

"Dicky, please—"

"Answer me!"

"I—I don't know what to say, honest, Dicky—"

"Did you like it?"

"I don't know— It hurt—"

"So why don't you say so?" He went to the mirror and retied his tie. "Get dressed," he said over his shoulder. "He ought to get here just about now."

Letty started to dress in the corner by the bed and Dicky watched her in the mirror.

"You didn't answer me when I asked you."

She stopped what she was doing and said, "Asked me what, Dicky? I don't remember."

"Why you didn't say so. Why you didn't say it hurt?"

She finished hooking her bra and didn't know what to answer.

"Well?" He sounded mean.

"Because—because I was afraid—"

He laughed loudly, but he said nothing else. Then he saw her put her arms into the slip and lift it up over her head.

"Hey, Letty."

She stopped and looked at him.

"I got this idea. Leave it off."

She looked at him without understanding. "But your friend is coming, this old man."

"That's why," said Dicky. "Make him all fidgety and embarrassed."

"No," said Letty.

"What did you say?"

She put on her slip. "No," she said again.

Dicky stared at her for a moment, watched her put on her dress, and then he started to laugh again. He got a bottle out of the closet and put it and a glass on the table. He poured himself a drink and then lit a cigarette. He said nothing else to the girl. Sometimes, when a certain tone came into her voice, he left her alone.

He drank for a while and watched Letty make up the bed and then he went to the window and looked out into the street. He couldn't see much, because of the fire escape in front, and because it was night and there were few lights on the street. He watched the hotel sign below his window. It had a border of blinking bulbs and Dicky held his breath to see how many blinks he could last.

"Is he going to the dance with us?" said Letty. "The old man that's com-ing?"

He let out his breath, making Letty start.

"Hell, no," he said. He went back to the table and when he passed Letty he slapped her behind. "Dalton won't stay long," he said. "One way or the other, there's just going to be one or two words spoken between us."

"About the job?"

"His job," said Dicky and suddenly he looked very cheerful. "How come you're wearing that deadbeat rag? Put on something with color, something that shines, Letty. Something that shines!" When she walked past him he gave her another slap on the rump.

He watched her change and then said, "Now some perfume, honey. Some-thing that makes their eyes water, Letty." It sounded so good to him he started laughing again. "And when I'm through with old Dalton...."

"Dicky," she said. "Stop drinking so much."

"I can't drink in my own place? Who in hell...."

"Dicky, I think I hear somebody coming."

"That's old reliable," Dicky said. He sat down in his chair, crossed one leg over the other and started to dip it. He gave a hoist to his tie and grinned. "Smile, honey," he said. "Here comes our future."

"If you want me to leave, Dicky...."

"Naw, stay. Just go over there and open that door. Open that door with a big shiny grin, and when...."

There was a knock.

"Open the door, lamebrain! Don't you hear?"

Letty ran to open the door, catching some of Dicky's excitement. She fum-bled it open, smiling the way she was told.

"Yes sir!" yelled Dicky. "Dalton rides again, huh, Dalton?" and he waved at the old man to come in. "And as soon as Letty gets the door shut tight— The door, lame-brain! Close that...."

Port came in and closed the door himself.

He came into the room and nobody said anything. Letty had nothing to say, Dalton was very nervous, and Dicky wasn't sure of the situation yet.

"What gives?" he said. "You know this guy, Dalton?"

The old man cleared his throat but Dicky didn't wait to hear.

"You bring this guy, Dalton? What is this, huh? You trying to...."

"I brought my friend," Dalton began. Then Dicky got up, pushed Dalton out of the way so that the old man staggered, and stepped up close to Port.

"Who are you?" he said, making it sound like an insult.

"My name's Port. Daniel Port. I'm a friend of Abe Dalton's and he asked me to come along."

"Why? You muscling in on this deal?"

"What deal?" said Port.

The question made Dicky frown and quickly he looked from one man to the other. Then he swiveled around fast and shouted at Dalton. "You got something in mind we wasn't planning? You come up here, maybe, to try...."

"If you'll stop shouting," Dalton said very clearly, "I'll explain this to you."

The voice was a surprise. It seemed calm suddenly, and Dalton was no longer the way he should be—old, scared, and too tired to kick.

"It's about this heist you want me to handle. I won't lie to you, Dicky, and say that I want to do it, and you know that I'm much too old to start double-crossing anyone now. So I won't say that I'm going through with it and then pull some trick to get out. But I brought my friend—" Dalton pointed— "and he thought, with him sitting in, maybe we can work something out. You see, Dicky...."

"Who is this guy? Cop?"

Dalton frowned, and Letty put in, "He just said, Dicky—he wouldn't double-cross."

She saw Dicky react and was sorry she had opened her mouth.

"I'm not the police," Port said, "and if you weren't such a stupid jerk I'd try explaining it to you, about Dalton, and what he's up against with this squeeze play you put him into. But I'll tell you this much, Corday—"

Port stopped when he saw the color change in Dicky's face. There was no point in talking to a man who was boiling with rage.

"Who is this?" said Dicky. "Who is this big shot?"

"He used to be with Stoker," said Dalton. "You remember the Stoker outfit?"

"A big shot—"

"He and Stoker were close," Dalton went on, but he didn't get any further.

"Big shot," Dicky said again, "trying to queer my setup, huh?" For a moment he didn't seem to know what to do next. Then he said, "I don't need no big shot the way I'm gonna run this." He grabbed Letty's arm and dragged her to the door.

"Dicky," said Dalton. "Wait. We haven't—"

"Go jump," said Dicky, and tore open the door. "I'm going dancing."

He saw Dalton's face change with surprise and before he banged the door behind him he started roaring with laughter. Port and Dalton could hear him laughing all the way down the stairs.

Chapter 4

It took Port a while to calm the old man.

"Danny," Dalton said when Dicky had left, "If he goes ahead now—"

"Don't get the shakes, Abe. He won't do a thing."

"You saw how crazy he is, Dan. You saw you can't tell what he'll do next."

"He's not so crazy as to send you back to jail and lose out on this deal he has in mind. All he knows now...."

"If he goes ahead, Dan—if he goes ahead—" The old man ended by shaking his head and sinking into a chair. He sat there, shaking his head and looking at the floor.

Port didn't say anything for a while. He went to the window and stood there, staring out. After a while he started to whistle, making a slow, tuneless sound.

"Dalton," he said. When he heard the old man sit up Port said, "If you just wait and do nothing you'll go back to prison for sure."

Dalton got up and Port turned to face him. There was real fear in the old man's face. His mouth started to work and he moved his hands in helpless gestures. When his voice came it was high, like a wail.

"Do you know what it's like? Do you know what it's like to sit on that rock remembering what it's like outside, and then trying harder and harder all the time to remember because you've begun to forget, and the worst thing of all when you start caring less and less and you think maybe it isn't so bad to sit inside a hole made out of concrete with the sky sliced up in the same black angles day after day! That's what it's like! And I'm not going to die that way!"

He was finished and breathing hard, and when he sat down on the chair again it was because he was tired. He looked at his hands and said, "I don't know. I don't know if you see it." And then, very low, "But I mean it."

Port sat down too. He played with a cigarette for a while, as if nothing else interested him. Then he said, "Where does Dicky go dancing?"

"Dancing?" said Dalton. He shrugged. "I don't know. Maybe Nick's—Nick's Palace—or the Off-Time."

"That's in the neighborhood?"

"Yeah," said Dalton. "He likes to hang around with his punk friends." He coughed. "Look, Danny. I've thought this over. I think the best thing is to go through with it. It's a risk either way—doing the job with Dicky or not doing the job—but maybe I got more of a chance if I do that heist."

"Don't be a fool," said Port.

"No, I mean it. There's a small toolmaking plant in this town, Newton, and the way I hear it the job isn't so bad."

"Dalton, you haven't even let me try to help you. I haven't even...."

Dalton went on as if he hadn't heard. "Their payroll is big—toolmakers' and diemakers' wages, that kind of thing—and it's one of the few places that still pays in cash."

"Listen to me, Abe—"

"The money goes to the plant Thursday night and lies there till pay time, Friday. Hell," Dalton said, "when I think of some of the jobs I pulled...."

"You forgetting the time you did for it?" said Port.

Dalton looked at Port, then away.

"And forgetting the crazy type you're going to be working with? I wouldn't even go stealing apples with that screwball punk. I'd be afraid he might not like the tone of my voice and start arguing manners with me, right there with the apples in his hands and pockets."

"I don't know," Dalton said, "I can't even think—"

"Listen to me," said Port.

Dalton sat and listened. It was the easiest thing to do.

"You're going home now. Go to bed and do nothing. Just sleep. I'll get to you by tomorrow noon and maybe we'll know more."

"What?" said Dalton. He did not seem to expect much of an answer.

"I don't know yet," said Port. He got up and tossed away the cigarette he had been mangling on the top of the table. "But know this, Abe. You won't have to pull that heist."

They left together. Dalton told Port where he lived and where Dicky might be. Then Dalton went one way and Port went the other.

It had stopped raining. There were shiny black puddles in the empty street and the night air was wet. Port walked down the empty tenement streets. He could see a white curtain flapping out of a window high up and sometimes the slow waving of sheets hanging in the dark shaft of a yard. He walked, smoking a cigarette and wishing for a cup of coffee. He did not know yet what he would do about Dalton and Dicky Corday.

Nick's Palace was a small, dark place crowded with a bar, booths, and a bandstand. A hard-looking female in dungarees was playing a steel guitar, singing mountain songs in a Hawaiian beat. The dance floor was crowded with working people and neighborhood punks. Port remembered that Dicky wasn't much taller than the girl Letty, and he tried spotting the couple that way. He might have done better had Dicky been tall, because everyone else seemed to be. Port looked in the booths, remembering that Letty had sandy brown hair, but there were many brown-haired women around, none of them Letty.

"You been staring at her long enough," somebody said, and when Port looked down the man in the booth took the toothpick out of his mouth and said, "You just looking, or buying?"

Port didn't know immediately what the man meant.

"You want her, or don't you?" The man thumbed at the girl sitting next to him.

"No," said Port. "I was looking for someone else," and he tried squeezing by the booth.

But the man had gotten up and he was in the way now, his face close to Port's. The man whispered, "She's all right. Low rates, too." Then he stepped aside to let the woman get out of the booth.

She was old. She was thin and old, the make-up she wore fixing a weird mask of youth on her face.

"Let's dance," she said to Port and put one arm over his shoulder. Past Port's ear she called, "A tango, Melissa!" at the woman who played the guitar.

The dungareed woman played a mountain song in tango tempo and the made-up face was close to Port's. "Come on," she said. "I love dancing."

"I don't tango," said Port. "I was looking for someone else. I didn't mean...."

"That's all right. Just move your hips."

"Look," said Port, "I don't mean to offend you...."

"That's all right." She stood close, because of the crush on the floor. Then she said without any banter, "Can't you just dance with me?"

"Sure," said Port.

"Just dance. No obligations."

Port held her around the waist and they danced.

She smelled of talcum powder. She moved with the rhythm and hummed the beat to herself. She said nothing else.

After a while Port said, "You really do like to dance, don't you?"

"Nothing but." She smiled at him. "I was going to be a dancer."

When the number was over she didn't give Port a chance. She said, "One more, huh? I don't get to dance much around here."

"I'm really sorry, but I told you I'm looking...."

"Come on, just one more. Maybe I can help." She laughed humorlessly. "I know everybody around here."

The dungareed woman started another song, and they danced again.

"You know somebody called Dicky Corday?" Port said into her ear.

"That nothing? Sure. What about him?"

"I'm looking for him. He went dancing tonight and I thought he might be here."

"He was," said the woman, "but Letty don't like it here."

"I didn't think Dicky was the type who listened to anyone."

"He does, to Letty. I seen her grow up. That kid, she'll do just about anything, but now and then—all of a sudden it comes—she says no."

"I wouldn't have thought Dicky'd take that sort of thing."

"He does, though," said the woman.

"Where did they go from here?" Port wanted to know.

"The Off-Time, I guess." And like an afterthought, "That Letty sure likes to dance."

"Dicky too?"

"He don't care. It's Letty. I used to know her mother," said the woman. "She was the same way."

"And her father?"

"Father. She's got a million of 'em, for all I know."

The set was over and the woman, without being asked, let go of Port and pushed her way back to the booth. Port had to hurry and lean close to her in order to make her hear him.

"Thank you for the dance," he told her. "I think you're good."

She started to smile, but then she stopped herself. She sounded off-hand. "The floor's too small. You can't really do nothing here."

"It was nice, though," said Port and then he nodded good-by.

"You'll be around again, maybe?" she said at the last moment.

"If I'm still in the neighborhood, I'll be back," said Port.

She smiled and then he turned away. He remembered, going out of the door, that she had not told him her name, and that she had not asked him his.

Chapter 5

The Off-Time was a roller-skating rink, but twice a week—on Tuesdays and Fridays—the management hired a combo of five and turned the rink into a dance floor. Bright lights glared over the rink but there were very few lights on the other side of the railing, where the tables were. There were setups on the tables and the men kept their bottles under the chairs. The women all looked alike. They giggled too much and wore the wrong kind of jewelry.

When Port had walked half the length of the railing toward the bandstand he saw Dicky and the girl. They were dancing close to the rail because Dicky was talking to someone. Letty danced with eyes closed, humming, waiting for Dicky to finish talking. The man who was talking across the rail looked like a delinquent grown-up. Dicky was telling him a joke.

He stopped talking suddenly. He stopped dancing, too. Letty opened her eyes, and Dicky's buddy, who had been ready with his laugh through the whole long story, put a cigarette in his mouth and took one nervous puff.

"Come on, man, don't stop now! What she say when...."

"You! Who in hell sent for you!"

Dicky's buddy cut loose with a loud haw-haw that shook him all over. He turned it off as quickly.

"What's the matter, there's more?"

Then he caught his mistake. He followed Dicky's eyes and saw the man Dicky was staring at. He didn't know Port, but he disliked him immediately. He didn't like the smile on Port's face, the way he was leaning against the rail, the suit he had on, the way his hair was cut.

"This square bothering you, Dicky?"

Dicky curled his mouth and said, "Ha!"

"You say the word, Dicky?"

"It's hard to tell," Port cut in. "He's the strong, grunty kind." Port smiled.

Dicky's buddy looked from one man to the other, wiped the backs of his hands as if stroking boxing gloves tight over the knuckles, and took a swift step forward. It looked very dramatic, but it ended right there.

He stiffened all over, and color spread all over his face from the effort to keep the scream out of his throat. Then air hissed through his clenched teeth as he slowly bent over and took hold of his knee.

Port's foot tapping into the man's shin had made only a small, wooden sound. The man limped to the nearest chair, still in slow motion, his breath a tight wheeze.

"I'm sorry," said Port, and looked at Dicky, "but I didn't come to see him."

"Yeah," Dicky said. For the moment he couldn't say anything else.

"I came to see you."

"Yeah."

"You and Letty ran out so fast I couldn't get a word in edgewise."

"Yeah."

Port cocked his head to one side and looked at Dicky. "Something bothering you?" He looked at Letty. "Or is he like this often?"

Letty didn't know what to say. She had no talent for banter but she knew it was foolish to answer Port seriously.

"You got troubles," said Dicky and he gave his voice a raw, ominous tone. He said the same thing again the same way, and it seemed to loosen him up. "Port, wasn't it?" He moved up to the railing. Letty followed him.

"Dan," said Port. "Might as well, since we'll be knowing each other much better before we're through."

"Before me and you are through," Dicky started but he stopped when he saw Port frown.

"Look," said Port, "It's no fun horsing around with you. Let's try it serious."

"You wanna step outside?" Dicky said. "Right now?"

"The hell with that." Port looked annoyed. "All I want is one brief word with you and you can go back to your dancing." He smiled at Letty when he said the last. "I just came to tell you...."

"You wanna go outside right now?" Dicky said again.

Port took a deep breath. He was sorry he had come to this place. He should have known that Dicky would show off in front of his girl, that he still would be sore at Dalton for bringing Port, and—maybe worst of all—that Dicky would be on home ground here.

Dicky's friend was no longer alone. He was still on the chair, leg bent and body crouched over, but now three punks in black-and-white satin jackets were standing by like an honor guard. The longer the injured punk crouched there the more fiercely the others looked around.

"No," said Port, "I don't want to go outside with you. All I want is to make an appointment with you. You, me, and Dalton. We can...."

"Who needs you?" said Dicky.

"Dalton does. You shouldn't push an old man like that. Your place, ten tomorrow. How's that?"

Dicky didn't answer.

"We don't have to make a production of this. How about it, Corday? Ten tomorrow?"

"Get out of my way," said Dicky. He was looking past Port. "You injured my buddy."

Port felt like smiling at Corday's choice of words, but when he saw Dicky start climbing over the railing he changed his mind.

"Letty," he said. "Can't you talk to him? All I'm asking...."

"You shut up," Dicky said to the girl.

"You going to leave Letty standing around here?" said Port.

Dicky pushed him out of the way and Port let him go. There were now five punks by the chair, not counting the sufferer, and all of them waiting for Dicky Corday. Port turned his back and swung his legs over the railing. Letty just stood there. And then Port had his hand on her arm.

"My pleasure," he said and danced the girl off toward the middle of the rink. He could see the tough boys all standing in the dark on the other side of the railing, their hands in their pockets, smoking the way Humphrey Bogart might.

Port thought he might have enjoyed dancing with Letty if he had met her some other way. Now he held the girl lightly, giving her plenty of room, and thought of other things. This was his night for dancing, all right.

"Letty," he said, "how long have you been with Corday?"

"Oh!" she said, disappointed, when the music stopped. She looked up at Port. "The set isn't over—"

He nodded and said, "Fine. We'll stay out here."

She moved back into position.

"Letty," he began again, but Letty said "Shh!" and waited for Port to move on the right beat because the music was playing again.

They danced to a slow, heavy rhythm, Letty with her eyes closed and Port looking up at the ceiling. The structural steel had been left open and paper garlands—red, white, and green—were wound around I-beams and struts.

"To do it right," said Letty, "you got to hold me closer." Then she moved closer to him and pushed his right hand lower on her back. She hitched her torso around so that they would fit properly.

"And you got to move more than just with the legs," she said, "or it isn't dancing."

She spoke very seriously and when she was satisfied with their position she kept still again and just danced.

"Better this way?" said Port.

"That's fine. Keep your steps short and smooth. You're doing fine now. It's different from walking."

Port sighed. "Does Dicky do this well?" he asked. He had to start somewhere.

"He's all right."

She started to hum.

"You known him long?"

"Hm-hm," she said.

Port chewed his lip. He looked up at the ceiling again, at the paper frills wound around the steel beams and at the dust up there. He started to feel very useless.

"You got to—to think you're in a wave, you know," Letty said. "And the music is the wave."

"Yes," said Port. "I'll try it."

"That's what I think of," she said and closed her eyes again.

It improved Port's dancing, but did not make him feel any better. "Letty," he said. "The reason I'm out here with you's got nothing to do with dancing." He waited a moment, but she said nothing. "I want to ask about Dicky."

"I don't care," she said. She started to hum again.

"You like Dicky?" Port asked her.

"Sure."

"He like you?"

She nodded, humming.

"I'm asking because he doesn't seem to like too many people."

"He doesn't like you," she said.

"You know why?" said Port.

"You're butting in," she said. "He doesn't like that."

"He's butting in on that old man, Dalton."

"That's because Dalton's a doublecrosser."

"What? Dalton?"

"That's what Dicky says."

"You've got that wrong, Letty."

"That's what Dicky says," she repeated and then the music stopped and the sax trailed off and the piece was over.

"There's one more in the set," Letty said. She stepped back, pulled her dress smooth in front, and waited.

Port nodded. He and Letty stood near the bandstand. He looked over at the darkened area where the tables were. It was not easy to see well, but Port saw that the table where the punks had been was empty. The black-and-white jackets were posted at regular intervals, one at each gate in the railing, two at the main exit, one each where a red bulb glowed over the side exits into the alleyway.

"The last one in a set is the longest," said Letty. "You know how to jitterbug?"

Port had started to whistle tunelessly.

"You know how to jitterbug?"

"We'll just dance," said Port. "Like before."

"You can let me go a few times, can't you? You just hold one hand, this hand here, and keep up the beat. Then I come back."

The music started with a crash from the bandstand, and then, without pause, went into a quick, nervous riff.

Port held Letty close.

"What's this doublecross Dalton pulled?"

"I can't hear you," said Letty .

She tried a breakaway but Port held on. He moved her away from the bandstand.

"What did Dalton do?"

"Listen, let's try...."

"You listen to me," said Port. "You know why I came here. Maybe you don't think it's important." He let go of her on the beat and pushed her left hip to show her which way to spin. She shot out, smiling, and at the right time made a full twist and came back like a whip. Port caught her so that she had to face toward the railing.

"See that gate? And that one, and that one? And the exits?" She looked where he told her, keeping the beat with the slightest movement. "That's for me," said Port. "That's how important it is."

He spun her around again and she came closer. She shifted her torso for the proper fit and danced close to him.

"What happened?" she said near his ear. "Why this?"

"I'm bothering Dicky," said Port. "Now what about Dalton?"

"Dicky says Dalton promised him—that the old man was gonna set him up right, the way Dalton himself used to do."

"When was that?"

"Before prison, he says, before that last time they worked together."

"Was that the heist that put Dalton away?"

"Before then. They used to work together, now and then. I didn't know Dicky then, but he told me."

"Listen," said Port. "There's no doublecross. All you told me is Dalton was going to show Dicky the ropes and then Dalton gets caught. And for the ten years he's on the rock he gets closer and closer to dying. He's sick, he's not the same any more, and what Dicky is doing is twisting an old man who's no good any more except to rest, who's got to stop running. There's nothing Dicky can learn any more, because Dalton is through."

She looked at Port when he finished, thinking about it. "Tell that to Dicky. Tell him the way I said it."

"I should?" she said.

"Do that. I can't get him to stand still long enough—"

"That's how he wanted it," Letty said. "That's what he told me when we left the room. He was going to keep out of your way till you left, and then he and Dalton...."

"What made him think I was going to leave?"

"He wasn't going to do anything. Not till you left. He told me you used to be somebody; he remembered, after a while you were somebody big in a different town—not this one."

She had said one important thing. Dicky Corday wasn't going to rush it. He wasn't going to sing the old man back into prison. He was going to bide his time, wait until Port went away, until the old man couldn't stand the threat any longer.

The five men in the combo were standing up now, whipping their bodies back and forth with the beat. The drummer was flying all over the traps and cracking the cymbals because this was the end of the number and also of the set.

"Tell him, Letty, the way I explained it," said Port, and they made a turn close to the railing.

"And then you'll leave?"

The noise was too much to be sure about Letty's voice, but Port thought she had sounded concerned; for the first time she had sounded involved.

"Why?" he asked, his head close to hers.

"It bothers Dicky," she said.

"You love him?" asked Port, but it seemed she was no longer interested in talking. She was lost in the music which was getting sharper and sharper. When Port caught her eye he asked her again. "Why do you stay with him?"

She heard him that time. She looked as if Port had interrupted something important.

"Stay with him? Because he loves me." She said it as if it were obvious.

At the end of the swing Port let her hand go and when she saw what he was doing she stopped dancing and stood there.

"You going?"

Port swung over the railing and waved. "I'm going to try hard as hell," he said. He didn't think she had heard him.

Chapter 6

Port headed for the nearest exit guarded by only one man. The band stopped before he made it, and the sudden quiet was unearthly. After the silence there was bedlam again; chairs scraped, people laughed, and a buzz of voices rose from the tables.

The kid at the door saw Port coming, but he didn't expect much from a man running away.

Then the kid's arm was suddenly bent double. The pain grew like a fire running up his arm and bursting hot and big in his shoulder.

"It hurts less if you walk," said Port's voice close beside him, and they moved out of the door and into the alley.

One wall of the alley was dirty bricks and Port, holding the kid before him, leaned against that. The other wall was stacked high with crates. One end of the alley was blind, the other led to the street.

They stood there in the mouth of the alley, five of the black-and-white jackets.

Next to Port the exit door of the dance hall opened slowly. Holding the kid in front of him Port moved back to the blind end of the alley. He did not want anyone behind him.

Dicky Corday came into the alley accompanied by one of the jackets. They closed the door and stood by the wall, getting used to the darkness. They looked back and forth, to the dark end where Port was and to the open end where the five jackets stood.

"Tim," said Dicky Corday. "You with that bastard?"

Tim was afraid to speak because of the way Port was holding his arm.

"He got a gun on you, Tim?"

Tim didn't answer.

The nervousness started to show in Corday's voice.

"Port? I can see you. You gonna stay there and wait forever?"

Port didn't move.

"There's seven of us, Port. You needn't try to be a hero."

The silence got so bad, that suddenly Corday giggled.

The men in the jackets waited, making no move, so that Dicky couldn't delay any longer.

"Port!" he yelled. "You yellow bastard!"

Port moved, but only because Corday, to save face, wouldn't be able to delay much longer.

Pushing the kid ahead of him, Port went close to the pile of crates.

Corday heard them. "Move in," he said. "Move in, men."

"Has he got a gun, Dicky?" one of them asked.

Dicky could risk his honor no longer. "That won't help him," he said and walked straight toward Port.

Port gave a twist to the arm he was holding and Tim's sudden scream stopped Corday. Then Corday laughed unpleasantly.

"He don't have no gun! He's holding Tim! I can see 'em!" The rest closed in fast now.

"Stay there!" said Port. They all stopped, straining to see him in the dark. "And watch this."

Port came forward, pushing Tim, and they saw how Tim was bent over. "What's going to happen to him is...."

"A talker," said Dicky, because he couldn't let Port go on. "A big talker and a shin kicker we got here. Wadjasay, Jerry?" He turned to the man Port had hurt. "You gonna let the shin kicker do it again?"

THE OUT IS DEATH

Jerry moved up, swinging a slat.

"Not the shin, this time," said Port. "Worse."

"You think you can do it twice?" Dicky said. "You think it's gonna impress twice in a row?"

"It'll hurt just as much," said Port. "Twice as much, really."

Jerry felt that with everyone looking he had the most at stake. "Feller," he said, and the anger made his voice raw. "You hiding behind my buddy there. You coming out?"

"Go take a jump," said Port.

"You gonna come out, feller? You and me, huh? Just you and me—" Jerry started to crouch.

Port knew better. He said, "How about it, Dicky? Whose fight is this? His or yours?" Jerry threw the slat. It made a sharp, vicious sound as it cartwheeled through the air and then clattered along the brick wall.

They didn't hear it fall. Port had kicked at the nearest crate, so that it had started to lean very slowly into the alley where Corday and his helpers were standing. They backed up a foot at a time.

It seemed to be happening very slowly. Nor was the sound of the falling crates loud—just a brittle bouncing and some snapping sounds and then there was stillness in the alley again. If Port had let go of Tim he might have gotten away, around the crates strewn all over and the six men flush against the opposite wall.

But he thought he should drag the man along with him, at least to the mouth of the alley. He started to move fast, but Tim didn't, and the boy's scream broke the spell. The men charged, all at once, and only the litter of crates slowed the rush.

"Corday!" called Port. He was breathing hard. "Do they know why you're pulling this? Do they know what they're helping you with?"

"Shut up, talker. You shut up and let's see...."

"You should tell 'em," said Port, talking fast now, "so they know how big this deal is—beating me up and getting me out of your hair. Did you tell 'em how much of a cut they'll get out of this caper?"

"I'll kill ya," Corday said. "So help me, I'll kill ya—"

"Or do they just get paid by that big feel of victory, huh? That big feel of seven guys beating up one—" But Port had said it too late and anyway the kick at Jerry had been an insult. The stalemated waiting had been an insult, the crate flying out and the pile falling over and Tim still bent over and groaning with pain was a sin and an insult.

"This was just gonna be sport," Corday was saying. "Till now, this was just gonna be...."

"Get this," Port interrupted, and his sudden anger made him talk through his teeth. "Call off your monkeys and beat it, or Tim pays for your trick."

"Crap," said Corday. He came closer, grinning. The jackets were following him. "Crap," said Corday. "You couldn't even...."

"I'll break his arm," said Port. "Watch it."

Corday laughed loudly but then he stopped.

Tim screamed.

For a moment they thought about Tim, but then they thought about insults again.

Corday stood up straight and looked around at the jackets. His grin was crazy, and his low voice was crazier still.

"Go ahead," he said. "Let's see it."

His followers stood around like curious cattle.

Port moved quickly and disjointed Tim's arm.

They were still looking at Tim writhe on the ground when Port broke Dicky's front teeth. He knew, with the next punch, that Dicky was going to double up and vomit. But Port didn't see it happen.

Chapter 7

Dalton had a bed in his room, a hotplate, and a small chest of drawers. Because of the size of the room the chest stood in front of the window and the backboard cut off the light. The wallpaper was brown with a motif of fall leaves and sepia shepherd scenes.

At five in the morning Dalton lay on his back, his eyes moving along the leaves where they curled and repeated themselves. He then looked at the shepherd scenes, one after the other, to find out if there were any differences. He did this until six when he got up. Between six and seven he washed, cooked gruel on the hotplate by the window, and then went to the washroom at the end of the hall to rinse off his plate, his spoon, and the pot.

He got dressed then, not knowing what else to do. By leaning over the dresser he could bend far enough out of the window to see the clock at the corner. It was only half an hour past seven. Port had said, "I'll see you by noon."

At eight Dalton thought about smoking a cigarette. Every day, since he had had to stop smoking, he had thought about having a cigarette at eight in the morning. By now he was able to say to himself that thinking of smoking was a keener pleasure than doing the real thing.

After this he cleaned his room and brushed his suit and overcoat. Then he sat on his bed and looked at his hands. He used to take very good care of his hands. He used to keep them very clean, the nails very short, and use salves and ointments to make the skin very supple at the fingertips. At one time he had always worn gloves. It had been his trademark. Gloves Dalton. He didn't know if the gloves kept his fingers more sensitive, but he had read about Arséne Lupin or some such French gentleman-thief and he had always felt elegant wearing gray gloves.

He touched the tips of his fingers now. They felt cold. His fingers looked like pale roots, just taken out of frozen ground.

It was barely past nine.

Dalton took a full, slow breath but had to stop in the middle. The deep pressure made the ache in his stomach a boring, hot rasp. He did not reach for the bottle of milk because he knew it would make him feel bloated. He might even get sick. He lay down on the bed holding very still so that his clothes would not wrinkle. He closed his eyes and imagined how it might be without the pain in his middle.

Then the pain was gone. He woke with a start that shook the bed. His pants legs slid up over his calves when he rushed to get his feet to the floor. The window. The street was bright with a high sun. The clock, at the corner, said one-thirty-five.

Dalton swallowed. Look again, slowly, he thought. The clock said one-thirty-six now.

If Port had been here, knocking, waiting, and he, Dalton, had slept.... Port had not come. Of course not. And if Port had not come it was worse.

The old man began to tremble. He sat down. He rubbed his mouth and the loose skin under his jaw. He could not afford to think about Port, to wonder about him, while Dicky—Dalton jumped up from the bed and tore his overcoat off the hook. Dicky Corday was crazy; he might do anything. Port had threatened him, maybe. To threaten Dicky Corday, crazy with glory dreams— Dalton ran down the street, not daring to look up at the clock again. He wished he had not taken the overcoat. The coat made him hot, slowed him down. Dicky lived far away for an old man, for the pain running made in the throat and in his legs.

Chapter 8

At first there was no answer when Dalton knocked on the hotel-room door. He knocked once more, and this time he heard a sound. He could not make it out at first, but then he heard Dicky's voice.

"Who in hell is it?"

"Me. Abe. Abe Dalton."

Dalton waited again, hearing nothing, and then Dicky started to laugh. "Come in!" Dicky called. "The door's open."

Dalton opened the door and walked in. When he saw Dicky and the girl Dalton did not know whether to stay or to leave.

"Close the door," said Dicky. "This ain't a public place."

Dalton came into the room and sat down by the table. He sat on the edge of the chair not knowing where to look, but the bed was right opposite him, with Letty and Dicky there.

Dicky was wearing his clothes, but Letty was not. She wore a slip which covered little and when she tired to get up Dicky pushed her back on the bed. He held her down and looked over to Dalton.

"About time you showed up," he said.

Dalton noticed the lisp. There was one front tooth missing and another one was broken.

"You staring at Letty or me?" Dicky said and the grin showed the hole in his teeth. He got off the bed and sat in the chair with the doilies.

"Take a shower, and then run down and get some coffee," he said to Letty. He looked at Dalton. "What's on your mind?" he said to the old man. "Anything I should know?"

"I can come back," said Dalton. "Any time you say I should be back, Dicky, I'll...."

"Letty's all right," said Dicky. "Don't you think Letty's all right?"

Dalton said, "Where's Dan Port?"

The shower went on in the bathroom and Dicky looked at the door.

"Listen to this," he said without looking at Dalton, and then they heard the girl make a sound.

"Every time," said Dicky. "Every time she goes in, the water's too hot." Then he leaned back in the chair, pulled a cigar out of his shirt pocket and lit it.

"Smoke, Dalton?"

Dalton shook his head. He looked at the wall and then at the window, and tried not to look the way he was feeling.

"What's that you asked me, Dalton?"

"I asked— I wondered if you knew where Port is. You remember—"

"Oh, him! What do you want him for, Dalton?"

Dalton knew that he could not take much more. He stood up and unbuttoned his coat. He took it off, hoping it would cool him, and then he sat down again.

"You tell me about Port," he said, "and then I'm ready to talk business with you. All right, Dicky?"

Dicky nodded and put the cigar in a tray. "Kinda makes you feel rotten the way you tried pulling a trick on me yesterday, don't it, Dalton?"

"Dicky, I'm here today...."

"Yeah. I know. Business. What makes you think I still wanna talk to you?"

There was a pause and then Dalton said, "No," like a groan.

"Scared you huh?" Dicky got up, went to the window, and threw the cigar down to the street. He turned back to the room with his hands in his pockets and leaned on the window sill. Dicky Corday looked very strong, very agile, but at rest for the moment.

"I'm no bastard, like you think. Don't worry, Dalton. I didn't sing to the cops."

For the moment that was all Dalton wanted to know. Right then nothing more mattered. He ran his hands over his face and let the tiredness come. He felt almost grateful to Corday.

"So now that you're ready for business, Dalton—" Dicky came away from the window—"let's you and me get this done." He hauled a trunk out from under the bed, unlocked it with a key from his pocket, and took out a long roll of paper. "You got a pencil, Dalton?" But before Dalton could answer Dicky slammed the trunk lid and came back to the table. He put the rolled papers on top of the table with a vigorous slap. "Like old times, huh, Dalton?" He laughed loud and hard.

Dalton sank into his chair. He had thought that he was ready for this, knowing it had been inevitable, but there also had been a hope—not large or convincing—but a hope.

"I asked you," he said, "and you never answered, Dicky. You know what happened to Port?"

Dicky ran his tongue over his teeth and then he turned his head to look at the bathroom door. The water was going off, and then Letty made that sound again, of breath drawn in sharply.

"What now?" he yelled. "Cold water all over your back?"

"I'm sorry, Dicky. I couldn't—"

"Lamebrain!" Dicky turned back to the table. He got out another cigar and ran the length of it back and forth under his nose. "Do I know what happened to Port?" he said. He sounded quiet and conversational. "I happened to Port." He stuck the cigar in his mouth.

"Oh," said Dalton, not knowing what else to say, and not wanting to hear any more.

"I'll tell you exactly," Dicky went on, "so you'll know." He lit his cigar and let the smoke run out of his mouth. "First of all, he comes mooching around and gives me a hard time. He wanted a cut, the way I see it. Then he don't get anywhere." Dicky leaned over the table. "You know what next?" He stopped and glanced at Letty, who, fully dressed, emerged from the bathroom.

Dalton didn't want to know. It was enough that Port wasn't here, that the whole thing had turned out a failure.

"Next he gives Letty here a hard time. So I see red, you understand, Dalton? I see red. There's some buddies of mine at the dance and they seen what happened, so when Danny leaves they tip me off—"

Dalton closed his eyes, trying not to pay any attention. Half of the story that Dicky was telling sounded like lies, but that didn't matter. Port wasn't here; that mattered.

"—and I stop him right there in the alley. He was leaving by way of the alley, understand? So," Dicky shrugged, stared at the ash on his cigar, "what can I do? I beat him up."

Dicky let it hang there, hoping for a reaction from Dalton.

"Cut him down to size, you understand?"

"Yes," said Dalton.

"He's outa town now," Dicky said. "My buddies throwed him out—what was left of him." Dicky knocked the ashes off the end of his cigar.

All of it might have been lies, but what mattered was that Port wasn't here. Dalton remembered Port the way he had been and he didn't understand any of this. He did not have the strength to try and understand it, he just nodded and said, "Yes," again. He put his hands on the table and rubbed them together. His fingers were cold.

"I forgot to ask you," said Dicky. "You in? Or out?"

"Show me what you have," said Dalton.

It was getting dark, and after Letty put on her coat and left, Dicky got up and turned on the light which hung from the ceiling. There were paper cups on the table, stained brown inside with cold coffee. Dicky sat down again and pushed up his shirt sleeves. Dalton was rubbing the top of his head. He pulled at his open collar, and then stared at the papers again. There were loose sheets of scrap paper and a large, springy roll of blueprints.

"For a guy who don't want to, you're doing fine," Dicky said. "I'll grant you."

Dalton nodded but he had been doing that all along, without meaning. Just nodding. He reached for the bottle of milk at his elbow and took a small sip.

The warm liquid revolted him but it dulled the pain.

"There isn't much more I can do," said Dalton. "To finish it off I need more information."

"You been saying that." Dicky stretched, making his shoulder joints crack.

Dalton put the papers in order, stacking most of them and crumpling some. Then he rolled up the blueprints.

"These are fine," he said, "unless they've changed the layout—added buildings or something."

"I told you the ground plans of that plant haven't changed. How often do I got to—"

"You go over it, and over it, and over it," said Dalton. He was tired too, but he was dogged and he was trying to work the way he used to. "So what you've got is the layout. Through the gate, cross the yard two hundred feet, pass the loading platform in front of shipping, and on past that. Next go to the right of the building—because you say there's a floodlight over the corner—and then take it from the parked trucks to the office building. Hit that through the front door, the shortest way. Hallway with time clock, up the stairs to the right to the second floor."

"You go straight and into the shop, Dalton, I told you there's another staircase going up to the—"

"First staircase from the hall," said Dalton. "You save twenty-five feet and nobody sees you for the whole length of the shop."

"Jesus, Dalton, how often do I have to tell you there's more doors going your way! I'm trying to tell you—"

"Let me finish," said Dalton.

They were both tired and both irritated, each for his own reasons.

"A door is no problem compared to a watchman coming through the shop."

"I told you a hundred times they got just one making the rounds and he's got four buildings and a quarter mile of fencing to do and you keep—"

"Let me finish!"

Dicky looked startled. He kept still.

"You don't know his schedule," said Dalton. "You're only guessing. I don't plan with guesses." He sighed and let his voice drop again. "We'll get to that later. First, we finish with what we got." He thought for a moment to get his mind organized. "Second-floor hall door, corridor, south wall of typists' room. You don't know how many desks there are. You ought to know." Before Dicky could say anything Dalton went on. "Hit the safe ten minutes after passing the gate; do better, if possible." Dicky was rocking his chair back and forth, hardly listening. Dalton did not notice. "The safe—two hours at the outside. No lights. The way you knock it over has to be figured without lights."

"You said that, you said that—"

Dalton looked up. He showed no emotion this time. "I say it again and then over again. So you know where the holes are. So you do it right. The safe is in the typists' room with windows the length of the wall. There's a railroad siding a quarter of a mile from the plant with a freight standing there and you don't know when he's pulling out. Another thing you don't know." Dalton tapped his hand on the table. "Next. You got, let's say, three hours at the outside for the safe. You don't know what kind of safe, so we'll say three hours—"

"I told you! I told you it's a Milton and Dunn! Christ, how often do I got to tell you—"

"You told me nothing. Milton and Dunn made nine different safes and six different types of each in nineteen forty-one. I don't know what they make now. I haven't checked since then and you haven't given me the information. Next." Dalton traced a pencil over the blueprint. "Back the same way, till you hit the trucks. New route. Crating yard to the fence—" Dicky bit his lips and stared up at the ceiling. "You need a new route because you save five hundred yards to the getaway. Five hundred yards of doubling back with a load, and nervous. I wouldn't trust you back out on the road when it's over. Cut the fence; go through the north field to that path going back to the road. The car at the railroad crossing, by the junkyard with all the old cars, where the driver can see you come out of the field. He meets you going north and you're off."

Dalton stopped and Dicky got up, slapping his hands against his thighs. "You done? Fine." He began to pace from one wall to the other. "I'm glad you're done repeating yourself because I like to get in a word edgewise. Okay, Dalton?" Dicky stopped pacing and gave Dalton a look, but the old man said nothing.

"Okay," Dicky said again. "Now here's how I got it figured, saving time. The watchman I don't worry about till we get there. I'll check him out myself. Same with the one at the gate. The train schedule I don't care about because I know for a fact no brakeman or anybody like that is gonna tell from a quarter of a mile away if there's an extra light in that plant or not. And if he does, he'll think it's the watchman coming through. So to hell with that. About the safe, you give me a guess. By the size and the make and the way the thing looks from the front, you can figure it's maybe this or that kind of lock. You take all the tools for what you think it might be and I get a man to carry the extra. That way we play it safe and no more horsing around with this planning. I been waiting long enough, Dalton. No more horsing around with that paperwork stuff." He looked at Dalton. "What now? You think up something else?"

"I didn't think it up. I just wasn't finished. You called three of the loopholes yourself. The guard, the train, the safe. Here's more. What's the alarm there, and where?"

"We don't break no windows, we don't have to worry."

"Does the safe have one? Did your man tell you?"

"No, he didn't tell me! How about you telling me? You're so hot with safes from way back, how come you don't—"

Dalton held up his hand. Then he leaned over to ease his stomach. He took a deep breath and said, "Your man," he said. "Is he a sweeper who's casing for you, or is he a caser who hired out there as a sweeper?"

"What in hell is the difference! Listen, Dalton—"

"You listen to me," said Dalton. The grinding inside his stomach made him curt. "I don't make mistakes if I know about them ahead of time. There's too many here, before even starting. How come, Dicky? You used to learn a lot. How come all this slipshod planning?"

Dicky stopped short, wheeled and came around to Dalton's side of the table. He hunched his shoulders. His face got livid.

"I'm running this thing, and what I want from you is toeing the line!" he shouted. "I don't want you to keep watering down what I been planning and figuring and I don't want you to try running it like an old man's card game! I got this planned from way back just waiting for you to get out. I don't wait any more. I can't sit around any more waiting for something to happen, you hear?"

When Dicky stopped for breath Dalton said, "You're rushing it, Dicky."

Dicky didn't say anything for a second and then he grated, "How old were you when you pulled that railroad job, huh? That Southern Pacific job? The one that was all over the papers, and they never pinned it on you till the statute ran out?"

"I was twenty-one," said Dalton.

"And I'm in the middle of thirty, you old son of a bitch, so don't hold me up, you hear me?"

Dalton said nothing. Dicky didn't say any more. He went up to the table and started knocking the coffee containers over, one by one.

"Where in hell is that lamebrain?" he said and then he started cursing Letty.

Dalton picked up his bottle of milk. He swirled the liquid for a moment, hoping that he would not have to drink it. But the pain was big and blue now, a heavy pain that weakened him and made him want to lie down.

"So, like I was saying," Dicky started again, "you got this all clear?"

"Dicky," said the old man. "Please listen to me."

"You've done fine," said Dicky and went to the window where he leaned out looking for Letty.

"Dicky," said the old man. When Dicky pulled in his head and came back to the table Dalton said, "I agreed to come in with you. I wouldn't, except you got me over a barrel. So I'm in. When I'm in, Dicky, I do a thing right. The only thing I want out of this is to stay out of prison. You want more. You want a job that's—"

"What's coming, Dalton? What's on your mind?"

"Do it right, is all. Like the alarm. You don't know a thing about the alarm."

"Look," said Corday. He talked fast. His tone was insulting. "There's a box, see? That's the alarm, see? It rings to beat hell if you trip it, and the guard comes running, get the picture? There's a million ways, see? Like the one this guy told me about he seen in a picture. You squirt a fire extinguisher into the box and the thing won't ring, see? You didn't know about that, did you? You don't short the wires, you don't fool with the tripper—"

"May not work," Dalton said. "The alarm may ring at the nearest station. There's that kind."

Corday almost stopped breathing. He held himself in, to check the rage he could feel flushing his face.

Then both men heard the steps approaching the door and Dicky held on because he wanted Letty to see this. Her big, dumb eyes were going to look bigger than hell when she saw how Corday handled Dalton, the pro.

"It's my way," Dicky shouted suddenly, "or back to the rock. Clear enough, Dalton?" Dicky kept eying the door.

"Say so right now, Dalton! One way or the other!"

Dalton just sat at the table and the pain inside him made him look hunched and small. He wished Corday would stop.

"And from now on you hop! You got a million notions I don't have all the dope? Get it! I'll drive you down, Dalton, and you case that place all you want. I'll give you a day—two days, seeing how old and slow you are—and then we knock that place over!"

Dicky stopped, waiting for some reaction, but Dalton just sat.

"You got that straight, Dalton?" he heard Dicky shout. "And now jump!"

"Don't! And you either, Corday."

Port was there in the room. He slammed the door shut behind him.

Chapter 9

Dicky stood crouched at the table, and he wished that there were more people watching this because the rage inside him made him feel as big as he wanted to be. Another step, Port, and another—

Port kept right on coming from the door to the table, and when Port swung the sudden, hard sound of his fist seemed to come out of nowhere.

Port stepped back to let Dicky fall and then took a deep breath. He waited for a while, but Dicky didn't move.

Dalton got out of his chair, not trusting himself to say anything yet, just staring at Port.

"You all right, Abe?" Port came closer.

Dalton nodded. His insides were churning, but he didn't feel it. It had all changed so quickly, Port coming back and Corday unconscious on the floor.

"What's this?" said Port and riffled through the notes and the stiff role of blueprints.

"When you didn't come," Dalton said, "when nothing happened—"

"Nothing happened?" said Port, and started to laugh. He stopped laughing quickly because of the pain that shot up the side of his chest.

"Sit down," said Dalton. "Maybe you shouldn't be on your feet. And a compress on that," he said, pointing at Port's left cheek.

A big scrape ran the length of Port's face from the temple down to the jaw, and when he moved Dalton noticed how Port kept one arm close to his ribs.

"How bad is it?" said Dalton. "Maybe you should...."

"I got away easy," said Port. He gave Dicky a brief look, then lit a cigarette and sat down. "The cops came to break it up. Or else he and his gang could have crippled me good." Port saw the stained paper cups on the table, but saw too that they were all empty. "That's why I'm late," he said. "I just got out of the cooler." He fingered the cups and waited for Dicky to wake up.

"Maybe you're too late, just the same," Dalton said. He waved at the notes and the rolled blueprints. "He's got me to start—"

Port looked at Dalton, and killed his cigarette in one of the cups.

"Just one thing, Abe." Port watched the old man and saw how sick he was. "You want out of this racket, or you want to stay in?"

Dalton started to raise his hands, then dropped them in a helpless gesture.

"It looks so— I don't know what to think, or to feel, Dan. It looks so far off—"

"I made it," said Port.

Dalton nodded and almost smiled.

"You're not sick. You don't have things hanging over you."

"Who doesn't?" said Port. "Is that what's stopping you?"

"There are things—like that job he's holding over my head—things you can't make up for."

"Maybe not. But you can stop doing them over."

"When I think," Dalton said. "When I think how I used to be—not sick—"

"That's why I'm helping you," Port told him. "If you want out."

"If I want out." Dalton paused. When he spoke again he was hardly audible. "I used to think that if I went back to prison, it'd kill me. I'd die." He closed his eyes. "That's not how it is, Dan. If I go back it'll be like living forever—and now that's the worst."

He bent over and didn't look up.

Port let go of the paper cup and went over to Dicky. He grabbed him under the arms, pulled him up, and tossed him into the chair.

"Pull out of it," he said and lifted Dicky's chin. Dicky moved his head. "Come on, you can make it," Port said and gave him a rough shake.

Dicky's face was silent and closed and Port started to frown. He caught on barely in time to get out of the way when Dicky kicked out with his foot. Dicky made it out of the chair and over to the wall with the dresser.

Port was boiling. Before Corday got the gun free of the top drawer Port was on top of him. Dicky leaned back over the dresser, gun held high, trying to reach Port with his knee. Port's left shot out aimed at the soft part where Dicky's ribs came together. Dicky doubled over and tried swinging the gun down like a club. Port slapped him sharply on the arm and Dicky, bending over, exposed the back of his neck.

He caught the rabbit punch there. It made his ears sing and his eyes burn and it shook up the insides of his head. He fell on his face, still conscious.

"On your feet," he heard Port say.

He balled himself up on the floor, tensed like a spring.

He heard Port curse and then felt himself yanked to his feet. Port's face was close to his. He hadn't known Port could look the way he did now.

"Corday, are you listening? Answer me!"

"Yes— I hear ya— Yes."

"You and me, Corday, we're through horsing around. You understand that?"

Dicky nodded. Then he nodded again because it made him feel as if his head were clearing.

"And pushing around, Corday. You're through pushing anyone around. You got that clear?"

Dicky's head was much better now. And Port didn't look as if he wanted to fight any more.

"And this heavy deal," said Port. He went to the table. "That's over." He picked up the notes and tore them in half. "And now I want to know how you were going to sing to the cops."

"Sing?" said Dicky. "I'm not gonna—"

Port came closer to Dicky and Dicky saw how Port was biting his lower lip, and how still Port's face looked. "I mean I was gonna sing, like I kept telling Dalton, but there wasn't anything...."

Port waved impatiently. "What was it? Come on, Corday."

"I was gonna tell 'em...."

"No. You wouldn't have been this sure about Dalton. What was it you were going to show them?"

"Show them?"

"Corday," said Port. "I'm getting tired of asking."

But Dicky knew something about Port by now—that Port wouldn't start swinging again just for the hell of it, and that he was waiting to hear. A talker, try talking around him or even try— Dicky started to think in long, flicking jumps, so busy trying to think his way out of it that he started nervously at a sound at the door.

Letty came in. She had a large bag in her hand. She looked at Port standing, at Dalton crouched in his chair, and at Dicky, at the dresser, his hair all mussed.

She said, "Hello. I didn't know you'd still be talking. I thought...."

"Close the door," said Port.

She didn't know what was going on but she sensed the tension in the room.

"It's all right," said Port. "You can close the door." Then he stooped to the floor and picked up Dicky's gun. He pushed the cylinder open, and ejected the shells into his hand, and when he dropped them into his pocket he began to whistle softly. He tossed the gun onto the bed.

"Did you bring some coffee?" he asked the girl.

Letty closed the door and went to the table. She put her packages down and opened the carton of coffee. White steam lifted off the black liquid. "There're some cups on the dresser," she said.

"Thank you."

Port held his hand out toward Dicky, who took a cup off the dresser and gave it to Port.

"You didn't finish your milk," said Letty. She looked at Dalton. "I brought you more."

Dalton said, "Thank you," but he sounded as if he were hardly there. When

Letty pushed the small carton across to him he didn't touch it.

She made more sounds with the paper bag, pulled out a hamburger, and then another one. The room was quiet. Everyone just stood around. Then Port went into the bathroom to run some cold water into his coffee. They all listened to the sound of the water running and looked at the bathroom door. When Port came back into the room no one had moved.

It would depend on Port, Dicky thought. He could figure this thing once Port made his move. But for the moment Port just stood by the wall, holding his cup in both hands. Now and then he took a sip. He watched Dalton, who sat in his chair looking as if he had been beaten.

"There's two ways we can do this," Port said without transition. "Are you listening, Abe?"

Dalton looked up and nodded.

"We can do it straight, or we can really cross him up." Dicky frowned, not understanding it.

"I don't care which way we do it," said Port. "Seeing it's Dicky at the receiving end."

"What do you mean?" Dalton leaned his arms on the table, trying to ignore the sharp stings inside him.

"We can do it straight and ask Corday here to hand over the evidence, whatever he's got."

Corday was starting to sweat. They were talking about him as if he were something you bought in a store.

"Or, if he thinks he's too smart for a straight deal, we can play it crooked." Port sipped some coffee, and then went on. "He can go ahead with his heist, but somewhere along the line he'll get crossed up. But good."

"Wait a minute." Corday came away from the dresser, but standing alone in the middle of the room suddenly made him self-conscious. He went back to the dresser and started to talk very fast. "Wait. You don't know what you're doing. Hell, you can't pull that on me! Or Dalton! You can't pull this on Dalton! Hell—" Dicky was loud and excited. "You'd do a thing like a double-cross? How crooked can you get?"

Port waited to see if Dicky had finished and then he said, "Not that crooked. Don't forget, I'm telling you ahead of time."

"I don't want it that way, Dan," Dalton said quietly. "If I say I'm going to do it, I'll do it. I told Dicky I wasn't going through with it, but if I ever say yes I'll do it."

"That's right," said Corday. "He's straight, anyway. He don't...."

"So we'll do it the other way," Port said. "Show me what you think will make Dalton work with you."

"Hell," Dicky started again, "I been telling you...."

"I'm through stalling!" Port was suddenly loud. He put down his cup and came a step closer.

Letty was watching. Arguing with Port might hold off things a while longer, but Letty was there, watching.

Dicky went to the closet and reached into the lining of one of his suits. When he felt what he wanted he hesitated for a moment. A lot rode on this thing—was he going to give it away?

"It's in there," said Letty. "Can't you find it, Dicky?"

Corday didn't say anything, but right then he hated her guts. He hated her guts for being there, for watching, for butting in and for being Letty.

"You're taking too long," Port said behind him.

Dicky wiped the sweat from his face and came back into the room. He had some folded papers in his hand, held together with a rubber band.

"Here." He tossed the small bundle on top of the table. "The works. It's worth...."

"Just shut up," said Port and picked up the papers.

"Dead to rights," Dicky said, chattering. "I got him dead to rights! This can...."

"You recognize this?" Port showed the papers to Dalton.

"... this can mean a mint, don't you get it? This can mean Dalton doing one job after another, big ones—" Nobody was listening to him but Dicky went on talking excitedly. "All right, so he's old maybe. Maybe he ain't so good any more at pulling a heist, but so what. I can see him laying it out—he does-n't have to go on the job, just lay it out. Sit in his chair and plan the job."

"Stop dreaming," said Port. Then, to Dalton, "What's he got on you here?"

Dalton went through the papers. One had a drawing on it, a ground plan of a building, studded with arrows and notes. Another sheet had a time schedule on it, a detailed schedule with minute-by-minute instructions—a well-planned blueprint for cracking a safe.

Dalton still looked sick, but excited now. His hands shook when he pushed the papers across the table.

"The Exchange Bank—that small town in Idaho—Bexley." He got up and stared at Dicky, furious now. "I never pulled that heist! I wasn't in it!"

There was a small silence. Dicky and Dalton stared at each other and then Dicky yelled, "That bank was knocked over in forty-one by this plan! And the plans here. They're in your handwriting, right?"

Dalton sat down again. The fury had gone out of his face but he was still excited. He sat down, reached for the bottle of milk and took a long swallow. Some of the milk ran down the side of his mouth.

"Abe," said Port. "Explain this."

Dalton put down the bottle and swallowed hard.

"I wasn't in on that job. It's my handwriting, yes, but I wrote that out later, much later, for Dicky. I knew about the job and how they were doing it and I wrote it all out for him, to show him how it was done. That's all!" he shouted. "That's all it is! I was never in on that job! I mean it—believe me!"

For a moment Port thought that this might end it. There was nothing here that could force Dalton back into jail—but the thought lasted only a moment. He did not think it was over. He looked out the window. He wished he were not here.

Then Dicky started to laugh. "He wasn't in on the job? So what! It looks like he was, and if not—so what!"

Port watched Dalton get out of his chair and go to the window. He was walking badly. He went to the window and stretched his neck as if fighting for air. Dicky saw it too, and laughed louder.

"Abe," said Port and went after the old man. He put his hand on Dalton's back. "Just hold out, Abe. We'll make it," he said softly. Then he turned back to the room.

"Corday," he said, "you got a point. And here's mine."

He didn't get any further. Dicky began to shout.

"You got plans, maybe, to take that evidence there on the table and tear it up like you did with the notes? Go ahead, Port, take it. And the first move you make, I yell cop. This hotel's got a regular pipeline to the next precinct. Wanna bet? Grab that evidence, and I yell cop. They'll find the stuff here unless you eat it. And if you do I can still make it hot." He stopped, and then his laugh came battering out again. "They'll find Dalton here. Dalton—you know—he's still on parole. He's on parole and associating with criminal elements. Me, a crook that served time, and you a crook that got away. They'll go hard on Dalton, understand?"

Port had tried waiting it out expressionlessly, but the more Dicky talked the closer Port got to losing his temper. It must have showed in his face because Dicky suddenly changed the tone of his voice. Now he was wheedling.

"Port, listen to me. I'll give you a chance. I shoulda caught on to you sooner, but better late than never. Listen!" Dicky leaned over the table. "I'll cut you in," he said hoarsely. "We can share the old man!"

"You make me sick," Port said.

All it meant to Corday was no, that he had missed the angle, that he didn't know the price.

"What?" he said. "What more? You want half? You want more than half? You wanna pick your own crew? Port, just don't foul up this job! Anything within reason."

"Dicky, please, I don't think you know—"

They had both forgotten about the girl. They looked at Letty where she sat on the bed and the silence made her lose her nerve.

Corday suddenly hated her guts. Hating Letty and fearing Port he went to the bottom and tried his last.

"You save me this setup, Port, and I'll trade you big. Here, take her! You want her? She's a lamebrain, but what the hell. Look what I'm trading you! She's...."

There was a dull sound from over near the window and Dalton sagged into a heap. He made only a small clatter.

"My God!" Letty was off the bed and standing over Dalton. "He's sick!"

Port knelt on the floor and turned the old man on his back. When the door slammed he looked up and there was only Letty in the room. Port did not have to look at the table to know that the plans in Dalton's writing were no longer there.

Port got up. There was no phone in the room and he went toward the door. He had to pass Letty. Before he passed her he stopped. He stood very close to her.

"He loves you?" he said, and then he went out.

Chapter 10

Port called the fire department because their ambulance service was the fastest. They came without a doctor so Port did not find out why Dalton had fainted. When the ambulance left Port stayed behind at the hotel.

Dicky's car was not on the street and the hotel desk clerk knew nothing. Port went to the stairs, but he did not go up because Letty came down, dressed for the street. She came into the lobby, saw Port, but said nothing to him. She went to the desk and gave the clerk her key. Port watched her do it and close her purse afterwards. When she looked up she looked out to the street, past Port's shoulder.

Her face seemed shut and the look of just waking up was gone.

She walked to the door, and then she stopped and waited for Port.

"Are you looking for Dicky?" she asked him.

"Can you help?"

She walked out onto the street and pointed left so that Port would know which way they were going. He did not try to talk to her. After ten minutes

Letty stopped at a corner and nodded.

"You see where it says Sport Parlor?"

Port saw the gold letters on the plate window.

"I have to go in there," she said. "That's his place—I mean where his friends are, and maybe they know."

"I'll go in," said Port. "I don't think women are welcome there."

"You think you are?" she said. "There's a diner, down this way. I'll meet you there."

She left Port and went towards the Sport Parlor.

They saw her coming when she crossed the street, and they all straightened up from the pool table to watch her. They knew her because she was Dicky's and because they all had grown up together in the same streets. They saw her stop for a passing car and then come toward the pool hall again. They saw her legs where the skirt ended and the way she set her feet. They saw the way her hips moved when she took a step. They watched the button that held her coat closed in the middle over her breasts.

"Here's your chance, Mac," one of them said, and they all looked at Mac to see how he would react.

"I ain't like you guys. I don't have to hang outa the window and imagine."

"Imagine, my foot! Lookit her. That's all solid, man. I mean solid."

They all looked out the pool-hall window and imagined what Letty was like.

And then, "Jesus—she's coming in!"

When Letty came into the pool-hall they all stood by the table and looked at her. She stopped in the aisle between the cigar counter and the big tables. She wished they would not look at her with waiting stares.

"Have you seen Dicky?" she said. "I'm looking for Dicky."

"Dicky?" said Mac. Then he looked at his buddies. "She needs Dicky," he said.

They all laughed, loudly and rawly.

Letty stood in the aisle and held her purse in both hands. She held it low, as if she were naked.

"Tell you what, though," said Mac. He hitched his rear onto the edge of the table and started swinging one leg. Then he grinned so everybody would know that now the next one came, and they should get ready.

"I'll tell you what, Letty. I'll play you some pool." He laughed loudly and they all joined in.

Letty waited for them to finish. She would have liked to leave but she stayed where she was and waited. The men at the table saw her take a deep breath. They saw that she did not mean to leave.

"You know where he is," she said. "I've got to find him."

"Oh," said Mac. "It's that way."

But this time nobody laughed. Letty had changed their mood for them.

Mac turned back to the table and picked up a cue stick. He started making passes at the low-number ball but didn't hit.

"A Coke, Letty?" he said, without turning around.

Letty had to walk to the table because all of them had followed Mac's lead. They had all turned away to watch the game.

"I don't want to bother you," Letty said, "I just want to ask...."

She broke off short because Mac moved his cue back and the butt of the stick nudged Letty in the soft of her stomach.

"Gee, I'm sorry," said Mac. "Where'd I tap you, here?" and he gave her a pat.

When Letty tried stepping out of his way she got caught from behind.

"Here," said the one who was holding her. "Mac didn't mean nothing, kid. Here, stand over by me." His hands held her arms from behind.

"Duff, she don't want you either," said Mac. "Come here, Duff, let her go."

But Duff didn't. He got next to Letty and put one arm around her. He kept his face close to the girl's and said something into her ear.

"All I asked her was to play pool," said Mac and they all stood back laughing and watching how Duff held onto the girl.

"Lemme go," said Letty. "Lemme go." The more she struggled the more they laughed and kept watching. She dropped her purse, her coat opened, and someone pulled it off her back. The laughing got much more quiet and a slow tension grew over the group. It wasn't just Duff now, holding her. They had all come close.

She could scream, she could weep, she thought she might faint, but Letty knew none of this would help her. They were all silent now. She heard only her own breathing. She caught a glimpse of the man at the counter, a fat man who had been asleep. He was awake now and watching. He had come to the end of the counter and stood there holding his lip in his teeth.

They were not really pawing her, they were pushing her one way. They had turned her so that she could see one of them holding a door open, waiting.

Letty moved by instinct. She didn't plan it or think it out.

"Jesus, you can let go. Don't you know that?"

They did let go. They stood there startled by her tone, by the lassitude in the movement she made when she pushed the hair out of her face. She put her hands on her hips. She took a deep breath and let it go. She ran her tongue over her teeth and said, "How many of you guys are there?"

They looked at each other but nobody spoke. One of them tried to laugh but it came out more like a cough.

"I'm asking," said Letty. "Whatsamatter, you never done business before? The rate goes by the number."

The man in the back closed the door.

"Get off my coat," said Letty and the man who had stepped on the hem of her coat moved away quickly.

"Give it to her," said Mac. "Ain't you got no manners?"

They gave her the coat and the purse, and they started to drift back to the table.

"Hell," said Mac, "how come you getting so serious, Letty? We was kidding around, is all, just trying to kid you."

Letty said, "Yeah?"

"Sure. Just fooling, you know?"

"I'm not," she said.

"Sure, Letty. And besides, we're Dicky's friends. Don't you know that? You ought to know that."

She tossed her coat over her shoulders, and when she followed them to the table, the coat flounced back and forth behind her.

"Sure," she said. "While he's around, maybe."

Duff started to line up a shot, then sank a ball. Mac was chalking.

"You got us wrong, Letty. What the hell, he's not gone for good. He'll be back, Dicky will."

"When?"

"When? I don't know. Duff, you know when?"

Duff straightened up and said, "Huh?" He looked very much interrupted.

"When's Dicky coming back? You got mud in your ears? Letty here wants to know when...."

"Oh, sure. He said maybe a week. Takes a day each way and he figures on a few days there."

"There? Where?" said Letty. "I asked you a dozen times."

"Oh, Newton. This burg Newton. You know."

"Yeah," said Letty. "The job." She looked down when she said it and opened her purse so that her face wouldn't show. She did not know how she might look. It was getting to be too much for her. Dicky was going to do it himself, rushing it for some reason, changing everything he had planned—

"Didn't he tell you?" said Duff.

"Sure, but I must have heard wrong. I thought he said next week. I thought—"

She was glad when she was interrupted. She did not know what to say next, and she was afraid that she could not carry it off for much longer. Anxiety touched her.

"He didn't know it himself," said Mac, "the way he came in here, all steamed. What happened? He wouldn't say."

"He thinks somebody is trying to butt in. That's why, I guess."

"Sure. He come in here asking for Loony. He needs Loony right away, so when we tell him that Loony's at work he hightails right outa here and to the shop."

"The shop?"

"Where Loony's working. That's why he's called Loony. He works in a shop." Mac laughed.

They all laughed, glad for the change.

"Maybe they know at the shop—" Letty started, but saw that she had made a mistake.

"You crazy or something? That's a legitimate job Loony's got there. They don't know from anything else. Christ—women!" said Mac and turned to the table.

"Christ, yes," somebody else said. "You want Loony to lose his job?"

"Maybe he'll lose it anyway," said Duff between shots. "The way he keeps taking off."

"Him? He's skilled. They don't fire the skilled ones."

They were through with Letty. They had a topic to haggle over, and they were absorbed in it. They turned it back and forth and held on to it, because it was better than boredom.

"He's always got a job. Hell, he can walk into any town—"

"That's what he said. He come in here for his cigars before taking off with Dicky, don't you remember? He come in here—"

"I was kidding him about getting fired. That's right—"

"… and he says he's taking a job in this burg. What was the name of this burg—"

Letty was at the door, no longer listening. She went out into the street. She went only as far as the end of the building, where she could not be seen from the pool-hall. Port was waiting and she would tell him all she could remember. But first she had to stop. She leaned against the brick wall and breathed deeply. She did this until she felt sure that the trembling would not start again.

Chapter 11

Port sat in the diner and tried looking the length of the street, but the window faced the wrong way. There were three cigarettes in his ashtray, the charred ends pushed flat. He moved his cup by the handle, moving it back and forth until some coffee spilled. Then he dragged his saucer over the puddle so that the stain would not show.

He did not see Letty until the draft from the door made him turn. She came to the booth, sat opposite Port, and said, "He left town. He...."

They had to wait while the waitress asked for the new order and until she got back with two cups of coffee. Letty didn't touch hers and Port pushed his own out of the way.

"You have any trouble?" Port asked her.

Letty looked at her handbag. "He left town," she said again. "He went to that Newton place." The concern showed in her face. "I think—"

"For how long? Do you know?"

"They said maybe a week. Do you think he's trying to do it alone?"

Port didn't know. He picked up his cup, but found the coffee too hot. He put the cup down again. "He's off the old man, anyway. He's not pushing him any more."

"Yes," she said. "That's good." She snapped her bag open and closed it again. "But do you think he should—do you think he's doing it on his own?"

Port looked up and gave her a brief smile.

"You worried about him?"

She said, "A little. He's no good at it—"

"If he gets caught maybe that'll mean something to him."

"He's been in before. The same thing. The second time they won't go easy."

"How come you're worried about him?"

"I don't like to see anyone go to prison."

Port looked out of the window and nodded at nothing. Then he turned back. "I don't know any of the details about this Newton job. I don't know if one man can do it alone."

"He didn't go by himself. He took Loony along."

"Loony?"

"He's somebody works in the shop down the next street. Dicky took him."

"They work together before?"

"I don't know what Loony does. He works in that shop."

Port frowned at the table. "Maybe he will try it alone. You'll just have to sweat it out."

He got out of the booth, put some change under his cup, and reached for Letty's arm.

"Try not to worry about it," he said. "Will you, Letty?"

"Sure," she said. "I'll try."

Port held the door for her and they went out into the street. "I'll take you home now," he said. "And thanks very much for your help." He paused. "Looks like rain." He took her arm to make her walk faster.

They turned the corner and Port saw the shop down the street. It said, *South Side Machine Co.*, and underneath, Toolmakers and Diemakers.

"That's where Loony works?" Port nodded at the small shop.

"Yes. He's something skilled, they said."

They walked by the shop.

"Toolmakers and diemakers," said Port. "The next best thing to being a locksmith—for Dicky's purposes."

It started to rain in slow drops and they walked bent over.

"You going after him?" Letty asked.

"No. There's no point."

The rain got heavier and they put their heads down, seeing only their feet.

"Will you let me know when Dicky gets back?" Port asked.

She didn't answer right away. She wiped rain off her nose and bit her lip.

"I don't know," she said. "I—I don't know yet." She looked at Port seriously. "You know what I mean?"

"Sure," said Port, and he nodded.

"Where do you live?" she asked.

"I'm leaving town," said Port. "I'll call you when I get back."

They turned into the door of the hotel and stood on the mat for a moment, shaking the rain off their clothes. Port felt the dampness through the back of his suit and he saw where Letty's coat had soaked through. She shook off the coat and moved her shoulders to keep the wet dress from clinging.

"You want to come up?" she said. "To dry off?"

"No," said Port, "Thanks. I'll come up just to get those notes out of the way. We left Dalton's notes on the table."

"I threw them into the wastebasket," she said. "Before the men from the ambulance came."

"I'll get them," said Port. They went to the desk to get Letty's key, and then they went upstairs.

The desk clerk made no comment and nobody saw them go up because the lobby was empty. There was just a man in the doorway who stood there shaking the rain out of his hair. He looked at them very briefly and then went out into the street again.

Letty closed the door to her room while Port went to the wastebasket. She watched him pull the torn papers out, stuff them into his pocket and then straighten up. She waited until he looked at her.

"And I want to thank you," she said, "for not pushing me."

"About what?"

"About Dicky. About helping you go after Dicky."

"I'm not really after him," Port said. "As long as he doesn't push the old man."

She went to the bed and sat down and pushed her shoes off with her feet. It struck Port as a tired gesture.

"Maybe Dicky will learn that, when he comes back," she said. She got off the bed and walked toward the bathroom. She had started unbuttoning the top of her dress.

"You're wet too," she said. "Can I make you some coffee? I got this hotplate over there"—and she nodded at it from the bathroom door.

Port thought she looked very tired. He thought it might have something to do with the way she felt about Dicky.

"No, thanks," he said. "I've got to go." He waved at her from the door and walked rapidly from the room.

When Port walked through the lobby the desk clerk looked up without interest, then looked back at the book he was holding. One page had print on it and the facing page a palmist's chart of a hand. The clerk was absorbed in it. Then a man stepped to the desk and the clerk looked up. He said, "Hi, Mac. Wet out?"

"Anyone else with her?"

"Who?"

"Dicky's dame."

"No," said the clerk.

"No visitors for an hour," said Mac, and went up the stairs. The clerk looked back at the chart again.

When Letty heard the door open she stopped shaking her dress out and closed her bathrobe in front.

"That's all right," said Mac. He leaned against the bathroom door and folded his arms.

"Please," said Letty. "Please go."

"That was fast," said Mac. He acted as if she hadn't said anything. "You and him, I mean. That bastard we beat up at the dance hall."

"He just walked me home," Letty said, not knowing what else to say. She did not think it would make much difference what she might say now.

"He in on this deal?"

"What? I don't know what—"

"He's butting in on Dicky, right? Dicky said so."

"He's leaving town. He just told me, Mac. Really, he's not even interested—"

"Leaving town? Coming back when?"

"I don't know. But he'll call me. When he comes back he'll call me up, and if you really want to know—"

"He gone to Newton?"

"Oh no. I told you, he's not...."

"But he's leaving, huh? A few days, a week?"

"More like a week. It sounded like a week. And when he left he...."

"That's okay," said Mac, "you done fine." He pushed away from the door and took Letty's arm.

It opened her bathrobe on top and she let it be. There was no point in trying to close it again.

Mac stayed for an hour. Then he left, got in his car, and drove out of town towards Newton.

Chapter 12

We are very glad you showed up," said the old woman at the reception desk. "He hasn't been able to answer questions."

"All right," said Port. "Then can I see him?"

"We'll call the floor," said the old woman. "After you fill out this form."

The clinic receiving desk was very busy and Port had to wait while the woman attended to something else. Then she took him into the office behind the desk while she searched for the form with the name Abraham Dalton at the top.

"What would you like to know?" Port tried to prompt her.

"The fire department brought him," she said. "There was a fire?"

"There was no fire. There was an emergency and...."

"Why didn't you call our service? Our drivers have their instructions about forms for Receiving. We always...."

"It was an emergency," Port said again.

"Nevertheless." She got up to get a bottle of ink so that she could fill her fountain pen.

For the next twenty minutes Port gave her Dalton's name again, because she wanted to hear it, Dalton's age, Dalton's address, and the facts that he was retired and had no known relatives.

"You want me to call the floor now?" the woman finally asked.

"Yes, please." Port sat watching her while she phoned Dalton's floor and explained that there was a visitor to see him.

"The nurse wants to know what the purpose of your visit is. Actually, the patient should not be seen for the next twelve hours. Actually...."

"I'm from the parole board," said Port. "Official business."

"Parole board? Dear—dear me—you mean Mr. Dalton is a criminal?"

"Was."

"Why didn't you say so? Why didn't you see to it that this fact was entered when I filled out the form?"

"I did." Port nodded at the form on the desk. "Former residence: Joliet. What did you think Joliet was?"

"Why—there's a town. I have a cousin in Joliet who's lived there for ten years."

"So did Mr. Dalton. May I go up now?"

There was some more hurried conversation on the phone and then Port got his pass. He took the elevator up to the second floor, gave his pass to a nurse who looked at it casually, and was led to a ward.

There were ten clean, white beds, with curtains between them, and progress reports hanging at their feet.

"Number Five," said the nurse, pointing, and left Port at the door. There was another nurse inside the ward. She sat at a small table where the row began and Port had to tell her whom he wanted to see.

"Number Five," she said, and smiled.

It was the first smile Port had seen in the place. He stopped at her table and said, "I'm the one who committed the patient. I wonder...."

"Only a physician can commit a patient. Are you his physician?" She smiled again. Port shook his head and smiled back.

"I called the ambulance was what I meant. Mr. Dalton had fainted. Could you tell me what happened?"

She reached for her records.

"Are you a relative?"

"He doesn't have any. About this fainting, I know he has a bad stomach—what's left of it."

She looked at the record. "He had a hemorrhage. Active ulcer. You knew that, I suppose."

"I don't know a thing. How bad is it?"

She looked again, moving her lips, and then put the record away.

"We don't know yet. His red count dropped badly in the beginning but it's leveled off now. If the bleeding doesn't start again he may improve slowly."

"May?" he said, and the nurse saw him frown.

"I can't tell you any more," she said. "Number Five. And just very briefly, all right?"

She smiled again and Port nodded. He walked down the row to the fifth bed. He did not recognize Dalton.

A tube that hung from a red bottle was taped to his arm and a tube that hung from a white bottle was taped to his nose. His nose looked very large. His face looked sunken and only his nose seemed to be the same.

"Abe?"

Dalton was awake. He rolled his eyes and when he saw Port he smiled with just his mouth.

"Dan," he said. "How are you?" He sounded very strange to Port. "Come around this way."

Port moved around the bed so that Dalton would not have to roll his eyes so far and Port would be able to hear him better. He sat on a chair next to the bed and leaned close.

"You're getting better," he said. "I just asked the nurse. The one that smiles."

"That's nice," said Dalton and closed his eyes.

"And I'm not to stay long, Abe. Can I ask you something right away, so it won't take long?"

Dalton opened his eyes, waiting.

"That Bexley job, the one Dicky is holding over you—where were you when that was pulled?"

Dalton was about to make a gesture but the needle in his arm stopped him. He bit his lip and lay still for a moment. Then he said, "That was in forty-one."

"I know, Abe. A long time ago. But you must have been some place, and wherever you were, maybe somebody remembers. You see how that would clear you, Abe?"

Dalton did not answer.

"Maybe Florida—New York—prison, maybe—or some small town where you holed up. Chicago?"

"I know where I was." Port waited, and then Dalton said, "There's no point, Dan. Just forget it. Let it go. I'm safer now than I ever was."

Port looked away for a moment because he did not want Dalton to see that he was shocked. He did not know whether Dalton was right and would not live long enough to fear anything else.

"Abe, listen to me."

"I'm listening."

"You can't live the way things have been for you. It keeps you sick, don't you know that? You can though, the way you had planned it. You can go home, have a room of your own, an easy job in the small town where you came from—" Port watched the old man, and saw how Dalton was trying to keep his face expressionless. "You let me help you, Abe, and pin down a witness, and you can go home. You know that, don't you?"

"I know."

"Well?"

"I—I don't want to, Dan. I don't think I can."

"Will you tell me why? Will you at least tell me why?"

Dalton looked up at the ceiling and said, "I was with a woman. She was a young girl then and now she's a woman. She has a husband and two or three children. You can't do it."

"To save your life, Abe?"

"She may not remember."

"Why not?"

"We lived together. For a while. I don't think she loved me or anything."

"Abe. Listen to me. Just to help a man who's down like you are, for that you don't have to love, the way you meant. She has to be a human being. She just has to have some feeling...."

"She had that," said Dalton. "But she's got a life now, different. Why should she spoil—"

"She won't. And you won't. I'll keep in mind how you feel, Abe. I won't give her any trouble. I'll just ask her, in a friendly way, to give a little help. That's all. She won't ever get involved the way this can be handled. Come on, Abe. Who? Where?"

"I don't know—"

"Where? Tell me. Look, maybe she'll be glad to hear from you. I can give her your regards, at least that—"

It was lame, but Port didn't know what else he could do.

And then Dalton said, "She might. She was nice. Eve Tomlin was her name. Eve Simmon now."

"Where, Abe?"

"Same town, Otter Bend. In Minnesota."

Port got up and touched Dalton's shoulder.

"See you, Abe. In a few days."

Dalton nodded as Port stepped away from the bed.

"If she remembers," he said, "give her my best."

Chapter 13

The train made the best connection to Otter Bend, and it took almost two days. There was a change on the second day, and at five in the morning Port stood for half an hour on a small, windy platform. He noticed how much colder it was here. Across the tracks was a young stand of pines, the tops whipping and twisting in the wind that came from the north. The tips of the trees had a silvery sheen, like hoarfrost.

There was a waiting room in the station, but Port stayed outside. The waiting room was not warm and had the feeling of a basement.

Two days both ways made four, leaving Dicky three days at the outside for his job. Port did not think he would need three days. If it took him three days it wouldn't be any good. He walked the length of the platform and felt the wind tugging at him. When the train came he sat by the window and watched how the landscape got bigger with wind-bare stretches and old woods getting deeper. Then he closed his eyes and slept most of the day.

The wind had stopped and Otter Bend looked warm in the late sun. The town did not look very large. Port could see almost all of it from the station platform. There was a long sheep shed along one side of the station and a diner opposite that. The town was behind the diner. The main street was short and very wide. Port could see the bank, the chain store, and the three car-dealer showrooms. The side streets had trees that were taller than most of the houses because there wasn't a building in town higher than two floors.

Port wondered whether he was looking at Eve Simmon's house. He picked up his bag, and went into the diner and sat down at the counter. There was a rancher at one end reading a two-page paper. A young boy with crowded teeth leaned his hands on the counter and asked Port what he would have.

"A cup of coffee," said Port. "Black."

The counterman drew the coffee and when he set the cup down it was half filled with milk. Port didn't say anything. He started drinking the coffee right away because it was cold enough.

"That all you want?" said the counterman.

Port put his cup down and pushed it over.

"Another cup, please. Black this time."

The counterman went to the urn and when he had drawn the coffee he turned and said, "That was black?"

"Black," said Port.

It was black and Port leaned over the cup to blow on the coffee.

"Anything else?" the counterman said.

"No, thanks."

The counterman took out a toothpick and started working inside his mouth. "My name's Curtis," he said. "What's yours?"

The boy was abrupt, Port thought, but all right otherwise, just eager for conversation.

"My name's Dan. How are you, Curtis?"

"Fine. You just off that train?"

"Yes. Just stopping over."

"Friends? Relatives? Business? You don't mind my asking, do you? Uh, what was your name again?"

"Dan."

"That's right. Dan. You don't mind my asking, do you, Dan?"

"No, go ahead. As a matter of fact I'm going to ask you a few things myself. You don't mind, do you, Curtis?"

"No, that's fine, Dan. That's fine with me." He leaned his elbows on the counter and lowered his voice. "I can always do with some intelligent conversation, if you know what I mean." Curtis looked sideways at the rancher who was still reading his paper. "I get to talk with everybody comes in here, you understand, but I mean intelligent conversation. These guys here—" He jerked his head at the rancher and made a face.

"He can hear you," said Port.

"Naw. He's deaf. And what if he could? He wouldn't know what I'm talking about. None of 'em do." Curtis sighed.

"I know what you mean," said Port and nodded seriously.

"I was born and reared here myself," Curtis said, "but I been away. I seen something, you know what I mean, and coming back after that—you know what I mean."

"Been around, huh?"

"Sure. I was in the Army."

"Ah," said Port. Then he picked up his coffee and tried it. It was lukewarm and he drank some of it.

"So where you from, Dan?"

"Chicago."

"Ah. That's a town."

"It certainly is, Curtis."

"I'll say." Curtis threw his toothpick away. "What's your business, Dan?"

"I'm in development. We represent production concerns interested in extending potential."

"Man. That's big business."

"Oh, yes."

"I'll say. And you're doing some of that up here, in this town?"

"Yes. Part of my job is incepting demand levels. I mean reconnoiter for incepting and at the same time recreate into repeater-consumption the senescent levels. That's how I get to see old customers too."

"That's a job!"

"I'll say. I don't repair them, you understand, but then they hardly ever need any repairing."

"Boy."

"Our line is for any part of the house, so you can imagine that our replacement department can't also be contained in the function of my division."

"No. Sure. I see that. Uh, are they expensive?"

"Not for the service. Anywhere from one-five to three-eighty-nine."

"Is that so? And they all work the same?"

"Sure. Just more chrome on the expensive ones. You know how it is."

"Hell, yes!"

"So I've got an introductory list of some customers here, and maybe I'll look some of them up. Just good will, you understand."

"Sure. How about new ones? You after new ones?"

"No. Not really. We don't need them, you see."

"Oh."

"You know everyone in town, don't you, Curtis?"

"I sure do. Anyone you want to know about?"

"Brown," said Port, "and there's—"

"Jimmy or Melvin?"

"Both. And Simmon—"

"Yeah. Him too."

"Where?"

"The store. That's on the left, the main street, where it says Simmon Hardware. He's there till eight or nine, mostly."

"Fine. And where do I catch him at home?"

"Elm Road. There's no elms there but they call it that. The big frame house with the lantern out front."

"And the Browns?" Port asked, to round out the conversation. After that he said Mrs. Eve Simmon was one of their best customers, to make sure the Simmon on Elm Street was the one he really wanted. Then he paid for his coffee and got up to leave. He had his bag in his hand when Curtis said, "Psst!"

Port turned back. He remembered for no special reason that nobody had said "Psst" to him since he had been a boy.

"I know how it is with you big concerns," Curtis said, "about forms and so forth." He hesitated when he saw Port frowning. "And, of course, you got this policy you been telling me of, about no new customers."

"Yes," said Port. "It would create competition. The complex kind. Creeping socialism, you know—"

"Yeah, I know all that, but just between you and me, Dan, one of those dollar-five kind—how about it, Dan, could you—"

"Out of the question." Port went to the door.

"Look I got the money right here, Dan." Curtis was holding a dollar and a nickel in his hand.

"Out of the question," said Port and opened the door. "It would cost eight bucks in bookkeeping alone."

"Hey, Dan—"

"I'll send you a catalog. That way it's cheaper." He got through the door before Curtis could say anything more.

Elm Street was not very far. Port walked past the Simmon hardware store and Elm Street branched off that. There was a hotel at the corner, a frail-posted building with a narrow porch running along Main Street and around into Elm. Port went inside. There was no train out of Otter Bend that night so he would have to sleep over. He signed the register and left without having looked at the room. He carried his bag. He would call at the Simmons' home looking like a salesman.

It would help if the husband were not there. Port went back to the hardware store and looked through the window. There was a confusion of tools and implements on display but Port saw no one so he went inside. When he saw the boy at the counter Port walked toward him, keeping his back partially turned. He walked as far as the boy that way and looked at the middle aisle.

"You know," he said, "you used to have—" Then he turned to the counter and laughed. "I thought I was talking to Simmon. I guess he's...."

"He's out back. Selling a tiller," said the boy.

"Good old Simmon, always selling something," said Port. "I thought maybe he'd be up home. Supper time." Port nodded at the clock on the wall. It was six.

"He's been and back," said the boy.

"Fine. I'll be in before closing."

"He's closing at nine," said the boy.

"Fine," said Port and went out.

With luck it would take until seven, maybe eight. Then back to the hotel, a shower if there was one, and, if it wasn't too late, a call to Dalton. A message for Dalton in bed with the tubes: *All set. Get well. Dan.* Or something like that.

It was a very large, very neat frame house, with a well-kept lawn, white curtains and milk-glass figurines in the windows. On the front porch was a bicycle, a tricycle and a foot-pedal car.

Eve Simmon had at least three children, and she baked her own bread. Port saw the loaves on the sill of a side window and he smelled the fresh smell of them.

He went to the front door and rang the bell. He could not see through the cut glass in the door but he heard steps almost immediately. When the door opened he said, "Mrs. Simmon?"

He barely caught a glimpse of the woman. He saw her shake her head. "I'm sorry, my husband isn't home," she said and the door closed again.

"I've just come from the store," he called through the door. "Mrs. Simmon. Your husband is at the store. I've just come from there!" He gave his voice a tone of alarm. The woman opened the door again, all the way this time. She was frowning.

"Yes?" she said. "Is anything—"

"No," said Port. "May I come in?" He walked through the door.

He watched her close it. She closed it quickly, worried now.

Two children came into the hall, a girl of about four and a boy of about eight. The boy said, "Hi, mister."

"Wait in the kitchen," said the woman. "Please, darling, wait there and close the door." She hustled the children out of the hall and then came back to Port.

"Mrs. Simmon," said Port, "I apologize if I have alarmed you. All I meant to say was that I knew your husband wasn't here because I saw him at the store when I passed there." Then he smiled at her but it did not make an impression. She was hostile.

"If you're selling something, please leave. I don't let strangers—"

"I know you and I are strangers. I have your name from a friend. When he heard I was coming through here...."

"I don't care what you're selling, but if you don't leave right this minute—"

"I'm not selling anything. But that's why I carried my bag. Anyone seeing me would think the way you did. That I'm selling something."

He had said the wrong thing because she turned on her heels and went to the phone that hung on the wall.

"Was your maiden name Tomlin? Eve Tomlin?"

She reacted quickly and angrily. "What do you want? You want to make trouble? Are you somebody that—"

"Can we sit down somewhere, Mrs. Simmon? I can tell you much faster."

Then he saw that he had lost her. She was controlled now, and whatever it had been that had upset her did not matter too much anymore. So Port said, "I'm to give you regards from Abe Dalton."

Port saw that now she would sit down and hear him out, but she would do it out of fear and dislike. It would make the rest harder.

Chapter 14

Eve Simmon sat in the chair at one side of the window and Port sat in the chair at the other. Eve looked as neat as the room. Her housedress was a catalog model with a small flowered print. The waves in her hair did not look like her own, and her hands were reddish from working with soap. She looked like most of the women in town.

If she were not so frightened, Port thought, or so hostile, her face would be pleasant.

"If you and Abe Dalton have some kind of trouble making in mind," she said, "don't think you're going to get away with anything. You sit right there all you want and when my husband comes home...."

"I'll leave now, if you want me to," Port told her. "I didn't think you would act this way." But he didn't move.

"Act what way?" she said, and sounded defensive.

"Angry about something. Did Abe ever harm you?"

She said nothing.

"He's sick. He may not get well. He just sends his regards."

She was still suspicious. "Don't tell me," she said. "Don't tell me you stopped in this town just to bring regards. I haven't seen him in—I don't know—it must be fifteen years." The thought made her remember. She had not intended that. "How old is he now, anyway?" Her voice sounded sharp again.

"He's very old, because of the things that have happened to him."

"I don't want to know anything about him."

She was in her early thirties, Port thought. She had put on some weight but she was a firm-skinned woman and her face could be pleasant. But she tried too hard to be prim. It took away her attractiveness.

"Mrs. Simmon," said Port. "I'd like to try to convince you that nobody means you any harm. Abe Dalton, I told you, is a sick man. He's in a hospital now. He doesn't want anything that could—"

"He's a criminal, isn't he? And you know him, so maybe you're one of them too. Or a lawyer. That's just as bad."

"*You* know him," Port said. "Does that make you a criminal?"

She caught her breath and jumped out of the chair. "I'm a married woman with a home and children! My husband has a good business here and we have standing in our town. We have nothing but friends in this town, and my children—"

"Someone's coming," said Port. The car that had stopped in the drive was a delivery truck but the sign on the side of it read *Simmon Hardware*. The man that jumped out of the cab was no delivery boy. He was big and blond and he laughed when two of the children ran toward him from the house. He grabbed the small girl and threw her up in the air and when he had caught her again he came straight into the house.

"Eve?" he yelled from the stairs. "You home, honey?"

Eve Simmon turned pale.

"Sit still. I'm a salesman." Port was bent over, busy with the catch of his bag when the door swung open and the man came in.

He had started to say, "Eve, honey" again when he saw Port. "Oh—" He put the small girl down on the floor and closed the door. Then his smile came back and he said, "I'm Jay Simmon. How are you," and came across the room with his hand out.

"How are you, Mr. Simmon? My name's Port. I don't mean to disturb you—"

"That's all right; you're not." Jay Simmon looked down at the bag. "You trying to sell my wife something?" He laughed. "I bet I know what happened!"

Port laughed too, and said, "Yes, I'm afraid you're right. Well, if you'll excuse me—" but nobody was listening to him. Jay Simmon was asking his wife if she'd seen the A.O. Smith catalog and Eve Simmon got up to show him where he had left it on the hall table. They all came out to the hall and Port was just at the door.

"Hey—uh, Port, wasn't it?"

"Yes?"

"Give you a lift? I'm leaving too."

"No, thanks, I'm just going to the hotel."

"Come on," said Jay Simmon. "I used to be on the road myself. I know how the feet feel this time of day." He kissed his wife, waved at the children, and ran after Port.

Port didn't argue. He felt tired, but he didn't care one way or another about walking or riding. He sat next to Jay Simmon in the truck, holding his bag on his knees. Simmon backed out and headed down the street.

"What are you selling?" he said in a friendly voice.

Port shrugged, wishing he were alone. "Why should I talk to the competition?"

"I bet I can guess. Can openers."

"Yes," said Port. "You're right."

"Business good?"

Port shook his head.

"Know how I guessed? By your looks. Next to encyclopedias there's no line makes a man look so discouraged at the end of the day as can openers. Why'nt you try something else? I myself can undersell any gadget you got to peddle. You're in the wrong line."

"I know that," said Port. "I get off here."

"You're not offended, are you?" Jay Simmon looked closely into Port's face. "Because all I meant was some friendly—"

"I know that," said Port. "And thanks for the lift."

That night Port sat at the window and looked out over the town. Soon after nine the town seemed deserted and most of the lights on the main street went off. Port lay down on the bed, but he could not sleep. He had slept too much on the train. He felt uneasy about walking into Eve Simmon's safe little world. And if he left her alone and went back to the old man, who was dying anyway— Port started to smoke. He smoked three cigarettes and then he got up and stood by the window. There was nothing to see. He could not do any harm to Eve Simmon which her safe little world wouldn't mend. But the old man, Dalton, had nothing. He should be allowed to die as he wanted.

Port undressed and slept until morning.

At nine Port walked into Simmon's hardware store and asked for Jay. Jay was in the yard, stacking drain tiles. When he saw Port he came over and shook hands again.

"Hi, Port. Feeling better today? I hope you didn't think.... Fact is, I was hoping you'd drop by or I'd run into you before you left."

"Good," said Port. "I was hoping—"

"I was thinking," Jay said without listening to Port, "that you might be interested in a proposition."

Port waited.

"You know anything about windmill pumps? No? Simple. Look, I need a man who goes out on the road—"

"Jay, I'm sorry. But I don't think—"

"You know what this job needs, mostly? A presentable guy, a guy that likes people, with—you know—appeal. You got that, Port. And if—"

"Jay, look, that's damn nice of you, but the fact is I have other obligations.

The reason I'm here is that it seems I left one of my sample boards at your place. Did your wife find it, or say anything?"

"No."

"Can I run over to your house and check? I thought I'd ask you first...."

Jay laughed. "Sure, go on over. And tell her I said it's all right for you to come in." He grinned at Port. "You thought maybe she wouldn't, huh?"

"Frankly, yes," said Port. "And thank you gain."

"Why don't you think over—"

Port said he would. He said that it was damn white of Jay to make the offer and that he'd think it over. Then he left and walked down Main Street to Elm, and all the way to Eve Simmon's house he was strangely comforted by the fact that he would always remember that once a man had offered him a job selling windmills to ranchers.

He rang the bell and heard Eve's steps in the hall. She opened the door without hesitation.

"My husband called me," she said. "You were coming over to pick up some samples you left here."

"Did you play it that way on the phone?"

"I don't intend having you mess up anything for me. Or for my husband." She held the door, waiting for Port to come in. She held it without welcome.

"I have said nothing to you that could make you think I want to mess up things for you," said Port. He went into the hall and when she had closed the door he followed her to the kitchen.

"You keep coming back," she said. "You must want something."

She was at the sink now, washing dishes, acting as if he weren't there.

"Where are the children?" asked Port.

She nodded out of the window. The little girl sat in the yard, patting her hands into the grass. The young boy was there, and an older one; they were painting a box.

"I'll tell you what I want and then I'll leave you alone. I can leave town tonight."

She washed dishes, waiting now.

"Abe Dalton just got out of prison. He's sick, and he's old. I told you that."

She kept washing with a slow, rotating motion.

"There's somebody who wants him to do one more job, and then another, and another. You know how it is with blackmailers."

"Not until now," she said tonelessly.

"The pressure on Dalton is an old job, a bank that was knocked over. He didn't do it, but it looks as if he did."

She was still washing the same dish without looking at it.

"He didn't do that job. He was with you."

Except for the slow, rotating motion she did not move.

"It can send Abe back to prison. He'll die there," said Port.

The circle of her movement over the dish got smaller.

"You can help him, Mrs. Simmon. You need not be involved, no one here need find out, and if your statement does become necessary—"

Port saw that she had stopped moving now.

"Mrs. Simmon," he said. "Do you hate him?"

She said it very low and fast, almost in a whisper. "You don't know what I have here, you don't know how much. I won't give it up. You come into all this and drag back every rotten thing I thought was buried!" Suddenly she turned toward Port and her wet hands hung at her sides, dripping water on the clean floor. Her face had a high color now and Port saw that she was close to tears. "You don't know how I met him, do you? You don't know how it used to be, who little Eve Tomlin used to be, do you? He knew my father. Abe Dalton was on the lam, and he knew my father. We lived out on a farm, in the bluff country where nothing's any good except that you're alone. He knew my father who was a drunk and a filthy thief and a crooked old man who always kept talking about the great times and the big deals he used to have in the city—a long time ago when he used to leave Mother and me alone out there and toot off to some city and come back broke and ragged. And when Mother died he really showed what he was, drinking and cursing and me in the middle of it, and then he had friends over—"

The tears were running down over her cheeks now but she didn't notice them.

"Friends, he used to call them, big-time friends from the big days in the city. They were crooks hiding out and they paid him for it and that's all that filthy old man ever cared about because that's how he bought his liquor. He'd sit in the kitchen all night talking to himself and to the bottle because his 'friend' got the one bedroom, the one with the double bed, because the bed I used to sleep on was too narrow for two, and when that filthy old drunk was ready to pass out he'd use my bed because I wasn't using it then."

She shook her hands violently, making the water spray off them.

"That's how I met Dalton, you understand? I was less than twenty and Abe Dalton was a stranger who came, stayed a while, and had bed and board. You understand?" Her voice got high with excitement. "He was as old as my father, almost, and a stranger! I don't want to talk any more. I don't want to think any more!"

Then she was silent. She turned away from Port and he was glad that she did because it was easier for him, not knowing what to say. He saw her shoulders move when she took a deep breath and then she stood still again. Port put his hands in his pockets and he had an urge to whistle, softly and for the short time it took him to see clearly again.

He said, "I'm glad you made it. And no one will take it away from you."

She went to the refrigerator and took out a bottle of milk. She carried it over to the stove and poured some into a pot.

"You made it, Mrs. Simmon. Dalton didn't." He waited a moment. "Do you remember him well enough to know that he wouldn't take anything from you?"

Port could not see her face because she had turned to the stove and was watching the milk she was heating.

"Isn't there anything you remember of him that wasn't bad?"

She went to a cupboard and took out a bottle. She gave Port one brief look but he couldn't tell what the look meant. Then she went back to the stove and poured milk into the bottle.

"You married a very short time after Dalton knew you. Perhaps that way you can remember about him. What I'm trying to make you see, Mrs. Simmon—"

"I remember."

The words were unexpected, and the tone of her voice was unexpected. It was as if she were no longer fighting it off, the time in the past, but was really thinking about it now.

"I remember because he was the last." She looked at Port. "He didn't tell you?"

"He didn't want me to come," said Port. "He just told me your name."

She put a nipple on the neck of the bottle but she didn't look away from Port.

"He took me with him," she said. "The night he left." She went to the window and looked out at her children. "My father was asleep in the kitchen—or passed out, I don't know which. Abe Dalton drove me to Grand Rapids, driving all that night and part of the next day. In Grand Rapids he found me a room. I must have been half dead with fear and excitement because I went to sleep as soon as we got there." She turned back to Port. "When I woke up he was gone. It was terrible being alone there. I must have cried myself to sleep again. That's why I didn't find it until I woke up the next morning. He had put five hundred dollars in my shoe."

Port said nothing when she was finished. He smiled at her briefly. It looked for a moment as if she were going to smile back but then she didn't. She looked down at the bottle and felt it for warmth.

"I know," she said. "This is all good. It's good as long as Jay doesn't know.

I met him very soon afterwards and he never knew about me."

"Don't you think...."

She didn't let Port finish. "He was from Otter Bend, but we had already known each other. We went back to Otter Bend very soon. We were married in the city and went back to Otter Bend, and it was as if I'd never seen the town before. This is my life now, and Jay will never know."

"You won't help Dalton?" said Port.

"You can force me," she said, "and ruin everything." She sounded almost indifferent. "And I would try to fight back."

She was at the window again looking out at the baby, so she didn't see Port frown.

"Jay doesn't know, and he never will." She went to the door that led out to the yard. "I must get my baby," she said and went out.

When she came back Port was gone.

She seemed very calm the rest of the day, and during the evening when her husband was home. She talked very little. Jay Simmon noticed this but he said nothing of it. When they went to bed he fell asleep quickly.

Eve Simmon lay awake for a long time and when she got up it was barely light. She went downstairs to the small desk in the living room. She sat there over a blank sheet of paper with pen in her hand. The sheet had a letterhead, *Mrs. Jay Simmon*, and Eve Simmon read it several times. Then she wrote her name, *Mrs. Jay Simmon*. She wrote it again, automatically, because she did not want to sit at the desk, with pen and paper, and do nothing at all.

Jay's truck was outside, under the window, and a swing in the yard was swaying in the cold morning wind.

She tried to write again. She wrote Mrs. Jay Simmon, over and over. She felt like crying, but she fought it.

"Eve?" Jay called from upstairs.

"Honey?" he called again.

She got up and went to the stairs. "Yes, Jay?"

He came downstairs, big and rumpled from sleep. "You all right, honey?"

She nodded.

"No, you're not," he said. "Come on out to the kitchen. I'll make us some coffee."

He put the coffee on and then sat down at the kitchen table with her.

"Like before we had the kids, huh, Eve?"

She nodded and almost smiled.

"Honey," he said. "You want me to leave you alone?"

This time she did cry. She could not hold it back. Jay Simmon put his arms around his wife and pulled her up. He patted her head and stroked her back. She relaxed after a while but did not let him go. They went back upstairs that way to their bed, and they made love the way she remembered before she had had any children.

She had not talked at all. She said nothing about it, ever.

Chapter 15

Letty was a sound sleeper, but when the bright light hit her face she woke up almost immediately. She sat up, more to get the glare from the ceiling out of her eyes than for any other reason. Then she saw Dicky standing in the door and came awake all the way.

"Dicky! You're back!" she said and smiled with her whole face. Then she threw back the covers and watched him come over to the bed. "You're back so soon," she said, smiling again.

She didn't see it coming but she heard him say, "Bitch!" and then the pain stung into her face and she fell sideways.

When she tried to get up out of the bed he hit her again, harder.

She could not think at all. She stayed curled on the bed at first, and then, when nothing else happened, she let the weakness come over her. She stayed there with the sheets rumpled around her and felt the burning on her face and a pain like a sharp singing inside her ear.

"Get some clothes on," she heard him say. "We got company." When she did not move immediately he snapped, "Get decent, you bitch!"

She sat up quickly, afraid he would hit her again. Dicky threw the bathrobe at her. It hit her in the face and wrapped itself halfway around her neck.

"Come on, come on—"

She put the robe on as fast as she could and when she had it tied securely Dicky went to the door and said, "It's all right now. You can come in."

Mac came in. He nodded at her but he didn't really look at her. He let his eyes wander along the walls and the floor.

"Get something going on that hotplate," said Dicky. "I been driving all night."

"Coffee?"

"What else, lamebrain?"

The two men sat down at the table while Letty started the coffee. They lit cigarettes and Mac said they really made time coming in and Dicky said yes, and wait till I put in that new carburetor but what he'd like to do best of all was to get one of those special transmissions, like the kind they had been talking about. Then he turned in his chair and watched Letty. She could feel his stare on her back.

"Come here, bitch," he said.

Letty turned around. She did not look sleepy and her eyes were much smaller than usual.

"Dicky, I don't want—"

"Shut up!" he said very loudly. "I'm talking, and you listen. Didn't think I'd be back this soon, did you? And as soon as I turn my back you think you can play the field?" His voice rose on a moral note. "I dress you up! I feed you to keep you in shape! I put a roof over your head and a bed under your rear and all you ever give back is what you give out for free anyway! I don't buy that, lamebrain! I don't go for that one little bit—" He gasped, almost choking himself. "And on top of that with a son of a bitch like Port! The first day I'm out of town shacking up with that—"

"Dicky!"

"I'm talking!"

"Dicky! You're wrong. I didn't do any such thing. What I was doing—"

"You calling my friend here a liar?" Dicky was out of his chair.

Letty stared at Mac. She didn't know what to say. Mac looked back at her, his face hurt yet mild, and Letty could think of nothing to say.

"The water's boiling. Let's have that coffee," Dicky grunted.

"Dicky. Will you listen to me, please?"

He got off his chair again and stepped very close to her.

"You want me to mark you up? For real?"

Her face got very still. "I'm leaving," she said.

"The hell you're leaving."

"Let go my arm, Dicky."

"Mac," Dicky said over his shoulder. "Shall I mark her up?"

"Naw. Don't mark her up." Mac looked at his cigarette.

"You still leaving?" Dicky asked her.

She did not answer.

"You wanna go join that Port bastard somewheres?"

She looked stubborn.

"You wanna tell me where he went?"

His grip on her arm became more and more painful.

"He's coming back," said Mac. "She said so the first time."

"Shut up, Mac." Dicky put his face close to Letty's. "He coming back after you?"

"You're wasting time, Dicky," said Mac. "We got things to do. If he comes back."

"Yeah." Dicky let go of her arm. "Get that coffee going."

"I'm leaving," she said.

"You stay till I tell you different," said Dicky. He gave her a violent shove that sent her flying back and over the bed. The shock showed in her face and she didn't try to get up. She lay there and made no sound.

"To hell with the coffee," said Dicky. He turned off the heat under the pot and went to the closet. "I'll be maybe two hours." He reached for a suit.

"You'll be?" said Mac. "You going alone?"

"This thing needs the right clothes," said Dicky. "Look-it you, with that rainbow shirt and the jacket."

Dicky shook out the suit he had in his hand and then started to change his clothes.

"What time, Mac?"

"Just past seven."

"Crap. I can't get in there till eight."

"Better go early just the same. Maybe you can figure more than one way."

"Sure," said Dicky. He was pulling his pants on. "Two, three hours," he said. "I'll meet you here."

Mac nodded and looked at the tip of his cigarette.

"I don't want her to leave," said Dicky and jerked his head at the bed.

"Sure," said Mac.

Letty sat up on the bed. Her eyes were wide and she wanted to say something.

"Shut up and keep still," said Dicky. "Or I'll mark you up."

"Don't mark her up," said Mac.

Letty sat where she was. Her hair slid down over the side of her face and she reached up to push it back. Dicky slammed the door shut behind him. She bent her head which made her hair slide down again.

Then she saw Mac's feet by the bed. She left her hair down the way it had fallen.

Chapter 16

There was a fan over the long desk, and each time the fan swung through its cycle it blew a draft of medicinal odors over Port's face. The smell irritated him but if he moved he would lose his place in the line and if he had to stay there much longer he would be ready to insult the receptionist, once the old

woman came his way. She was busy with forms, nodding and chatting with
the man who sat in the visitor's chair by her desk.

"Maybe I'll drop to the floor and have a fit," said someone in the line behind Port. "Maybe then I'll get some attention."

"Don't kid yourself," said someone else. "In this clinic you got to be dead
to get service."

"If you tell 'em you died, maybe."

"That old woman there, she's still here. And she's dead."

The old woman behind the reception desk finished with the visitor and
swiveled around to look at the line. It pleased her to see such activity and
to know that it was all coming her way. When she saw Port she smiled, because to remember a customer gave her a special pleasure.

"Mr. Port, wasn't it? From the parole board, isn't that right?" She reached
for the pad she used for the passes.

She asked Port whom he was going to see, and Port told her the name and
the floor and the ward. He got his pass, he got past the floor nurse, and he
left his slip on the table at the door of the ward. The nurse who usually sat
there was busy distributing pills.

It would not be easy to tell Dalton about Eve Simmon, but Port went down
the length of the ward fast, because he had been away so long.

Dalton did not have the tubes going into his arm and his nose, and when
Port got to the side of the bed he saw that the man asleep in the bed was
not Abe Dalton.

Port bit his lip. He went back to the door, almost running, to speak to the
nurse who was back at her desk now.

"Dalton? Abraham Dalton?" She checked in her book. She looked up once
to give Port a stern glance because he had started to whistle.

"He's not here," she said.

"I know that. I want to know where he is!"

"Would you mind keeping your voice—"

"Don't try humoring me, lady. Look it up. What happened to Dalton!"

She had to look in another book and, being offended, was awkward about
it.

"Dalton! D-a-l-t—"

"Oh, him," she said. "Yes, he's been discharged."

"Discharged? He walked out of here?"

"We don't call it *discharged* when they're deceased," said the nurse huffily.

For a moment Port let the relief sweep through him and he could feel the
tension go out of his muscles. The nurse was talking again.

"There was some question about the matter, but there's nothing we can do in a case like that."

"What? What case?"

"The patient leaving. The resident had to sign him out but warned him, of course, to get back into bed. And to consult a physician."

'You let him go? Didn't he—"

"He paid his bill," said the nurse. "The young man paid the bill."

Port held very still for a moment. He wet his lips and said slowly, "This young man. Sort of short, muscular type? Black hair with a wave in it?"

"You know him?"

Port left without another word. He had made the mistake of leaving Dalton alone, the mistake of chasing after Eve Simmon, and the mistake of treating Corday like a human being.

He took a cab to Dalton's place. The landlady said Dalton hadn't been in for almost a week, and his rent was due. Port gave her two weeks' rent and left. He took another cab to Dicky's hotel, sitting with his arms on the driver's back rest staring out of the window. He didn't say a word.

"Look," the cabby said. "I can't go any faster—"

"I didn't ask you to. Just drive."

The cabby didn't say anything more. He could feel his customer's mood. It was a mood that hung over his shoulder like a gun with the hair trigger cocked.

"Here it is," said the cabby. "Here's the hotel." The cab rolled up to the curb. The back door to the cab was half open already.

"One-twenty-five," said the cabby but Port had a bill out by then and let it fall on the driver's seat.

"Count it later," he said and was gone.

He went past the desk and the clerk looked up, opened his mouth, and shut it again. At the door to Dicky's room Port knocked once and walked in.

There were clothes strewn over a chair, two cups and a jar of coffee on the table. The cups were clean.

It was late afternoon. Letty was still in bed.

"Letty—you awake?"

She turned her head toward him but the rest of her stayed toward the wall.

"Letty! Snap out of it."

The bed sheet was twisted around one of her legs and the blanket was mostly bunched over her hips. She was wearing a nightgown.

"Come on, girl. Whatever it was, it's over. Up with you." Port gave her a boost by one arm.

She wasn't drunk, Port saw, and she wasn't tired, but she was down to a key where nothing could trouble her much.

"Was Dicky here? Letty!"

"He's gone."

"Was Dalton with him? Letty, answer me!"

She let herself drop back onto the bed and turned to the wall. She mumbled something but Port didn't catch it. He tried again but she wouldn't answer. She shook his hand off her shoulder when he tried to turn her around. He decided to give her a chance to recover from whatever it had been.

"Letty, get up now, come on, girl." He helped her up again, but this time he held her arm and led her across the room. "Now you go in there and take a shower. I'll turn it on for you. You like it hot? Medium? Never mind, I'll set it the way it should be." He adjusted the taps and arranged the curtain so that the water wouldn't spray out. "Now get in there and—Christ, take that shirt off first. All right, take your shower, then get dressed, and meanwhile I'll make you some coffee. All right?"

She nodded and started to pull off her nightgown before Port was out of the door.

He boiled the water that was on the hotplate and smoked a cigarette while he waited. The shower went off in the bathroom and Letty stuck her head out of the door. She was still wet.

"Will you hand me my clothes?" she said. "On the closet door. Inside."

Port gave her the clothes and then waited some more, pacing back and forth, whistling low, and tonelessly.

She came into the room, dressed, with a towel wrapped around her wet hair. A hank of it showed over the green towel, and Port noticed how blonde her hair could look.

"Here's yours," said Port and handed her a cup of hot water mixed with instant coffee. He fixed his own, sat down and said, "You act as if Dicky ran out on you."

"I don't like him any more." Her tone was flat.

"The same," said Port. He was bent over, sipping coffee, so he didn't see the look she gave him. When he lifted his head she was looking elsewhere.

"You think so?" she said.

She had been hurt, Port thought. She looked very quiet. She didn't seem to care very much, and Port felt he would have to go slowly. She might help, but he would have to watch her.

"Where is Dicky?" Port asked.

"He left. He went to Newton."

The long trip to Otter Bend, the careful handling of Eve Simmon, the waiting for Letty—that was over now.

"Where is Abe Dalton?"

"He went—Dicky took him along."

"To do a job?"

"Yes."

"When?"

"Soon. I don't know when."

"How sick was Dalton? Did he walk, eat—"

"He wasn't here long. He didn't look good, but he got around."

"He's going to be in on that job in person?"

"Dicky said yes, and Dalton didn't argue long. He just said to wait two more days—two anyway—so he'd have his strength back."

"And Dicky said?"

"He said okay. He had to say okay. Dalton made that very clear. Dalton can get that way, I guess. Besides, he was so weak they could see it."

"Corday and Dalton are going, to pull this alone?"

"And two more. Mac and Loony."

"Mac? You know this Mac?"

"Yes," she said. "I know this Mac."

"He does what?"

"I don't know. Wheel man, I think."

"And Loony? That's the machinist guy, isn't he?"

"Loony's there now. Dicky left him there."

"You know what he does?"

"I don't know. He's got himself hired at the plant and he's working there. That's why Dicky and him went there in the first place. To find out more things about everything there."

"And they left when—with Dalton, I mean?"

"Today. Before noon."

"Today," said Port. "Today is Monday. The money is there on Thursday night."

Port looked down at his cup. Then he clinked his fingernail against the side of the cup. "Monday, Tuesday, Wednesday," he said. "Monday, Tuesday, Wednesday."

Letty got up and brought back the pot of water. She put more coffee powder in both of the cups and then poured water over it. Port was still clinking his fingernail against the rim of his cup and as the water ran into the cup the sound changed, getting flatter and harder. Then he got up and went to the window.

It was getting dark outside and the hotel sign had come on, going blink,

blink, blink.

"Letty." Port turned and looked at her. "You going to help?"

She shrugged. "I tried helping you once before."

"What happened wasn't your fault."

"I know. That's what I mean."

Port came back to the table and stood beside Letty. He understood that she meant something other than not having helped enough with the information she had gotten at the pool room.

"What, Letty? Tell me."

Her face got sullen and she turned her head so that he could not see it. He put his hand on her shoulder and said, "What, Letty."

"I'm disappointed," she said.

Port did not ask any more. She had told him what was important.

Then Port walked around so he could see her. He said, "If this works, Letty, what happened to you needn't happen again."

He wanted to say something else but she didn't let him finish.

"I'll help you," she said. "What is it?"

He pulled his chair close to hers and then talked. It was clear and very impersonal.

"You have any money?"

"No."

He gave her money.

"You know where Dalton lives?"

"No."

"I'll take you there later. I want you out of here."

She nodded.

"I want you to stay there for twenty-four hours. There's a phone in the hall outside his room. I'll need to call you."

She nodded.

"You want to know what I'm going to do?"

"No."

"You don't care about Dicky?"

"I don't care."

"Just as well."

They left and Port took her to Dalton's room. Since Port had just paid the landlady her rent the landlady didn't care, so Letty took over the room without any trouble. Port left immediately.

It was now eight in the evening, and he did not have much time.

Chapter 17

Port called a man whom he had never met, but that didn't matter too much. They both knew of each other. Port reached the man at his home, a legitimate home with a listed number, because most men like him had legitimate fronts. The conversation was short.

"I'm Port. Daniel Port. I'm in town and I need some advice."

"Who did you say? You're who?"

"Stop horsing around. You know I'm in town."

"I know Port's in town. We keep track."

"What I need—"

"How do I know you're him?"

"Because I know you."

"So do the cops."

"Do they know you put Gassman in office? Do they know you're up to your neck in a thing with the liquor commission—"

"Shut up! Christ, shut up on the phone!"

"So who am I?"

"All right, so you're Port. Christ, you sound like him. Nobody else would have the gall to—"

"Here's what I need."

"Listen, if you're gonna stir up—"

"It's nothing. You're just the only one I know of in town, and I need a small hand."

"What? If this is—"

"Shut up and listen, all right?"

"All right."

"I've got to see a pawnbroker big enough to carry some value. Not a fence, a legitimate pawnbroker. But he's got to be willing to play some ball."

"How you gonna find a legitimate anything that's—"

"What's the matter with you in this town? Haven't you got a man that looks clean but you know about him?"

"That's all you want? A pawnbroker like that?"

"Who?"

"Schneider on Ninth. Corner Ninth and Commercial."

"Call him and tell him I'm coming. And tell him to hear me out."

"All right. If that's all."

"One more thing. You know anybody on the local paper?"

"Sure. Who?"

"Somebody who'll do you a favor about what to print and how big."

"Listen, Port. This paper we got here in town is clean almost all the way through. This town's proud to have—"

"Stop it, stop it. I'll get sick. All I want is a boost on some news. Local news. Can you get it some space?"

"If it's got anything to do with cleaning up this town, I can maybe get the night desk to shuffle the space. Anything to do with cleaning up—"

"You said that. I'll have Schneider call you back. He'll tell you when it's time to plug the news."

"What news?"

"Schneider will tell you."

"If that's all—"

"That's all. No strain, was it? So long."

"Hey! Wait—"

"What?"

"You leaving town, Port?"

"You're so big you don't know?" Port hung up in the middle of the other man's cursing.

He took a taxi to Ninth and Commercial and walked into Schneider's just before closing time.

For a pawnshop Schneider's place had a look of elegance. Bright lights made the choice pieces of jewelry sparkle in the long glass cases, and the cabinets with musical instruments on the right and optical instruments on the left were arranged neatly and with an eye for display. Nothing was crowded and there was no junk. Port ignored the two salesmen and walked to the cage in back. There was a small, worried man sitting there.

"Are you Schneider?" said Port.

"Yes. But we're closing. If you want—"

"I'm Daniel Port. You're expecting me."

The small man looked even more worried and ran his hand over his bald skull. "Yes, yes," he said without looking up. "This way, please. There's a table. We can sit at this table—"

Port came around to the back where Schneider had a place fixed up for making loan applications. Schneider was at the desk already, but Port didn't sit down.

"Let me look around first."

"Around? You mean here?" Schneider ran his hand over his skull again. "Just to look around."

He looked around, and then he sat down at the table and he and Schneider had a detailed talk. It lasted until after closing, and when Port left he did so by the back door.

It was ten now. Port had a drink at a bar, looked in on Letty, saw that she was fine, went to Dicky's hotel and left there in a very short time. He killed time until twelve, and in one of the neighborhood bars he made a point of finding out what Loony's real name was. Then he checked once more with the man whom he knew in this town. After that Port went to sleep.

He left town very early in the morning in a rented car. There were street-cleaning machines making rounds through the empty city, and milkmen and paper boys. At a corner where the light was red, Port bought the morning edition from a boy. He glanced at the first page and at the second but when the light changed he took off immediately. Further out he bought a bottle of milk from a wagon because he had not found any restaurants open. Once on the highway he drove very fast. He took the cap off the bottle and drank some milk. It was very cold and without taste. He drank some more and then let the bottle fly into a ditch. He rolled up the window again. He was smiling. He was smiling about something else.

Chapter 18

Newton was a small town with pretensions toward a kind of cozy age. There were store fronts with casement windows and leaded windows, and trim fences outside the houses. Almost everybody belonged to the big happy fake family that worked for the Newton Tool and Die Works.

The plant was out at the edge of town, home-owned, home-managed, and home-staffed. The gate was built like a bastion, though the plant wasn't very old—or was the Newton family. There was a statue on the town square, not of the usual Civil War soldier but of Sherman Newton, who was still alive and running his plant.

The plant had no gatehouse. You could walk into the yard without being stopped. There were no signs saying admittance to personnel only and there were no numbers on the various buildings. The one visible sign said Enter. Port entered, looking for the employment office where they could tell him how to find Kostanovitch, which was Loony's last name.

Port walked into a long room with a ramp. On one side of the ramp were three time clocks, and on the other side was an old lady, wearing celluloid cuffs buttoned over her wrists.

"May I help you, sir?" She sounded nice and old-fashioned.

"I'm looking for the employment office," said Port.

"I'm the employment office." Then her face turned almost sad. "But it's almost five, sir. Wouldn't you like to come back tomorrow?"

"This won't take long. All I want to ask—"

"It's almost five, sir," she said again, but this time with an old-fashioned chiding sound.

"I know, but all—"

She smiled sadly and walked away from the ramp as if she didn't see anyone there. She went to her desk and started to dust.

Port sucked in his breath and held it for a moment.

It made a sound when he let out his breath and the old lady looked at him, but Port wasn't looking at her. Behind the casement windows lined with cute figurines converted into ivy plants Port saw the parking lot and the car. Dicky Corday had had the rear end lowered, the bumper moved back to make room for a spare, and lights, reflectors, and antennae added. Dalton could not be too well, or he wouldn't have let Corday show that car on the streets.

It was almost five, and the workers would be emerging at any moment. Port left without another word. At the door he heard the old lady call, "See you tomorrow—" as if they had a date.

Port sat in his car outside the gate. When the rush started, Port didn't worry about missing the car because there was only one like it in Newton. The car came out and headed for an across-the-tracks part of the town. It stopped in front of a three-story house with a patchy lawn in front. The house wasn't old-fashioned, it was just old. A man, big and blond, got out of the car, carrying a lunch bucket under his arm. That was Loony, Port thought. Loony lived here, and maybe the rest of them, too.

Port sat and smoked for a while. It was getting dark and nobody came in or out of the house. Port flipped his cigarette out onto the street but sat for a while longer. His hands were on the wheel and his thumbs rubbed slowly back and forth. He made a slow, breathy whistle in the same rhythm.

Finally Port stopped whistling. It was very dark and very quiet inside the car. There was a small click when he opened the glove compartment but no sound at all when he dropped the revolver into his pocket. Then he went into the house.

Dicky would be the kind to take a room way up on top. It would feel out of the way to him and much safer. Dalton would take a room on the bottom. It would attract no more or no less attention and it would be easier to get out fast.

Port tried the downstairs first.

The landlady's apartment had a sign on the door—*Day, Week, or Month. No Pets or Children.* The door next to it was open, but there wasn't even any furniture inside the room. Port roamed down the hall until he saw a door in front of which were six empty milk bottles. Port almost knocked one of them over. No pets or children, and six bottles of milk? Port listened at the door and he heard, "... so then I put the screw end in the turntable and...."

"Loony, please! I don't give a damn if you turned a screw or screwed a tern."

"That boy loves his work," said somebody else. "Always jamming about screws, grinders, Bridgeports."

"Bridgeports," said Loony. "That's a machine what—"

"I'm telling you, this keeps up and you can stay on that job. We get done here you can stay in this Newton burg and work permanent!"

"I may do that! I may just do that," said Loony. "It's a good job. And very—sort of—old-fashioned, you could call it. I might just—"

"All right!"

That was Dicky Corday. And then there was Loony and somebody else. Mac, the one Letty didn't seem to like.

If Dalton were there, he wasn't talking. Perhaps he was too sick.

Port turned the door handle and entered the room almost in one movement. He closed the door behind him so quietly that the men in the room had barely focused on him.

"All around," said Port. "Sit still."

Dicky jumped up and then stopped because Port was showing the gun. The little black hole looked steady and large to Dicky. For a moment they all stared at the gun in Port's hand, staring and letting his presence sink in.

Port saw Dalton standing at the far end of the room. The old man had been stirring something in a pot. He didn't seem to know what to do with his spoon.

"Don't let it burn," said Port. He was grinning. Then he turned back to the others because they were coming to life.

"I came for two things. Abe Dalton, and Abe Dalton's notes."

"Whatcha gonna do?" said Mac. "Shoot everybody?"

"Shut up," said Dicky.

"No, I mean it," Mac said. "You got an idea this is some kinda Western?"

"Listen to Corday," said Port. He didn't like Mac, and it showed. "Listen to him and this'll be short." His voice was quiet. "I can make this long, if you want."

Mac looked at Loony without turning his head. "Rush him!" he said suddenly.

Loony didn't move. He stood near the table, the lunch bucket still in his hands. He didn't know what to do with it. Then he said, "Can I sit down?"

Port nodded and watched Loony sit down.

"Loony—" Mac started again.

"You running this?" Port looked at Dicky.

"Dicky," said Mac, and his voice sounded almost uninterested. "Ain't he the one who took over your dame?"

The needle worked.

"Let's see you ain't bluffing," said Dicky. He was sweating, and a slow flush crept under his skin. "You think you're so hot—"

"He's bluffing," said Mac. "I can tell. Here!" He moved quickly, as if reaching for something to throw at Port. Port only moved the gun in a small arc. He moved his mouth too, and Mac got the impression that Port was going to whistle. Mac got confused. He had to do something else.

"A slow one, ain'tcha?" He laughed. "Speaking of slow, has Letty—"

He let it drop when he saw Port begin to move. Port walked toward Mac. "You're bluffing—" said Mac.

Port came closer. Mac was unable to laugh, but he managed a grin. He held the grin and tried outstaring Port. He still had his eyes wide open when the gunsight cut through his nose.

First he trembled and then he fell to the floor. He lay there holding his face and breathing in sharp gusts.

"I'm sick of that guy," said Port. "I get sick enough, Corday, and I do worse!"

But Dicky hardly heard. His rage burst out, raw and ugly.

"You son of a bitch—you stinking son of a bitch! I'm gonna get you if it takes from now till hell! I hate your guts worse than anyone that ever crossed me up and nobody crosses me up, nobody's gonna keep—"

"Stop dreaming and listen."

"I'll get you! I'll frame you up and then I'll step on you! You think squeezing Dalton was something? You think squeezing Dalton was the best can be done? Lemme tell you what's gonna—"

"Here!" Port reached into his pocket and pulled out a newspaper. He tossed it on the table where Dicky could reach it. "Here, Corday. Lemme show you how it's done!"

Dicky stopped shouting.

"Read it," said Port. "The column on the right about routine crime and routine pursuit."

It meant nothing to Dicky but it held his attention. He picked up the paper.

"First and second paragraph is all you need. The rest is just the same thing all over." Port's gun tapped the column. "Read." The last tap was sharp and tore the paper, and then the gun pointed at Dicky again. Dicky read:

Our police, like any large institutional body, need the occasional bite of public criticism. This column is meant to furnish that bite.

"Keep reading," said Port.

Maybe it's routine for a thief to make a living off the efforts of others—that's his crime. Does that justify the crime of routine on the part of a lethargic police force which contents itself with filing a complaint, stacking it away by hour and alphabet, and then—if the man can be spared—sending out a disinterested employee to see if the crime really occurred?

"Did you come to the part about Schneider?" said Port.
Dicky looked up, impatient. The prose made him feel stupid and he had lost interest.
"I know it's an effort," said Port. "But it may save your skin. Read."

Schneider's Pawnshop was robbed of five thousand dollars in cash and twenty-five thousand dollars in jewelry. Of course, it wasn't jewelry stolen from the home of a leading citizen—just from Schneider's pawnshop. Maybe that isn't enough of an incentive for the police to—

"You seen the part about Schneider?"
"Yeah," said Dicky. "I can read."
"What's it say?"
"He was robbed. Twenty-five grand hard and five cash."
"What else?"
"The cops are getting the needle."
"Don't bother reading the rest. They really get it by the time it's over."
"I'm worried," said Dicky. "I'm already shaking."
"The guy who pulled that heist is worried," Port said. "It's going to be as tough as if he stole the queen's garter."
"I'm shaking," said Dicky.
"You should. That fall guy is you!"
Dalton had long since stopped stirring his pot. He was now standing near Mac, who was still lying on the floor, curled into a ball. At Port's last words there was such a deep silence in the room that Mac turned slowly to look up. No one moved and no one made sound.
The tableau held for a long moment. Then Dicky Corday started to laugh,

loudly and violently, until he was winded and had to stop. "Sucker bluff,"
he kept saying. "Sucker bluff—" He was hoarse now.

Port put the gun back into his pocket and said, "It's in your apartment."

"Huh?"

"The loot from the Schneider robbery. It's in your apartment. Robbery. I
hear you've been up for the same thing once before. You know what the second offense carries in this state?"

Dicky stared at Port and turned pale.

"I guess you know," said Port. "So help me, Corday, I'll nail it on you. I made
that frame so it won't come apart. It's over you, solid."

"No—"

"Yes. Unless you want to give me Dalton's notes." Then Port shrugged.
"They wouldn't help you any after ten or twenty years in jail. How old are
you now, in your thirties? When you get out you'll be just a little younger
than Dalton, you know that?"

Dicky looked at Dalton and so did everyone else. Mac was sitting up on
the floor, his hands cupped over his face. He looked up over his hands at Dalton. The old man turned away then, and went to the stove.

"All right, Corday. Make up your mind," Port said.

"How do I know—"

"You don't—if you want to end up in stir."

"How do I know you—you'll trade even? The frame I got on Dalton for
the frame you got on me?"

"You got a phone?" Port asked.

"There's one at the end of the hall," said Loony.

Port took the gun out of his pocket and nodded at Dalton. "Hold this. Loony
can sit at the table and Mac should stay on the floor."

"All right," said Dalton, and took the gun.

Corday and Port went to the end of the hall.

"You got any silver?" asked Port.

Dicky was too nervous to argue now. He handed Port some change and
Port dialed long distance.

Corday began to suck his teeth. Then he shifted his weight from one foot
to the other, looked at the cracks in the wall, and avoided turning in Port's
direction. His brain was going frantically, but it solved nothing for him and
made him feel tired.

"Corday."

He turned almost with a jerk, and saw Port with the phone to his ear. "Better listen to this," said Port and then he spoke into the phone. "This is Daniel
Port," he said to Letty. "Can you hear me?"

She could hear him and Port went on, without using her name. Dicky heard only what Port was saying.

"Now listen close. Last night there was a robbery in town. Schneider's pawnshop. Yes, the one that got written up. Listen. The loot from the robbery is in Dicky Corday's hotel room. No. Leave it there. It's behind the small access door to the plumbing, that little door in the bathroom next to the sink. You know where I mean? Right. Now, here's what you do." Port looked at his watch. "What time do you have? Right, good enough. Here's what you do. If I don't call you back within fifteen minutes—fifteen minutes—you phone the police and tell them where they can find the loot from the Schneider robbery. Clear? You got it. Yes. Sure looks like it, doesn't it. All right now, you wait fifteen minutes. If I don't call, Corday is it." Port hung up.

He looked at Corday and said, "Made up your mind?"

Chapter 19

There were only twelve minutes left and it showed on everyone. Port had stayed by the door, because that way he could get to the phone more quickly. Dalton was standing next to him. He was still holding the gun, making small, nervous arcs with it from Loony to Dicky, to Mac and then back to Loony again. Dalton did not want anything to go wrong. He wanted this to be over, to be able to lie down and to cover himself with a warm blanket.

Loony still sat at the table. The perspiration on his forehead made his blond hair damp at the edges, staining it dark. He was worried about Dicky. He was worried that Dicky might be crazy and do something wrong.

Mac had pushed himself up onto the couch. His breathing was careful and noisy. His nose was swollen and tight and crusted with dried blood. He blinked his eyes as if they were too dry or as if he had something in them.

"Ten minutes, Corday."

Port watched Dicky standing there where the four men could see him. Dicky seemed to be dying with indecision.

"Eight minutes," said Port. "And remember the four minutes it takes for the call. You now have less than five."

"Dicky," said Dalton. "Better give him the paper. He'll go through with it otherwise."

Finally Dicky spoke. He seemed to be almost pleading.

"How do I know? You keep saying he'll do this, he'll do that—how do I know the whole thing isn't—"

"Dan isn't that way," Dalton said. "That's all. I know him."

"You know him, you know him! How do I know—"

"I wouldn't deal with him," Dalton said, "if he were different."

Dicky knew one thing at least; that Dalton had always been straight. In Dalton's life there had always been that one island of honesty. It made his word good and it made him different from others who lived the way he had.

"You say so?" Dicky said.

"Don't you know me?" Dalton was no longer holding the gun on the room.

"A bargain's a bargain," said Dicky. "You say so."

"It's my word," said Dalton. Everyone knew it was so.

"Two minutes, and I phone." Port opened the door. He stood that way, holding the door, and watched Dicky Corday move fast now. Dicky pulled off his right shoe. He put it on top of the table and fumbled inside it until he had the thin leather out of the sole. He reached into the toe, pressing his hand into the shoe, and held up the folded papers. He looked as if he had been running.

"Put them on the table and open them up."

Dicky did that.

"Abe, take a look."

Dalton went to the table and looked at the papers. "They're all here."

"Take them," said Port. "Corday?"

Dicky looked up, waiting. He was no longer trying to think. It would make no difference.

"You and me make a phone call."

Dicky and Port left the room and Port placed the call. Dicky was not nervous any more. He felt dull. He saw Port look at his watch while he held the phone, waiting.

"What time?" said Dicky.

"Time's up. Now."

Dicky saw Port purse his mouth, as if he were whistling. He was still holding the phone to his ear. Dicky felt the skin draw up on his scalp. He wanted to say something but he was afraid.

He saw that Port was frowning.

"Line's busy," said Port.

Chapter 20

The three men in the room never knew what had happened out in the hall; that Port had had to grab Dicky by the throat to keep him from screaming, that he had pressed him against the wall until Dicky had calmed down enough to listen to Port and to wait. Port had called again and this time there had been an answer. Port hadn't said much, just, "Where were you?" and "I know it was busy. All right. Never mind." Then he spoke the words that Dicky wanted to hear: "The deal's off. Don't call the police."

What the three men in the room saw was Port who looked at Dalton and smiled. "All right, Abe," he said. "Burn it." Dicky said nothing. What they didn't see was how Dicky felt, that he was alive again, hating Port and Dalton as he had never hated anyone before.

Dalton burned the notes on the stove and Dicky packed his bag. Mac didn't have one. He stood waiting for Dicky to finish. Loony sat at the table as before.

"I think I'll stay," he said. "I got an idea this job I got here—"

He let it go when Mac gave him a look. Mac's eyes were slitted from the swelling and his face was ugly. Then Dicky snapped the bag shut and straightened up.

"One more thing," he said to Port. "What about that loot?"

"I'll pick it up before you get there."

"And give it back?"

"How else do you think the cops are going to stop looking for it?" said Port.

Dicky shrugged, then jerked his head at Loony and Mac. Loony said again, "I think I'm staying," and watched Dicky anxiously, but there was no argument. Dicky didn't even look at Loony. He said, "Come on, Mac," and then went through the door. Mac went with him.

The room looked as if nothing had happened there. There was a man at the table who had just come from work, and a pot with a spoon on the stove, something left over from somebody's meal.

Port took Dalton's arm and led him out of the door. He nodded at Loony and Loony nodded back. Loony sat a while longer, until he heard the car pull away down the street. Then he ate what the old man had been cooking.

"I'll drive through the night," said Port. He watched the curve in the highway and waited until he hit the straight stretch again. "That way you can go back to the hospital in the morning."

"No," said Dalton. "Not there." He rested his head on the back of the seat and breathed slowly and carefully. "I'll go home now," he said. "Thank you, Port."

It was the only time Dalton had thanked Port, and it was enough.

Port said, "You think you're well enough?"

"It feels fair," said Dalton. "I can make it home." He paused. Then he said, "I had a letter from my nephew there, when I was still in jail. He says that they have a hospital now, new since I was there last."

"How long will you have to stay in it?"

"Maybe not at all. Maybe it'll heal at home."

"But you'll need a doctor, won't you?"

"I'll have a doctor. But I think it'll heal fine, when I get home."

"Yes," said Port and then they drove without talking. Dalton was sitting up with one arm on the back of the seat, and he saw the lights first.

"A car's coming," he said.

Port looked in the mirror and nodded. "Yeah, I see it."

Dalton kept watching it. "It's coming very fast," he said. "Notice how fast."

Port looked in the mirror again.

"There are lots of cars faster than this one."

"And the lights," said Dalton. "He's got five lights in front."

Port said, "You mean Dicky Corday?"

"If he gets back to town first, I don't know—"

"You're worried he'll go for the loot I put in his room? Don't."

"Why? You don't have to bring it back? You paid for it?"

"No. I've got to return it, or pay for it."

The car had drawn close now.

"Can you tell?" asked Dalton.

The car behind swung into the passing lane and pulled away at a fast clip. The rear end seemed to be scooting along the ground and the two antennae in back weaved and dipped.

"That was Corday," said Port.

They watched the car move away fast. It had a bank of red and blue lights in the back. They got dimmer and then disappeared altogether.

"I don't want you to have any more trouble," said Dalton. "I wish you could get to town before he does."

"Look, Abe, he'd be a fool to go near that stuff. The way it's set up, the last place Dicky would want to go is his hotel room."

"And if he does?"

"They'll find him. He'll have walked into the frame of his own free will." Port looked at his watch. They had more than four hours to go. "I know he's crazy. But not that crazy."

It did not seem to concern Port and Dalton tried not to worry about it. After a while he slept....

They reached town at eight in the morning, and when the car stopped at Dalton's place Port explained to him about Letty, how she had helped and that she was using his room. Dalton said that that was all right, and he wished he could do something for the girl, now that it was over. She could keep the room, if she wanted to, and he would pay her a month's rent, because as for himself he was leaving now. He knew the train schedule by heart, and he could catch his train at noon. Dalton showed Port his ticket and when he put it back into his pocket and got out of the car, Port saw that the old man was smiling. He had not smiled since leaving the hospital.

The room was clean and Letty had made the bed. There was nothing lying around. Letty was gone.

Dalton sat down on the bed and unbuttoned his coat.

"I thought you said the girl was here."

"Yes. I thought so."

Dalton took his ticket out of his pocket and put it on the table next to his bed. Then he took off his coat and his shoes.

"She left nothing here?"

Port shook his head. He was walking around the room. He stopped at the window and looked out.

"I would like to offer her—as I said— If she wants this room—"

"Fine," said Port, and came back to the bed. "Maybe I'll see her. If I do I'll give her your message." He pulled a blanket back on the bed and motioned to Dalton. "You lie down now. Get some sleep, and I'll wake you when I come back."

Dalton lay back. He stretched out and looked up at the ceiling. He was smiling again.

"I won't see it much longer, the crack up there. You know, when I took this place after coming out, this room and the things here—the crack, the window with the rattle in it—all that looked so good to me. After ten years." He folded his hands on his stomach and looked at Port. "And now I'm leaving." He laughed shortly. "I'm just going to lie here now, Dan, and feel sentimental. You know? I can lie here and afford to feel sentimental." He laughed again and watched Port go to the door.

"I'm picking up the stuff from Corday's place. I'll drive you to the station when I come back."

Dalton had closed his eyes. He just nodded. When Port was halfway through the door he called after him, "And if you see that girl, tell her—"

Port left. When he got into his car he was whistling. He looked at his watch, started the car, and made a sharp U-turn.

The pickup wouldn't take long, less than an hour. Port drove, whistling tunelessly.

He wondered where Letty was. He wished he knew her better and did not have to wonder about her. On the way to Dicky's hotel he passed the Off-Time, where Dicky had cornered him in the alley. The big building was closed now.

He wondered where Letty was.

Past the next corner he remembered the other place, Nick's Palace or something, and the woman with the old face who liked nothing better than dancing, and who knew everybody. Nick's Palace was right, because Port could see it now. The neon sign was on. From here to the hotel it took about five minutes' driving. Perhaps the woman who knew everybody was in the bar. Perhaps she knew where Letty was.

Port stopped the car in front of the bar. If he did not find the woman here it would not make any difference, one way or the other. The hotel was down the next street. He would go there next.

At the hotel, Dicky Corday told Mac to stand by the door to the hall and he himself had gone into the bathroom. He knelt on the floor next to the sink, but he could not get the plumbing door open. Mac could hear him rattling the wood and cursing. Mac stood by the door with nothing to do, waiting and listening to Dicky in the bathroom. Mac's face hurt worse than ever now, and sounds set his teeth on edge. He could hear every footstep down on the street and a car coming by, or stopping, made him jump.

"Dicky. Hey. You getting anywhere?"

There was no answer, just the scraping behind the closed door and Dicky's cursing, low and intense. Mac looked out along the corridor and then he closed the door. There had been nothing out there and the waiting was getting him. He went to the bathroom and looked in. It made Dicky jerk around suddenly so that he hit his head on the edge of the sink.

"Don't get so jumpy," said Mac. He was whispering. He kept saying this while Dicky swore at him and until Dicky turned back to the small door.

"Aren't you done yet?" said Mac, leaning closer.

"Get back to the door." Dicky didn't look up. He was whispering like Mac and breathing hard from the effort of trying to pry at the door.

"There's a screw; don't you see the screw?"

"Shut up, willya?"

"Stop prying the edge there. Try—"

Dicky looked up. He thought he had never seen a face as ugly as Mac's. The two men glared at each other without saying a word. Then Corday turned away abruptly. There was no time.

He had a knife in his hand, and he went on prying at the edge of the door.
"If we had a screwdriver—" said Mac.

"Get my coat. I mean get the gun in my coat. Over there on the chair."

Mac brought the gun, a short Smith and Wesson with a gunsight that looked like a big, stiff fin. Dicky took the gun and worked the sight into the screw.

"Does it give?"

Corday was grunting.

"Try the knife on that—"

"Shut up. It's coming." Slowly, with an effort that made both of them hold their breath, the screw gave in small fractions.

"Now try the knife. Maybe with the screw loose now—"

Dicky picked up the knife and tried that. "Get back to the door," he said.

Mac stayed. He was watching the screw come loose slowly. The crack in the small door showed black now, like a wedge. Dicky dropped the knife and squeezed his fingers into the crack. Then he strained.

"There's another one, another screw, here on the bottom."

"I'm breaking it out. Here, get your hands in there—"

They both pulled now. The effort agonized their faces.

"Watch it. Now—"

"Not that way. Here. Try here!" The wood gave with a sudden snap.

They both fell backward and Corday, in his scramble to get back to the hole, jabbed Mac's face with his elbow. He had not even known he had done it until he heard the groan. And then Mac hit him.

They fought in the small space between the bathtub and the sink. They fought silently, a grotesque straining without motion.

A door slammed, down the hall, and both men jerked apart.

They had not even seen the loot yet. They did not even know if it was there. Corday reached into the hole and felt the pipes. Mac had stood up. He wanted to run to the door but first he wanted to see the loot.

"Well? Come on!"

"Wait," said Dicky. "Wait." The word seemed to help him search. There were pipes, one big and one small, going off to one side. And a valve, it felt like a valve with a string holding a bag—a string holding a bag! Then....

Dicky yanked and the thing came out, a small bag which looked lumpy inside.

They both rushed into the room and over to the table. Corday said, "Check the door; lock the door," and Mac said, "Open it up, on the table. Open it—"

Corday tore the string to get at the inside.

First there was a wad of odd bills.

"What he say, five thousand? Man, look at that!"

And then a tangled pile of jewelry with the hard, expensive glitter of real gems.

"Twenty-five grand worth? Twenty-five grand worth is what?"

"What?"

"Under the counter!"

"Hell, I can take it to Wint and—"

"You nuts or something? That guy's a crook, nothing but a crook. We're taking the stuff to—"

"Polly. She's got a good outlet where—"

"And cut her in? Listen—"

"You trying to tell me—"

They both stopped at once, turned to the door at once, and knew at once what was coming. Mac got to the door. Dicky ran to the bathroom to get his gun. Mac wanted first crack at Port and was pulling a spring knife from his belt when the door made a sound. It looked as if Mac was drawing a gun. Dicky came back into the room, the gun held behind him so that Port wouldn't see it. His grin was big.

One cop was in mufti, the other one in uniform. Each held a gun.

It wasn't real to Dicky until the shot. The bullet hit Mac. Mac, with his hand on the knife looking as if he were drawing a gun, caught the slug full in the shoulder. He spun back into Dicky and with a last effort swung up the arm with the knife so that the cop shied and shot a second time.

The knife sliced Dicky under the ear as Mac fell. Not dead yet, Mac clawed at the man behind him.

They fell together, one dead the other one stiff with the fear in his bones.

"Got them both," said the cop in uniform.

"Jesus. I didn't think—"

"Look, here's the jewels and everything on the table."

"Jesus!" said the other one, and the voice was close to Dicky now. "I got both of them—"

"The chest. And the other one in the neck. He still bleeding?"

"Jesus!" said the near voice again and then the feet went toward the bathroom, where water started to run.

Dicky lay still. He felt his gun under him, pressing into his belly. If nobody moved them— Don't think. Just lie still and live, lie still and let the strength bunch up in a ball to get ready.

There was the sound of feet again for a moment. There was talk. "Get the rest—tell Jack to call in for an ambulance—" Then he heard just one pair of shoes making a slow creak near the window. Corday saw the heels. The toes were pointed toward the wall under the window.

They swiveled around very fast then, but Dicky shot the cop dead. Before the body fell Dicky was running.

Chapter 21

The whore recognized Port before he was sure it was she. He went to her booth when he saw her wave, and then he saw why he hadn't been sure. Her hair was tied back and she wasn't wearing any make-up.

"The dancing fool," she said and grinned at him. "You come to see me?"

"Yes," said Port.

It surprised her. She looked down at her beer and her hand went up to her hair.

"You know," she said, "at eight or nine in the morning I usually just don't do nothing at all. I usually only—"

"I just want to talk," said Port. "Buy you a beer?"

"Oh," she said. "No, thank you. You don't have to buy me a beer."

Port said he knew that and he was sorry if it had sounded wrong, but he would like her to have a fresh beer if she wanted one, because he was going to have one too. Then they both waited for their fresh beers and the whore saw that Port was nervous.

"You don't have to wait," she said. "Ask me."

The beers came. Port paid for them and said, "I'm looking for a friend of mine who—"

"Same one?"

"Huh?"

"Dicky Corday."

"No. Letty."

"You was looking for Letty last time I seen you."

"That's right," said Port. "I was. I'm looking for her again."

"That's real steady of you," said the woman. "It's been days." She was grinning at him when she said it, but she was not especially friendly—or helpful, thought Port.

"Then you know who I mean," he said. "Have you seen her around?"

"Off and on. Why?"

Port said, "I've seen her in the meantime, since I talked to you last. But I've been out of town and when I came back we missed each other."

"Oh. Yeah. I see what you mean." She took a long pull at her beer. "That little girl's got a lot of admirers."

It was too much talk with no results. Port moved in his seat and coughed. When he looked up at the woman he sounded different.

"Look," he said. "There may be trouble. That's why I'm looking for her."

"In that case," said the woman, "maybe Letty better not show."

"All right," said Port. "You know where she is and you don't want her harmed." He picked up his beer and drained it.

"Who are you?" said the woman.

Port put his glass down and said, "Daniel Port." He looked at his watch and made a move to get out of the booth.

"Oh," said the woman. "You're the one!"

Port looked at the woman.

She said, "So you're the one been cutting in on poor Dicky." She watched him after that. She saw he wasn't patient enough now to explain himself and that he wanted to leave.

"No. You got that wrong." He got up. "You say Letty's all right?"

The woman smiled and nodded. She motioned for Port to sit down again. "I know I had it wrong," she said. "If you weren't Port I think you would have said something else."

Port sat down again, because now the woman was going to talk. He was still anxious to leave but it wouldn't take long.

"You know," said the woman, "I told you once how I've known the girl for a long time. Used to know her mother." She lit a cigarette and talked through the smoke. "So naturally, when the girl don't feel good or something like that, she comes to me."

"I understand," said Port. "I'm glad she has somebody."

"Yes," said the woman. "And she's told me about you."

"She was supposed to be somewhere when I came back. So when she wasn't there—"

"She's with me. She'll be all right. When that little girl has troubles—"

"What happened?"

The woman looked at her beer. She shrugged. "Ever since she was a baby, she's always been stubborn. It comes over her, and when she don't want to talk she won't talk." She leaned over the table and pushed the beer out of the way. "She's in bed now, sleeping. She come over in the middle of the night, practically, and I can see she's upset. I try talking to her, asking her, and she starts crying. She cried a long time."

"I'm sorry she's so upset. I—"

"No, no. That's all right. If she can't talk about it, it's good if she can cry about it."

"I tell you," said Port. "I made her do a few things, I don't think she was used to anything like it."

"I know. She isn't. She told me that part."

"That part?"

"She didn't tell more. There is more, though," said the woman. "All I know is, she's afraid of Dicky now. I don't mean like before, I mean real afraid. And even of you."

"Me?" Port frowned. A hundred pieces of doubt came together and made one large fear in Port.

"She won't say what but it's something she done."

"Christ!" said Port. He got out of the booth and wanted to run. "Look, you keep that girl where she is, hear? Don't let her out till I tell you. Where do you live?"

The woman told him.

"And don't tell anyone else, understand?"

"I'll take care," said the woman and then Port was gone.

He did not get into the car. He saw that he would only get stuck further up because there was a crowd in front of the hotel. He ran down the street and saw the ambulance. It took off before Port got there and the police cars took off too and a lot of cops spread out the length of the street. Port reached the nearest policeman and then he got stopped.

"Who are you?"

Port told him.

"Identification?"

Port showed him.

"All right. Now keep walking," said the cop.

"One get away?" Port asked. It did not sound casual.

"Not for long." The cop started walking.

"Which one?"

"The son of a bitch that didn't get shot."

Dicky, or Mac.

It was close to ten. Better get Dalton. Better make sure about Letty and then take care of Dalton. His train did not leave till twelve.

Chapter 22

When Abe Dalton woke up he knew immediately where he was, for how much longer he would be here, and that the next bed he'd sleep in would be one at home. He smiled at the ceiling, where the crack was, and when he heard the steps in the hall he smiled at the door. He said, "Come in," before anyone had knocked, because he felt relaxed after his sleep. "The door's open, Dan," he said and watched for the handle to turn.

It snapped over, the door opened and shut, and Dicky Corday was in the room.

Dalton stared. He could not sit up for the moment. Dicky Corday leaned against the door. His breathing was labored. When Dalton sat up he saw blood down the side of Dicky's neck, dirt on his face, and dirt on his hands. Then Dicky came over to the bed and took Dalton by the front of the shirt. He pulled the old man up until he was very close. Then he spat in Dalton's face.

Dalton sat down on the bed. He did not wipe the spittle off his face until much later.

"The old bastard with the word as good as gold," Dicky said. "The filthy old son of a bitch learning the double-cross this late in life." Dicky stared at Dalton, hoping for one wrong move.

There was nothing but blank confusion in Dalton's face. Dicky sucked in his breath. "I walked into that frame! Cops, loot, and everything!"

"What?" Dalton was up.

"Didn't work, did it? Because I got away! And right now I'm here, so—"

"You mean—you mean Dan hadn't called the thing off?"

"There was cops waiting and cops chasing and Mac got shot in the head and you got the nerve to ask—"

"No! It's a mistake. Something went wrong—"

"You're damn right something went wrong. And you, Dalton, you're gonna make it right!"

"Dan wouldn't pull—"

"And maybe you didn't know about this?"

"No, Dicky. Nothing!"

"And I'm telling you they sprung it on me! And you—you're in on that double-cross."

"Are they after you?"

"What do you think they do when a cop killer gets away, huh?"

"No—"

"Yes! And you got to make it good, Dalton, fast."

"What—"

"I need dough. I got to get out of the city. You catch on, don't you?"

"You need my money? I have—"

"You know what day this is, Dalton? Thursday! Thursday night they put the money in the safe back in Newton. Follow me, Dalton?"

"Dicky, listen—" Dalton was up, his voice high. "You can't do it like this. You're running, you got no tools, the job needs— I've been telling you it needs much better planning. You got to—"

"That's what I got you for, Dalton. Come on. Move." Dicky's gun was out, nodding at Dalton.

The old man did not have the strength to argue. He leaned on the small table next to his bed and shook his head.

"Dicky, I'm too tired to be pushed any more. You can push and nothing would happen. I'm too tired."

He was not surprised when Dicky put the gun away. He was not surprised when Dicky changed his style and talked rapidly in the urgent tone he had used before, pleading with Port and trying to trade Letty.

"They're gonna have a ring around this town like a vise. I can still make it. I slipped the neighborhood where they're looking. Get me out, Dalton. I got a car I can use. You can drive. Me in the trunk and you driving—"

"I'm slow. I'm slow, Dicky. If you need a wheel man—"

"I don't need a wheel man, you stupid jerk, I need you! We're going to Newton and make it!"

"Dicky—"

"Now you hear this," said Dicky. His voice was suddenly low, and he was spacing his words. "You gave me your word; remember? And I went along. I traded you one frame for another. Your word wasn't good, Dalton, was it?" Dicky waited.

"No," said Dalton. "It wasn't good."

"You double-crossed me, Dalton. I'm running now, and it's your fault. I'm running and I need your help because your word wasn't good."

When Port slammed into the room he saw that for the second time in a day he had been too late. There was one chair and Port sat down in it for a moment. He took a deep breath to slow himself down, and rubbed his hands over his face. Then he looked around the room again. The bed showed where a man had been lying on it, the hook on the door was empty, the railroad ticket lay on the table next to the bed. Dalton would only have forgotten it if there had been no point in remembering it.

Port got up. He went over to the table and picked up the ticket and stuffed it into his pocket. He did it with a violence that showed how the tension inside was growing stronger. When his hand was in his pocket he felt the gun. He took it out, flicked the cylinder open, and counted the shells even though he knew the gun had not been fired. Then he stuck it into his belt and buttoned his jacket.

Mac or Corday? It would help to know which, because one of the two would take Dalton back to the plant in Newton.

Port went out of the room and downstairs. His heels made hard clicks.

He could call the hospital and find out who had been admitted, shot up. It would take a while to find the right hospital. He could call the morgue, he could call the police, he could call the man he knew here in town, or he could ask almost anyone on the street in Dicky's neighborhood. For that matter, he could ask anyone who had been listening to the radio. The landlady's room was on the ground floor and the old lady was sweeping the hall. She had left her door open and the radio was droning on, something about soap so pure—

"You been listening to the news?" Port asked the woman.

"Couldn't help it," she said. "They even cut in on my program."

"About the shooting on the South Side?"

"Yes. One got away."

"Which one?"

"I don't know, but I know which one got killed."

"Who?"

"Maximilian Kloos. And one of the detectives got killed, by the one who got away. The detective's name was—"

"Thank you," said Port, and was gone.

Maximilian Kloos. Not Dicky Corday. Port got into his car, slammed the door, and punched the starter. Dicky Corday was out of town on his way to Newton with the old man—because this was Thursday, when they put the money into the safe.

The car tore away from the curb. Port didn't slow down until he got near the center of town. Traffic was heavy here and he had to crawl. The same would have happened to Dicky. Maybe he was still in town, lying low, waiting. That wouldn't make sense. This was Thursday, and he had Dalton along at the point of a gun.

The car was in low, whining, crawling.

Port wasn't the only one looking for Corday. The police were looking, an army of them, because of Port's own maneuver and because Corday had killed a cop.

And Abe Dalton was in the middle of it—unless Port got there first.

The light turned green but by the time Port reached it it had turned red again. He kept his foot on the throttle, gunning the motor in short, fast jabs. The light changed finally, and Port crossed the intersection, then crawled again, joining the traffic. He turned the radio on and he turned the dial till he found the station for police calls.

"... two, eight, eight. No activity, over," and without pause, "Central to two, eight, eight. The accident is on corner Field and Bennington. Correcting previous instructions, corner Field and Bennington. Bicycle and truck. Over, out."

It crackled and went dead. Truck hit bicycle. Port fiddled with the knobs and heard music. He found his station again and heard, "... tow-truck. We blew a tire. Over."

They blew a tire. Some cruiser was parked somewhere waiting for a tire. Nothing about Corday. Perhaps they had him. Perhaps— He fiddled with the dial some more and that was when he found the other station.

They were using two wave lengths.

"... gray-blue Buick, fifty-six. License number LF twelve. Reported stolen in Sector B. All cars not on regular assignment abandon Sector B, proceed to M. Buick reported in Sector M. Fugitive believed to be driving stolen Buick, gray-blue, fifty-six, license number LF twelve. Observe extreme caution. Fugitive is armed. All cars...."

They had him tagged!

Loud horns made Port look up. He was still crawling, but the street ahead was clear and he was holding up a line of cars behind him. Port drove faster.

"... cover Brook Road, Harwood, Eighth—"

Where was that?

"... confirmed in Sector M. Fugitive last seen in Sector M—" A crackle, then the voice. "Correction. Last report from Sector Q. All odd numbers from Sectors O, P, R, proceed to Q. The fugitive is armed. Observe—"

Port's hand slipped on the wheel from sweat. They had him tagged, but where? The more he listened, the more they told him, and none of it meant a thing. Port was heading out now, going faster, going fast and straight to Newton while Corday and the old man were some place in a police grid sector in the city which they might never leave.

He had to get to Dalton first!

Port hit the brakes and pulled in to the curb. He stopped beside the policeman.

"Officer!"

The cop was big and bored. He turned to look at Port and chewed his gum.

"Officer, I'm from the *Courier*; my name is Port." Port held out a card which he stuck back into his pocket when the cop moved closer.

The press? The cop stopped chewing gum and came up to the car. The press, on this beat? The cop smiled down at Port.

"Need some help?"

"I do. You heard about the cop killer loose in Sector Q?"

"Q? I didn't know he was in Q. The one shot his way outa that hotel on the South Side?"

"Right. He's in Q, and I'm supposed to cover that. Where's Q, officer? I've got to...."

The cop spat out his gum and looked animated.

"You sure? Christ, you're in it! Where'd you hear it, on the radio? Come on, come on, turn that thing up!" The cop leaned through the window.

"... North Trumbull, South Trumbull, Ward Street, covered as requested. Over." And without pause, "Central to all cars. Follow plan W...."

There was more that Port did not understand. The cop was leaning in at the window and unwrapping some more gum listening to the radio and playing cops and robbers.

Port felt like screaming. The more he listened the more he knew, and the more they could tell him, the more they knew!

But Port had to get to Dalton first! If he could find out which way they were going, what chance Corday had of getting away—

"... Sectors S and T," said the voice.

"What now? You know what that means?" Port asked the cop.

"Hold it, just hold it—"

"... plan W in Sectors S and T. Call Precinct Thirty for local instructions. Out."

"Boy!" said the cop.

"Well? Christ, don't let me sit here and—"

"You gonna mention in your column who give you the information?" said the cop. He offered Port a stick of gum.

"Hell, yes, I'd be pleased to, but let's have it."

"S and T, that's further out. See this?" The cop drew a circle on the windshield. "That's the city. You're here, the Highland district, what we call Sector Q, or part of it, anyway. Pretty far out, you see that?"

"Christ, yes. Come on, come on."

"That's out of the city!"

"Suburbs. Now you wanna know what they mean by plan W?"

Port groaned and nodded.

"That means all procedures relative to roadblock techniques. What we mean by that—"

"You mean roadblocks out there, out of the city?"

"Like I told you. He's heading out, the way Central describes it. Now, what we mean by roadblock—"

"So where's he going, heading that way?"

Port was very anxious now. He knew one town that lay out in that direction.

"Open country. He can take Highway Ten or alternate Twenty. One goes to Pittering and the other joins Six further south."

If Corday made it he would take Ten. He would take a cutoff to Newton before reaching the cross-country highway.

"That means they're bound to stop at the edge of one of those two sectors."

"Maybe."

"There're only two highways, you say—"

"But the country starts there. Remember what it said, to call the precinct for local dope? That's so the local men can direct the search out there, seeing there's open country and small roads and that kind of thing. You can't have a roadblock on a field, you know, and if that cop killer should—"

"I get it," said Port and shifted his gears.

"Now, I was telling you about this procedure we—"

"Look, thanks a lot, officer, thanks—" Port started moving.

The last thing Port heard was the cop yelling his name so that Port could put it in the paper.

If all this information were correct he would hit a roadblock in less than half an hour.

The cop's story was true. The roadblock itself was an impressive affair of six cars and scores of troopers and city police equipped with riot guns, lights, and a radio truck. It meant that they didn't have Dalton and Corday yet. It might mean the pair had turned back; it might mean they were trying some other way.

The police had been looking for them on the South Side when Port had been halfway into the middle of town. Then they had switched to a sector far away in alphabetical order. Corday had a good start. He might make it.

When Port went through the roadblock they warned him about taking the trip.

Corday might make it. Even the police thought he might. Port drove off, and, hours later, when it was dark, he turned off on the road going to Newton. There were no more patrol cars racing by, no more motorcycles. The police wave length had long since died out and the calls from the highway stations had made no sense to Port.

The dark country rolled and the air smelled of rain. Port drove steadily. The wind shot past the windows and killed every other sound, except for Port's whistling, an irritating, unfinished sound. He kept it up far into the night. He didn't stop until he saw the Newton Plant, big and black on the landscape. Then he stopped whistling. He parked before the street ended and walked down the highway where the country began.

The plant looked bigger in the dark than it did in the daytime. Three lights in the court gave a dank, deserted look to the place. For some reason Port could smell hay.

The grilled gate was shut. Port took out his revolver and looked at the gate.

Chapter 23

They stood in the dark and talked in whispers. The small light was on the dial.

"My hands aren't good enough any more," said Dalton. "Even if there were no timer."

There was silence, except for Dicky's breathing and Loony's feet shifting. Dalton was making no sound.

"Well? Don't gimme no list of what you can't do. There's something like thirty-five grand on the other side of this door and you stand there—"

"Be quiet," said Dalton.

Dicky was quiet. Dalton was working, and his voice was authoritative, without emotion.

"We have no tools," Dalton said.

"You think I was gonna stop and—"

"That means we have to find what we need here in the shop. Loony?"

"Yes," said Loony.

"A tank of acetylene, two of oxygen. If they're the big ones, just one each. Bring two torches and a handful of extra heads, new ones."

"I know where they are."

"A ball peen and wedge. Find some punches. Here. They have to fit here." Dalton pointed. "And a chisel, twelve-inch, and a sledge."

"Whyn't you go down with him and get it?" said Dicky.

Dalton ignored Dicky.

"Biggest electric drill you can find, and a handful of bits—quarter-inch, nothing bigger. And high carbon. Unless you got something harder?"

"We got. I know where."

"And lubricant, mixed well. That's all."

Loony left.

"You go with him," said Dicky. "That dumb ox—"

"Please. Let me sit."

Dicky had the light off and he couldn't see Dalton's face, only his outline as he sat down on a chair near a desk that stood by the window. Dicky saw how careful the movement was. He heard Dalton breathe carefully.

"You all right?" said Dicky.

Dalton ignored it. "I want you to take that light," he said, "and find the power line that goes into the alarm. It'll be sheathed. You can—"

"I know what I'm looking for."

"Find where it comes out of the main line. Or find out if it's independent."

Dicky didn't argue. He left. The old man stayed there and tried not to move. He was facing a window. It was very large, and he could look very far out over the countryside. He saw changing shades where fields must be, and thick black which had to be woods.

He turned back to the room. It was darker there, and it would help to get used to the darkness.

Dicky was the first one back.

"It came out of a main," he said. "I jumped it."

Dalton said, "The next time I tell you to check, just check. You don't—"

At first the voice had been clipped but then it faltered after a sudden hesitation. Dicky didn't know why, but Dalton did. He had said, "The next time."

"Go help Loony with the tanks," Dalton said wearily.

Dicky left and Dalton sat in his chair. His head was down as if he were looking at his hands. He could see nothing and he had stopped thinking. There was nothing to think about. He was doing this job and there was nothing to think about.

They made quite a racket returning with the tanks. They brought those and the other things Dalton had wanted. They dropped everything at the door of the safe and Dalton got up and went over to them.

"Plug in the drill," he said.

Then he picked out a bit and set it into the drill. "Ready there?"

"I got it plugged in," said Loony.

"All right. Dicky, get set with the coolant, and you, Loony, stand outside."

Dicky held the can of lubricant ready and Dalton flicked the drill trigger a few times. It made a high, noisy whirr. Loony went out through the door. He stood on the dark stairs where he could see the entrance to the office building and the metal stairs that went down to the shop. He stood there and lit a cigarette.

Then Loony's cigarette jumped out of his mouth.

Port caught him from behind. Port lowered him gently, felt the back of his head, and then straightened up with a faint sound of exhaling.

The swinging door to the room with the safe had large glass panels on it. Behind it was the dark room, the shadow of desks, and the bright, busy spot of light. Dalton was raising the drill, using both hands. Dicky held the light in one hand and the oil can in the other. He would drop the light first.

There were two sharp whirrs from the drill and when the sound died the drill went into position.

"Now," said Dalton.

"Drop it!"

For a long, still instant there was nothing, just the sigh of the swinging door behind Port.

Dicky dropped the light and scuttled away from the safe. He was not very fast. The shot rang out before the sound of his movement was over.

Silence.

"You shoot often enough, Corday, and they'll hear you in town."

Dicky used all the profanity he could think of, cursing into the dark at Port. But he did not know where Port was.

When it was over the scene was as before. Dalton had not moved. The light was still at his feet. It shone at the safe and it highlighted Dalton's face with a weird effect of long shadows running up his features.

"Dan!"

It was hard to tell what the intonation in the voice meant. It was not relief and it was not a question.

"You move, Dalton," said Dicky, "you move or kick that light and you're dead. Port! You hear that?"

Port didn't answer. There was no point.

"Now get up, Port. You hear me?"

Port told Dicky what he could do.

"Quiet, both of you!"

They both listened to Dalton. They both strained into the dark as if Dalton might solve everything.

"Go away, Dan."

"Tell him to throw out his rod," said Dicky.

"Quiet," said Dalton.

It was the light, Port thought, the way it hit Dalton's face from below. His face was set, without movement. "Dan," said Dalton. "I want you to go away."

"You're rattled," said Port. "Just stand still. I'm—"

"No, Dan. It's no use."

"Abe, I know he's got a gun on you now but—"

"He can put the gun down if he wants. I'm staying. I'm going through with the job."

Chapter 24

Port felt as if he had been hit. He caught his breath and held so still behind his desk that the gun in his hand started to tremble.

"Dalton," he said. "You're out of your mind."

Dalton lowered the drill and held it along his side. He turned slightly, so that Port could see him full-face.

"You sprung that frame on Corday. I won't take that, Dan. I gave my word."

"Abe, for God's sake don't talk like an idiot. You had nothing to do with that! A slip-up. A bad slip-up but you had nothing to do with it!"

"I gave my word," said Dalton and turned back to the safe. "I haven't much else." He lifted the drill.

"Abe! Listen!" Port yelled, but the drill was going with a hard whine and Dalton aimed at a spot near the dial. The sound of the drill would change when he set it into the metal. He was cautious about it, and precise. It drew Port's eyes, made him watch—and the same would happen to Corday. Dalton was aiming the drill and Corday must be watching— Port jumped. The wall wasn't far behind him. Port hit the switch near the door, flicked it, and when the ceiling lights came on Port was down on the floor again.

Dicky's shot broke the glass in the swinging door. Then he shot twice more, at the light in the ceiling. One fluorescent tube shattered, but there were nine more of them.

"Kill that light, damn you! The whole town can see it!"

"Right," said Port.

Dalton had dropped the drill. He looked sick in the white light. He was leaning against the safe, shaking his head. His eyes seemed to be closed.

Port forgot about Dalton then. His turn would come later. Corday was cursing across the room and his feet made sliding noises. Port lay down on the floor, flat, his head sideways. Then he aimed and shot Corday in one foot.

It couldn't have been very bad. Corday yelled, started scrambling, and ran crouched along the far wall. He reached a partition with a door that said Private and when Port shot again the door slammed shut with a hole in it.

Somebody would see the light.

The office and the partitions were like a maze, and both men had to go by sound, Port after Corday and Corday running to find a way out.

He made it. Port heard him in the hall, where Loony was lying, and then he heard the fast click of heels on metal steps.

Port ran back into the office. Dalton was sitting now. He had slid down along the door of the safe and he was sitting on the floor where the tools were lying.

"Abe. Up! Take my hand—"

Dalton didn't raise his hand. He sat slumped, shaking his head.

"Abe, damn it, you're coming with me!"

Port had to drag him. He had Dalton halfway up on his shoulder when the siren cut loose back in town.

Not the shop stairs—too narrow— Port made it down, sliding and stumbling, and crashed into the door that led outside.

A laugh. Somebody laughed in the yard. Then Corday fired from the truck ramp. Unless he had reloaded he had only one shot left.

The siren got bigger and much more urgent. Two sirens now!

Port thought he saw Corday in the yard, but they had to get out now.

"Left," said Dalton. "There is a way left—better—"

Port dragged Dalton through the door and went left. He would have to cross where a yard light was. Dalton was wrong. Then Port saw Corday run through a light on the right and disappear behind the edge of a building. Port ran, dragging. Past the light there were no buildings, a fence— Too much in the open.

"Keep going," Port heard. "There is a fence close."

Port couldn't see it.

Then he did, as if it jumped at him, jumped with the reflection on wire loops along the whole width of vision. Port let Dalton drop and threw himself down next to him.

Behind them, off to one side, the yard near the gate suddenly exploded into brilliance. Two lights on the towers that held the gate and lights from the road on the other side went on. The space looked huge and bare and Dicky Corday was in it. He stopped dead and then waved his arms as if fighting the beams. He had one shot left. He fired. A light went out on one tower. Corday cursed and screamed in the empty yard and then tossed his gun away.

He didn't hit anyone. The men running at him had Corday in a circle. It was over.

Port and Dalton got over the fence where trucks were parked. The trucks made the climb possible. Port and Dalton made it across a wild field, through muddy water and around bushes. Then came a road, then the highway, and while Dalton lay in a ditch Port walked into town and got his car.

He found Dalton where he had left him and they drove off.

Port didn't notice until they were far out of town and the car was roaring steadily along the black highway that Dalton was sick. His face was an inhuman gray and his skin was clammy with sweat. He sat doubled over, groaning.

"I'll stop, Abe, if you say the word. Can you hold out three hours until we get to the hospital?"

The old man did not answer.

There were just two small towns on the way, nothing big enough for a hospital. But maybe there was a doctor. "Abe. Another fifteen minutes and I'll be able to look for a doctor."

The old man just sat.

"Shall I stop? You want to rest?"

The old man would not talk. For the moment the pain seemed to have gone because he sat up and his face wasn't as strained as before. He looked straight ahead and would not answer.

"Abe, what is it? You talked before. You told me how to get away. What now?"

"I did not want to get caught," said Dalton.

It was a relief to hear him say something. Port took out a cigarette and lit it.

"You feel better?"

"Yes."

"Abe, if something's eating you—"

"I told you before, in the plant. What else is there to say?"

Port took a deep drag.

"It went wrong, Abe. I told you. I called the frame off, right there with Corday next to me. In that hallway, you remember?"

"I thought you had."

Port was very tired. He had not slept in two days and too much had gone wrong.

"I could tell you how it went wrong, how it wasn't my fault and why your word was good."

Dalton leaned over. He looked as if he were dizzy. He kept his head down and said, "I've never gone back on my word, Dan. And now, this late—"

"Look, Abe. You—"

Port stopped talking because Dalton was in no shape to listen. Dalton had winced and the movement forced a sound out of his throat. Then he leaned back, looking exhausted. When Port slowed, not knowing what to do, Dalton moved his head. He said, "Drive. No difference."

Port drove. He wanted to get to the hospital.

"Abe, I don't know about your condition. Is it dangerous to go on? Should I stop? Tell me."

"It makes no difference," said Dalton.

"Lean back more, over this way. Or do you want to lie on the back seat?"

There was a long moment before Dalton spoke. "Dan," he said, "I've been wrong all my life, but I don't think—" The rest died into a mumble.

Port knew there was only one thing to do—drive as fast as he possibly could. The car raced down the highway, chasing the beam that sliced the darkness ahead and it seemed as if the black road in front of the car had no end. The sound of the motor was like the roar of a fever and the speed was like a fever too.

"Almost," said Port, "almost there." He did not dare say how many hours it would take. He did not even look at his watch.

"All my life—" Dalton mumbled again.

"Abe, I know what's bothering you. But you didn't lie about the frame. Because I didn't. Abe, listen. If I had arranged it so Dicky got caught, would I have left you in your room, sleeping? Do you think I would have left you alone?"

Port tore around a curve, holding himself by the wheel.

"I'm all right," Dalton said. He sounded much better. "I believe you," he said, "because you didn't blame it on Letty."

Port looked sideways once but said nothing.

"I know she did it," said Dalton, "but you didn't blame it on her." He rested for a while and then said, "It will be hard on her. Perhaps—" His voice suddenly wandered and he said a few words that made no sense.

Port was afraid to talk to him.

Once Dalton said, "Hemorrhage—"

Port drove like fury.

Then Dalton tried once more. "It's all right now. I've been wrong, but I don't think I've—"

Then he fainted. He did not wake up, and Port chased the beam and the car seemed to swallow the road.

He slowed down later. He drove automatically at a sensible speed. When Port got to town with Dalton the old man was already cold.

Dan Port left the city very soon afterwards. He saw that Abe Dalton was buried, and he saw Letty once more. It was best that the girl should leave town. Abe Dalton had left a railroad ticket and Port had found the old man's five hundred dollars. He exchanged the ticket for Letty, to a town where she had some friends. And he gave her the money.

It reminded Port of the thing Dalton had done with Eve Simmon. He was sorry that Eve Simmon could not have helped. The old man, Port thought, had been wrong most of his life, but he had not been bad.

THE END

It's My Funeral
by Peter Rabe

To
"Uncle Murray"

Chapter 1

Daniel Port held the wheel of his new MG as if he had never driven before. He had a persistent feeling that his feet stuck out through the grille and that any minute his bottom would scrape. Most of all he would have liked to pull over and stop, but the Wilshire traffic through Beverly Hills wouldn't let him. The Cadillacs got thicker. They shot from one lane into another, their tail fins following the bulk of the car like two sharks in formation.

They stopped swarming by the time he got closer to Santa Monica and Port sat a little straighter, a little more confident, even crossed from one lane into the other. After a while he also looked right and left, and into the rearview mirror. There were still plenty of Cadillacs. There was one, further back, a white one, that had been there before Port had come through Beverly Hills, that had been there all the way down La Brea, in fact, a big white Cadillac with zebra upholstery which had caught Port's eye when he had seen it across the street from the place where he had bought his MG early that morning. Port frowned, then looked front again. This feeling, he thought, had something to do with sitting so low to the ground. This feeling of being followed was all tied up with sitting clamped into a car whose rear wheels were next to his elbows and whose front wheels were attached to his ankles.

And for that matter, if he felt persecuted, all he would have to do is scurry straight ahead and under the belly of the truck in front of him and out again between the truck's two front wheels.

At the next light Port took time to get a cigarette out and when the light changed he even leaned back into his seat and kept his left arm on the side of the car. At the end of Wilshire, Port turned left, keeping his bearings by watching for the roller coaster on the pier past the hotels. After a few small streets he had worked his way close to the pier and since it was early forenoon and his car was so small he found a parking place by one of the bars near the pier. Port shoehorned himself out of the seat and walked to the archway where the pier started out into the ocean.

She wasn't there.

The booths on the pier weren't open yet so she couldn't have wandered off in that direction. It wasn't likely she had gone into one of the bars down the street, not at this hour, and the delicatessen nearby was almost empty.

Port put his hands in his pockets and started to whistle. It sounded mostly like air, but he whistled that way as if he were concentrating on a real tune. When an empty ice cream cone came rolling by he nudged his foot at it. There was always a breeze. It blew in from the Pacific but it didn't smell like the sea.

That had been the first thing Port had noticed about the place. Sand, breakers, seawind, sun on the water, but it didn't smell like the sea, the way he remembered the sea smelled in the East. Not enough kelp, maybe. If he stayed in Los Angeles a while longer perhaps he would look for a part of the beach where it smelled as the sea should. Or he would ask Tessy about it, except that she hadn't showed up. Thinking about it, there was no good reason why she should. She didn't know him except for a drink at the bar between acts, and he didn't know her except to watch her on the stage, with the microphone coming up to her chin after lowering it almost a foot because she was just a little more than five feet tall. Someone in the club always laughed when she came back to the mike, reached up, and worked it down to her size. After that nobody made a snicker. Tessy could sing and Tessy looked good. She had light blue eyes in the tanned face and tanned arms and shoulders and the rest that was visible over the gown she was wearing. Later, when he had bought her the drink at the bar, Port had been happy to notice that her voice sounded as good from close up, talking to him, as the mike voice up on the stage.

He could go back to the bar that night, and try again. When it came to something as nice as Tessy, as nice in several ways as Tessy, Port wasn't proud. He looked down the pier again, down the street, and then the length of the beach, but saw nothing.

Or maybe he'd leave town. L.A. meant nothing to him and the week he had spent there hadn't changed that any. He'd go down to the beach, lie around, do some swimming, and he would think about leaving L.A. If the sun got too hot, or for that matter, if it clouded up with that haze which turned yellow when it hit Santa Monica, maybe he'd leave town right then.

He turned toward the beach, because the sun was still out and he would first take a swim. Then he would lie in the sand for a while. He might even think about where he might go from here.

"Hey, buddy!"

Port turned around and saw a man with an apron in the door to the delicatessen. Port didn't know him.

"That's right, you," said the man. "Your name, uh, Sherry, or something? Daniel Sherry?"

"Daniel Port."

"That's what I mean."

Port came a little closer and then the man said, "Somebody on the phone for you. She said you were waiting outside by the pier and I should...."

"Where's the phone?"

The phone was past the tables in a booth by the back wall, and on the way there Port suddenly caught himself smoothing his hair back, as if he wanted to make a good impression, once in the booth.

"Hello? This is Port."

"So it is Port. I wasn't sure whether it wasn't Sherry, perhaps," and then Tessy laughed.

Port laughed too but didn't feel much like it. "Where are you?" he said. "You sound half asleep."

"I am. I'm in bed."

"Oh? Where are you?"

She laughed again, much more awake now, and then she said, "Dan, I'm sorry about not being there, but...."

"That's all right. Just tell me where you are...."

"I just overslept, Dan. You know I work till four in the morning and I should never have made the date for so early. Forgive me?"

"Sure."

"Will I see you again?"

"Very sure."

"Come to the club? Late?"

"I'll take you home."

"Nice." She laughed again, and said, "You can wake me up in the morning." Then she hung up.

When Port came out of the booth he was grinning to himself.

"Right party?" said the man with the apron.

Port nodded. He felt very benign then and thought he should order something, if only to express his thanks. "Coffee," he said. "Leave it black."

The man drew the coffee without enthusiasm and put it down on the counter.

"And something to eat," said Port. "What you got that's special."

"You want breakfast?"

There were some chickens turning on a spit in the window and a good crisp odor in the air.

"I'll take one of those," said Port. "And some bread." Port saw it made the man happy, and Port felt a huge appetite, and when he got the chicken he ordered some beer with it. When he was through he drank his cold coffee and smoked a cigarette.

Back outside Port felt that the sun was brighter and the wind smelled fresher, even smelling a little bit like the sea should. Down the pier some of the booths had opened and a few kids had lined up at the roller coaster. Port decided to go to the pier first and then to the beach because there was no rush, seeing he had all day. He took a ride on the roller coaster and thought it felt so good he would take Tessy tomorrow for sure. Way up on one of the loops he could see the street with the bars and he saw his new MG parked by the curb. The car looked smaller than ever, squeezed between two normal-sized cars, and Port thought he should have parked on the sidewalk perhaps. To be really safe he should have picked up the car and leaned it up against a wall somewhere, to be out of the way and safe. Just before the roller coaster tore down the steep incline Port saw the Cadillac again, a white Cadillac parked further back.

When Port came off the pier and turned to go down to the beach he reminded himself that he didn't know a soul in L.A. He saw the white Cadillac down the street; there was the zebra upholstery. This time Port also saw the man that went with the car. He was short, wearing a big, light-colored jacket, and the way it draped the man underneath must have been slight. He was wearing big sunglasses and didn't look like anyone Port could remember. The man was rubbing his nails on the lapel of the jacket and then he looked at them. Then the man pushed away from the wall and went into the bar next to him.

Port went down to the beach. He staked his claim by spreading the towel he had brought in his back pocket, took off his shirt and his pants. He had his swim trunks underneath.

There was a good surf that day. Port swam, sunned, slept. When he woke up there were two-tone shoes next to his face, further up slacks with a weird purple sheen, then the jacket which turned out white cashmere, and the thin face with the black glasses.

"I bet it's Port," said the face. "And I win. You owe me a buck, Danny."

Chapter 2

Port sat up and cursed. He spat some sand off his lip, but even if there hadn't been sand he might have spat because he didn't like seeing the guy. There was no chance of being mistaken, and when Joko Mulnik took off the glasses and stretched his thin mouth to make that noiseless laugh he practiced, Port spat again.

"Beat it," said Port. "You're ruining my day."

"First pay me my buck," said Joko, and laughed again.

Port got up and brushed sand off his arms.

"When did you get out? I thought they gave it to you good, last time."

"Time flies."

"Go join it," said Port and pulled on his pants. The trunks were still moist, but he didn't feel like staying any longer. He didn't want Mulnik around and he didn't want to remember what went with the guy.

"So I heard right," said Joko. "About what happened back East, huh?"

"Joko," said Port. He pulled on his shirt and sounded patient. "Don't you know I don't like you?"

"I don't mind, Danny, honest I don't. Besides, that was years ago. When was it, Danny, you and me worked for Stoker?"

"What makes you say you ever worked for Stoker?"

Joko laughed and started to peel cellophane off a cigar.

"You know, just an expression."

"I grant you."

"That was years ago, Danny. How come you carry a grudge from years ago?"

"I don't. I just don't like chiselers."

Port shook out his towel and started to walk up the beach to the paved walk that led back to the pier. Joko followed behind him. He didn't talk, being busy keeping the sand out of his shoes. It made him walk like a crab, with careful knee-bending and foot-placing, but once he got to the paved walk he caught up with Port and held on to his arm.

"Come on, Danny, I'll buy you a beer."

"That'll be the day."

"Honest."

"It'll cost me. Beat it. With you in the picture...."

"I been following you all day," said Joko. "I been...."

"Yeah. How come?"

"I heard you was in town so I went to the place you live. You were just coming out, taking a bus."

"Then you parked at the place where I bought my car. What was that for?"

"I wasn't sure it was you. Hell, Danny, I haven't seen you in years."

"And you couldn't stand it."

"That's right."

"Anyway," said Port, "you gave me long enough to have some time on the beach before ruining my day."

"I was watching your car from the bar."

Port didn't answer. He was wondering how to shake Joko. Tell him to blow was no good; insult him, same thing; hit him—so what?

"This way," said Joko, and waved at the bar next to the delicatessen.

"All right," said Port. "One beer, and it's on you."

After the bright sun and the heat on the beach the inside of the bar was like a dark cave. Port buttoned his shirt and put the towel around his neck while Joko ordered two beers. Then he led the way to a table in back and they sat down. Port lit a cigarette and watched Joko. Joko chewed his unlit cigar and watched Port. Then he smiled.

"You know, you and me got something in common. You know?"

"We both breathe air."

Joko laughed, shaking his shoulders and stretching his mouth. He rarely made sounds when he laughed. "I mean it. Here we are, both legit."

"You're giving me cramps, Joko."

"Why? Ain't it true? I even read it in the papers."

"You didn't read about me in the papers," said Port.

Mulnik leaned over the table, smiling, trying to get through to Port.

"I read the papers from the East. It said right there how the Stoker machine blew sky high and how the racket king's right-hand man went scot-free. That was you, Danny. Stoker's right-hand man."

Mulnik sat back, looking pleased, as if it pleased him to know such a person as Daniel Port. Then he looked at his fingernails and said without looking up, "I also hear—not from the papers, mind you—that they couldn't have cleaned up Stoker's outfit without inside help." Then Mulnik looked up. "How come you fingered your buddies, Danny?"

Port didn't seem bothered by the insult in Mulnik's remark. He said, "Old man Stoker died. It didn't need me to make his outfit go to pieces after that."

The beer came and Joko pulled out a roll of bills. He flipped through it, frowned, and made a small sound to show how embarrassed he was.

"Look—hey, Danny, I got nothing less than a C-note and I can't ask the man...."

"Just ask him."

"Seventy cents," said the waiter.

"Seventy cents," said Joko. "Give him the change, Danny, and I pay you back soon as...."

"No."

Joko frowned, peeved this time, but then he found a ten-dollar bill. He gave it to the waiter and told him to bring back nine dollars change.

"Same son of a bitch as always," said Port and poured beer into his glass.

"So like I was saying—" Mulnik leaned closer again—"you work in the rackets for years, a brain-truster no less, and then you walk out. How come?"

"Stoker died."

"Personal loyalty made you such a hot crook?"

Port didn't answer. He didn't feel like explaining things and besides, Mulnik would hardly have understood. Mulnik had never worked with anyone whom he didn't end up robbing blind. Mulnik couldn't have understood how old man Stoker and Port were close to each other, even though Mulnik had used the word loyalty in the right place. When Stoker had died Port had left the organization. He had wanted to leave for a long time, after the filth and the conniving had gotten too much for him. Except for the way he had felt about Stoker—a sick man and old who had helped Port out of the gutter—except for that he wouldn't take the machine discipline, the cold acts for profit, and all the small, greedy men who made up the organization. So when Stoker had died—

"You still didn't say, Dan. After Stoker was dead, why did you finger the rest of the outfit?"

They hadn't wanted to let him go. They had never heard of a hood that quit out, except dead, and they wouldn't let him leave quietly.

"You push hard enough," said Port, "and I'm liable to do any number of things."

"Like fingering the only friends you ever had?"

"That's how I got clean."

The waiter brought back the change, nine one-dollar bills, and left again. Joko laid the bills out like cards.

"How come you're alive?" he asked.

"Because I'm legit."

"You're a legitimate ex-hood. I never heard of an ex-hood who wasn't dead or running from it."

"I got insurance," said Port.

"You mean they hit you and it means they get more of the finger?"

"Shaking up Stoker's machine was just a small sample."

"Gee!" said Mulnik, because he admired that sort of thing. Then he drank beer, plunked the glass down with a flourish, and reached across the table to pat Port on the arm.

"You're for me, Danny; you're for me and I'm with you all the way. And welcome to L.A. A good place for you and me to hang out, believe me. I been here for a couple of years...."

"You sound as if everybody in town is crooked."

"I'm legit, I told you! Listen, there's a lot of people here are legit. I mean it!"

"How would you know?"

"Danny, don't act like such a bastard." Joko drank beer, then looked at Port with a superior air. "I'm an agent," he said.

Port laughed.

"Listen," said Joko, "I got an office, I'm in the book, and I drive a car that can knock your foot-power vehicle out there clear into...."

"Where'd you steal those seats you got in that car—El Morocco?"

"I paid for 'em, cash. And to show you the size of my operation, I got right now three lawsuits handled by my lawyer for breaching—for breaking contracts with me, clients trying to break contracts with me."

"Who?"

"Talent! I handle talent! I help 'em up out of the gutter, I do all the leg work and all the brain work, and then, when I got them set up—and the way I operate, I set 'em up talent or no talent—they...."

"Joko," said Port. He leaned over the table and made it look confidential. "You a pimp?"

For a moment Port thought that Joko would grab his glass and throw it across the table, but he put it down again, gnawed on his lip for a while, and then talked in an even voice.

"You can quit acting the bastard," he said. "Come on, I show you my office." He got up, looked down at Port, but Port didn't move. "Come on, I show you."

"I don't want to see your office."

Joko put the cigar on the table and put his hands into the large pockets of the cashmere jacket he was wearing. Except for his build he stood there like a fashion plate.

"You know why I'm talking to you?"

"I've been wondering," said Port.

"Because you and me can do business. I got a proposition in mind that can mean...."

"Nix," said Port.

"Listen to me, you bastard." Joko leaned closer, hissing. "I'm talking business! On the up-and-up with pay in advance. Did I ever rob you?"

"No."

"I ever do you a dirty turn?"

"Not yet."

"So maybe you're afraid you wouldn't be smart enough working with me?"

"I don't know, Joko."

"That's why I'm asking you, Danny, because you got qualifications."

"Ex-hood?"

"No, no, no. You got brains and can think on your feet. I need somebody legit who can do that, and that's hard to come by. All I ask, you listen to me, make up your mind, and then tell me. You don't want the job, say so. You walk out and I don't bother you any more...."

There was something disarming about Joko Mulnik. He could brag with unmatched affrontery but do it so plainly, with such show of honest belief, that it was hard to take real offense. Or he could lie, and be so naively crest-fallen about it when he was found out that it was hard to hold him responsible.

"Maybe you're still worried about what happened when you and me was working for Stoker."

"I'm not worried. I just don't like it."

Port had helped Mulnik get a job in the Stoker machine. They had needed a brazen, fast-talking type to wheedle collections. That's how Port picked Mulnik. And then, very soon, Mulnik had started to rob Stoker blind.

"But that's all done with," said Mulnik. "I got fired and I even paid back some."

That hadn't been the end of it, though. It turned out Mulnik had sold part of the territory to some other outfit for rake-offs, something that hadn't come out until after Mulnik had disappeared. It made it bad for Stoker. It made it bad for him with his underlings and put him in hot water higher up. And Mulnik had been the one who had tipped it off higher up.

"So how come you don't like me?" said Mulnik. "Honest, Dan, this was years ago."

"I don't like a man as greedy as you. You're too greedy."

"But I'm sharing!" said Mulnik. "I'm asking you to come in out of the rain...."

"I'm not looking for work."

Mulnik put his hands in his pockets and sounded disgusted. "So you made a lot of dough being a crook. Maybe now you're afraid you can't do it legit."

Port stared up at Mulnik, but after a moment he gave up trying to think of an answer. He didn't know how he could put Mulnik down.

"Let me up," he said and pushed Mulnik out of the way. "And thanks for the beer."

He walked to the door fast but wasn't surprised when Mulnik came up beside him, talking again.

"... and all you have to do is hear me out and give it a chance. If you don't want any part of it, Danny, then you can say so and I won't bother you any more. Honest, all you have to do...."

Port thought it might be the easiest way out. He had nothing to do between now and the evening and maybe there was a point where Mulnik talked himself out.

"All right," he said. "Let's see that office you got."

They walked out of the bar and Joko kept slapping Port on the back and explained how grateful he was.

"Don't be," said Port. "You know that I don't like you."

"That's all right, Danny, that's all right. I don't mind."

They walked down the street to Port's car and stopped there.

"How about it," said Joko. "You wanna put it in my trunk, and we ride in my car?"

"You're giving me pains, Joko."

"Never mind, Danny, I didn't mean it, but let me give you a hand. You grab this end and I take the rear and we just lift it out on the street so you don't have to...."

Port mumbled something and waited for Joko to go to his car before climbing into his own.

Chapter 3

Port wasn't used to the distances in Los Angeles. When Joko's Cadillac swung into a lot on Vine it was almost two hours later and Port kept cursing himself for not having turned off some place on the way and forgotten about Joko. They parked on the lot and Joko stood by while Port paid a buck in advance. Joko didn't have to pay. He had a monthly permit at reduced rates.

Joko Mulnik really did have an office, in the building next to the parking lot, on the second floor. The fact impressed Port. He tried not to show it and just nodded his head when Joko told him to sit down, just sit down, just sit down anywhere, while he went to the next room to make a call.

It wasn't a two-bit layout. There had been the waiting room, then the office where Port looked out the window at Vine, two stories below, and the room where Joko was on the phone. The door was half open and Port was really making a call. There was also a piano and a microphone visible.

Port went back to the window, and then walked along the walls. They were covered with publicity stills, most of them signed. *To dear Joko with thanks*, or *To Joko, a great guy, my best*, and then somebody's name. They were actors, or singers, or comedians, and one—full length—was most like burlesque. And there were a lot of known film stars. They said *With best wishes*, or *Lots of Luck*, and then the well-known name signed at the bottom. Port noticed that on the movie star pictures Joko's name wasn't part of the message.

But legitimate, just like Joko had said. Port sighed and went to the desk. He sat down and waited for Joko. It was a long conversation, and legitimate probably, just like Joko had said.

A bell went *ding* in the waiting room and then Port heard the front door close. Next, the office door opened.

This female was something!

Her head was held like a queen's, her bosom was defined beauty, and her hips and thighs were the absolute. Her walk into the room was like an affair of state, and when she nodded at Port, nodding with the casual smile that might come from long years of intimate friendship, Port managed to smile back at her, too late for her to see, because she had crossed the room, gone into a little hallway, and opened a closet door. In the dark there she was taking her hat off, and her jacket.

Port got up and went back to the window. He looked out, seeing nothing, and started to light a cigarette. That was a secretary, he thought. Such a secretary; to have such a secretary! How in hell did Joko rate such— Port heard those steps again, measured, sure, and he turned around. He took the cigarette out of his mouth, tearing his lip.

It had all been true. She had been altogether the absolute truth, all of it, because—except for the high-heeled shoes—she now stood there quite naked.

She cocked one hip, froze her arms in a graceful gesture, posed her head. Then she said, "Okay?"

After a moment she looked at Port. She was frowning.

"Do I get the job or don't I?"

Port started to say something, he didn't know what, when Joko came back into the room. He nodded at the girl, sat down at his desk, looked up again.

"Beat it," he said. "I'm busy."

The girl relaxed her pose, looking just as good, and got angry.

"Which one of you guys is this Mulnik?"

"Him," said Port, and nodded at Joko.

"I'm Mulnik," said Joko. "What do you want?"

"The audition, you jerk. I called you up and you said…."

"Oh, yeah. I forgot. Now beat it, I'm busy."

"What about the job? I come down here…."

"It's yours. Christ, what kind of question. Get your clothes on and beat it. You know the address?"

"I know it," she said, and went back into the alcove with the closet.

She was dressed in no time at all and came back to stop at the desk.

"Pick up your check at the end of the week," said Joko. "This office."

The girl nodded and went out.

"Okay," said Joko. He peeled cellophane off a new cigar and waved it at Port. "Sit down over here and we talk."

"What was that?" said Port.

Joko looked up.

"I didn't hear anything."

"What was, I mean, who was this...."

"Come on, sit here. She?" Joko put the cigar in his mouth, holding it up at an angle. "I'm her agent. She's talent."

Port nodded to himself and sat down. Then he looked up at the walls where the pictures were hanging.

"I don't see her anywhere. How come you haven't got a picture of her any place?"

"She hasn't got a name," said Joko.

"But it seems to me, Joko, with such talent—"

"I'm working on it." Joko was getting impatient. "Forget about her for a minute and listen to me."

"Okay, Joko. I'm listening to you. I much rather listen to you than think about that talent you...."

"Danny, please, don't act like a bastard all the time. Please."

Port smiled across the desk and waited.

Joko sat back and took a breath.

"Only reason I asked you up is because this thing is big."

"Talent?"

"Danny, please stop acting the...."

"I know."

"All right. You think she was talent? She's no-talent! Strictly nothing compared."

"What?"

"Strictly no-talent compared."

"Compared to what?"

Joko went through his laugh. Then he said, "I was waiting for you to ask. You follow the movies, Danny?"

"Faithfully."

"Good. They're big business, they're here to stay, they make money."

"You mean that, Joko?"

Joko ignored it. "Who are the greatest? Mention some."

"Some what, movies?"

"Movies? Who knows from movies? I mean stars. The biggest."

Port blew smoke up, watching it drift. "Well," he said, "there's Sarah Bernhardt, Theda Bara...."

"Stars, you jerk! I mean stars!"

"I was working toward that, Joko."

"So let's hear if you know what you're talking about."

"You mean contemporary?"

"What?" But Joko didn't wait for an answer. He made an impatient gesture and said, "Look, Port, I'm talking business. I'm taking time doing it so you get the importance of this thing. Do me a favor and please stop horsing around with my time like a bastard and show a little...."

"Sure, Joko, sure."

"All right. Who's the biggest today?"

"Well, sir, there are some mighty fine actors in today's...."

"Danny, please! Actors, shmactors. I'm talking about stars! I'm talking strictly about the talent department!"

"Ah."

"Well?"

"Putting it that way, I'd say Ella Anders."

There was a silence after that and then Port saw how Joko was smiling. After a moment he said, "She's really something, isn't she?"

"She certainly is," and Port thought about Ella Anders the way everybody thought about Ella Anders.

"And now I'm going to tell you why Ella Anders is strictly talent."

"You don't have to," said Port.

"Yes, I do." Joko leaned over the desk and sounded professional. "Fifteen or sixteen minutes ago a dish was in here and you thought *she* was talent. But she wasn't. Not like Ella Anders. You know why?"

"No name. She hasn't got...."

"That's part of it, but here's the real difference. This dame here in the office with no clothes on, all she's got is a body."

"Yes. It's a shame. All she had...."

"Shut up and listen. Now there's lots of bodies. Talent all over the place. But Ella Anders, she's got that and plus."

"Yes?"

"She's got plus. She can move it, she can make it talk, she can make it live. I bet you," and Joko Mulnik's voice rose with emphasis, "I bet you Ella Anders would have the real talent even if she *didn't* have a body!" Port thought about it and there was something to it. But it was a surprise to hear Mulnik say it.

"You know how old she is, Danny?"

Port didn't know.

"What if I told you she's thirty."

Port thought about it. "Could be true," he said.

"Or twenty?"

"That could be true."

"You're damn right that could be true. And thirty." Joko took the cigar out of his mouth. "You get it now? It shows that she's good."

"I see what you mean."

After a moment Joko turned the cigar around and stuck the unchewed end in his mouth. He crossed his arms on top of the desk, making his false shoulders stick out. It reminded Port of the fenders on Joko's car, like two sharks in formation.

"Know how old that kid really is?"

Port shook his head.

"She's thirty-one. She's been in pictures for maybe ten years, and now she's thirty-one." Joko looked at Port, his head low between the shoulders. "That means she's good for twenty more years. Maybe more."

"You sound callous as hell, Joko."

"If she wasn't Ella Anders but that doll here in the office a while ago, she'd have, at the most, five more years."

"You talking about a horse?"

"I'm an agent. I'm talking about talent."

Port put out his cigarette and leaned back. He said, "You're showing such interest, Joko, how come you don't own her?"

"I will," said Mulnick. "I will."

Chapter 4

Something changed in the air, making Port feel uncomfortable. He remembered that it had started when Joko had leaned over the desk, his false shoulders sticking out like fins, and had turned to talking about Ella Anders as if he were judging a horse. Port also remembered how little he liked Joko Mulnik and that he could have spent the time better lying in the sand on the beach or swimming.

"Don't go yet," said Joko. "Here. Take a look."

He reached over the desk with his hand, waving at Port to hold out his. When Port did Joko dropped a small piece of cellophane into Port's palm.

It was a small piece of film, one frame from a 16-mm. strip.

"Hold it up to the light," said Joko.

Port did.

"What do you see?"

Port squinted and said, "She looks naked."

"Know her?"

"Her back is turned."

"Let me show you the rest of the film. I can…."

"Never mind," said Port and put the frame back on the desk. "Not my kind of kick."

Mulnik laughed. "I just bet."

Port shrugged, got out of his chair. "I'm really not interested."

Mulnick laughed again, loud this time. "The hell you say. That's Ella Anders!"

Joko leaned back in his chair and let his feet come off the ground. He watched Port sit down again, he saw Port give him a smile, and then Joko grinned back. He misunderstood what Port meant and said, "I thought you would see it, Danny."

Port was still smiling. "All I see is a small-time punk who's got a hold of a pornographic film and he's sitting on it and sitting on it while it goes to his head."

"At least I got a head. And I'm gonna use it."

"I thought you said you'd gone legit, Joko?"

"I have. What's more legit than selling something that somebody wants?"

"You know, Joko, there's only two or three crimes that get a worse rap than blackmail."

"Rap? Danny, please! You and me…."

"Forget it. I'm not going in with you."

"For dough? Can't you see the dough?"

"I like Ella Anders. And I don't like you."

"I understand that, Danny, believe me I do. But what's that got to do with—Look. You like Ella? Then make it easy for her. You got the finesse, I know that. So do you. I know it by the way you got to be Stoker's top man and by the way you walked out of the thing without even a scratch. And I also know…."

Joko was off again. Port sat back, smiling down at his hands, listening to the bland flattery and to the self-effacement when Joko described how helpless he was without Port. When Joko ran down a little he had achieved at least one thing. Port had gotten curious.

"If I'm going to give this some thought, Joko, you got to explain more. Some details."

"What, Danny? What do you want to know? Ask me!"

"That little piece there, that's a positive, isn't it?"

"That's right. Right now there's just that one positive."

"And the negative?"

"I got that."

"How come?"

"The guy who took the film gave it to me. I mean I bought it from him."

"How come you aren't broke, Joko?"

"Look, that's got nothing to do with nothing. He didn't know what he had then. That film's fifteen years old."

"And the negative is still good?"

"Good enough."

"Let me see it."

"You don't know beans from photography, Danny, so don't even ask. Next question."

"Fifteen years old. She was sixteen then."

"She looked the same, believe me. If you want to see...."

"Maybe later." Port got up and went to the window sill. He sat down there and crossed his legs.

"Did you make contact yet?"

"Just a letter. Two letters."

"To her or the studio?"

"The studio, naturally. They got more money."

"And more of everything else. Once they take you seriously...."

"I got even more than they do. I got the film. Danny, just look at the setup." Joko got up, excited. "She's good for at least twenty years, twenty years of high-income property that...."

"What setup? You haven't set up a thing yet."

"That's why you and me...."

"Have they contacted you?"

"I haven't asked them. So far, I've just told them what's what. Let 'em stew, you know what I mean. Just the needle at first and...."

"Stop talking. You haven't gone any further because you don't know how."

Joko was frank and disarming about it. "That's right, Danny. I don't know how. I'm sitting on it and it's driving me crazy. That's why I need you, Danny."

"For what?"

"Contact man. I need a guy smart as you who nobody knows around here and can make a good contact man...."

Joko trailed off because Port had started to laugh. He kept laughing till it got under Joko's skin and he felt like throwing something.

"What did you call it?" said Port. "Contact man?"

"Yeah, that's what I called it."

"You mean fall guy, you son of a bitch." Port started to laugh again.

After a moment he stopped very suddenly. He came back to the desk and gave Joko a push, just a light one, to tell him that he should sit down. Joko sat and looked up at Port.

"I keep forgetting what a smart snake in the grass you are, Joko. You didn't need me to figure this thing out for you and make it a setup. You had that all worked out. All you needed was the jackass dumb enough to run such an errand and deluded enough to keep you out of it when the contact man got picked up and became the fall guy." Port sat on the desk and reached over to flip Joko's tie up in the air. "What made you think I'd go for a lame-brained stunt like that?"

"There was nothing lame-brained about it, the way I was going to tell you about it."

For a moment Port just stared. The gall of the man, his wide-eyed, blank-faced admission was difficult to grasp.

"And the money," said Joko. "You know there's money in it."

"For me too?"

"Sure. Just to bring over the film, for instance, I was gonna give you a thousand, five thousand, I mean."

"I'll be damned!"

"And then something extra, each time we negotiate. You know what I mean? They don't get the negative, you understand. The way I'm going to do this—"

"Jesus," said Port. "You don't give up, do you?"

"Give up what?"

"Count me out," Port said. "You told me your setup and it's no good."

"Look, Danny, if it's no good we can fix it." He came around from behind his desk, came over to Port, and took hold of the towel Port had over his shoulder. "If it's no good I don't know it, Danny. Why is it no good?"

"What are you asking? Free information?"

"No, not free, Danny. You tell me and I...."

"Let go of me," and Port, suddenly irritated, clapped Joko's hand off his shoulder. Then he controlled himself, because there was no sense getting riled up over Mulnik. "This deal you got in mind makes you as stupid as every dumb blackmail artist behind bars."

"Tell me why!"

"Because you're running it as blackmail. You start out right from the be-ginning as the sucker they're all going to look for. And more power to them."
Port turned away and opened the door again.

"How, Danny, how else?"

Port wanted to get away. He was getting disgusted and it was so bad that he didn't want Mulnik standing so close to him.

"Remember Delray? He played it smart. Of course he's dead now, but Del-ray had a smart system."

"Yeah, I remember Delray; wait a minute, Danny, let's talk about Delray...."

"He's dead, I told you," said Port from across the waiting room.

"Danny, I'll raise your ante! Six thousand!"

Port looked back and gave Joko a smile. "Hell, Joko, I could get more hir-ing out to the studio, chasing you down."

Joko Mulnik didn't say anything else, just watched Port close the door and listened to his footsteps going away.

Chapter 5

After Port left the parking lot he drove around for a while to get the bad air out of his system. He went down to the Hollywood freeway and prac-ticed driving. When the downtown skyline came clear through the smog he tried to head back, took the first turnoff that came along, and got lost in a series of underpasses and loops which funneled him toward Pasadena. Once he discovered this it was too late to do anything about it. He noticed there were hardly any Cadillacs in Pasadena, which was a relief in itself. Be-fore heading back he stopped in a hamburger place which was called Bovine Boudoir and had a revolving cow on the roof, a cow which seemed to be leaping into the wide open mouth of a face which was also revolving.

Inside, the waitresses were mostly plain. No use wasting talent on people in Pasadena. Port ate his hamburger plain, foregoing sesame seeds, exotic herbs, and secret sauces. He sat around for a while, waiting for his coffee to cool, and wondered how long he should stay in L.A. Tessy or no Tessy, he didn't like Joko Mulnik so close, and no matter how big L.A. was, Mulnik could find him if he wanted to. But by now even Mulnik should know how Port felt about him and his deal, and if worse came to worst, Port could al-ways threaten to queer things for Joko. But Port didn't feel like expending the effort, not when it came to something like Mulnik. To mix in and maybe call Ella Anders—if there was such a thing as calling up Ella Anders—that never occurred to him.

He drove back to his room in Los Angeles proper, just below Hollywood, and took a shower to get the feeling of salt water off his skin. Then he changed and went to a movie. At the time there were three Ella Anders films running in town and Port picked the first one he passed because he hadn't seen any of them. The film stank, but Ella was a delight. When Port came out it was dark, a warm darkness with the sting of the smog gone out of the air, and Port drove slowly. He went up to the place where Tessy was singing, and sat by the bar, drinking rye with water, and watching Tessy, who was all talent even if there had been no body. She didn't spot him until after her second set and came to the bar.

"Mad at me?" she said, and looked up at him. She was standing and Port was sitting perched on a barstool, but she still had to look up at him.

"*For*, Tessy, not *at*."

She took his arm and started to yank.

"I got forty-five minutes this time. Come sit with me?"

Port picked up his drink and took Tessy to a small table. They passed the couches by the fireplace and the low cocktail tables which cluttered most of the room, and took a table by the far wall.

"You can't sit here," she said, "unless you eat." She sat down and folded her hands on the tablecloth. "I'll have a steak."

"I knew you would," said Port and put his drink on the table. "Raw, probably."

"Just middling. I'm doing ballads today."

"And a drink?"

"No, thank you. I'm singing."

"You sing beautifully."

"All you want is my body," she said and gave a hoist to her neckline.

"No, honestly, Tessy...."

"You said no?"

"Honestly. I mean yes."

She grinned at him and he laughed back at her.

When he ordered the steak for her she said that she didn't want the salad that came with it, but the waiter was the kind who didn't understand such extravagance and kept insisting the salad went with it. Port told him to bring it and while Tess ate the steak Port ate the salad. It had a strong flavor of cheese which went well with the rye he was drinking. After that Tess wanted tea and Port stuck to the rye.

"What did you do, Danny, after I called you that I wasn't coming?"

"I jumped in the ocean."

She liked that, but then she said, "Not that it meant anything, seeing you came out again to show up here."

"I couldn't hold my breath any longer."

"You don't seem winded to me."

"I'm controlling myself. After all...."

"Stop staring, Danny."

"What else can I do? Take your eyes, for instance. They are the damnedest blue I've ever seen."

"It just looks that way, because I have dark hair."

"And the tan."

She looked at her arm, turning it back and forth.

"It's fading. Will you go to the beach with me tomorrow?"

"All day."

"After we get up."

"Of course. I forgot about that."

"That's why I reminded you."

"Do, Tessy. Lean over a little."

"What?"

"Over the table. I want to give you a kiss."

She said, "Oh," and then leaned over the table and they had a short kiss which pleased both of them.

"I got to go," she said then. "I'm on in ten minutes."

"But ten minutes—"

"You know, lipstick and everything."

"As far as I'm concerned...."

"Not with those lights."

"Doesn't that get on your nerves, night after night?"

"But I'm a singer."

"So make records."

She shook her head, smiling. "Then nobody would see me."

"That's why I think records are just exactly the thing in a case like this. How long have you been singing?"

"Oh, a long time. Since I was a little girl."

"In public, like this?"

"No, no. Just for myself. I like singing."

"There, you see? Nobody saw you and you enjoyed it just as much. Now, it's my feeling...."

"But I was a little girl then. I wasn't like now."

"You're a wanton, that's all."

"That's how I got you."

"Gimme another kiss."

"No," and she got up. "But if you want to wait till I'm off," she said, "I'll give you one after the show." She waved at him and was gone.

She wasn't through until four in the morning and when Port and Tessy left the club they were both very tired. Everything felt very slow and warm, and even the morning air didn't change that feeling. She had changed into a suit with big pockets and she stuck her hands in there, which gave her a wrapped-up look.

"You want breakfast, Tessy?"

"No. Let's go to bed."

They walked across the deserted street in the thin morning light and went to Port's car.

"Is it cute," said Tessy. "How do I get in?"

"Any more of that and I'll make you walk."

"You could steer and I could push."

Port grabbed her and lifted her off her feet, making her laugh, and then plunked her into the right seat.

"Where do you live, Tessy?"

"Up in one of the canyons. Up there."

They could see the length of La Cienega reaching straight up the long hill toward Sunset and the hills behind that where Tessy lived.

"That's too far, Tessy. Let's go to my place."

"Is it closer?"

"Much."

"Let's go to your place. I'm ready for bed."

She yawned. When Port swung out of the parking lot it made Tessy lean up against him and they smiled.

Ten minutes later they went up to the room Port had rented, a place called an efficiency apartment with wide windows looking down on a tropical court. Tess hummed to herself and Port was working the lock. He swung the door open, watched Tess walk in ahead of him, and then she stopped humming abruptly. The door closed, barely missing Port, yanking right out of his hand.

Chapter 6

The one in the chair had a gun on Port and the one by the door was reaching under his coat. He said, "Police. Detective Bureau," and he held out his badge. "Are you Daniel Port?"

"Let's see that badge," said Port.

The officer was putting it back into his pocket.

"Let's see your warrant."

"Are you Mr. Port?"

"You need a warrant, busting in here."

"You're under arrest, Mr. Port."

"And the warrant for that."

"Get the cuffs," said the one in the chair and got up. He kept his gun on Port and came closer.

They both looked like cops wearing mufti. They moved slowly, like men doing a routine, looking sure but a little tired, and they acted as if they could be polite. The one with the gun had gray at his temples and a big frame. The one by the door was younger, but the lines in his face made him look as if he had seen plenty of wear. He said, "Raise your hands, Mr. Port."

The other one still had the gun out, so Port raised his hands. He got a fast frisk, almost too fast, but it was efficient enough. Then he turned to Tessy and said, "Just routine, ma'am," and while the old one stood by Port the young one went over and gave her hips, where the big pockets were, a brief pat. Then he nodded and said,

"Thank you, ma'am, that's all."

"Who are you?" said the older one to Tess.

"None of your business," said Tess.

He shrugged and turned back to Port. "Come along. We're going to headquarters."

"Like hell!"

"Pat, get the cuffs," he said to the young one.

Port didn't want any cuffs. The young one didn't have the cuffs out yet so Port said, "Never mind, I'll come."

"Fine. Go quietly and there won't be any trouble."

"What about the lady?" said Port.

The two cops looked at each other, then the old one shrugged. "She's not wanted."

"Stay here," said Port. "I'll be back."

He walked out the door with the gun in his back, and then the young one followed.

Port got to the street, still without handcuffs, and they guided him to a car by the curb. When the old one opened the door Port said, "I know his name; it's Pat. What would yours be, Mike, maybe?"

"Just get into the car, Mr. Port."

"You know something, Mike, you and Pat...."

"Get into the car, please. No more delay."

"You look like a cop, walk like one, talk like one. I know all this very well because I watch TV all the time. You two, just like TV cops—" which was as far as Port got because he got sapped from behind and passed out.

The headache woke him up, but it woke him only enough to know where he was, not to move. He was still in the car, in the back seat, next to Mike, whose pants leg he could see next to him, and either it was a very long drive or he hadn't been sapped very hard. Don't move yet, just wait a while longer till the strength comes back wait and see— Port saw the gun in the man's hand, on his knee, held there like a prop.

A prop cop. No warrant, no handcuffs; they didn't take Tessy along, didn't even ask who she was, where she lived. And a prop gun, because Port could see the holes in the cylinder, black holes where the round snouts of the bullets should be if the gun were loaded.

"Don't try it," said Mike suddenly and held the gun close to Port's ribs.

Right then the car swerved hard, and Port's swing went wild and the gun exploded, with a strong stink of powder and burned upholstery. Blanks. He should have thought of that. If that gun had gone off in his side, or his face— Pat had stopped the car with a hard jerk and came up with his sap. And behind Pat, on the veranda in front of a house, stood a man, hands on his hips, craning his neck to see what went on in the car.

"Don't!" yelled Port and in case Pat wouldn't be able to stop Port dragged Mike over in front of him so the sap would be stopped by somebody else.

"Don't, I'll go quietly!"

Inside the car they were all piled up on top of each other, breathing into each other's faces and waiting. Then Port smiled. He was at the bottom and the other two saw it. He smiled and said, "Get off me, please?" and when they made room for him he got out of the car. He stood there with the gun on him and waited for the other two to come out. He straightened his jacket and watched them climb out of the car.

"I got to see this," he said. He was still smiling. But the first surprise came when Port looked back at the man on the veranda. He was still standing there, seeing everything, and hadn't moved.

Then the second surprise. The two TV cops took Port by the arms and went straight to the veranda.

The next surprise, though less than the others, came when Port realized they hadn't parked on a street. The road was paved but there was no other house except the one with the veranda. A house—a big one—in a park with a drive. Quite a way back was a wall and the gates to the street.

After that it was no surprise when the man on the veranda went to the door of the house, held it wide, and stepped aside to let Port and his TV cops pass.

He could have made a break for it then, but he didn't. He was blowing his tuneless whistle when he walked into the house.

A low beamed hall with white plaster between the dark oak, but very expensive; King Arthur's Round Table looking small in the expanse of the place; tapestries hanging heavy, armor with the metal looking pitted and oiled, crossed halberds and—naturally—coats of arms. Then a subtle change when they all walked into the room off the hall. King Arthur's Round Table again but this time with the legs sawed off to make it a cocktail table; suits of armor again but this time in miniature, chrome plated, and by allowing the visor to spring aside a flame would go on to light cigarettes; and once more halberds, swords, daggers, and even several Iron Marys all artfully arranged in a printed pattern that covered the big-cushioned seats in the room. There was only one coat of arms this time. It started just over the fireplace, flared out, and reached up to the ceiling. The ceiling in this room was beamed, too, but high steepled, so the coat of arms made it almost up to the saddle of the roof. A simple coat of arms. All it said was *R.S.L. II.*

Port turned to look at the man from the veranda who was just closing the door to the room.

"How are you, R.S.L.?"

The man frowned and went to the low table to pick up one of the knights in armor and light his cigarette. It didn't work. One of the TV cops went over to give R.S.L. a light from a matchbook and then R.S.L. took several nervous puffs. He was short, bald, and young. A roomy sports coat covered the soft little belly and heavy crepe soles gave him an unbalanced look. For collegiate effect he wore heavily shell-rimmed glasses, but that didn't come off so good either, because of no hair.

"You got it?" said R.S.L.

"Yes, Mr. Luden. But we have to report to—"

Luden! Of course. RSL Studios. And this R. S. Luden the Second, heir apparent, mostly apparent in the movie mags, but with some kind of a title at his old man's studio. And RSL Studios owned Ella Anders.

"Ah! Here are my men!" said a voice and Port knew who it was before he turned around to look.

Joko Mulnik came through an archway next to the fireplace. He was car-rying a drink, his pants legs were flapping so his thin ankles showed, and he was smiling from ear to ear.

"Well, R. S., here we are," he said, and then to the TV policemen. "Have you got it?"

"Yes sir, Mr. Mulnik," and one of them handed him a reel of 16-mm. film.

Joko showed a lot of excitement when he grabbed for the reel. He rolled out a length of the film, held it up to the window, and kept saying, "Uh-huh. Ah, yes. Uh-huh." When he turned back to Luden he seemed to swell out in the chest and even grow a few inches.

"Mr. Luden, our search has come to an end."

But Luden hardly heard. He had been coming around King Arthur's table as fast as he could and when he got within reach of Joko he made a nerv-ous grab for the reel. Joko didn't let him. He held it out of the way, up to the light, so that Luden stopped reaching and looked instead.

"Remarkable," he kept saying. "Remarkable."

They seemed to have forgotten all about Port, but Port wasn't leaving. He sat down on a couch, crossed his legs, and waited. He wasn't going to miss any of this. Not that he was sure about what was going on, but he didn't feel that there was any real danger. There were no police involved, no real po-lice, which alone showed that it wasn't all kosher—aside from the fact that Mulnik was in it, which left kosher out of the question.

Joko rewound the reel and stepped over to the big fireplace. He stepped up on the apron and it was clear there was going to be a speech.

"Mr. Luden," with a nod, "men," another one, "we have come to the end of a grueling search. We have come to the end and I'm glad. A reputation has been saved, and a lot of money. Mr. Luden," there was the nod once more, "I hand over to you the blackmailer of Ella Anders, the man who by taking advantage of someone's youthful mistake...."

"Mr. Mulnik," said Luden, and the anxiety showed in his voice, "I appre-ciate the way you feel at this moment, but let's just have that...."

"In a moment, R. S."

"Now! And take this man out of here."

"You mean Port?"

"Whatever his name is."

"I thought, R. S., you might want to hand him over to the police."

"Are you out of your mind? The main reason I hired you...."

"I understand." Joko coughed. "You got the check?"

Luden was already fumbling inside his jacket and pulled out a check.

"Twenty thousand, certified. Here you are, Mr. Mulnik, and made out to your organization. And now if you will...."

"Let's see that."

Joko took the check and looked it over. It looked very good to him and he nodded at Luden.

"Here," he said, handing over the reel. "Your troubles are over." And then he walked to the door very quickly.

"Come on, Port, let's go."

Port grinned and shook his head.

"Come on, Port, I'm doing you a favor. Mr. Luden doing you a favor. If we wanted to...."

Port shook his head again and grinned.

"What does he want?" said Luden. "I don't understand."

"I just want to stay a while longer. Five minutes, maybe, that's all."

"Port, I'm warning you! Come on and let's go or I set my men on you."

"Don't try it," said Port and he wasn't grinning any more.

"Mr. Port," said Luden, "I'm trying to have as little to do with you as I can. You've tried blackmail, and you've failed. If you're trying to hold me up with some kind of threat to cause a stink about this, let me promise you that...."

"I just don't want to leave with that Mulnik character," said Port. "Give him a five-minute head start and then I leave."

"If you're trying to hold me up with some kind—"

"I'm not. I told you."

"Then leave my house!" yelled Luden.

"I don't want to leave with that Mulnik bastard," said Port.

"Come on, you crook," and Joko took a step towards Port.

"Beat it."

"I got you once, I'll get you again. You're trying some kind of squeeze play on my client."

"Why don't you make sense!" said Port, sounding angry. "Would I stir anything up that'll get me a rap?" He looked over at Luden and said, "Would I? I lost out on the caper but at least I look clean!"

"Yes, that makes sense," said Luden.

But Joko was now very nervous. Port was acting the part of the blackmailer, just as if he and Joko had rehearsed it that way. Port mustn't stay behind. Joko jerked his head at the two cops and they came toward Port, one with the blackjack, the other with the gun.

"Joko," said Port. "It's almost nine a.m." He said it with voice very even, no special emphasis, and what he said didn't seem to make any sense.

But Joko reacted. He gave Port a fast, mean look, then waved off his men.

While he did this he was already on his way out of the door.

"Mr. Mulnik! I insist…" Luden began.

"I'm staying five minutes," said Port.

"I demand protection! Mr. Mulnik!"

Joko stopped in the hall, came part way back to snap at one of his men. "Stay with him, Rodnick."

"His name is Pat," Port corrected him.

Joko gave Port another quick look, then turned and rushed out of the house. Mike went with him, but the young one stayed behind. He didn't know what was wanted of him but he stayed behind because Joko had said so. He stood by the door and watched Port sit down in a couch and Luden, by the fireplace, looking ill at ease under his large coat of arms. After a moment they all heard the car take off and then Luden cleared his throat.

"All right. I'm giving you five minutes, that's all. After that I make trouble."

Port smiled at Luden and said, "Don't you want to know what just happened?"

Luden didn't understand what Port meant.

"You've just been suckered," said Port. "Don't you want to know how?"

Chapter 7

The first thing Luden did was run to the window and pull a long strip off the reel in his hand. He looked at it against the light, felt it, turned it, looked at it again. When he faced the room he rolled up the film very slowly, walked toward Port very slowly, and put a lot of heaviness into his voice.

"Port, I'm in the film business, every phase, meaning I know what I'm talking about. This reel is of Ella Anders and this reel is the negative. That's what I paid for, that's what I got."

He paused, waiting for Port to find something to say, but Port didn't say anything for a moment. Then he rubbed one hand over his face and looked up.

"It can't be. I don't care what you got there."

But Luden wasn't impressed. He waved a hand at Mulnik's man and said, "Five minutes are up. Throw him out of here."

But Mulnik's man wasn't a cop any more. All he said was, "All right, Mr. Port, let's go," and started to walk out of the door.

"Wait a minute, Pat—"

"I'm leaving."

"Pat. I'll stick you for impersonating an officer."

The man came back to the door.

"Stick around, Pat. I need a ride back to town."

"You can stop calling me Pat. The name happens to be Rodnick."

"Okay, Patnick. Just sit down till I'm through."

The man did and Port turned back to Luden, who had understood none of this.

"You've been suckered, Mr. Luden. I'll tell you why."

"Look—"

"Just sit down," said Port.

Luden did, looking confused, on the edge of the big round table.

"The reason I know that you paid for nothing is because I told Mulnik how to do it."

"You what?!"

"Unintentionally, but I told him."

"You mean you and he—you mean you know him?"

"Jesus, do I know him," said Port. Then he got back to business. "There was a guy once, Mulnik and I both knew him, who worked it pretty much the same way. This guy Delray used to blackmail anonymously, and after the victim had stewed for a while, and after Delray was sure that nobody had gone to the police, he'd show up at the victim's place as a detective. As a private eye. He would say that in the course of some kind of investigation he'd stumbled across...."

"Oh no!" said Luden.

"So he did, huh?"

Luden swallowed, unable to answer.

"Well, this con man, Delray, worked that racket on a pretty permanent basis. He really did have an office, he even did have a license, and he never asked for money except that one, first time. Even if somebody went to the police, Delray could show he was doing legitimate business."

"But—but—" Luden raised the reel.

"Then there was a wrinkle. Delray improved his method and wouldn't deliver the right merchandise. It looked all right, but it wasn't. Delray would come back, excuse himself for having made a mistake, however unfortunately, but for an additional fee...."

"But this is the film!" yelled Luden. "This is it!"

"Was I right so far?"

"I don't...."

"Did he say he was a private eye?"

"Yes! And I checked! Confidential Services; they're in the book!"

"So what?"

"I called up and the girl said she knew Mr. Mulnik."

"She probably did. Now, that check you handed to Mulnik. Whose idea was it to have it certified?"

"His."

"Sure it was. You remember my telling him it was almost nine o'clock?"

"Yes."

"And he rushed out of here like he was stung?"

"Yes, but I don't...."

"He can cash that check, certified and with the Luden name on it, in any bank in this town."

Luden jumped up and started to race for a phone that stood in a niche by the door.

"Don't bother," said Port. "It isn't nine yet, so you can't even get through to the bank. He'll walk in at nine sharp and cash it without interference."

"I can get through! There isn't a bank in this town...."

"At which bank in L.A. is he going to cash it?"

Luden looked beat.

"And a general stop order takes time, plenty of time for Mulnik."

Luden's frustration was too much for him. He wasn't used to this kind of treatment. His face seemed to swell with the red color in it and he started to pound one hand on the reel he was holding.

"But I have here in my hand—right here in my hand—"

"Unroll it."

When Luden didn't move Port got up and took the reel out of his hand. He held on to the end of the strip and threw the reel across the room.

There were maybe ten feet of negative. Then came a splice. The rest of the film was a lot of footage of plain, opaque leader. No pictures, just dead black film,

Then Luden came to life. He tore the film and kicked at it. He promised death for Mulnik, death for whoever got in his way, and when nobody in the room put up an argument he started to kick the furniture. Then he stopped very suddenly, sat down, and looked sullen.

"You needn't take it so hard, Mr. Luden," said Port. "As a matter of fact...."

"I'll handle this."

"Good," and Port leaned against the fireplace, waiting to hear.

"Every means at my disposal," Luden was mumbling, and then, louder, "I'll get my father on this!"

Port didn't say anything, but Luden caught the way Port looked at his shoes, then out of the window, as if he didn't think much of the idea.

"The police!" Luden went on. "Or the FBI!"

But that's all Luden did, talk about it, and sit on the couch with a sullen look. When Port still didn't say anything and just stood there, looking unimpressed, Luden started to yell again.

"Well? Maybe you think I should let this go by? You realize how much Ella Anders is worth? You realize what it means when somebody tries to cross me?"

"Tries? He did it."

Luden was, at the most, in his late twenties. The paunch and the baldness sometimes distracted from that but he was young and he acted even younger. He could start acting like a ten year old at the drop of an insult but while Port was looking at him he suddenly looked old.

"It isn't that bad," said Port.

"Bad—"

"Don't forget, Mulnik isn't this Delray I was talking about. Mulnik had to improvise."

"I don't care what you call it—"

"I happen to know that he didn't set up this caper till some time yesterday afternoon. Besides, I know Joko pretty well."

Luden turned his head toward Port very slowly and the look he gave him got more and more hostile. "How come you know all this?"

"I happen to know Mulnik several years now."

"Who are you?"

"Nobody. I just got into town."

"What do you do?"

"I'll tell you what I will do, if...."

"You another one of those crooks? Maybe Mulnik is working for you?"

"No."

"Daniel Port? I can check into you; I think I will check into you."

"Go ahead. I've been in L.A. a week and a half, unemployed."

"How come? You so rich you can afford it?"

"I'm not broke. And for the past five years I've worked in the same place out East."

"Doing what?"

Port made a short laugh, and said, "I'll even tell you that. I used to work for the Stoker outfit."

"Stoker! That racketeer who died and his whole organization blew up in headlines?"

"I'm the one who got away."

"That's very strange, Mr. Port."

"Not at all. I've got a clean record."

"I think I'll turn you over to the police."

"Wouldn't do any good. But I'll tell you what you should do—hire me."

Luden got off the couch and tried to make himself tall. His voice got heavy, a board-meeting voice, and he said, "You underestimate me. You must have the idea, from where I don't know, that...."

Port took the wind out of him with one short sentence. "You don't have to pay me a thing."

He had to laugh when he saw Luden's face. Then he said, "You gave Joko twenty thousand? Well, I'll collect that."

Luden liked that idea, but suddenly he had another one. "How do I know you won't collect the film too, and keep that."

"I won't, that's all."

But that didn't impress Luden. "I'll make it worth your while, returning the negative. You deliver that negative and I pay you ten thousand in cash. Plus expenses."

"I'll take it."

"But if you don't, if there is one more attempt to...."

"I know. You'll tell your father. Now look, there's one more thing. Just in case I get fouled up in some way, and I've got that negative on me...."

"What do you mean, fouled up?"

"A million things can happen. So just in case, I want you to give me a statement where you say I've been authorized by you to bring that film to you. That you're paying for it, and that I'm the messenger picking it up."

When it came to signed statements, contracts and so forth, Luden wasn't so gullible. His father had taught him never to sign anything until their staff of lawyers had checked the thing through, and Luden had stuck to that order, because it relieved him of a lot of thinking.

"I'll do that," he said. "You come to my office tomorrow and I'll have it for you."

"Why not today?"

"Because I'm going to check up on you."

"Go ahead. Where do I find you tomorrow?"

"Come to the studio. Building Twelve. I'll leave word at the gate."

Port grinned. "And do I get to meet Ella Anders?"

"I can arrange it," said Luden, looking bored. Mulnik's man still sat at the door and when Port walked out he waved at him and said, "All right, Lieutenant, drive me home."

They got into the car and drove out of R. S. Luden's park.

"Tell me, Rodwick," said Port.

"The name's Rodnick."

"I better call you Pat, for short. So tell me, Lieutenant, what precinct you working out of?"

"Mulnik's precinct. I'm one of his clients."

"How come I didn't see your picture on his wall?"

"I didn't have one to give him. I ran out and I'm broke."

"Ah. An actor."

"I was a comic."

"Was?"

Pat turned his tired face toward Port and then he looked front again.

"Would you mind answering me a question?"

"You got to ask it first."

"When you walked into your place and found me there, with the other one, did I look like a cop?"

"Absolutely, Lieutenant."

Pat thought about it, and then, "I think I'll try TV. With all the tired-cop programs they got, maybe—"

"Why don't you try Luden? Now that you've met him...."

"Don't make me laugh."

"Not big enough for you?"

"Look," said Pat, "first of all I didn't meet him. Second, it wouldn't make any difference. You know what he is? He works in production, but he isn't a producer, he isn't an associate producer, or an assistant producer. He is an assistant *to* the producer."

"What's that?"

"Whatever you like. And then it doesn't mean anything."

"So how come he's in on this Anders shuffle? That's big."

"He's assistant to Ella Anders's producer. And the only reason he's in on it now is because he thought he could come up with a fast, brilliant conclusion to the whole mess. I know, because that's how Joko played it. He made that phone call to Luden the Second direct, and for once Luden didn't check with the lawyers because it all happened so fast. Not to mention the chance he saw here to make a big splash at the studio."

It made sense. And it also meant, the way Port saw it, that Luden might turn out a second Mulnik. Not as sure as Joko, and with much less practice, but the motive was there. Luden was out to make himself a mark, and the more it looked like a sure thing, the less he would care who got hurt. He hadn't looked like the type who liked people.

Chapter 8

When Port got back to his room he saw the wall bed was down and everything else was in order. But Tessy had left. There was a note on the floor where Port couldn't miss it. It said, *If you get back here before I can reach you at the police, please please call me. Love Tess.*

I would like to, he said to himself.

Then he decided to call her right away and tell her to stop looking for him at the police, because the jerks that had picked him up had been actors. They'd have a laugh about it, over the phone, and then he would get her and they would have a good time at the beach some place.

He even picked up the telephone before he remembered that he didn't know what her number was or where she lived. He blinked his eyes, feeling the tiredness, and started to look for her name in the book. Then he remembered he only knew her stage name, which, as it turned out, was shared by a construction company in the telephone book and by a party who was a retired Army major. When Port called the club the cleaning lady answered the phone and after she got the boss on the line Port was told that it wasn't the policy of the club to reveal personal information about their entertainers over the telephone. And even if Port were told Tessy's real last name that wouldn't be of much help. She had an unlisted number.

Port hung up and stood by the window. The sun was up strong now, making reflections on the growths in the courtyard below. It hurt Port's eyes and made him feel tired. He would go and eat something. He would lie down on the bed for a moment and rest, then go out and eat something....

When he woke up he was ravenous. Except for that he felt remarkably well, fresh and rested. One look out of the window explained that to him, because the sun seemed to be going down. Port jumped up fast and ran into a chair which was standing in the middle of the room. The whole thing gave him quite a start. There was a nightgown over the chair, a wonderful thing made out of nothing, and on top of that another note.

It was very short and Tessy had printed it big. It said, *NUTS!*

That evening Port walked into the club when it was still practically empty. Tess was at the microphone singing a ballad and it seemed to make no difference to her that there were only a handful of people. She saw Port come in but finished her set without showing a ripple. Port waited for her at the same table and since you had to eat at that table Port ordered. He ordered two steaks, and not wanting to argue with the waiter again he also ordered two salads. In the meantime he wanted a cup of coffee.

When Tessy was through she made no hocus-pocus about deciding which she would do: go over to Port's table or snub him and go to the back. She came straight to the table, with steps much too long for her size, and then she stopped by Port's chair and put her hands on her hips. Port didn't say anything right away, just looked at her, because she looked that good. Then he said, "All right, Tessy. Before you bust, say the worst thing you can think of."

She flared her nostrils, keeping her lips tight together. "What's the worst you can call me, Tessy?"

"Rip Van Winkle!"

Before her next set they both had a steak and ate the salad. Then Tessy had tea and Port sipped his cold coffee. They had a long discussion about all that had gone before, and Tessy told him she'd been to the police and then the police had come to see her and how happy she had been finding him safely at home, sleeping in bed, when she had dropped over in the afternoon. She would rather, if he didn't mind, not discuss what she thought of that situation as the afternoon had worn on, because far be it from her to wake up a boy who needed his sleep. However, just to show her good faith, not to speak of her good will, she had arranged to sing just one more set and they could both leave in just about forty-five minutes. That, she pointed out, was a gain of almost six hours.

Port kept nodding and saying yes and smiling at her and interrupted her now and then to say that he thought she was wonderful.

"Of course, I'll have to get up very early, Dan."

"Sure."

"I do. I'm leaving town for a three-day engagement."

"Where?"

"The hotel at Palmedo."

"Make it two days and we can spend tomorrow...."

"I'll be back, you know. I'll be back after a mere three days."

They argued a little while longer, Tess about having a three-day stand out of town and Port trying to change the subject, and then she went up to sing.

When she was finished she didn't bother to change into her street clothes, but only carried a wrap which she didn't bother to put over her shoulders. The evening was warm and the lights on the street made beautiful shadows and highlights on her bare skin.

They started to cross the street.

"Miss Dolphin?" said a voice, and they both turned around.

He wore mufti, had a tired face, and kept his hat on his head. He was polite but fatalistic about it. "I'm Sergeant Fritter, Miss Dolphin. Excuse me," and he turned to Port. "Daniel Port?"

"Yes."

The sergeant looked past Port and said, "Hey, Pat, I got him."

It was probably the name Pat that did it, but Port felt suddenly angry. He didn't see Fritter wave a gun at him and nobody asked Pat to get ready with the handcuffs, but Port blew his top.

"Sergeant what? You mean Sergeant Friday, don't you? Let's see your badge, Friday, I mean your equity card. And tell me, Rodnick…."

"Is he drunk, Miss Dolphin?"

Port said, "He isn't drunk, Friday, he's just sick and tired of…."

"I know what he's sick and tired of," said Tessy. "As a matter of fact, I myself…."

"Just routine, Miss Dolphin. It's about your report to us, about that bogus arrest."

"I'm sick and tired of any and all kinds of arrest and as far as I'm concerned."

"This is no arrest, Mr. Port. It's just that we've been looking for you, and now that we've found you we'd like to clear up that story Miss Dolphin gave us."

"It didn't happen. I wasn't even there. And the two guys that did it to me were old buddies of mine pulling a joke."

It didn't go over. There was a silence, during which Port lost the mood he had been in, and then Sergeant Fritter started all over, but much more definite this time.

"We'd like both of you to come along to the precinct and we'll clear this thing up in no time at all."

"How long will it take?" asked Port. "Miss Dolphin and I have to know just how long…."

"You're wasting time right now," said Fritter, so instead of driving home with the MG, Port and Tessy drove to the precinct in the back of Fritter's sedan.

They let Tessy go after fifteen minutes, but Port had to stay longer. They didn't like to hear reports of somebody impersonating an officer and pulling a fake arrest and then get no cooperation from the guy who had been victimized. They really got bothered when they realized who Port was, and what with his racket background they kept him under the lights for a number of hours.

He made them swallow it finally, that it had been a private joke, committed on the premises of his own home, and Miss Dolphin was an excitable creature who had misunderstood the whole thing.

When Port got home he found Tessy's nightgown across his bed. The note that was pinned to it read, *You wear it*, and, of course, Tess wasn't there any more.

Chapter 9

Port called the studio at ten in the morning and was told that Mr. Luden the Second would be ready for him any time after one. That gave Port three hours with nothing to do. He could have tried doing something about Mulnik but didn't feel like it yet. He first wanted that paper from Luden, the statement which would keep him in the clear should something go wrong and he got caught with that filthy film in his pocket. Port didn't know what might go wrong, or who might try to nail him, but considering the people he was dealing with and the things that were at stake—he just felt better having that paper.

As far as Mulnik's getting away was concerned, Port didn't worry. If worse came to worst Port could always stick it out till Mulnik would try his next contact. He would do that eventually. Mulnik wasn't the kind to consider twenty thousand enough for the kind of merchandise he had.

And finally, Port wanted to meet Ella Anders herself. As far as he was concerned he'd be working for her, anyway. Not counting the fact that he was sore at Mulnik.

When Port drove up to the studio gate it reminded him of the entrance to Luden's estate. The same corner posts, the same wrought-iron scroll work arching across, and the big letters *R.S.L.* worked into the design. The difference was the guard house and no park on the other side. Just rows of hangars, it seemed.

There was another Cadillac in the way when Port moved his MG into position, but it didn't stay very long. The guard nodded, the kid in the Cadillac nodded back, and then the car tore off. The two exhausts made a racket like a four-engine aircraft. The mufflers had been taken off. Port didn't see who the kid was.

The guard took longer this time. He checked Port's driver's license, made a phone call in his booth, and then came back with the pass, which had all this time been lying in a little file box. Together with the pass Port got a small, geometric map of the studio grounds, and both the gate and Building Twelve had been marked with a circle. The route was marked in between those two points. Last, the guard stamped Port's time of entry on the pass and waved him through.

"Have the time stamped on when you get there. Shouldn't take you more than five minutes."

At Building Twelve, a fussy colonial affair with three stories, there were several more security checks and then Port waited in Luden's anteroom, a large silent room with a silent receptionist. She watched Port and he watched her.

Luden came to the door himself. He gave Port a busy nod and waved him into his office without saying hello.

Luden almost disappeared behind his desk, but by coming halfway around Port could see pretty well where Luden had sunk into a green leather chair which was sighing.

"We checked you," said Luden.

"You got the paper for me?"

"Quite a background." It sounded as if Luden resented it.

"Do I pass?"

Luden opened a drawer and took out a paper. He gave it to Port to read, and it said that for one dollar and other valuable considerations Daniel Port was something to the effect of messenger for the studio in the task of transporting and delivering a certain film—delicately described—to the studio. Luden the Second had signed it, somebody had countersigned it, and the letterhead was R.S.L. Studios.

"Fine," said Port. "And now...."

"I've arranged to have Miss Anders picked up."

"I was going to say something about that."

"Yes. At any rate, there will have to be a brief conference before you begin your work."

It sounded almost ominous, or as if Luden meant it to be ominous, but that was Luden's way of creating importance.

"Is she coming here?" asked Port.

"Shortly. She will be through in about fifteen minutes."

"She's working?"

Luden nodded and got busy reading some papers.

"You mean she's making a film?"

"What else? What else does she make?"

"Can I watch?"

"I doubt it. We have rules, you know."

"If she's through in fifteen minutes, perhaps I could just walk in and see where she works, how it's done." Luden looked coldly at Port, but then he shrugged and picked up the phone. The pose he took seemed to give him pleasure.

"Miss Elroy. Have someone take Mr. Port to Stage Two." Then he turned to Port and said, "Wait outside."

A young man in severe charcoal took Port to the stage. By way of a short cut they walked through a piece of the casbah which was backed up to a view of Washington Square.

Stage Two was in one of those hangars. The red light over the door was off and then the door opened to let out a man in a bathing suit and a girl in an evening dress. Then several other people came out. It was all right for Port to walk in and the young man who was with him started explaining the inside. The big lights and the cables all over the floor, the folding chairs near the camera boom, and the tricky, soft lights that illuminated a pent-house terrace with a flat of a skyline behind it. Port couldn't figure out where the man in the bathing suit fitted in.

Then Port saw the knot of people, a dressed-up female with notebook and pencil, a man with flash camera, and a few others, all talking at the same time, to Ella Anders. She stood by a concrete wall and a light bulb was hanging high overhead. She stood in the worst light imaginable and she looked beautiful.

Port walked closer and watched. Exactly like in her movies, he thought. The hair very silky and thick, her improbable eyes with the last-minute tilt at the corners, the small nose that made her mouth look so wide. She talked, she laughed, she pushed her hair back over her ears, and whatever she did had magnetism. She wasn't all sex, she wasn't all manners, she wasn't all gentleness. But she had all of it. She was completely female.

Ella Anders said something and laughed. Then she gave the photographer a pat on the cheek and when she left the group nobody stopped her. The young man in charcoal had raised his hand, waving to her, and she came over. Port watched her and thought what a frank figure she had.

"Hi, Charley, I'm sorry I'm late." Then she looked at Port. The look seemed so uncomplicated that Port just kept staring at her.

"This is Mr. Port, Miss Anders. He...."

"Oh, yes." She shook his hand, smiling at him.

"If you don't mind going back alone," said Charley. "I have to see Cooper on something."

"He's standing at Number Two," she said, pointing. "Come along, Mr. Port. I'll drive you back."

Port felt like taking her arm, but before he could think about it she had taken his. She said, "Careful," and showed him where he was going to trip over the cables. Then she walked ahead of him, out of the door, and went to the motor scooter that stood by the building.

"If you hold on you can sit behind me," she said, so for a five-minute ride Port sat close behind her, stiff and precarious, because he didn't know where to put his hands.

They hadn't talked during the ride, and when she got off she still didn't say anything. It wasn't as if she ignored him, she just was quiet. The way it struck Port, it made her warmer. They didn't speak a word all the way up to Luden's office, though she smiled at him once when he took a wrong turn, and when Port closed the door to the office she still said nothing and seemed to be waiting for Luden.

He got up and came around his desk. The way they looked at each other Port didn't know what their relationship was.

"Have a seat, Elly. Port here might want to ask you a few questions after we're through, so let me first clear up the thing with this film."

Ella Anders didn't sit down. Her face had changed. She was plain angry.

"I never made that lousy picture!" she said very loud.

Chapter 10

Luden gave her an indulgent smile. It was ridiculous because next to Ella Anders he looked like a school-boy.

"Elly, it's absolutely no use. I'm not talking from hearsay."

"I don't care what you are talking from! If you've got any notion of pressuring me because of...."

"Nothing of the sort, Elly, nothing of the sort. But since you do mention it, it does seem as if I'll be the one to handle that matter; or at least, will be in on the thing."

It wasn't clear to Port what he was going to be in on, but it must have been pretty important because Luden sounded nasty about it and Ella Anders was getting more and more furious. "Why am I talking to you, anyway? I want to see Rosenstein. Why should I waste my time...."

"You'd be wasting it if you try to see Rosenstein. At least in the matter of this filthy picture you made...."

"My God," she said. She ran her hands through her hair. "How often do I have to tell you!"

"Don't bother."

"Luden," she said, very calm now. "You've been trying for a long time now, Luden. As long as I've been with this studio you've been trying."

"I don't know what you're talking about. Now, as far as this filthy picture you made—" he took great care to repeat the whole phrase—"as far as that goes, I'm the one who's handling that matter. Rosenstein assigned me to the business, and I've got approval from my father's office."

"Why? Because you're the hot-shot on pornography in this company?" Port felt glad she didn't dislike him.

"Because I've done some fast, constructive work on the deal."

"I'm sure you have, Luden."

"And that's what I'm going to keep right on doing," he said. He chewed his lip and looked at her.

"Luden," she said, "I'm not going to bed with you just because you're the boss's son. You've found that out. And I'm not going to bed with you just because you're now the vice president on pornography."

He gave her an ugly look. "Every time one of you females gets provoked you pull the same...."

"When it comes to your kind, what else is there?" She gave him an insolent smile and leaned against the desk.

Luden was boiling. "Don't kid yourself! Perhaps you think because you got special equipment that...."

"You're drooling right now," she said, leaning, so he could look her over. She should have known it would make him more vicious, but perhaps she didn't care.

"Anybody—" he had to swallow, "anybody who's slept their way to the top like you did—"

"I know how you feel, Luden, because there you were, without the right kind of executive position to get in line and get yours. That's what you think, isn't it?"

"Why, you lousy bitch!"

"Anyway. I sleep only with men, not offices."

She turned away from the desk and went to sit down on a couch. She took a cigarette from the small table and Port lit it for her. It had given Luden some time to recover. He came over to the couch and talked very low.

"All I'm going to do from now on, Elly, is treat you like merchandise. I'm the front office...."

"Not yet, Luden."

"I'm the front office and you are the merchandise. No personal feelings, no human element, but just impersonal facts and figures."

"I consider that an improvement, Luden."

"And I'm going to show you a piece of those impersonal facts and figures right now!"

He ran back to the desk. He got a key out of one of the drawers, took it to a small safe in the wall, and after he had turned the key he worked the combination. Then he brought Ella Anders the film.

"It's part of the negative, but enough. I'm going to show it to you."

"I bet you know it by heart," she said.

"So do you, I'm sure."

Ella Anders just sighed and shook her head. She didn't say any more until Luden had set up the small projector and screen, and had drawn the blinds. Then she said, very simply, "I didn't make it. Whatever you've got."

Luden ignored it. He was threading the film and said, "I'm going to run the negative. You will have to use your imagination somewhat."

"Don't you have a positive, Luden?"

"No. And we don't intend making any," he said.

Then it whirred and the white light glowed on where the screen stood.

Port noticed that Ella Anders wasn't as calm as she had seemed. She sat on the edge of the couch, very straight, with her hands holding her thighs.

For a moment there was just black leader. Luden cut down the speed and the image came on. It showed a bedroom. A dressed woman walked into the frame and when she came to the bed she kicked off her shoes. She didn't turn toward the camera until she had halfway unbuttoned her jacket. Then she did.

It was Ella Anders. She seemed to be tired and shook back her hair. That's when she was finished unbuttoning. Without changing the distance of the shot the camera made an artless pan up to her face so when Ella Anders took off her jacket only her face, neck, and one bare shoulder showed. There was a pan down which didn't get very far, but enough to suggest that Ella Anders hadn't been wearing anything under that jacket.

The screen blanked and Luden let it run till the leader flapped off the upper reel.

When Luden had opened the shades he turned back to the couch and put his hands in his pockets. There was a studied smile on his face.

"Don't worry, Elly. I'll get the rest of it."

Ella Anders sat without answering. Her face was flushed and her breath came in short, shallow gasps, as if she were going to say something but didn't know when. At first she just looked from one to the other, to Port who was sitting next to her, then to Luden who stood there having his moment of glory. With an impulsive move she turned back to Port and her hands clasped his arm.

"That was me!" She didn't say anything else.

She looked so completely bewildered that Port started to pat her hands on his arm. In a moment Port felt her relax, and then her face seemed to shut itself. She leaned back in the couch and stared quietly across the room.

"Well, Elly?"

Port offered her a cigarette and she smoked it with complete concentration.

"I can see there's going to be a change in our relationship," said Luden, needling her. When she didn't answer he went on. "Our business relationship is going to be something to see." No response. "You still don't think I'll be in front office?" He got irritated then and changed his tack. "When did you make it, Elly?"

She looked up as if nothing had happened, as if they were talking about something you discuss over tea. "When?" she said. "I never made that picture."

Luden started to laugh. Then he simmered down but kept interrupting himself with an occasional chuckle.

"You don't remember? You mean you can't rightly place that particular one?"

Port expected her to get angry again, but she didn't. She looked annoyed, but somehow didn't seem bothered by Luden, but she gave it back to him in the same way he had put it.

"You know, Luden, in a way you must be quite disappointed."

"I'll get the rest."

"I didn't mean that. I meant, there I was, getting undressed. I get undressed every night. Usually a few times during the day, in addition."

"And that trick with the jacket? You weren't wearing a thing under that."

"I often don't. Some jackets are made that way."

"And in front of the camera? That, I suppose, happens too, several times a day."

"In a way, yes," she said, but she had lost interest in the baiting. She put out her cigarette and got up. "Luden, I don't know what to say. I have to think about it and I'll let you know." Then she walked to the door.

"There's nothing to let me know, Elly. There's the film and that's it."

"I didn't make that film," she said and opened the door.

"Miss Anders," said Port and came after her.

She closed the door and looked at Port, frankly curious, but wishing he would hurry it up.

"You don't understand one thing, Miss Anders. What's really important here is the film, not how you feel about it."

"I don't know how I feel about it. I actually don't."

"You keep saying you didn't make that film, as if all we were worried about here are your morals."

She smiled at that, and then Port went out.

"We're worried about the film, which really exists, and we're mostly worried about the part we don't have. What's on it?"

"I don't know what's on it," said Ella Anders.

"Perhaps this was made quite some time ago," said Port. "It would help me to find it, if you can tell me some details."

"Honestly," and she spread out her arms, then dropped them again. "Honestly, Mr. Port—"

"The man who sold us the piece you saw said you were sixteen at the time." She laughed.

"That's ridiculous. When I was sixteen I was going to high school in Arizona and in my spare time I was practicing the piano."

"So what?" said Luden.

"I never was inside a hotel room till I was twenty-two."

"How come you know that was a hotel room?" said Luden.

This time she got angry again. "I don't know. I just said that. And I'm not staying here any longer to help you get your kicks, Luden. Besides, I got a rehearsal."

When she turned to the door again Port said, "We can't just leave it there, Miss Anders."

"Yes, I know. But—"

"Could I see you after that rehearsal?"

"Come to my house, after nine. You know where I live? The office can give you the address."

She acted very off-hand about it and left, closing the door behind her, but Port thought she was really disturbed. At that moment, all she had wanted to do was get away. With her last remarks she hadn't looked at anyone, and her parting crack at Luden seemed to have come with an effort.

Port left shortly after. If only Luden had been in this deal, Port didn't think he would have cared about going through with it. But there was Mulnik, and there was Ella Anders.

Chapter 11

Confidential Services had office space at a Broadway address. Port walked up three flights of stairs and through the door which said *Confidential Services*.

He had hoped it would be cooler inside, but there was no air conditioner, just a fan from a dime store, blowing the smog into the room. The girl at the desk hung up the phone when Port came in.

"I'd like to see Joko," said Port.

"Huh?"

"Mulnik. You know Mulnik."

"Oh, him." She laughed.

"You know him?"

"Sure. Who are you?"

"Daniel Port. Mulnik's a friend of mine."

"He's got friends?"

"Don't slam him," said Port. "He's a friend of mine. Where is he?"

"Tell you the truth, I don't know."

"You seen him lately?"

"Sure. Off and on."

"Come on, honey, help a little. I've got to find him."

"That's our business: find 'em."

Port sighed and looked around.

"All right," he said. "I'm a client. Now tell me again."

"I'll announce you," she said and got up to go to the door marked Private. Then she came back. "I forgot. He went to the washroom."

Port sighed again and leaned against a wall. After a while he said, "Is he coming back?"

"Always has, in the past."

Then they had silence again, while Port felt uncomfortable in his shirt, which was moist on the back, and the girl at the desk kept drawing a hat with a feather on a notebook. Then she turned around.

"What did you call me before?"

"Uh—I?"

She smiled and cocked her head to one side.

"You called me honey."

"Oh. Yes, so I did."

She held the smile a moment longer, then shrugged and turned back to her desk.

The hall door opened and a thin man who looked like a farmhand came in. He was wearing a business suit but the haircut and the bones in his face made Port think of a farmer. He was barely inside the door when the girl spoke up.

"Mr. Flint, this is a client of yours. Mr.— What was that?"

"Port."

"Ah, yes," said Flint and walked to the door with the Private on it. "Let me have the file."

"He's new," said the girl. "There's no file yet."

"Well, in that case," he said, very animated, "come right in." He opened his door. "No calls," he told the girl. "Just take messages." Flint walked into his office, closed the door.

They sat very close together, because the office was small.

"I have here," said Flint, "our questionnaire. That's how the file starts."

"Look, maybe—"

"Everything recorded. That's plain good sense. Now, Mr. Port...."

"Maybe you don't want to record this," said Port. Flint sat back, put both hands on the desk in front of him. His big fingers beat a few drums, in cadence.

"Let's see your badge," said Flint.

Port laughed and made a gesture to show that he didn't have one. "I'm a client. I'll pay."

Flint just looked cagey.

"That's much better," said Port. "Isn't it?"

Flint let go a deep breath, then hunched over the desk. "Go ahead. Don't be ashamed. We keep everything confidential."

"I want to buy one of your confidences."

Flint drummed again.

"I'm ashamed to admit it," Port went on, "but I know a guy by the name of Mulnik."

Port saw that Flint did too.

"And I want to know where he is."

"Yes?"

"You know where he is?"

"First tell me more about this."

"It's about a doublecross."

"That's Mulnik," said Flint, and then, "A doublecross will cost you double—a hundred even."

Port got bills out of his pocket and counted fifty dollars on top of the desk. Flint picked it up, counted it twice, and then folded it into his wallet.

"Mulnik said he was going to Canada. He does hunting and fishing there. Lethbridge, Alberta."

Port nodded to himself, and then he reached back into his pocket. He counted another fifty dollars out on the desk and sat back.

"He went to Palmedo," said Flint and folded the money into his wallet.

"Palmedo. Where's that, in Canada?"

"You mean you don't know where it is?"

Port remembered that Tessy had gone there. It couldn't be far.

"I'm new around here."

"Well, it's right over in Arizona, out in the desert. One of those new places they got, all refrigerated and irrigated."

"What's there? Why there?"

"Why I don't know. He goes there off and on, for a vacation."

"Any particular place in that town?"

"It's not a town. Just some dude ranches and one of those big hotels. All landscaped. I've seen the pictures."

"Okay, Flint, thanks a lot." But Port didn't get up. "And now I'll tell you how you fit into the picture."

Flint got very upset. His Adam's apple started to jiggle and his big mouth was working without a sound. He even started to reach for his wallet, probably with the thought of giving Port back his money.

"It doesn't mean that you have to worry about it, Flint. Just know about it."

Flint held still and listened.

"You cashed an R. S. Luden check yesterday and gave Joko the money. Maybe you don't know what that was for?"

Flint couldn't talk, but Port thought Flint was in the dark when it came to that check.

"That was blackmail money."

"Oh, Christ!"

"Well," said Port. "You know Joko Mulnik."

"But I—just cashed it for him. All I did—"

"That may be, but the check was made out to you."

"Joko explained that. He explained how that happened. He said I should-n't be sore for his using my name like at, but he needed the moniker to make an impression."

"He told you right."

"He was doing a job for the studio, as a consultant, an expert on one of those gangster pictures. He wouldn't got the job, he says, if he hadn't been able to use the name of my firm."

"Did he pay you for that piece of swindle?"

"Twenty dollars!" Flint hunched in his chair. "I have the receipt."

Port sat up. "You have it?"

"So what?" Flint looked very dejected.

Flint looked up, puzzled, and then he couldn't remember what it said on the receipt. He got up, went to the files that were in the outer office, and started to go through a drawer.

Port followed him. He stood by the girl's desk and said, "You got a call from someone at the Luden Studios a couple of days ago. Remember what you told them?"

She frowned and looked hostile.

"You told them that you knew Mulnik, isn't that right?"

"How do you know?"

"I was on the other end of the phone."

"Oh—"

"Did Mulnik want you to answer that he was the head of this Confidential Service outfit here?"

"Yes, he tried. And then he said it was good enough I said he was working here, but I told him I don't do anything that is illegal. All I'd say was that I'd say I know him."

"Why'd you do that for him?"

She really looked hostile now and turned back to her doodling without answering.

"And then he stood you up, huh?"

Even though she had her head down over the desk Port thought she was close to tears.

"It's all right, honey," he said, "you don't need him." Port went back into the other office.

When Flint came in he was carrying the receipt. It was true what he had said about keeping a record of everything. The receipt said, *$25.00 received from J. Mulnik for service of cashing check for him.* Then the check number, the date, and J. Mulnik's signature.

"Very nice," said Port, "and hold on to it. If you get involved in this blackmail thing, it'll help to show what you cashed that check for."

"Involved—"

"No reason why you should be," said Port. "You've been very helpful." He started to leave.

But Flint suddenly felt so grateful he had to shake Port's hand and then he insisted that Port take the money back.

"Keep it," said Port, "as long as you don't make a record of it."

"Oh yes. Oh no—all that money—" he kept saying.

"Buy the office girl a corsage," said Port, and when he left he thought that Flint might.

Chapter 12

When he was back in his car Port had an impulse to drive to Palmedo immediately, except that would have meant he'd miss his appointment with Ella Anders. He didn't want to miss that; there was too much left unexplained. As for Joko, he wasn't likely to do anything rash. He had worked like a beaver, improvising right and left, and so far he had made it. Port didn't think he would keep rushing around. He would sit still, check the course he'd been taking, and when he thought Luden had simmered enough, Joko would make his next move.

At five to nine Port drove his car through the gateway that led into Belair. He hadn't expected the roads to wind quite so much or that the houses would be so far from the street. And there weren't any mail boxes planted out on a stick, with the tenant's name on it, because these were estates. Whole streets of estates. When Port thought he had found Ella Anders's house he only recognized it by the abstract sculpture on the big lawn. They had told him at the studio he'd recognize her place by that sculpture on the lawn.

Port swung in and headed for the back. What with all the remarkable trees and bushes he didn't see the house till the last minute, and then there it was. In the dark he got an idea of the place by all the lighted windows. There were lighted windows as far as the eye could reach, and some seemed to be in the oddest places. It turned out that some of them were car windows, because there were cars all over including some in the bushes.

Port left his MG where he had happened to stop because that's what everybody else had been doing. Then he walked up to the door which was really a gate. The racket on the other side was very strong. Next to the door, inside the mouth of a little lion, there was a button and Port kept pressing that for a while. Nobody heard the bell. Port walked in.

No sooner was he inside than he was pinned right back against the door he had just closed. It seemed everybody was passing through the hall to get from one room to another. Port saw that a carpet had been set on fire.

"There you are! There you are!" yelled the man, and when he started dragging Port by one arm he whispered, "I thought you weren't coming."

The whisper told Port how drunk the man was, so Port didn't bother to answer. Once in the next room, the crowd thinned out. Some were in evening clothes, but a few were wearing bathing suits. It reminded Port of the set he had visited, with the girl in an evening gown and the man wearing swimming trunks. It no longer struck Port as outlandish.

The man let go of Port's arm and stood back. He eyed Port for a moment and said, "Who are you? Why were you holding my arm?" and again Port didn't answer because the man had already left.

How to find Ella Anders. Port saw a maid and he stopped her. First he had to take a drink off her tray and then he asked her where Ella Anders was.

"I ain't seen Elly today," said the maid and walked off.

The next one was a movie star. Port had forgotten her name, but when she looked up at Port's question she turned out to be a really big movie star.

"I ain't seen Elly today," she said, and Port walked someplace else.

Somebody said, "How are you, J.J." to him, and one blonde gave him a dirty look, but aside from that no one cared who he was. Port asked for Ella Anders a few more times but it didn't do any good. He had another drink and walked around. That's how he got into the library. When the door swung shut behind him it was remarkably still in the place. The room was big and dark, except for the light where the man sat in front of a chess board. He looked up and waved at Port to come over, to sit down at the other side of the chess board. Port did and saw that it was his friend from before.

"I thought you said you weren't coming to this party," said the man. "Under no circumstances."

"Well, you know—"

The man eyed Port as he had once before. "Don't lie to me, you, you— What's your name?"

"Dan Port."

"Don't lie to me, Dan Port. I've never seen you before in my life."

"Well, you know—"

"Let's play chess," said the man.

Port looked at the board, but all the men were in the wrong positions. They were lined up by size. Port decided to take advantage of the man's moment of soberness and ask him the question.

"Have you seen Ella Anders?"

"Not since the time she made *Scaffold*. Good, wasn't she?"

"I mean in the flesh."

"When you say flesh like that, Port, just exactly what do you mean?"

"I mean I'm looking for her."

"Here?"

"If she isn't in her own house— Besides, I had an appointment with her."

"I congratulate you. But this isn't her house."

"Not her house?"

"I told you once, I told you twice. You had no intention of coming here."

"You know that statue out on the lawn?"

"I'd rather not."

"They told me I should look for that thing on the lawn, and that's where she lived."

"Funny story about that. She does have one."

"There're two of them?"

"She commissioned the artist to create this thing for her—it's called *Time Warp*, by the way—and for the munificent sum of thirty-five thousand dollars plus materials and labor, coming to an additional twelve hundred dollars and fifty-seven cents—it was created. Only one in the world. Well, sir, Elly and her *Time Warp* got into all the art mags and arty mags which is one medium of publicity usually denied our local artists. Now, the lady of this house is a lot like Elly except she's with a different studio. Different measurements here and there and maybe a little dumber, but just about the same ratings as Elly. So her studio ups and figures that their queen bee wasn't to be denied the publicity Elly was getting in art mags. They went to the creator of *Time Warp* with this problem and the bastard makes another of those things. Same castings, as a matter of fact, saving twelve hundred dollars and fifty-seven cents. But to be ethical he didn't repeat on the original. This one on this lawn cost forty-five thousand dollars and is called *Time Lapse*."

The man sat back and nodded at Port to say something admiring.

"Which one's the better one?" asked Port.

"The one on this lawn. It cost more."

"Is that what the art mags say?"

"I don't care what they say. I'm the bastard—this artist I'm talking about—who built both of them."

Port got away then because a girl came into the library who distracted the artist. She was very pretty and wore only a bathrobe. Her wet bathing suit was in her hand. When Port closed the door he saw them sitting opposite each other, playing chess.

Now that Port knew that this wasn't Ella Anders's house he got somebody to tell him where she lived. It was only a few houses down the street, but by now he was very late. It bothered him. It bothered him even more when he saw that her house was almost completely dark. Only the hall had a light in it and one room to the side.

Port rang the bell. A maid opened and he told her his name. The maid said that he was expected, to go through those rooms to the left, and Miss Anders was in the last one.

The light from the hall helped him through the empty rooms because they were all connected arches. There was a glass door at the last one which slid sideways with a small, oiled sound.

He didn't see her at first because she didn't move on the couch. She sat with her back to him, hunched over, and when she sat up to look at him she did it slowly.

"I'm sorry I'm late," he started, and looked for a chair to sit down on.

She was wearing glasses with big rims and after she took them off she rubbed the back of her neck as if she were dog-tired. "Is it nine yet?" she said.

There was a mimeographed script in front of her, a pencil, and loose pages of paper. She was wearing black slacks and a shirt with the sleeves rolled up. Port saw that the shirt tail had come out in back.

"I'm sorry to bother you, Miss Anders, but I feel that this film thing we're working on...."

"That's all right." She got up and tucked her shirt into the slacks. "Can you give me a cigarette?"

When she took it and Port gave her a light he saw she wasn't just tired. Her face showed the effort of control and he thought her hands were flighty.

He tried to sound easy.

"Look, Miss Anders, the more you can tell me about this thing the less you have to worry about it."

She exhaled the smoke with a deep breath, sat down again. She wasn't vivacious, as she'd been the first time he had seen her, and she wasn't angry. Port saw that she was just plain beat. She leaned back in the couch and looked over Port's head. They were silent for a while. Port started to wonder what else she was showing, more than just being exhausted, because she was not relaxed. Then Port thought that if she got only a little bit of the wrong kind of push, she might give up.

When she talked it sounded very impersonal, and she put nothing into her voice but the words.

"You know what makes Luden so happy?"

"I didn't know he...."

"That's right. You don't know him." She sat forward and opened her collar button because the neck was too tight. "He's very happy because this thing came up." She made an impatient gesture and looked to the far side of the room. "Anyway, my contract runs out."

Port had never thought of Ella Anders as someone who needed a contract, or as someone who had to worry about one.

"But—" he laughed—"but you're Ella Anders."

"Right now I'm somebody on a pornographic film."

"I'm here to fix that."

"And since this thing has come up," she went on, "little Luden is in on the contract negotiations. He's making it hard."

"I don't see how he can keep you from getting a new one. After all—"

"I'll get a new one. The question is how much. Luden keeps stressing the damage to my name and to the studio, something that's bound to happen, he says."

"Don't listen to him. I can think of a couple of cases where something like this hit the public—and your troubles haven't, you know—and all that happened was improved billing."

"In my case it would be out of character."

"You're hardly the girl next door, you know."

"No," she said, looking out the window.

"Why don't you switch studios if Luden gives you a hard time?"

She looked at Port from across the room and gave a halfhearted laugh.

"You don't know Luden Junior. This thing isn't public yet, but it wouldn't take long."

Port didn't think this important. If they cut Ella Anders's income because of some squeeze play in the front office, she wasn't going to be out on the street.

"It wouldn't put you in the poorhouse," he said. "A little economy...."

"Economy?" She came across the room fast and looked furious. "You know what I make? I'll give you round figures: I make three quarters of a million a year! My agent gets twenty-five thousand, personal publicity costs twenty thousand, the business manager gets forty thousand, my manager takes thirty thousand, the house costs twenty-five thousand a year and thirty thousand to run it. Personal expenses come to forty-five thousand with whatever is left over going to taxes; and the difference I owe made up from investments which my forty-thousand-a-year business manager is managing. Cut down on any of that? I can't! By contract most of the money I told you about is paid by the studio, and taken off my check. The expense was part of the build-up when I needed it and part of the front now that I've hit. You think I want to live in this house? I'm alone, unmarried, with no children! Do I need eighteen rooms? Do I need a hundred guests for the parties they schedule for me? Do I need this address, except that it's part of the arrangement?" She seemed breathless, and when she went on she talked as if she were bored. "I've got a personal checking account. They don't even know about it." Then she laughed. "I have five hundred and twelve dollars to my name."

She had turned her back again, looking at the script that lay on the table by the couch, and Port couldn't tell what she felt like. "Would you give me another cigarette?" she said.

Port got up to give it to her and when he saw her face he saw that there was a shimmer in her eyes. She was trying not to cry. Port lit the cigarette for her and said, "I don't think you ought to worry about that money so much."

"I'm not." She sat down.

"Your reputation?"

After a moment she said, "I hate this life. I'm sitting here thinking about that contract—so I can hate this life for another ten years." Then she put out the cigarette and put her arms on the back of the couch.

"About this film, now."

Port thought it was a little abrupt and he didn't know how to start. Especially since she had insisted she never made the film.

"Did you recognize yourself, when we looked at the film?"

"Of course."

"And you didn't make it?"

"I just—I can't figure it out."

"You thought back, in the meantime, when you might have...."

"Look, Mr. Port, I've thought back over every drunken party I've ever been to, every weekend and every man I spent it with. I can't place it, I can't understand it, and I don't believe it."

"How far back did you go?"

"I went back eleven years. I'm thirty-one now and until I was twenty, my life was sheltered."

"I mentioned this once before, but the man who had that film said you were sixteen when you made it."

"He flatters me."

Port took a breath and rubbed his palms together.

"Let's try something else. Did you recognize the room?"

"No. There was a bed, a bed stand, a vanity, and a door in the back. That's what I saw in the film. It meant nothing to me."

"But as our friend Luden pointed out, for some reason you called it a hotel room."

"Didn't it look like one to you?"

Port smiled. "It did, at that."

He watched her frown, and then she leaned forward a little. "Sixteen! It couldn't have been sixteen. When I was that age I had long hair, down to here. I remember I always wore dresses with high collars because I couldn't stand it when the long hair got entangled with—" She hesitated and her mouth stayed open. Then she snapped her finger. "Clothes! That picture couldn't have been made when I was sixteen! You remember the suit I was wearing in that film?"

"Uh—yes, quite well."

Ella Anders jumped up and ran out of the door. Port sat waiting. When Ella Anders came back she was carrying the jacket she had worn in the film.

"Watch this," she said and rolled down the sleeves of her shirt. At first Port had the thought that she might take the shirt off, since she hadn't been wearing one under that jacket when the film had been taken, but she kept it on. Then she put the jacket on and buttoned it.

"Well? Do you see something?"

Port looked her over and chewed on his lip. Then he said, "What am I looking for?"

"Idiot. The jacket. The style! What year was it?" Port smiled at her, then kept looking again. "Tell you the truth, I couldn't say."

She smiled back at him and took off the jacket. "It's incredible. Every year dozens of overpaid couturiers go through a million dollars' worth of birth pangs, and you don't remember when."

"When was it born?"

"Four years ago!"

Port shrugged, smiling apologetically. "I should have known."

"Anyway, that helps, doesn't it? It couldn't have been when I was sixteen."

"Except for the jacket, you couldn't have proved it by me."

She liked the compliment, but didn't want to take it up. "Could I have another cigarette?" she said. "I'm very nervous tonight."

Port lit her one; then he said, "I'd like you to try to think about four years ago. Where were you, what did you do, whom did you know?"

She thought for a while, then shook her head. "I don't know—something like that should stand out in one's mind, something like that picture."

"Well?"

"Well what?" She was suddenly angry. "What do you think it means because I don't remember?"

"I didn't mean it that way. All I meant...."

"You're puzzled, is that it? You can't understand it. Maybe you'd like it better if I told the real dirt: I made that picture, in fact I make one every year. It comes over me like the rutting season and that's been happening ever since I was sixteen. All right?"

Port didn't answer and waited for her to calm down. He watched her put her face into her hands and she sat that way for a while, trying to control her breathing. When she looked up again she just shrugged. "Ask me again," she said. "I'll try to remember."

"About four years ago. I know your schedule and your activities must be quite something, but if what you say about that jacket is true, then you can see how important it is for you to remember that year."

"I remember that year." She was thinking about it. "My real build-up started a little more than four years ago. I was in Hollywood for perhaps ten per cent of the time, and the rest I was all over. Guest appearances, benefits, night-club work, and a couple of romantic junkets thrown in which had been staged by the publicity office."

"What about three years ago? Didn't you wear that suit then?"

"I wouldn't dare," she said. "I still own it because I like the skirt. I can still wear the skirt."

"Oh."

Port didn't say any more for the moment, because he was thinking about the schedule she must have had during that year. And even if she remembered all of it and he went over it with her, there was still her insistence that she never made the picture. And by now she was getting sensitive about it.

Perhaps he should let it go as a blind alley, not waste time in L.A. while Mulnik was someplace in the desert, in Palmedo, Flint had said.

"What I could do," she said suddenly, "is to look up that year's schedule. It's sort of a scrap book I have. All my engagements or public appearances since my first role."

Port sat up, a little more hopeful now. "Let's do that. Perhaps a name, or a place, might suggest something."

"What's the use," she said, and let her arms drop between her knees. "I did-n't make it. Maybe it wasn't even me in that picture. I didn't make it."

It was late and Port felt he was wasting his time. He got up and said he was leaving, there was some other lead he would have to check and he would let her know what developed.

"And about that schedule you have. Could you let me have it? I'll bring it back to you in two days, maybe."

She said yes and got it for him. It was a spiral-back notebook with a list of dates and places. It showed where she had been and for how long, and what her official duties had been.

"I'll be careful with it," he said. "I'll bring it back."

Her nod interrupted him, and the way she closed her eyes when she did it. Ella Anders wasn't much interested. Her beautiful face looked tired, her movements were tired, and since all this was about her, and her career, it showed Port how close she was to giving up.

Chapter 13

Before Port went home he stopped at a gas station, tanked up, and got a map from the attendant. He looked up Palmedo and checked how long it would take him. Traffic willing, he should be there in the afternoon if he left in the morning.

He left in the morning but didn't get there until evening. Going toward the desert it got hot during the day and his car couldn't take the sustained speed.

The first thing Port saw of the place was the neon sign far off in the desert. Then came palm trees, lining the road, short palm trees, because they had been planted only a few years ago.

Suddenly there was Palmedo. Low, rustic buildings with hitching posts and swinging doors at the bars, and all along the hitching posts stood the Cadillacs. There were other cars, but the Cadillacs took most of the room. A traffic light hung over the main intersection and right under it, for the authentic touch, was the local policeman in black cowboy garb with white piping, high up on a well-fed pinto. Every time the traffic light changed the horse twitched one foot and the policeman gave a pat to the pinto's neck. At other times the policeman waved at cars driving by and said, "Howdy, stranger."

And then there was the hotel. The structure was built like an old adobe house, except that this one was ten stories high. Port drove to the side of it, where the parking lot was, but the white Cadillac with zebra upholstery wasn't there. He didn't worry about it. If Joko Mulnik were around, Port would find him.

When Port walked into the lobby the first thing he saw was the big sign that said *Tess Dolphin Sings Here*. There was a beautiful picture of her and Port started to smile when he thought how surprised she would be when she saw him.

He tried to get a room at the hotel, but they were all filled up. He should try one of the dude ranches. Port said he might but without much conviction, and when he walked past Tessy's picture he smiled again. It was ten in the evening. It said on the sign that Tess's last show wasn't until one in the morning, so Port walked back into town to see what he could see.

He didn't see Mulnik, and he didn't meet anyone he cared to ask about him. If Joko were here to lay low on the side, Port would run into him by a gradual process of combing the place. Port started making the rounds of the bars and some of the poker places, coming back to some of them once or twice. Nobody knew who Port was or that he was looking for anybody, which was all right with Port.

A little while before one he went back to the hotel and walked into the room where Tess was singing. She was singing when he came in. The music had little to do with the decor and the name of the place, which was fitted out in the Gay Nineties manner, but nobody seemed to mind. Port could see her on the stage with the fake foot lights, dressed in something sleek and singing something slow and rhythmic. He sidled along the crowded bar and made his way to the doorway where Tess would be leaving.

Port wasn't the first one. A bouncer was guarding the way and a kid in a tuxedo was there. The kid had the cleancut but tired look of an expensive upbringing. When Port stopped by the door the kid looked at him as if he owned the place; Port thought that perhaps he did. Then the kid said something to the bouncer, who nodded and came over to Port.

"You waiting for a performer?"

"That one," said Port and nodded up to the stage. "Miss Dolphin."

The bouncer shook his head slowly. "We don't allow that."

"You don't allow what?"

At first the bouncer was going to say something else, but then controlled himself and tried to sound confidential. "Mr. Semper won't like it. Mr. Semper was here first and he carries an awful lot of weight."

"Where?" and Port looked at the kid's back of the pants.

The Semper kid noticed that, especially after having heard Port's remark, and he came right over.

"Throw him out," he said to the bouncer, looking at Port.

Semper wasn't so young. In spite of the smooth skin and the boyish look Port noticed he was by no means a kid.

"If you do," said Port, looking at Semper, "I'll ruffle your hair for you."

It couldn't have been Port's remark, but just the same the bouncer didn't do what he had been told.

"I'll have you fired," said Semper, but since he was still looking at Port, Port answered.

"He'll be worse off if he tries doing his job," he said. "And as for you, I don't think Miss Dolphin would like you. I know her likes and dislikes and you'd be out of the latter, for sure."

He was barely finished when Semper gave Port a backhand. It was nothing dangerous, just a slap in the face to defend his honor and to force the bouncer to do his job.

He tried. He tried so hard to prevent a commotion and to rush Port at the same time that he tangled with Semper in his excitement and missed his chance. But Port didn't. He clouted the bouncer behind one of his ears, making him crowd Semper, and Port took advantage of that and returned Semper's backhand. That one wasn't for show. It made a big smack and raised a big welt, and Port thought that would be the end of it.

But it only made the kid come to life. In a moment Port had the bouncer hard in his midriff, because that's where Semper had tossed him, and next Port felt the wind where a short hook just missed him. The next one didn't. It clipped him hard on the nose, with sensations all through his head and through the eyeballs, while the bouncer was trying a clinch. He managed it until Port gave him the knee, but in the meantime Semper was swinging again. It caught Port's ear, making it sing, and then Port really got mad.

But they had attracted some attention. A crowd of admirers had formed, pressing closer because the ones in the back couldn't see. It kept Port from swinging the way he had wanted to and it kept Semper from leaving the way he meant to. The two men found themselves close together, almost nose to nose, and if it hadn't been for the bouncer, who was underfoot, they might have stepped on each other's toes. Pinned up close that way and having to waltz around in order to keep their balance Port didn't know what to do with his anger because the whole thing now seemed ridiculous. It felt even more so when Port saw Tess. She stood on the stage, watching Port, and when she caught his eyes she burst out laughing. Port looked back at Semper, into one of his eyes, and said, "Excuse me."

But Semper didn't have any humor. He tried to grab low, which made Port angry again. Without any room to swing he smacked both open hands against Semper's ears, and when Semper gasped, almost paralyzed with the shock, Port knew what Semper was going through because his own ear was still ringing.

He pushed Semper out of the way and made the door. He stood there for a moment while Tess came down from the stage, and the crowd opened up to let her through. Port grabbed her arm and they took off down the corridor.

They stood by the swimming pool where all the lights had been turned off and caught their breath. Tess smoothed down her dress and Port felt his nose.

"You didn't have to go to all that trouble," said Tess, "just to attract my attention."

Port grunted. His nose was sore over the bridge but there wasn't much swelling.

"It looks fine," she said. "Almost as good as a disguise."

There was a large swarm of insects buzzing inside of Port's ear. He cocked his head at Tess and said, "What?"

She cocked her head too and talked very low. "How come you people with one deaf ear always try to hear with the deaf one? Why not use the other?"

"You don't need to shout," he said. "I can hear you fine."

Then he pulled her close, with both arms, and gave her a kiss. She gave it right back to him.

"That was sweet of you," she said, "coming here to surprise me. But you didn't have to go to all that trouble just to...."

"Because you're such a cold fish, and aloof. I had to shake you out of that damn indifference somehow." He gave her another kiss. But when she came back at him he suddenly winced and drew back his head.

"Can't take it, huh?" and she stood back, arms on her hips.

Port didn't answer, but stood still waiting for the pain to die down. He felt sure his nose was glowing. She gave him a moment and then she said, "Are you staying the night?"

He just nodded.

"A lot of good you're going to do me."

"Don't worry," he said. "Just don't you worry."

"Where are you staying?"

He cleared his throat and said, "As a matter of fact, seeing how expensive this place is, I had an idea—just an idea, you understand...."

"I'd like that," she said. "I've got two big rooms and a big bed, and tomorrow we can go back to L.A. together."

"Two rooms? If you're making that much here, why not stay a little longer?"

"I have just a three-day engagement, I told you, and it's up. If I stayed through tomorrow I'd have to pay for that suite."

"Who pays for it now?"

"It's for free. For the entertainer. I get the suite, free meals, free drinks, and a free horse."

"And they pay you?"

"Little bit."

"You must have some pull here."

"Oh no. That's standard procedure. Every entertainer gets those privileges. And it's always the same suite, so they call it the Star Suite."

Port felt much better by now and his nose seemed to have shrunk again. "Let's you and me go stargazing," he said.

"Let's."

She walked to the parking lot with him, where he got his canvas bag with his extra shirt. Then she took him upstairs, to the top floor, where the Star Suite was.

It was nice. It was out of the way, at the end of the corridor, with just a linen room and a service staircase nearby. They went into the suite, without turning the lights on, because Tess wanted Port to see how the desert looked through the large windows. It looked blue and white in the moonlight and as if nothing had ever moved there, or ever would. Then they walked into the bedroom and Tess turned on the lights.

They made a startling blaze. There were two on the ceiling, two flanking the bed, two on the vanity, and a standing lamp with a beam each, up and down. And there wasn't a cozy twenty-five watt bulb among them.

"This, I suppose," said Port, "is meant to make you professionals feel right at home. Like on the stage."

"Isn't it something?"

"Let's turn some of them off, Tessy."

"You can't. Only one switch for all of them. But you don't have to worry about it," she said. "Pretty soon I'm going to turn off the lot of them."

She went to the wall mirror and looked at her face and then she reached back to unhook herself.

"Let's leave them on," said Port. "The whole damn lot of them."

She smiled at him but then she stopped unhooking herself. "Hook me up, Danny. I've got to go downstairs again."

"What?"

"I'll just be a moment. With the commotion you made I forgot about going back to my dressing room. I'm supposed to clear out after my last performance."

"Let it go till tomorrow. We'll get to it early in the morning."

"Sure."

"And I'll give you a hand. Tessy! Don't go."

"Suffer," she said and was gone.

Port tried to distract himself by unpacking his bag.

There wasn't much in there and he was done in no time. Then he picked up Ella's notebook with the list of engagements. Sitting down on the bed he leafed through the pages, and when he found the engagements she had had four years ago he looked them over. There was New York, Chicago, Detroit, San Francisco, St. Louis, Miami, and each with a note of what she was doing there. Singing, a comedy sketch, walk-ons just to say hello—

Port put her notebook down and listened for Tessy. He didn't hear her. One ear was still buzzing and he knew he heard things only because he was impatient. The lights started to bother him, and the buzz in his ear got on his nerves. Then there was the wall mirror on the wall opposite him. He could see his face and the room's reflections. The lights didn't bother him but the face did. He walked again, and when he passed the mirror he gave it a push. They had it nailed to the wall, and when the thing didn't budge that got on his nerves too. He sat down on the bed again and tried to concentrate on the lists in Ella's book. Palm Springs, Winter Gardens, Palmedo, Las Vegas, Hollywood Bowl, and a whole mess more. They'd kept her busy.

Then Port heard Tess come into the next room. By the time she was in the bedroom he had put the notebook back on the dresser and made himself look casual. Tess closed the door behind her and said, "You look nervous, Danny. Did you suffer?"

"I wouldn't tell you even if I didn't," he said and followed her across the room.

She stopped by the vanity and moved a few things around.

"What did you do while I was gone?" And then, "Hmm," she said, "you shaved for me." She pushed him away and moved things around on the vanity. She put some of the jars into a kit she had. "What else did you do, Danny?"

She'd laugh if he told her he'd been reading. Then she'd laugh some more if he told her he'd been reading a list, reading names like a dumb ox without remembering the last— Like a dumb ox!

Ella Anders had been in Palmedo.

Four years ago, and every performer at the hotel got the Star Suite.

"Unhook me?"

He came back to the present without an effort and started unhooking her. He didn't do very well, especially since she kept walking around. She walked to the night stand, to the vanity, and back to the bed.

"Hold still," he said.

"You all thumbs?"

"Just hold still." He continued unhooking.

He caught sight of Tessy in the mirror, and she smiled back at him. She was holding the front of her dress so it wouldn't come down and kept smiling at him.

"The longer you take," she said, but he wasn't listening. She looked strange in the mirror, and exciting. All the shadows were deeper and all the highlights were dimmed. It was the darkest damn mirror.

"You're done," she said. "I can feel it. Why don't you let go of my dress?"

"Dress?"

"Or I will," she said, but Port didn't hear it.

In the mirror his face showed a sudden grimace of rage, and then he pushed her aside. He grabbed up a chair and flung it hard, running after it before it had hit the mirror.

The glass crashed into pieces and the hole behind wasn't empty. It showed a white, startled face and the movie camera with the wide-angle lens.

Chapter 14

At first the man in the laundry room thought he would die with fright and surprise, but when he saw that Port couldn't get through the smashed one-way mirror he got his breath back and bolted. He even grabbed the camera. The corridor was still empty, and even if the man who had smashed the mirror would run through the two rooms of the suite and come out in the hall, that would be enough time. Holding the camera, he rushed through the door to the service stairs and ran down.

There weren't any carpets, and the racket of running was enough to wake up the town. The racket of his breathing would have been enough to do that. But the staircase was empty at that time of night and one flight down he started to feel better. Just an occupational hazard. Forget about the living rage of the man who had smashed the glass and think of it all as an occupational hazard. That felt better.

He suddenly felt so much worse he stumbled and almost dropped the camera. The fast, sharp steps he heard at that moment came from above, charging closer. He started to clamber down as if the devil were after him, and remembering the face coming at him in the one-way mirror it had looked like the devil for sure. But he had a two-story lead.

He made the door on the ground floor. In his haste he yanked at the knob without turning it—with the following steps getting louder. He got the door open and ran out into the night, with the frantic feeling that now he was invisible, toward the pool, where all the lights had been turned off. Once he made it past the pool, over the hedges and the lawn where the eternal sprinklers were waving back and forth in the moonlight, he'd make the bushes where the desert pushed in, and then over the waste stretch of thistles and sand. But so far he had made the pool. The concrete under his feet jolted him to the top of his head, his lungs feeling thick with the air he couldn't breathe out fast enough, and the hard jolting up through his legs. He wasn't aware of much else, when a crazy noise burst loose in his head and he flew sideways, out of control, and then crashed into the water.

He panicked before he came back to the surface. He came up thrashing and choking and didn't see the safe rim of the pool and the figure that stood there until a while later. Then he saw the figure still standing there, without moving, and one arm was stretched out to help him. He reached for it and was pulled up, standing safe again.

It didn't last. The fist smashed his face and he fell back into the water. Port couldn't stop. He yanked the man out, beat him again till he dropped; pulled him out, beat him again till he dropped. Then he let him lie on the rim and watched the water spread around the man's body and listened to the spasmodic breathing and the weak coughs.

Port's hands were sore and he held them in the pool for a while. He could see the camera on the bottom. A black blob that must be the camera. Then he waited for the man to come around.

There was something familiar, but Port didn't think that he knew him. When it finally came to him who the man was Port almost started to beat him again. A rotten apple! The cop on the pinto, the one who said "Howdy, stranger," and had white piping on the black outfit he wore. This time he had on khaki pants and a light-colored shirt, wet and torn.

"Get up," said Port, when he saw the man looking at him.

The man made a movement, as if he meant to squeeze himself into the cement.

"Get up or I start all over," said Port.

The man got up, almost fell into the pool again, and kept watching Port.

"Get the camera out of that pool."

At first the man hesitated, but then Port unfolded his arms and the man went back into the water. He did it slowly this time, hating the feel of it, and bent under in the chest-high water to bring up the camera. He put it on the edge of the pool and shivered a little.

Port picked up the camera but didn't know how to open it. He smashed it down on the cement, watched it burst open, and pulled out the film. It glistened like a wet snake and made live sounds and movements when Port stuffed it into his pocket. The camera stayed on the concrete.

"Get out of the water."

The man tried, groaning a little. Port gave him a hand so the man stood at the pool's edge again, afraid and clammy.

"I haven't got a very long list of things that want to make me throw up," said Port, "but you combine two of them: a rotten cop, and a Peeping Tom."

The man shivered in his wet shirt.

"So don't cross me," said Port. "Do you hear?"

The man nodded.

"You run this racket?"

The man shook his head.

"You know Joko Mulnik?"

No, the man didn't.

"Who's your head man?"

"I don't know."

"Who?"

"I don't know. Honest—"

"You say honest as if you knew what it meant."

"Honest, please."

"Is the hotel in on this thing?"

"I don't know. I figure they must be."

"Who runs the hotel?"

"McCabe. But he couldn't be in on it. He's local and just does the managing."

"You're local."

"I know," said the man, and he added, "But McCabe couldn't be in on it."

"Where were you going with the film?"

The man made a half-hearted gesture toward the hedge, the lawn with the sprinklers, and the desert beyond that.

"Show me the way," said Port.

It was a short cut to one of the dude ranches. Once past the bushes Port could see it, off to one side, with the main house under black looking trees and the cottages dotted around in the open. Each cottage had a big cactus growing in front.

"How much they paying you?" Port wanted to know.

"Fifty. Each time I tended the camera I got fifty."

"That's cheap for the risk you've been running."

It seemed the man wanted to say something to Port, perhaps plead with him, but he didn't have the nerve to do it.

"You're the fall guy," Port went on. "You get it in the neck for the smallest pickings."

The man didn't know what to answer. He kept walking painfully, and tried to keep his steps smooth so his head wouldn't jar. His face was swelling up badly. When they got close to the cottages Port stopped.

"To which one are you going?"

The man pointed, and Port saw a small light on inside. "Who's in there?"

"The guy I always give the film to. They call him Joe."

"Joe who?"

"I don't know."

Then the man started walking again, but Port told him to stop.

"Beat it. I don't need you," he said.

"You mean— You mean I can—"

"Beat it," said Port.

When Port stood by the door of the cottage he felt himself getting angry again, but not like before. It was more like a nice, hot fire, not too big, but all you had to do was blow on it some and the heat would leap up.

Port opened the door and walked straight in. What he saw made him grin. "Hi, Joko."

Port stood there enjoying the way Joko looked. His weasel head had snapped around and it looked for a moment as if his eyeballs were going to jump out. Then he jerked up from his chair, sat down again, and his hands started rubbing up and down on his legs.

"You look restless," said Port. "Here it's close to three, middle of the night, and you look restless."

Joko got back his presence fast and started to grin at Port. "So would you be," he said. "How come you're here?"

"I was looking for you."

"You mean you're sore about that caper with Luden? Hell, Danny, looking back on it the whole thing comes out real funny, don't you think?" He laughed to show how funny it was, and then kept right on going. "Here I was pulling the deal, just like you told me to; there you were, a wooden Indian, right in the middle of it but at the wrong end. Wasn't that funny?"

"Come to think of it, yes," said Port.

"Why'd you stay behind when I left? You talk to Luden?"

"I told you I'd make more going after you than working for you, remember?"

They grinned at each other and Mulnik said, "I can match it. Listen to me, Danny, I'll match it."

"I can't hear you. And remember, working for Luden I got an added reward. I'm going after you."

"But Danny, how long can the job last? With me—" He started to rummage in the small desk drawer. "With me it's a long-term thing. And the compensations, Danny—there's more than money involved. Here, take a look." He handed Port a small roll of film which he pulled open so that Port could see what was on it.

Port was still smiling, so that the sharp punch in the face came as a real surprise to Joko. Port bent down to pick up the film Joko had dropped and Joko came back to life. He reached out quickly, but only got another punch.

"Don't get me riled up," said Port and watched Joko draw back. "Besides, I brought you this." He pulled out the tangled film he had taken out of the camera, back at the swimming pool.

"Christ!" Joko yelled. "Don't! The light!"

But he didn't dare move. The negative was turning slowly to an even black and Port kept rattling it back and forth, to be sure it got exposed all over.

"I don't think you know where I got this," said Port, and he told Mulnik about it. In the telling he kept hoping that Mulnik would give him an excuse. Mulnik did.

"That's what you get for hanging around a dame like Tess Dolphin. You didn't know about her and her sideline?"

Port swung so hard that a seam busted open in the back of his jacket and Mulnik caught it full face. Mulnik sank down to cover his face, but then his neck seemed to break with the punch he got from behind. Mulnik sighed and fainted.

When he came to he saw Port on the floor by the miniature fireplace and thick, yellow smoke going up the chimney. Port prodded the burning film with a poker.

When Port turned around Mulnik lay quiet.

Port was still holding the poker. He said, "Get up, you son of a bitch," very calmly, and kept dipping the poker up and down.

Mulnik jumped up.

"How come you picked Tessy Dolphin?"

"Look, Danny, let me explain something to you."

He stopped when Port stopped dipping the poker. Then he went on.

"Because she was in the suite, the Star Suite. But believe me, Danny, if you'll just listen a—"

Port dropped the poker, got up, went over to Mulnik, and shook him back and forth a few times, by the front of his shirt. Then he let go, letting Mulnik drop into a chair.

"Just answer me, will you, please? Don't keep preaching at me." Port picked up the poker and held the point on the floor. "Is that where you took the picture of Ella Anders?"

"I didn't, Danny, believe me. I can explain."

"Don't. I believe you. You were in jail at the time."

"That's right; you remember right, Danny."

"But this outfit took the picture of her, up there in that suite?"

"Yes. That's how the thing was set up. They'd do it to the celebrities."

"Why wait with the Ella Anders thing? It's been four years."

"She wasn't so big then, just starting. They figured she was a comer and to hit her with it when she was big."

"Good, patient planning, Joko." Port waited a moment and then he said, "Then how come you were trying to push that film in such a hurry?"

"Hurry? Me? Hell, Danny, I wasn't in any hurry. That's just the way I operate when I'm on to something. Honest."

"All that planning and waiting and then you go and pull a stunt like you did with Flint?"

"Stunt? Flint?"

"You used Flint's name in your deal with Luden and never told Flint about it. He could have rocked the boat. He could have said, 'I'm going to report this and keep my nose clean.'"

"Money. I was going to pay him plenty for that."

"But you didn't. You didn't have time to set it up with him beforehand and you didn't have time to pay him off afterward. How long do you think he's going to hold still."

"Honest, Danny, honest, I...."

"Don't keep saying that word."

Mulnik looked at the poker and then up at Port. "I was going to take care of him. Except right then...."

"You were in too much of a hurry."

Joko sat still, trying to look as bland as he could.

"Why the hurry, Joko?"

"Nothing. I just told you."

Port raised his voice. "Some kind of doublecross, that's all I can figure. Come on, Joko, tell it. Or I'll tell the head man."

That made Joko lively. "You want in on it, Danny? You're in! Remember, right in the beginning I asked you to come in. I don't hold no grudge with you, Danny, if you want in."

"Why the hurry, selling that Anders film? The part you sold, anyway."

"All right, it's this way. They got films—the kind they took in that suite—they got those in a place here, in the hotel. After I joined up, every so often, they kept dropping it about Ella Anders and how they were holding her picture till the time was ripe, and pretty soon, maybe, they'd make their touch." Joko shrugged and looked modest. "Well, in my opinion, she was ripe just about now. That's the whole story."

"That's how you got hold of the film—but why the hurry?"

"They don't look in that safe with those pictures, except to put something in or to take something out. There've been a string of male performers up in the suite, so nobody was likely to look in that safe for a while. Then this singer got her engagement, this Miss Dolphin." Joko watched Port carefully when he said it. "And that meant we'd put her film in the safe. That's how I had to set up my deal with the Ella Anders thing fast, before her reel was found missing."

"She's been here for three days. Any other pictures of her been taken?"

"Sure," said Joko. "But you just burned them."

"All right. Up on your feet."

Joko got up fast, but not willingly. "Danny, if you got in mind...."

"That's it. Show me that safe."

When Joko wanted to argue Port gave him a fast slap over the mouth, but when he saw that Joko was willing he let it go at that and they left the cottage.

They walked back the way Port had come with the policeman. One question was on Port's mind. "How many prints did you guys make of those films?"

"Just one. Just one before we make the touch."

Joko led the way down into the basement of the hotel.

The room was for storage. Tables and upturned chairs, bar stools and beach chairs. They made disorganized shadows which moved slowly back and forth because the overhead light was swinging. Why it moved Port couldn't figure. There was a supporting wall in the back, not completely across, and behind it more storage space. There were file cabinets with old papers and two dusty safes with doors ajar. There was even a desk which wasn't in use.

Joko went to one of the safes and opened the door all the way. The safe was empty, except for the dust. Joko reached in, and when Port heard the sound he figured that one of the drawers inside must have a tumbler lock on it.

"How come they gave the combination to you?" said Port.

"They didn't. And how do you figure I could see it in this light?"

That was true. There was only light from the room in front, hitting part of the safe from the side. Besides, Joko's eyes were closed. When Joko pulled out a plastic bag Port watched very closely. He hadn't known about Joko's talented fingers.

"Before I give it to you, Danny, I just want to say one thing."

"Don't bother."

Port took the bag out of Joko's hand and opened the top. Then he shook the contents on the floor where the light was.

They were little cans, each with a label: some said positive, some negative, and all bore names.

Port opened all the cans and shook them out, except the one that said *Ella Anders, negative.* He put that in his pocket.

"Burn those," he said to Joko.

Joko gasped. He couldn't find words, could hardly breathe, because he saw a fortune there on the floor and what Port had said was sheer blasphemy.

Port got up and stood waiting.

"Danny," Joko managed, "you out of your mind? Danny, you and me—"

"You and me, Joko, are all alone down here," and when Port said it he rubbed one fist into the palm of the other hand. "So better burn it."

Joko did. He put a match to the pile of film, several matches, because the film didn't catch very well. Then he stood back watching the smoke. He watched like someone condemned.

"Stinks, doesn't it?" said Port.

When they were outside again Port took Joko's arm.

"It's a switch," he said, "but this time I'm taking you back to Luden."

Joko just shrugged, but when Port led him toward the front of the hotel he pulled his arm away and stopped.

"Just let me get back to the cottage, just for a minute."

"More merchandise?"

"You know better. You burned it. I just want my stuff. If I'm clearing out, let me get my stuff."

They turned around and went back the same way.

"I didn't ask you yet," Port said, "but who heads up this filth factory?"

"What's the difference?"

"Lot of difference to you. They'll be after you."

Joko kept still, too depressed to apply himself to the problem.

Port didn't remember having left the door to the cottage open. It stood ajar and a thin line of light was lying across the gravel. Port made Joko stop.

"He'll be back," said a voice. "Just sit and wait till he gets here."

Chapter 15

Port didn't place the voice, but Joko apparently did. With a small sound he jerked free from Port's hand and dashed down the gravel path that wound itself past the scattered cottages.

"You hear that?" said another voice behind the door with the light, but Port didn't stay to listen to the conversation. He took off after Joko.

Once out of the light from the cottage, and after having stared at the beam that came out of the crack in the door, the night was black as ink. There was no other sound from Joko, who had probably left the gravel, and all Port could see were shapes of cacti and small houses. The lights further on didn't help. They were the pinpoints of windows at the main house of the dude ranch, and other small ones to one side, where the hotel stood near the town square.

Then a horse whinnied.

Joko had turned to the right. Port heard the commotion behind him, because the men in the cottage had come out, had heard the horse, and because of that were now following Port.

It turned out there was more than one horse. They all started to mill around the corral, snorting anxiously. Then there were three men, none of them Mulnik, and horses all over the place, and clods flying, and the men grunting and saying low, quick words. Port crouched, trying to keep out of the way and to get his bearings. He put one hand on the pocket where he had Ella Anders's million-dollar film and then, being low, he saw the three men against the sky and they were all running in different directions. At least one of them was going to find Mulnik. Which one to follow? A horse came clambering up, snorted, and reared out of the way. The men kept running. Before it would be too late Port stood up, and took off after the one who had headed toward the hotel, but the man disappeared. Then Port heard the motor.

Port turned and ran past the main house, where an outdoor light was now visible. Mulnik's white Cadillac shot briefly through the spot of light and then off. Port didn't care who else had heard the sound, or who else might be running with him. He could hear the hard breathing nearby and then suddenly he ran into the man.

They held each other for balance, straining to see, both of them nervous and winded.

"Copper," said Port under his breath, and started to swing at the man.

The man dropped to one knee, hands up. He said, "No, please, not again, please—"

Port let go of him, thinking fast. "Copper, you got a patrol car?"

The man nodded anxiously.

"Let's go," said Port, and pulled him up by the shirt.

They had to run all the way from the dude ranch back into town because the cop kept the car in a shed by his house. It was his own car, except there was a red light on the top, *Police* on the trunk, and—as Port found out later—a special transmission inside.

"How come you're after Mulnik?" asked Port.

"I—I'm not after anybody. They saw me walking past the hotel. That's when they started to wonder about the way I looked."

"Who, your boss?"

"The one that pays me, and his buddy."

"You spilled the beans to them?"

"I tried just to go away and then, when they asked me what was going on,

I just tried to say nothing. They got real suspicious then."

"What did you tell them?"

"I didn't want any part of this deal."

"Brother, you really must have calmed their feelings when you said that."

"So they said we were all going to go over to Joe's. And then he wasn't there."

"Did you tell them who beat you up?"

"Joe."

"You mean Mulnik. His name's Joko Mulnik."

"Mulnik, then. All I said was that I brought the film to him and then he got to acting funny. I got suspicious about it and he beat me up and took off."

"So how come they were waiting for him there?"

"All his stuff was still there. Money, even."

"That clinched it."

They drove in silence for a while. Ahead of the car nothing showed but the straight road cutting the desert in two and disappearing up front.

"You know this country?" asked Port.

"Pretty well."

"When Mulnik hits the main highway, which way is he likely to go?"

"Left, I figure. Unless he's hitting out for more of the desert."

"Any towns that way, where the desert is?"

"Nothing. Just those tiny ones."

Port didn't think it was likely that Mulnik was heading for open country; he wasn't the kind, and besides, Mulnik wasn't likely to be through. And to pick up the pieces he would have to head back for L.A.

They were going so fast Port almost missed it. A dust cloud, still and thick as a solid body, hung over the ground to the right of the road. When Port shot by he saw the dirt road winding into the terrain. Mulnik hadn't only headed out for the desert but had taken to the desert right away.

Port stopped, reversed, swung into the road.

"Where's it going?"

"Nowhere," said the cop. "That's open country out that way."

It didn't make sense. "But there's a road," said Port. "Where's it going?"

"Nowhere. It gets worse further on and then swings back to the main highway. Used to be a talcum mine out that way. It gave out years ago."

Maybe Joko just thought this was a short cut back to the highway getting him back to the main drag further ahead. Or maybe he meant to lie low for a few hours, till morning, maybe, and let the chase go past him.

They were going so fast that when the road got soft Port thought the car was going to dig in. He slowed, hoping Joko had been doing the same, and kept watching for tire tracks. He could see them, wide and heavy, and he avoided the places where Joko's Cadillac had been having a hard time with the sand. Then came the bend where the road turned to head toward the highway. And suddenly there were no more tracks. The night air was clear up ahead, because the dust cloud had disappeared too.

Port reversed and crawled back slowly. Mulnik had turned off into the desert.

"Where's he going now?" Port asked.

"That road goes off to the mine I been telling you of."

"Where's the road?"

But he followed the tracks which wound past rocks and through dips, and with some imagining it could have been a road. Port cut out his lights after a while, thinking that Joko could not be so far ahead any more, and after a stretch of slow driving, to get used to the light, he speeded up again. The moon had gone, but the East sky was clearing.

"What are you after?" said the cop.

"Mulnik's got something I want," Port said. And then, very suddenly, they saw the street.

It was less than a ghost town, just two lines of shacks, some almost intact, but one of them had two stories, which made it all look more impressive than it actually was. Port slowed down immediately, to lessen the motor sound and to look for the Cadillac. If he turned on the lights he would see the tracks in the blown sand but that way, if Joko was really here—

He was. The two shark fins of his car shot out from between two buildings, the motor making a high whine in reverse. Port jammed on the brake. The two fins and then the long bulk of the body shot by in front of the hood, then bucked to a sudden stop, ready to swing. Port shifted and shot ahead, but the blocking didn't faze Joko. He crashed into the side of Port's car, hard enough to make the door spring open wide. The Cadillac had to back up again. Port was out of the door, trying to dash toward the other car, when he stumbled.

He could hear the roar of the Cadillac's motor. There was sand in his eyes.

Joko wouldn't! Joko was a bastard but not that much. But Port rolled. In spite of the pain he tore open his eyes, when the metal cones on the Cadillac's bumper shot toward him like two pointed fists. Port tensed with fear. His body relaxed only when he passed out.

"I told you. He forced me along."

"There's no gun on him."

"Well, he just forced me."

"Why come here?"

"I told you—"

"You don't know. Yeah, you told me."

They talked more, arguing, but now Port heard only the rush in his ears, and then the pounding. Not his ears, it was in his head, and more so when he moved. Was he moving? After a moment the pain slowed down and he concentrated on breathing. He felt over his body after a while, and it seemed he was all there. No pain, just in the head. He opened his eyes.

Semper's groomed face was looking at him. It looked down the way a face might when inspecting something to buy.

Somebody grabbed Port under the arms and made him sit up. He knew he was sitting after the flood of pain had drained back out of his skull.

"Come on, come on." Semper sounded impatient.

Port saw where he was. It must be one of the large shacks. A buckled wood floor, broken table, a potbelly stove red with rust, nothing else. No romantic ghost town trappings, like stuffed deer heads on the wall or lines of liquor bottles hung with cobwebs. The light came from outside. Early morning.

"He's all right. Just a headache, I bet."

The bouncer. Semper and the bouncer. The cop was there too but he didn't seem to matter.

"Daniel Port," and Semper tossed Port's wallet between his feet. "What's your part in this?"

They didn't know, but why should they? Port reached for his pocket. He tried to cover the movement, and maybe he did, because none of them seemed to be interested.

Port felt his pocket. Ella Anders' film roll was gone.

"Let's have some answers," said Semper. He nodded at the bouncer who came over to Port and hoisted him up on his feet. They all watched Port weave, but he stood. He even felt better about it. Except for his headache he felt all right.

"Who conked you?" asked the bouncer.

"The car door," the cop said.

"How come?" Semper wanted to know.

It was Port's turn. He couldn't figure it all, but they clearly didn't know why he was out here, just as he wasn't sure why they were here.

"Why are you here?" Port asked.

Semper stepped up and hit Port under the nose and when Port's head stopped churning there was nothing he could do about Semper.

"Just answer," said Semper, "unless you're big enough to buck this gun."

Port didn't feel big at all, gun or no gun, and he made himself breathe very steadily. Give a little, he said to himself. Give a little and make them open up.

"I'm here for the same reason you are. Looking for Mulnik."

"Why here?"

"Same reason you came. The dust over the road."

The way Semper grunted Port saw he had figured it right. "You don't answer right." Semper was irritated. It made him look elegant, like a pose. "How come you're after Mulnik?"

None of it was clear. Didn't they have the film out of his pocket? Didn't that tell them why he had been with Mulnik? Port looked at Semper standing there with the gun, a fancy pose, the gun held with practiced ease. And he also looked expectant, wanting Port's answer. Port guessed and said, "He's got a film I want."

"Film? What are you talking about?"

It didn't impress Port, and he started to smile.

"You didn't know he was playing the field? You don't know Mulnik very well."

"What film?" This time Semper was angry.

"The best. Ella Anders."

It hit like a bomb. It hit with a big, powerful impact that left everybody afraid to make a move.

Port followed it up fast, to take the best advantage.

"How would I know about it, except from Mulnik? Did you bother to check your safe in the basement? Did you find it on me? I haven't got it and it isn't in the safe. Mulnik has it. Ask your cop if he wasn't here; check the tracks outside in the sand. You want it back, get him."

They all swiveled to look at the cop, who nodded at them, and when they turned back to Port he started again.

"Take a look at your basement, at the safe—if you think you can spare the time while Mulnik hits it back to L.A.! Don't stand there like jerks. He suckered me; now he's doing the same thing to you!"

Semper was running already and he waved at the bouncer to stop wasting time and to follow him. They rushed out of the shack into the street, where the morning made a flat, shadowless light and they made jerky movements looking back and forth at the tracks in the street, the gouges where Mulnik had turned his car, hit the door of the police cruiser, and taken off between two of the buildings where he must have jolted out into the open to avoid their car which had been coming down the road into the street.

Port didn't take a deep breath till they took off, with sand flying and a strained noise of the motor.

The morning air made Port shiver, but the coolness helped his head. He walked to the side of the cop's car and leaned there, breathing deeply, feeling his lack of sleep. When the cop came out of the shack Port watched him as if he had never seen the man.

"Is it true," asked the cop, "what you said about Mulnik stealing a film?"

"Didn't you see him take it?"

"Huh?"

"I had it right here in my pocket."

The cop gaped, then shook his head. "Your pocket? He never stopped. He hit the open door of my car so it clipped you over the head, but he never stopped."

At first Port just stood there, to let it sink in, and then he was almost afraid to look. He got down on his hands and knees where the dirt was churned up from his fall. Then he found it, partway under the car. He picked up the can, shook the sand off, and saw inside the film of Ella Anders.

Chapter 16

The cop drove him back to Palmedo. They didn't talk because Port felt sore and tired and the cop had his own problems. When they got close to the town the cop said, "What's—what happens now?"

"Just drop me off at the hotel."

"I mean about me?"

Port lit a cigarette. He didn't feel like a discussion. He shrugged and said, "You're the cop."

He got out at the hotel and didn't even wait to watch the cop drive off. He went into the empty lobby and up to the desk.

The clerk shook his head.

"She's been taken to the airport, maybe an hour ago."

"Oh. Any message for—any message at all?"

"No, sir. Was she expecting you?"

"I doubt it," and Port walked to the breakfast room.

There wasn't anyone there except the two waitresses and a couple that couldn't make up their minds to go up to bed. Port ordered coffee and when it came he told the waitress to leave it there, he'd be right back. He went up to the tenth floor, tried the door to Tessy's suite, but found it locked. He went into the laundry room and saw where a closet door was standing ajar. Inside the closet was a stool and a tripod, both on their sides. Port used the stool to climb through the square hole in the wall where the mirror had been and got his things from the bedroom; his bag, the few clothes he had put on the dresser, and his toilet things in the bathroom. Then he picked up the notebook Ella Anders had given him, and left the same way he had come. When he was back downstairs, drinking his lukewarm coffee, he kept worrying about the fact that this time Tessy hadn't left a note for him.

They wouldn't let him in at the studio gate. He looked like hell, didn't have a pass, and the guard refused to call Luden's office. He argued with the guard, but it didn't do any good. Port walked back to his car and sat down. He was dog-tired. He had been hit on the ear, punched in the nose, rolled in the sand, and clipped over the head. He thought about that and when he felt good and mad he went back to the gate.

"Officer," he said, "call up R. S. Luden the Second or I'll tear off your badge."

"Beat it, bum."

Port reached over and tore the guard's badge off his chest. It made a hole in the uniform.

"Call up R. S. Luden the Second or I'll tear off...."

The guard had meant to make a lunge for Port, but right then a two-block-long car rolled up to the gate with a double-breasted girl at the wheel. She wore dark glasses which concealed more than her dress did, and instead of lunging at Port the guard lunged past him and pressed the button that swiveled the striped barrier out of the way.

"Why, Jamie," said the girl, "your costume is open."

Then she hummed the car through the gate and the guard pushed the button again.

Port was waiting in the booth when the guard came running back.

"I didn't know what button to press here," said Port and nodded at the phone, "or else I would have called myself. So please get me R. S. Luden the Second."

The guard made a grab for Port's arm, got shoved out of the way, and then Port's expression took the spunk out of him. He went to the phone and yelled into it, "Gate One! Emergency!"

Port had his arms folded, leaning against the wall, and ignored the guard's look of victory.

The guard rushed out again, but it was only a sightseeing bus that had slowed down to let the faces behind the window get a look at the magic of the studio gate. All the faces looked at the guard with his torn uniform and then the bus took off for some other high spot in the tour.

"They thought you were a bum," said Port when the guard came back, but the guard could ignore it. A jeep with howling siren came down the studio main street, and after making a smart swivel at the gate it stopped and four storm-trooper types jumped out of the jeep and piled into the guard house ready to tear Port apart. At the last minute—he hadn't moved in the meantime—he held out his folded sheet of paper. They stopped as if a spell had been cast.

"May I see that?" said one of them.

"Of course," said Port and handed it over. "It states I am a special assistant to R. S. Luden the Second, on a confidential mission. Take a look at that letterhead. And the signature."

They did, and from troopers turned into an honor guard. "We'll have to check that, of course. Will you come with us, please?" one of them asked politely.

Port nodded and followed them.

"Why in hell didn't you say so?" said the guard.

"This way it's faster," said Port.

"Gimme back my badge."

"Of course." Port gave it to him.

At Building Twelve there were no shenanigans with passes, phoned verifications, or any such thing. They all marched straight up to Luden's floor and the decorative secretary in Luden's front office sat wide-eyed, as if watching a movie.

"Is Mr. Luden in?"

"I'll have to ask—checkifyoullwaitaminute," she caught herself.

"Just to verify a document."

Luden, it seemed, couldn't make head or tails of the receptionist's phone call, and finally came out himself.

Port nodded at him, smiled and held up the roll of film he had brought. For a moment it looked as if Luden would jump at it, but he checked himself, looked stern, and used his executive voice.

"Thank you, men, you may go. Mr. Port—" He stood aside to let Port enter his office.

First Port took his paper back from one of the guards and then he went into Luden's office.

Luden closed the door. It banged shut when he was already halfway across the room, very eager, and holding out his hand for the film.

"A great day! This is a great day!" He took the small can from Port and fumbled it open.

For the next few minutes nobody talked. Luden unrolled the film and looked at it by the light of the window. Port looked at Luden. It wasn't clear to Port what excited Luden: the end of the chase, the salvation of the studio's star, or the woman on the film. Then Luden started to frown. Perhaps he was thinking about the contract negotiations and that now he had no longer the whip hand. Or the film didn't please him.

He said, "Why, all she does is—she gets undressed and goes to bed!"

"Disappointed?"

Port got a vicious look, but he shrugged it off. "Is it Ella Anders?"

"It certainly is."

"You owe me ten thousand."

Luden put the film down on the desk and re-rolled it. He put it back in the small can, carried the can to his safe, and locked it up.

"Well, Port, we are grateful. My organization is grateful. Have a drink?"

"No, thank you."

"Have you seen Elly about this?"

"No. I just got in."

Port stood by the desk, watching Luden rummage around in a drawer. If that bastard was stalling it wouldn't be a surprise. Perhaps Port should have gotten a statement to show that Luden owed him ten thousand for delivering. But Luden couldn't be that stupid. If Port wanted to make up the ten thousand all he had to do was sell what he knew to the public, hold Luden up for the money, or else. Luden would be the kind to expect such a threat.

"Do you want it certified?" asked Luden and opened the large book with the checks.

"Won't be necessary," said Port. "I trust you."

They exchanged smiles, Luden politely and Port with relief.

"Here you are." Luden handed the check over the desk. Port took it, then stuck it into his pocket.

It was over. Delivered and paid for, it was over. "I've changed my mind about that drink," he said. "Are you still serving?"

"Certainly, Port, certainly." Luden got up to get busy at the small bar he had in a cabinet.

Luden seemed very relaxed now, and looking at him Port was reminded of a fat hen. Luden poured the rye Port asked for and took the same. He made a benign nod when Port saluted his glass at him and sipped, looking satisfied. They had nothing to say to each other any more and it was clear to Port that he could leave any time. Luden wasn't anxious about it, he just didn't care. Perhaps he was off on something else. Big executive.

"Okay," and Port put down his glass. "I'll be leaving."

"Fine. And thank you again."

He made no move to shake hands and Port went to the door.

"Will you pick up your pass at the girl's desk?" said Luden. "And sign the receipt the girl has typed for you."

"Receipt?"

"For the money. You know."

"Fine. Good-by," and Port went out.

When he got to the receptionist's desk she was on the office phone taking down the check number Luden was giving her. She entered it on a receipt, showed Port where to sign, and after he had done so she filed it. It said that Port had delivered, Luden had received, and had paid such and such. Luden's signature had already been on it. No matter what the merchandise, business is business.

There was no problem about getting out of the studio gate and the guard, a different one, took the pass. Outside Port got into his car and drove off. He felt dog-tired.

What about Tess? He'd go home and call her. Then it struck him that it had to be this way, because the affair wasn't finished until he saw Ella Anders and told her that it was finished. That would top it. He liked Ella Anders, he had finished the job for her, and he and Elly would have a drink over it. After that, he'd go and see Tessy.

When he got to his room he felt edgy about Tess. How much would she care about all his good reasons? How much could she take?

"May I speak to Miss Dolphin, please?"

"She's in rehearsal."

"Would you tell her that...."

"I'm sorry, sir. We have a policy...."

"I know. Please tell her Daniel Port is on the phone."

"We make it a policy...."

"Tell her, for God's sakes! She's been waiting for this call!"

"What was the name?"

"Port."

"She didn't leave a message. When she expects a call Miss Dolphin always leaves a message."

"It's about her engagement at Palmedo. She just left there this morning. Maybe she doesn't know it yet, but she left something behind. That's why I'm calling."

"What did she leave behind?"

"Don't get nosy, just tell her. Tell her Port is on the phone."

Port listened for more but the man must have put the receiver down to tell Tessy. Port sat by his phone, very anxious, wondering where she was rehearsing. It took long enough for her to go across the street, get a hamburger—no. She'd eat steak. Raw, probably.

"Yes? Hello? Here I am."

But it wasn't Tess.

"Miss Dolphin sends a message. She said she couldn't take any more of this and I should hang up on you."

"Don't you dare!" yelled Port, but the phone was dead already.

He slammed the receiver down, hoping to break something, but the phone took it. He paced around a few times and then decided to take a shower. When he was undressed he decided to hell with the shower and lay down on the bed to think it over. A little while later he was asleep.

He drove into Bel Air, and when he came to the first abstract sculpture he noticed that the house where the party had been was totally dark, very quiet. The way they had been going Port had been sure it would have lasted a few days. When he came to the second abstract sculpture he got ready to turn in but stopped partway up the drive. It wasn't Ella Anders's house. This meant only one thing. There were now three of those things. The third one was a few houses up, where Ella Anders lived. He turned into her drive but didn't get very far. The cars were parked almost all the way down to the street, and every window was lit in the house.

"Must be her turn," he said to himself.

When he came to the door he relied on his past experience and didn't bother to ring. He was stopped immediately.

"I thought you said you weren't coming to this one?" said the sculptor.

"No," said Port. "That was the other one, the other party."

"This is the same party," said the sculptor.

Port believed it. He recognized some of the faces and there was even the blonde from the first time, who gave him a dirty look.

"Have you seen Miss Anders?" Port asked the sculptor. "And before you say 'Elly isn't here' I happen to know this is her house."

"So what?" said the sculptor.

Port walked away from him and tried asking some other people. They didn't know about Elly. The house was big and the party mood was running high, and no one knew anything about Ella Anders. Port thought he'd wait; she would show after a while. There was no real reason to rush because by the looks of the high spirits around Elly probably knew the good news already and this was her party to end all parties.

Then the sculptor was back.

"Are you sure this is the right house?" he said.

"I'm sure," said Port. "I've been here before."

"That's nothing," said the sculptor. His hands speared out when a tray came by and he took two cocktails, giving one to Port.

The sculptor took the red cherry out of Port's drink and swallowed it.

"Now. What was I saying?"

"You said that's nothing."

"It wasn't? Wait till you hear this. One day—evening, rather—I went to this house which I knew full well, having been there several times and on good terms every time—"

Port could tell this was going to be a long one, so he interrupted and said, "By the way, I see you sold Number Three."

"I beg your pardon?"

"The sculpture, the third one. What's the name of it this time?"

"Oh, that! Next door!"

"Yeah. What's the name this time. It was *Time Lapse* before the last one."

"Time, spelled T-H-Y-M-E."

"How apt. How much did you charge?"

"Hell, nothing. This one was good will."

"Can you afford it?"

"I had to. It's on my own lawn."

Port found another cherry in his drink and gave it to the sculptor. Then the sculptor went away. Port spotted the maid he had seen in the house on his first visit and he asked her where Miss Anders was. She recognized him but didn't say anything right away.

"Isn't she home?" Port asked.

"Yes, she is, Mr. Port, but I don't think she wants to come down."

"She's upstairs?"

The maid nodded.

"All right for me to go up there?" Port asked.

"I don't think she wants to be disturbed."

"Oh," said Port.

"It's the second room on the left," and the maid went away, giving Port a look he didn't understand.

It was getting late and no sign of Ella Anders. Port wanted to leave. He went back to the hall and then upstairs.

Somebody was ahead of him. The man stood by her door, swaying a little, and by the time Port made the landing the man had opened the door and walked in.

If he hadn't left the door open Port would have gone downstairs again. He heard the man say something and then a laugh. Port went towards the door.

"Come on, Elly. Good God!"

He got no answer.

"You maybe a prude all of a sudden?"

It sounded drunk and belligerent, but still no answer. Port pushed the door open all the way.

Ella Anders was sitting on a low stool where a blue telephone stood on a table, and she was pushing the man's hand out of the way. But she didn't look angry, or any other way that showed emotion. She was wearing a slinky silvery dress which was like a mold, but none of that caught the eye. Only her face did: cold, as if she wasn't there.

"Now listen to me, Elly—"

"Blow," said Port.

The man turned around and started to say something when Port grabbed his arm and doubled it back. He said, "Blow," once more and pushed the man out of the door. Then he closed the door and came back.

"Miss Anders?"

She looked up at him, and her eyes narrowed.

"You don't look as if you've heard the good news yet, Miss Anders. I got the film back."

All she did was take a deep breath.

"I gave it to Luden, this afternoon."

"I know. He just called me."

"Well? Now that Luden's got it, your troubles are over."

"No, they're not. Luden just called me. He's the blackmailer now."

Chapter 17

Luden's telephone call had been very specific. There were going to be contract changes to save the studio money, there were going to be binders to keep her from signing with anybody else, there were going to be contract additions which made Luden the Second the top arbiter in decisions covering her career, and there were other details, such as a new business manager, more studio supervision over her personal budget, and so forth. Of course, all this—Luden had added—could be liberalized on the basis of personal considerations. Elly should think it all over.

Ella Anders recited the whole thing to him, and the more impervious she had acted the more furious had Port become. But it didn't help, not right then, so he kept it inside.

"Come on, Miss Anders, you've got to shake it."

"As if I couldn't breathe," she kept saying. "As if I couldn't breathe...."

He took her arm and made her get up.

"Come along. We'll take a ride. It'll do you good."

"But don't you see—"

"Come outside. In a while you'll feel better and we'll talk it over."

They went out the back way but had to pass through the garden, where the tables and the sun umbrellas were standing. Nobody paid any attention to them. Port took her down the drive, to his car, and they drove back to Sunset. There he turned right where Sunset wound the rest of the way down to the ocean and from there he took the shore highway going north.

She had forgotten to wear something over her dress and Port could see that she was cold. But she didn't try to keep out of the wind and didn't want Port to give her his jacket.

"We'll stop for a while," he said, "And I can put on the heater."

He stopped, facing the ocean, but when he wanted to close the top of the car she shook her head.

"Leave it. Maybe the cold will bite me out of this."

They sat and listened to the ocean below. The surf wasn't visible, only the water further away. The shaded moon made a dark lead color on the Pacific, a cold, stony color which moved between black and blue-white.

"Want me to turn up the heater some?"

He had to look at her to find her answer. She sat with her bare arms crossed. "Could I have your jacket now?" she asked.

"If Luden asked me to go to bed with him now, I don't think I would care," she said.

"You probably wouldn't. So don't do it."

She looked at Port, then away again. He wasn't sure if she had smiled.

"Reason I wanted to talk to you," he went on. "I wanted to tell you I'm going after him."

"I don't know," she said. "He's not just one man."

"I've got some experience."

She asked for a cigarette. When she was smoking she said. "You know how much money I have. About five hundred dollars."

"I want Luden," said Port.

She watched the end of her cigarette, moving it back and forth to make it glow in the breeze.

"You know, Dan, there's a much easier way. I know one easy way."

He waited.

"Walk right out of it. Take my five hundred dollars and go."

"All your work gone to hell? You just made it."

"Made what?"

Port didn't know what.

"The magazine covers? The ads? A million eyes staring at me?" She threw the cigarette away. "I don't need that many," she said.

"You're good at your work," said Port.

"I don't like what it costs, anymore."

"Miss Anders...."

"Elly."

"Look, Elly, don't walk out under a cloud. It'll hang on."

She tried to say something, but then she didn't.

"I'll help you. Luden paid me already, but this time I'm really going to collect from him. You just sit tight, will you?"

She tried to be light about it, but her voice sounded unsure. "You're doing this for nothing?"

"I'll get mine. I'm going to get Luden."

She put her hand out, making the jacket slide off one shoulder, and touched the side of his neck.

"You sound as if you will, Dan."

"Just sit tight. I'll keep you out of it."

"I don't care. Get me into it," she said, and she sounded alive again. Then she turned his face with her hand. "Give me a kiss."

He bent over and kissed her and then she laughed and looked again as she ought to look.

Port knew there wasn't a chance of getting back into the studio. Next time the jeep wouldn't pick him up, they would probably run him down. So at eight in the morning he was inside Luden the Second's own park. Port didn't think it was likely that Luden was gone at that hour and he stood by the shrubbery watching the silent house. He might not even be able to get into Luden's house. A window? There was most likely a burglar alarm.

Port went to the side door and rang the bell. There were footsteps and someone unlocked the door.

"May I help you?" said the houseboy.

If necessary, Port thought, this one wouldn't be any problem. He was a slight, dark-haired Oriental. Unless, of course, the houseboy knew jujitsu. Port decided to try something else first.

"Is Mr. Luden up yet?"

"No. May I ask who is calling?"

"I'm the masseur, from the studio. Mr. Luden asked me to be here at eight, and if he wasn't up you should wake him."

"Masseur?"

"Yes, masseur. I also do roadwork. I didn't bring my equipment, because today we do roadwork. May I wait inside while you call him?"

The houseboy seemed puzzled, but looking at Port he felt reassured. A frank face, guileless eyes, and an expectant smile. The houseboy thought that this man could never look any other way.

"Come in." He held the door. "Come right through the kitchen." He led the way to the hall and pointed to the room where Port had been once before. "Wait there, please. I'll wake Mr. Luden."

Port sat down in one of the chairs facing the window. It would get Luden further into the room, before he saw who it was.

Port lit a cigarette and sat thinking. He thought about how Luden would feel, getting called out of bed at eight in the morning to do "roadwork."

Port heard Luden when he was still at the top of the stairs. He was taking his foul mood out on the houseboy.

"In the sitting room," said the houseboy, and Port could hear him retreating across the tiled hall. He also heard Luden.

"All right! What is the meaning of this? Are you here?"

"Here by the window," said Port.

Luden rushed into the room, unable to place the voice and not seeing anyone.

"I demand—" he started, when Port got up.

Port said, "Come here."

Luden stopped still, wide awake now, but unable to move. The hairs around his skull stood up in odd bunches and his unshaven face seemed to quiver. Port came right to the point, because the sight of the man had made him lose all humor.

"I'm here for the film."

Port walked over to Luden. "I'm going to make this between you and me. Either hand over that film or I'm going to cripple you."

"You—you are what?"

"Like this," and Port whipped his hand under Luden's nose. Luden staggered and sat down.

This wasn't going to take very long, Port could see. "So you know how I feel about this," he said, "I'm going to do it again." He did.

When Luden recovered enough to use his voice he didn't know what to do with it. It slid up and down a few times, broke, and he started to stammer.

"I paid—paid you. I paid—I got the receipt— How much do you want?

How much—"

"You make me sick, Luden."

Port watched the man get to his feet. "Where is it?" he demanded.

"Criminal—you're a criminal!"

"I'm going to break your arm," said Port, and when Luden saw Port's face he believed it.

"Wait, let me—"

Port reached out, yanked Luden's arm into position, and then he held it there.

"Let me explain it," said a voice.

Joko Mulnik seemed lost in the smoking jacket. There was an R. S. L. crest on the breast pocket, a silk ascot around Mulnik's throat, and he had even found time to comb his hair.

They stared at each other without disguises. They didn't like each other and it stuck out plain.

"I should have known," Port was hoarse. "I should have known that fat idiot didn't have the brains for this twist."

"Now you know." Mulnik came into the room.

"My arm," Luden managed, "he's got my arm."

Port dropped it and went over to Mulnik. Mulnik looked very brave.

"You don't carry a gun, Danny, do you? You never did."

"I don't need it," said Port.

Mulnik held up his hand, and it was enough to make Port hesitate. Mulnik wasn't acting a bluff. Mulnik had something big, and Port waited.

"You will now," said Mulnik. "Wanna hear about it?"

"Go ahead. It won't make any difference."

"Wanna bet?"

Port sat down on the coffee table and held his hands between his knees. He knew when to switch tactics. He knew when to take a man seriously. "How come you moved in here?" he asked. "Scared of somebody?"

"Me? Hell, no. I moved in because it's headquarters right now. R. S. and me, we're a team."

"And you're the general. What's that make the idiot boy there?"

"Don't let him faze you," said Mulnik to Luden. "He's trying to make you and me split."

Luden was glad to agree, because it saved him the trouble of working up indignation. His face hurt and he wished he were someplace else. He was glad Mulnik was there, and he nodded at him.

"Didn't work, did it?" Mulnik said to Port. "What you gonna try next?"

"Hear you out."

"My boy!" said Mulnik spreading his mouth for the laugh.

"How funny is it?" said Port. "Are you here because you're hiding from your buddies or because you don't trust Luden alone with the merchandise?"

"I'm not afraid of them; I'm in touch with them."

"Except they don't know where you are."

"And I trust Luden, because we're a team."

"How about that little white lie about your being a detective instead of a blackmailer, he forgive you for that?"

"Sure. Him and me's a team. We do blackmail together."

Luden cringed, but he didn't say anything.

"Can't live without each other," said Port.

"That's right. Or at least, we wouldn't get what we want."

"I know what Luden wants," said Port, and looked at him.

Luden was coming back to life. A useless rage came into his face, which stayed there long after Port had looked away again.

"And you?" he said to Mulnik.

"I'm going to get a piece of her too. By contract." He made a pause for effect. "I'm going to be the new business manager. By contract."

Port had to get up and walk across the room. He was glad for the size of the room. It gave him more time to distract himself. "As if I couldn't breathe," Ella Anders had said. Port started to whistle, the sound monotonous. He looked at the two leeches back by the coffee table, and Luden had moved over to be closer to Mulnik. They both sat still, watching Port, but it seemed to him as if he could almost see them feeling where to latch on and not to let go. Port walked back and said, "Ella Anders won't take it. Ever think of that?"

"Don't have to," said Mulnik. "There isn't a dame won't give her eyes teeth for the place Elly's got." Mulnik grinned. "She already give more than eye teeth to get where she is."

"Maybe she's got nothing else to give any more."

"Elly?" Mulnik laughed.

Port controlled himself and kept it conversational. "I'm going to be in the way, Mulnik. Count on it."

"I am. And I got that all set up for you."

"How much this time?"

"You're too late to get in. This time, you bastard, you're getting out!"

"You make it sound easy, Mulnik."

"Sure. Why not? Listen to this, Danny Port."

Mulnik saw that Port was listening and he couldn't let the moment go by without some kind of performance. He got up, redraped the smoking jacket, and stood by the fireplace like a high executioner waiting.

"Gimme a light, R. S."

Luden handed him one of the lighters that looked like a knight in armor and Mulnik worked the visor. When his cigarette was lit he kept tapping the lighter into the palm of his hand, swinging it like a sap.

"Maybe all along you've been thinking, Danny, and wondering about my two buddies I left back there in Palmedo. They're right here in town, if you want to know."

"Looking for you."

"Not no more they ain't, buddy. They're looking for you!"

"Sure. Call them in. We should all have a talk about who is who and who did what."

"That's taken care of, too. They know I'm in close with Luden, who's the real man to handle the Anders caper, and all we need now is the film. So while I'm keeping Luden warm, they're looking for you. They think you got it."

"As I said, any time we can get together...."

"So are they, except they don't talk the way you do. That's why I asked you before if you had a gun. Are they ever sore at you, Danny! After I got through talking to them, were they ever sore!"

"Wait'll I talk to them."

"Won't do any good. I talked to them first. And seeing how they're happy about the way I've set up this thing with Mr. Luden himself, me being his confidant and so forth, you can picture it what their feelings are. Why, they never been so close to a permanent deal in all their career."

"Then how come you don't let them know where you are?"

"Later, after the contract. Right now their appearance may upset Mr. Luden, I told them."

Port thought about it and it looked like Mulnik had covered all the angles. He had Luden, he had his buddies, and he had even managed to be the top man of the deal.

"So here is what it is," said Mulnik, and he gestured to show that it was the conclusion. "You stay in town, Danny Port, and you're gonna get hurt. But remembering what buddies we was, back with Stoker, I'm gonna give you one chance. Blow town, and I won't set my men on you. I haven't told them yet where you are. That's it, Port. Or else."

Mulnik was waiting for Port to talk back. Maybe he'd give away what he had in mind next. And Luden was waiting for Port, because things were going fine and perhaps Port would start crawling.

Port stood where he was for a moment, looked from one to the other, and then he walked out.

Chapter 18

He drove around slowly for a while, with precise control. If it had been any other way he would have gone back, cracked their heads together, torn it out of them where they had stashed that thin strip of celluloid that made all this filthy conniving possible. Except that wouldn't have worked, not with a thing that had gotten so complicated. There was only one simple thing about it. They were not going to win. They were not going to win because Port was after them now, in earnest. No more laughs, no more lenient favors, no more letting things go. And there wasn't going to be time for a waiting game. Port drove downtown, thinking it out. They had set the tempo; he would call the shots.

He parked on a lot on Main Street and went into a drugstore to make a call. When the girl answered, Port said he wanted Flint.

"Who is calling, pl—"

"Just get him, will you?"

Flint came on right away.

"This is Port. Remember me?"

Flint remembered right away. "Well, you're back. How was Palmedo, Mr. Port?"

"Where can I get a gun in this town?"

"Did you say...."

"Where, Flint? Come on."

Flint told him, and Port hung up.

The address wasn't far and in the room behind the cigar store Port paid double for a .38 Magnum, because that's what they wanted to sell him and not because he would need that much firing power. The gun had hardly been used and had no serial numbers. Then Port drove home.

He parked the MG in front of the house and locked the door to his room. Then he slept until nightfall. He got up, boiled coffee, unlocked the door, sat down in a chair. It was now dark in the room. He sat to one side of the door, across the room near the windows. Now and then he took a slow sip from his cup of coffee.

He sat like that till long after midnight. He could see well in the dark, by then, seeing each part of the room, and the door, and the faint shine of the door knob. Now and then he heard someone walking outside, going to some other apartment, but mostly he only heard the faint stirring of the plants in the yard, leaf sounds.

If nothing happened, there'd be another night, though Port didn't see why. He thought it would be soon.

Sometimes traffic sounds from the distance, less now than before, and leaf sounds now and then. He held the Magnum in his lap and waited.

When it came it wasn't the door. He didn't know how they had managed it quite so silently, but they had come from the outside landing which circled the yard like a balcony and had climbed over the railing to creep their way over, along the ledge. It wasn't far from the landing. They had made a shuffle coming that way and next they were trying the window screen. Port could see one man. The other one was still out of sight.

Port sat still, changing his mind about how he would do it. Not a play for a stalemate, the way he had thought, but more impressive. They were playing it right into his hand.

They took a while with the screen, pausing after every small sound, and Port was starting to boil. This part was taking longer than the rest of the night.

The first one came in, but Port didn't want him. The first one walked past Port, unsure of the layout, then waited in the room till the other got through the window. The second man climbed in, gun first, holding his breath with each movement. Once through the window he paused, to take a deep slow breath, and when he had done that Port swung on the exhale and the sound on the skull was like slapping wood.

Before Semper was down the Magnum had come up and Port said, "Stand still, bouncer."

He hadn't meant to move anyway.

"Turn on the light," said Port.

"Where is it?"

Port could see the switch, because he had been in the dark much longer. It was good to know that the bouncer's eyes hadn't adjusted. Semper's gun had slid up close to his feet.

"Turn right," said Port. "Walk with your arms out."

When the bouncer hit the wall Port told him to feel with his hand, till he found the switch. Then he told him to turn it on. A standing lamp on a low table came on, hitting the bouncer full in the eyes, so it would take him longer than Port to get used to the light.

But Port needn't have been that cautious. Without Semper to tell him things the bouncer didn't feel very active. Port told him to sit, to keep still, and to watch what would happen. Then he picked up the gun from the floor and put it on one of the window sills. Semper was still out. Port sat in his chair and by the time he had done with a cigarette he saw that Semper was starting to twitch. Port went for a waterglass, filled it up, and threw the cold water in Semper's face.

"Easy," said Port.

Semper got up on one arm and looked as if he had been dreaming badly. He moved his head slowly from side to side, and very slowly got his legs under him. His gun wasn't far, on the window sill.

Port had thought he might and because he was mad he let Semper get as far as he did, but when Semper had lunged halfway to the sill Port's foot caught him in the chest and before Semper fell again he got another kick to the side of the head. Semper took a while to get back his breath.

"All right, up," said Port.

Semper got up, trembling. Port didn't know if it was weakness from shock or pure frustration.

"You wouldn't be able to tell, would you, what a gentle person I am most of the time?"

Port waited a while and then, "Well? Answer me."

Semper shook his head.

"Good. Now, sometimes, I put myself out, just to impress bastards like you. You impressed?"

Semper looked at the bouncer and then back at Port. He felt plenty vicious by now, for what Port was doing, and in front of his flunky.

Port waited just so long, then got up, walked over to Semper, and hit him hard in the stomach. "Answer me."

This time Semper was impressed. He could hardly talk, but he got it out that he was impressed.

"Fine. You can sit in this chair."

Port sat down too, put his gun down and took out his pack of cigarettes. After lighting one he threw the pack at Semper who caught it and lit one.

"Give it to the bouncer," said Port. "Maybe he wants one too."

The bouncer caught the pack but shook his head. He said he was in training and never smoked anyway.

"And now we'll discuss something," said Port.

"Go to hell."

"Or I'll make garbage out of you, Semper."

"You think because you sit there with a gun—"

"Yes, I do," said Port.

Semper took a deep breath, then stopped because something hurt him.

When he relaxed again he crossed his legs and talked with the special air he had, cold and from way up. "If you didn't have that gun, I'd tell you what I think."

Port didn't feel like horsing around. He didn't feel he had the time, and he didn't feel like it with a person like Semper. "Get up and come over here," he said.

He was still holding the gun and Semper just sat, starting a thin, supercilious smile. Then Port tossed the gun on the floor, out of reach. "Get up and come over here," he said again, low but very clear, and his eyes were the only thing that seemed to have movement. Except, the way Semper saw it, Port may not be moving right then, but when he did it would be like a flash and like murder.

Semper had to clear his throat. He looked at his shoes and said, "What—what do you want?"

Port got up, got his gun off the floor, then sat down again. He put the gun in his pocket and asked, "You said if I didn't have the gun. Then what? Go ahead, you can tell me."

Semper answered because he now was afraid of Port. "I was going to say—What I meant before was, without you with that gun there—"

"I wouldn't shoot you for talk. Say it."

But Semper couldn't. He wasn't himself enough to remember what he had meant to say.

"All right, Semper. We'll start over. To discuss something."

"What do you want?" asked Semper.

"What do you want, Semper, the film?"

"So you've got it!"

"No. But I want it."

Semper's aches and discomforts helped him cover his confusion. He concentrated on the feeling of pain in his chest and the hot throb under his skull. That way he didn't have to decide right away what to think of Port's remark.

"You and me want the same thing, so I'll brief you," said Port.

"You're a liar!"

Semper felt like crouching, as soon as he had said it, but Port surprised him again. He shrugged and pulled a paper out of his pocket.

"Read it. Here."

Semper got up to take the paper, sat down again and started to read. It said Port had been authorized to transport and deliver to R. S. Luden Studios a sixteen millimeter film by Ella Anders. Signed and countersigned.

"So what," said Semper. He gave back the paper and sat down again.

"And I delivered it," said Port.

He took out his ten-thousand-dollar check and showed it to Semper.

Semper didn't speak. He sat thinking and wondering. Even his pains did-n't bother him at that moment.

"I got it from Mulnik—not that he was willing—and delivered it back to Luden. Follow me?"

Semper was frowning, suspicion and anger making him look like he was boiling inside.

"Just as I told you back in that ghost town, Mulnik stole it from you, crossed you, blackmailed the studio on his own. I was hired by Luden to break that up."

"Why you—why, that little creep told me—"

"I know. He talked all over you when you caught up with him here in L.A."

"We didn't catch up with him, he called us!"

"Smart. So it looked like he wasn't trying to keep out of your way, but all he did was set you on the wrong trail, after me."

After a moment, Semper yelled, "Wrong trail? It's still his word against yours."

"Word, my foot. Why didn't Mulnik tell you where he is?"

Semper didn't answer.

"So you can't mess with his deal. He tell you he's setting things up with Luden himself?"

"Yes, and...."

"And he is, but without you. You know why?"

Semper had an idea, but was afraid to think about it.

"Because he doesn't need you. Know why he doesn't need you?"

"You son of a bitch. You talk as smooth as that Mulnik does."

"He doesn't need you because he's got the film. That makes you the dumb son of a bitch, Semper."

Port had him where he wanted him. Semper was thrown off his track, crazy with doubt, sweating with impatience.

"You want to be sure, Semper?"

"If this is all on the level, why'd he bother getting me back into it?"

"To get rid of me, idiot. Because, as I told you, I'm after him."

"And you! Why are you pulling me into it?"

"So you'll stay off my back."

"Hell, there's better ways than this, and you know it," said Semper, feel-ing his head.

"And because you can do me some good."

"Huh?"

"I told you I'm after that film."

"You think for one minute...."

"I do, Semper, because it's your only chance to get at the film yourself. An even chance. You and me after the same thing."

Semper got quiet again. He sat up, crossed his legs, and waited for the business end of the conversation.

"I figure Mulnik got the film," Port said, "not Luden, and to crack this thing I got to pry Luden and Mulnik apart."

"Go ahead," said Semper, waiting.

"I can't. I'd have to convince Luden that Mulnik is a bastard, and I can't."

"How come?"

"Because the way it is now, those two are in on the film together. They're buddies."

"What do I care? All I want is that film."

"Same here. One of them has to talk, or one of them has to run. That's how we'll know." Port took time to let it sink in, and then he said, "I want Luden to talk, and I want Mulnik to run."

"Go ahead. A smart bastard like you...."

"Like I said. That's where I need you."

"I'm not working for you."

"You want to know who's been snowing you, don't you? Mulnik or me. I'll let you hear it from the horse's mouth. Luden himself."

"Luden—"

"He scares easy, better than you even. And when he hears it from you, that Mulnik isn't as safe and as smart as he says, because now you're after him, maybe Luden will scare enough to part company."

"Where's Luden?"

Port got up. "I don't know how you been managing without me," he said. "Follow me."

Chapter 19

They got there much too early. There was dew on the shrubs and lawns and the air had a cold sting in it. Port had left his MG by the curb, further back, and had joined the bouncer and Semper in their car. They were parked close to the corner, and by stretching their necks they could see Luden's gate further up the street.

It didn't take the sun long to steam off the dew, and after a while some of the sprinklers on the big lawns came on. But there were no people in sight.

After eight a few cars came by, but except for that the streets were as empty as in the early morning.

Port had counted on that. They had to wait until after nine. Port's throat was raw from too much smoking and he wanted a cup of coffee. Or food. Just plain breakfast food would have been good.

They sat in the car, not talking, because they had nothing between them except one thing, and that had been talked about as much as it had to be. They got on each other's nerves without talking; Semper impatient to make good the raw deal and the raw treatment he had been getting; Port impatient to be done with the filthy turn in his filthy job.

"I saw something," said the bouncer.

They all jumped. They craned their necks to see movement along Luden's drive, but not enough of the drive showed.

Nothing else showed either.

"I was sure," the bouncer started, but Semper didn't let him finish.

"Shut up. Just shut up and hold that wheel."

"Don't worry about me," said the bouncer. "When I was wheel man for Pinky...."

"Shut up, damn it!" They all kept still for a short while, but with the atmosphere full of suspicion Semper had to say more or bust. He barely mumbled it but he said it was time the bouncer learned to keep his trap shut in front of strangers.

"You got things to say about me, say 'em out loud," and Port gave Semper a look.

"I'm not talking to you."

"Just keep it that way, just shut up and keep it that way," said Port. The irritation made him gnaw on his lip.

"I will. I'm just waiting my turn," said Semper.

"You'll get it. Count on it, Semper. You'll get it."

"If he ever shows," and with a short look at Port. "Or if he doesn't."

When it came, it came from the wrong direction. The big limousine rolled up the street, slowed at Luden's gate, and turned in.

"He's been out all this time!"

"He wasn't in the car, you dumb jerk. He's getting picked up."

And after a while, "What if there's two gates out of that park of his. What if...."

"That car didn't turn in there more than three minutes ago. Don't start getting upset."

"What makes you so sure? Maybe this whole stupid deal—"

"You got brains enough to work up a better one?"

They didn't get any further, and glad of it. The limousine nosed out of the gate, swinging their way, slowly.

Port was the only one with a gun. He got out of the car fast, crossed the intersection, and by the time he had reached the curb Luden had recognized him. He must have yelled it at the chauffeur, maybe giving him a start, but the limousine jerked and then picked up speed.

It missed Port, not that the chauffeur had meant to run into him, but then—with a nervous bounce—the big car came to a stop.

Semper's car had rolled across and just when the chauffeur started explaining to Luden, Semper's car pulled out of the way, the door to the limousine opened quietly, and Port sat down next to Luden.

"It's a gun," said Port. "And you, chauffeur, follow that car."

The chauffeur wanted to object, but Port had no patience.

"I'll beat your head in with it, believe me," and Port's tone of voice, and a slight move of the gun made the chauffeur drive.

Semper's car went at normal speed. Luden's car went at normal speed. From the residential parts they switched to a highway going through the hills and from there they drove partway into the valley, to a point where three motels lined the road. Semper's car took the third and the limousine followed. They had reserved the cabin at five in the morning, by phone, and while Semper walked back to the office the rest sat in their cars, sat with an evil quaking inside, wishing that whatever it was that would happen weren't true and were over.

Port had to help Luden when they got out of the car.

The cabin was small and hot. The five men in the cabin didn't look at each other, tried to stand as if they were alone.

"Sit down, Luden," said Port.

Semper looked as nervous as Luden. For other reasons. "What about him?" he said, and jerked his hand at the chauffeur.

"Bouncer," said Port, sounding too loud, "I got to spell it for you?"

At the last moment the chauffeur covered his face with his hands and when the sap hit his head he dropped straight down to the floor.

"Pick him up," said Port.

"Leave him there!" Semper's voice had an edge.

"On the bed," said Port.

The bouncer obeyed and put the unconscious chauffeur on the bed.

Meanwhile, Luden had started to cry. They all stood around Luden and waited for him to listen.

"Ask him!" screamed Semper.

Port said, "Luden. Where's the film?"

Luden didn't talk and Semper hit him.

"Luden," said Port, "where's the film?"

When Semper tried to hit him again Port caught the arm and twisted it down. Then he looked back at Luden. "See your man on the bed? He's well off, Luden—" They stood in the close room, sweating, hating each other, and waited for Luden to get over the terrible fear which made him gag on his crying.

Port had his gun out. It made Semper wait too.

"Where is it, Luden?"

"I have— I don't have it, Mulnik."

"Where," yelled Semper. "Where's he got it?"

"I don't know!"

"Why not? How come you don't know?" Port said immediately.

"He's got it. He's handling that."

"He doesn't trust you; why should he trust you, Luden?"

"He and I—we—"

"Where's he keep it?"

"I don't know!" Luden screamed.

Port waited till Luden had his breath back, and then asked, "How come, Luden?"

Luden sat still, either scared by his own scream or suddenly frozen with doubt.

"Because he's looking out for his own, Luden. He's got his ways, doing that. Tell him, Semper. Tell him about Mulnik."

"Ever hear of the doublecross, you fat bastard?"

Luden jerked back, fearful again, because Semper had bent close, still yelling.

"Luden," said Port, "tell this hood here what Mulnik said about him. His name's Semper. You recall the name?"

"Semper—"

Luden was ready to freeze again so Port grabbed his shirtfront and gave him a shake.

"What did he tell you about Semper?"

"Please—he said they used to work together."

"Used to?" Semper was livid.

"You heard him, Semper." Port stood close by Luden and went on. "What else did he say, last time I was there. What did he say about Semper?"

"He told you to lay off, or he'd set his men on you."

"What men?"

"His men. Semper and his helper."

"Did he say something else? Did he ever say you and him and his men were in on this thing together?" Port gave Luden a prod, to make him answer.

"No. Just he and I. Just Mulnik and I."

Semper hauled out, but Port was in the way, so instead of hitting Luden he started to curse, long and filthy.

When Semper was through there was an exhausted silence. Then Port stood back. He talked fast and sharp.

"How was Mulnik going to keep these hoods out of it?"

"They didn't know where he was."

"How was he going to keep it that way?"

"He wasn't sure yet, he said. But a frame, some kind of a frame."

Port pushed Semper back with the gun and told him to hear this thing out. He turned back to Luden. "Why keep them out? Was he scared?"

"No."

"But they might mess it up, for you and him?"

"Yes, he said he didn't want them in."

"Now they're in, Luden. They're back in. The going's gonna be rough. You've never seen it so rough. Not the kind of thing you're used to."

"When I get my hands on you," Semper started but then he let it drift, waiting to hear what Port's play was. "You thought being a crook's easy, Luden?"

There was no answer. Just fear.

"You think you can hold your own?"

Luden shrunk.

"You gonna stay in on this or you gonna get out?"

"No, please—"

"Look at your man on the bed there, and then answer me!"

"No! Please! I never meant—all I meant—"

"You quitting, Luden?"

"Yes! Please, yes!"

Port straightened up, wiped the sweat from his face. "Now for the clincher," he said, and he could have been saying it to himself. His voice got clear again when he pulled Luden up on his feet and said, "You're going to tell that to Mulnik. You're in deep water, too deep for you, and you're going to tell Mulnik that you're getting out. Right?"

"I will, yes."

"And tell him why. Tell him his buddies are back in on the play and it's getting too rough for you. Right?"

"I will!"

Port let go of Luden and took a deep breath. He lit a cigarette and smoked for a moment. Semper's breathing made sounds, and a floor board creaked, but nothing else happened. It felt like they were almost through.

"Semper," said Port. "Did he talk?"

"Yeah. He talked."

"And now he's going to make Mulnik run."

"Yeah. You said that."

"You came in handy." Port stepped on his cigarette. He didn't want it any more. "One more thing, Semper, and we can part company."

"Yeah?"

"I'm driving back to where Mulnik is."

"Where's that?"

"I'm driving back there and it shouldn't take more than half an hour. In forty-five minutes I want you to get Luden to make that call."

"Me? I'm staying here? Not on your life!"

"Make sense! We got to time this. I've got to be there, waiting, when Mulnik takes a powder. That's the only sure way I can get him with the merchandise on him."

"What makes you think...."

"If he hasn't got it on him he'll be going where it is. Whichever, I've got to be there."

"Like hell. I'm going to be in on this!"

Port had known it, that this was the weak spot of the whole scheme, but there hadn't been time for doing it differently. He bit his lip and then said, "All right. Leave the bouncer here. Somebody's got to time that phone call."

"You got that straight?" Semper said to the bouncer.

The bouncer nodded. He looked at Luden, but he didn't worry him. Then he looked at the chauffeur, on the bed, and he jiggled the sap in his hand.

"Maybe I better have me a gun. If they both...."

"Tie them up."

"There's no rope."

Port made an angry frown, then waved at Semper to go out of the door.

"Where's Mulnik staying?" Semper asked again.

Port didn't bother to answer him. He reached into his pocket, pulled out Semper's gun.

"Catch," he said, and the bouncer caught the gun. There was one brief moment of hesitation, as Semper's mind started to race and weighed possibilities.

"Forget it," said Port. "You don't know where Mulnik is, and I still have a gun of my own."

Semper turned abruptly and got into the car.

Chapter 20

Port drove. Neither of them talked. They sat, making the least possible movements, because had they moved as they wanted to, too much would have been destroyed. There was no air in the car, just mistrust. They breathed it, they sweated it, they heard it creak with the slightest movement.

How to get rid of each other, neither knew. That they had to get rid of each other, they both knew.

Semper raised his hand slowly, to make sure Port could see what he was going to do. He wiped his eye, then lowered his hand. He saw how Port tensed, how he controlled himself to keep going steadily.

"Look out back," said Port, very hoarse.

Semper moved as slowly as before and only at the last moment did he turn enough to look out the back window. Even then he was ready for Port's trick.

The police cruiser was charging straight down the white mid-line and the few cars on the highway didn't even move over. There was no siren, no flashing light, just the speed of the car along the white line.

"Hit it!" and Semper made a sound like at the end of a scream. "Hit it, you lousy…."

"Sit still; look ahead and sit still—"

They talked in fast whispers to keep themselves bottled up, talking fast, as if they meant to match the speed of the black bug of a car chasing up the road, chasing closer.

"Can't be for us."

"I don't care. The chance—"

"It gets worse if we race them."

"Race them? Gimme that gun."

"Keep your head, damn it."

Port didn't finish but pulled the car into an abrupt turn off the highway. Halfway through he was in second and flooring the pedal he made the wheels suddenly spin till they bit and the car churned ahead, over the gravel road, and they both sat tense waiting for the speed.

Maybe the bouncer should have been driving, maybe a regular wheelman should have been in the car, because for a long, trembling moment it was almost as if they were standing still. It felt that way when they saw the patrol car lean into the road behind them, then straighten out in their direction as if drawn by a magnet.

"How come?" Semper kept saying.

"Something went wrong, something must have gone wrong back at the motel."

They couldn't gain. They couldn't even keep the distance they had, and when the patrol car crept closer, edging to one side, and one of the cops leaned out of the window; then Semper's restraint broke. He threw himself across Port's middle, clawing for the gun in his lap, ripping Port's hands off the wheel without caring about it, and after a few crazy twists sideways with Port's desperate braking, the car lost footing at the edge of the ditch and jammed to a stop.

They didn't hear a thing outside, as if they were alone. There was a slow dust cloud over the car, the creak of hot metal under the hood, nothing else.

But when they moved, they saw him. The cop looked like he had been standing there for a while, leaning into the side window which was now on top, and he held his gun as if he didn't think he needed it.

"Can you move?" he said.

Semper scrambled around, stood on Port's hand. "You can move. Get out." This time the gun looked like business.

When Semper was sliding through the window, feet still in the air, Port found the gun. When the cop looked back in again and told Port to get out, the gun wasn't in sight any more.

On the road Semper had his arms up already. Then Port did the same and while one cop covered, the other gave them a fast frisk.

"Get in the car," and they sat down in the back seat, with one cop taking the wheel and the other looking at them over his gun.

"What for," said Port. "What's all this?"

"You're under arrest," said the cop.

"What for?"

"The book," said the cop. "That's what for."

The car started, then hunted for a turn, so they could head back to the highway.

"You lousy coppers are...."

"Shut up," said the cop to Semper.

"I wanna know what for!"

"Speeding, for one," said the cop. He thought that was very funny and laughed.

"All right, look," said Semper. "I'll give...."

"And assault and battery. And kidnaping, maybe."

They knew the works. They had found out in no more than twenty-five minutes, since Port had left the motel, what had taken him a whole day of frantic hours to figure out.

"Who tipped you?" said Port.

"Nobody tipped him. He's got delusions of grandeur."

"Who?" Port said again.

"A guy who says he's R. S. Luden's chauffeur."

"You got him?"

"Sure. He called in and we picked him up."

"You got the others?"

"Huh? Oh, yeah, sure. We found Mr. Luden in the motel. And the others."

They had Luden, and the chauffeur, but they didn't have the bouncer. Port tried to think it through fast, because the car was starting to back at a wide part of the road, and then they were going to head back for the highway. Before they got to the highway he had to decide.

The chauffeur had gotten away, far enough to make a phone call. That meant the bouncer didn't go after him. Then they had found Luden in the motel alone, because when the cop said they had found the others he was just talking. And if the bouncer didn't go after the chauffeur, stayed behind with Luden, then maybe the phone call was made.

It was worth the chance.

But Semper was ahead of him. He suddenly slapped the cop's gun in Port's direction and opened the door at his side. It happened fast then. Semper jumped and ran, Port held the cop's gun by the barrel, took his own out of his sleeve, and knocked the cop out. And by the time the driver had stopped and twisted to reach for his gun, Port was ready for him.

"I've got this gun thrown on you, so hold still," he said, and jabbed the cop in the back of the neck. "Now, get out."

The cop did, and then Port followed after.

"Look across," said Port, and waved at the overgrown field where Semper was dodging around bushes. "Go after him. He hasn't got a gun." When the cop hesitated Port said, "But I have."

The cop figured he'd get one of them anyway and started to sprint after Semper.

Then he saw that the cop who was running across the field had taken the key out of the ignition. Go after him? He had a gun too. He may have thrown the key away. No time. Mulnik must have gotten the call. Port ran.

In a way it felt better now, running back to the highway, and then the short stretch to the cut-off where the streets began. The strong, muscular work and the heavy breathing seemed like a tonic after the time in the car. Port ran without saving his strength, and when the strain grew bigger he still ran, thinking of Mulnik. His breath felt like a blow-torch in his throat and his ribs seemed to grow tighter, but he ran till he thought he would split.

After that he still kept it up, even more so, he thought, because not until then did it strike him what he had left behind. He wasn't just running after Joko Mulnik. He was running from Semper. And from the cops.

Chapter 21

When Port came up the drive to Luden's house he wasn't running on strength any more, just pure will power. And he didn't knock on any doors or ring bells, just pushed through the side entrance and stumbled into the kitchen.

The houseboy jumped up, spilling a salad he was mixing in a bowl on his lap.

"Where's Mulnik?" said Port, but the houseboy couldn't have understood and he smiled because something about Port struck him funny.

"That roadwork," he said. "You're taking it much too seriously."

"Mulnik, where is he?" said Port, and all the tension came back to him.

"Mulnik? He left, maybe twenty minutes ago."

Port felt the strength drain out of him and he let himself fall on a chair. "The bastard left," he mumbled, "he got the call and he left."

After a moment he got up and walked back and forth in the kitchen. It felt better to walk, to let his breathing catch up with him. The houseboy swept the spilled salad into a scoop and followed Port with his eyes.

"Drink a little water," said the houseboy. "Just a little. It helps settle things."

Port went to the faucet, ran water into a glass, sipped it. Then he sat down at the table again.

"Okay, now tell me about it. Mulnik left."

"You're not Mr. Luden's masseur, from the studio, are you?"

"No."

"Don't tell me about it," said the houseboy. "I'm not involved and don't want to be."

"Involved in what?"

"You and Mulnik. Whatever it is. I never thought Mr. Mulnik should have come to this house, and now that he's gone I just as soon...."

"Okay. Fine. Let me ask you something."

"Of course, go ahead." He started to make another salad and waited.

"Mulnik left," said Port. "Did he leave because of a phone call?"

"Yes. Mr. Luden called, asking for Mr. Mulnik."

Port found a cigarette and said, "You can stop calling the son of a bitch Mister all the time."

"Whom do you mean?"

"Anyway, Mulnik took the phone, and then he left?"

"Yes, very much in a hurry."

"He take his things?"

"He certainly did. He also took Mr. Luden's smoking jacket, as I discovered after."

"How did he go? Car, taxi, walk—"

"I think he walked out to find a taxi. I offered to ring him one, but...."

"Why? What about his car?"

"His car hasn't been here for the past day and a half. One fender was badly crushed."

"What garage? Where?"

Port had to wait while the houseboy put the bowl on the table and thought.

"I don't remember. Mr. Luden recommended it." Then he got up and walked to the door. "I may be able to find it in the book."

All Port could do was follow and wait.

"I'm sure that's the one," said the houseboy, and handed Port the small book they kept by the phone in the hall.

Port had the phone off the hook before he had read the number.

"Cadillac Service," said the girl.

"Gimme service," said Port.

"This is Cadillac Service," said the girl.

"Service, garage, where they fix the cars!"

"Yes, sir, I'll give you Mr. Dodge, our shop foreman."

Before Dodge was through introducing himself with his credentials Port was talking.

"Now listen close, Dodge. You got a Cadillac there, a—"

"We have *only* Cadillacs here."

Port controlled himself and exhaled through his nose. "Fine," he said. "Very good. I'm looking for one of your customers, a Mr. Mulnik...."

"One moment, please." A sharp sound jumped into Port's ear when the foreman dropped the phone on his desk.

The foreman came back when Port thought he had been forgotten. "Sorry, sir. No Mr. Mulnik in our customer book."

"Wait!"

Port didn't want the man to hang up. After a moment he said, "Perhaps I got the name wrong. I mostly know him by his first, but the car he drives is a white Cadillac convertible. It has zebra upholstery and the left front fender is shot. You're fixing it."

"Well? What do you want me to do?"

"Tell me if the car is still there!"

"Listen, mister, you don't seem to know how big a place we got here. I can't waste my time."

"I've got to reach that guy. When he finds out I tried to locate him and you didn't cooperate…."

"Look, if you say it's here, it's here. I haven't checked out one like that, so maybe it's here."

"Dodge, do me one favor. Walk down the length of the shop you got there and just…."

"Are you one of our customers, sir?"

"I drive an MG," said Port and hung up.

The address of the garage was on Western, and Port checked with the houseboy, because he wanted to know how far away the garage was.

"Way down on Western. Near downtown."

Port cursed, feeling the time shrink in on him from all sides. He rushed back to the hall and picked up the phone again. He got Flint on the line immediately and Flint started talking before Port had a chance.

"Look, Mr. Port, I know you done me a favor and all, but…."

"Shut up and listen, you haven't even heard what I want."

"I know, but the last thing you wanted could get me in trouble, you know."

"I need a detective. You want the job?"

"Yes!" said Flint.

"There's a garage on Western." Port gave him the address. "Go down there and check if they got Mulnik's car. You know Mulnik's car?"

"White, with leopard…."

"Zebra! Zebra upholstery."

"Yes, zebra."

"Hightail it down there right away, and call me back as soon as you've checked."

"Have I got your number?"

Port gave it to him. "And if you see Mulnik there, don't let him spot you! If he does, make up anything, just so my name isn't in it. Understand?"

"Absolutely."

"And call back immediately. Is the car there, where did it go if it isn't, when is Mulnik going to pick it up if it is, et cetera. Understand?"

"Right. I'll ring you in fifteen minutes."

Not to go crazy for fifteen minutes Port had the houseboy show him the room where Joko Mulnik used to stay, and he went over it completely and furiously. But no better than Mulnik had. There wasn't a thing.

"Did Mulnik have any valuables along, something he might have put in a safe?"

"We can look," said the houseboy.

Port swallowed his surprise and followed.

The safe was empty, except for some bonds and a personal letter. The letter was old and pink, with some penciled crosses on the back flap.

"You are surprised?" said the houseboy and smiled.

"No. I'm sure he had a girl friend one time or another."

Port put the letter back and watched the houseboy close the safe.

"I've read it," said the houseboy. "It's very old."

Port walked away, wishing the phone would ring.

It rang when he passed it, in the hall, making him jump.

"Hello?"

"Mr. Port?"

"I'm listening, Flint. What?"

"It's here. I found it."

"Mulnik's car? When do they expect him."

"Well, I had a time finding...."

"Come on, Flint, come on. When's he gonna pick it up?"

"He's been here."

"What!"

"I found the car, like I said, and talking there to the helper I spot Mulnik. He just comes in."

"Where is he?"

"He comes in, goes out again. He didn't see me, I'm sure, because he never looked around and I saw him first. He's real busy, the way he can look sometimes, goes to his car, fiddles around a while, then goes out again."

"You let him go, you stupid...."

"Now, wait a minute, wait a minute. I couldn't help that right then, and besides, I didn't think it was that urgent."

"Flint. What in hell made you think—"

"He's coming back. You didn't let me finish."

"When?"

"He talks to the foreman here and the way the place is arranged, and from where I'm standing, I hear him ask the foreman when he can have the car. At ten in the evening, the foreman said. Mulnik's gonna pick it up at ten in the evening."

"Did he talk to that Dodge, the foreman called Dodge?"

"No. That one's in the body shop. Mulnik's car is in the paint shop."

"Ten in the evening," said Port. "You're sure? That's a hell of a long time to wait for a fender to get painted up, if you're in a hurry."

"Fender nothing, he's having the whole car painted up! Painted black."

"Jesus!" said Port.

After a while Flint asked if Port was still on the line, and if Port wanted him to do something else.

"No— Yes, you did fine, Flint. Real fine."

"Looks like he's leaving town, doesn't it, Mr. Port?"

"Yeah. For serious. Look, Flint. When he came in and walked out again. What did he do at the car?"

"Nothing. He just looked it over."

"Did he bring any luggage?"

"No, nothing. He just walked around the car, sort of checking it over. The trunk even."

"Trunk?"

"Yes. Looked inside, even checked all the tools."

"That's all?"

"From where I was standing. Anyway, he didn't have any luggage or any-thing. He just walked in, and then out. Except for checking the car and talk-ing to the paint shop foreman."

"Good," said Port. "Very good."

"Want me to do anything else?"

"No, nothing now."

"You want me to look for Mulnik?"

"I don't think that would do much good, Flint. You can check around, on my time, but I doubt if you'll have any luck."

"I know some of the places and people he used to hang around with, you know."

"He's all set to leave town tonight, so why should he queer it for himself by hanging out where he's known."

"He's got to stay someplace."

"So he'll go to a movie. Or some hole in the wall."

"Sounds most likely."

"Anyway, thanks. If you hear anything, call me up at this number."

"Sure will."

"I'll be up to pay you," said Port and hung up.

Port felt much better. Mulnik was sneaking around with the feeling of eyes on the back of his neck. He was going to run and for the few hours in be-tween he wasn't going to make any mistakes. Even showing up at the garage, just to hang around and chitchat with the help, even that wasn't the thing Mulnik would do. Mulnik felt too close to winning and too close to losing the lot, for any carelessness now. He wouldn't even walk around town, or sit in a movie, or hide in some hole in the wall, without figuring how it would be if he were caught. He wasn't going to be caught with any Ella Anders film on his person. And Port thought he knew now where the film was.

Chapter 22

Of course there was still Semper, and, more important, the police. But they hadn't been here yet; Semper, because he was running the wrong way when Port last saw him, and because the cop had most likely caught up with him; and the police hadn't showed up yet, because they didn't seem to know any good reason to do so. What could Luden tell them—that Port was at his house? No reason why he should think so. No reason why he should even tell the police that there was or had been a blackmailer in his house. The longer Luden could keep Mulnik out of his conversations, the better off he'd think he was.

Port left the house by the front and walked fast through the park. No need to creep along bushes. It would be different once he got out on the streets, once he drove through the city to get to the garage. If Luden had dropped the name Port, they'd know a lot. They had written down a lot the last time they hauled him in, including the car he was driving.

They both stopped dead at the gate, to keep from running into each other, to keep from killing each other on sight.

"You're in a hurry," said Semper. "You had an idea, maybe, you were gonna make it?"

They stood tense, hands like claws, and Port knew that if he tried drawing his gun Semper would jump him because he stood close enough and was that far gone.

"Don't hold me up now," said Port "Move over."

"Where's the film?"

"Mulnik has it."

"You got here first, you double-crossing creep, so don't tell me Mulnik has it."

Port made a move to get by when Semper jumped him. They held for a while, deadlocked.

"Semper, you're going to ruin it. Mulnik's gone. There's nothing here."

"I'm coming along."

Port tried kneeing Semper, but it didn't work. They held like before, deadlocked.

"I'm coming along, after Mulnik, or we stay here till it's too late," said Semper.

They breathed at each other, each could see the small veins in the other man's eyeballs.

"It's your loss too."

"I got more to lose," said Semper, "letting you go."

Port knew he could break the grip, then shoot the man. He wouldn't get rid of him any other way. No other way. No other way, unless he took him along. Shake him later, somehow.

"I'm coming along," Semper said again.

"All right. Let's go."

"You shoot me, and it's over. Somebody's gonna come outa their park or look up from the teacup...."

"I'm not dumb. Let's go."

They walked down the street together, fast and very close. They came to the corner and stopped.

Port's MG was still there, as it had been early in the morning. And now a patrolman stood by the curb, leafing the pages of the notebook he had, and keeping one finger on the pages that was open he looked at the MG—at the license plate, then back at the book. He slapped the book shut and ran down the street.

Port and Semper saw the last part after they had already turned back the way they had come. The move was automatic, just to get away, but by the time Port decided to do something else they were halfway back to the Luden gate and there was the houseboy.

"Mr. Port!"

Port turned on his heel; he wanted to get back to his car while the cop was still at his callbox.

"Mr. *Port!*" The houseboy had run up, talking. "The phone for you. Somebody named Flint on the phone...."

"Not now—"

"Very important. He insists it's very important."

The cop had made his call. He was coming back. He was going to guard that MG.

They all turned back and went through the Luden gate, through the park, into the house. The phone was lying on the table, waiting.

"Hello, Flint?"

"Yes, now listen to this. I got Joko."

"You what?"

"He walked in just a few minutes ago, to pay me off for that check deal a while back. Pay me off to forget all about it, he said."

"Where is he now?"

"I'm coming to that. He's here, out front with the girl. He wants me to put him up till evening!"

It was a setup, but it wasn't any good. Mulnik would sit there, wait his time until ten o'clock, and Port couldn't get to him. Semper had fouled that for him. Port couldn't get out of here without being spotted in no time at all, assuming the cops that would start swarming into the neighborhood didn't nail him right on the steps of Luden's front door.

"Flint. Hang up. Stay by the phone, because I'm calling right back."

Flint didn't get it but the phone went dead and then Port hung up. He didn't hang up the receiver, just pressed down the buttons. Then he dialed Flint's number, and Flint himself said hello.

"Do what I say, Flint. Say: 'Ah, yes, sir, yes, sir!'" Flint said it. He sounded overwhelmed and honored. "Can Mulnik hear you if you raise your voice?"

"Sure, he—uh—yes sir, indeed!"

"He's not in the room with you."

"No sir."

"Fine. You're now listening to a call from R. S. Luden. Understand? I'm R. S. Luden. I'm trying to locate Joko Mulnik, or leave a message for him, and I'm calling you because I can't locate Mulnik anywhere but I remember your name from the check I made out to your firm. Got that?"

"Of course, sir. I will!"

"Don't overdo it. Now here's what Luden said: The cops got Port, and they got Semper. Luden is alone in his house and wants Mulnik to hightail it over here. Very important that he come as fast as he can. Port and Semper are out of the way, the cops have been thrown off, and Mulnik should rush over here because of some contract matter. Got it?"

"Yes sir, Mr. L...."

"Don't say that name, for God's sake, or he'll rush in on you and want to speak to me!"

"Ah—of course, sir. I will."

Flint hung up, but the phone wasn't all cradled yet when his door flew open and Mulnik dashed in.

"What did you say? Luden? You just talk to...."

"Oh—I thought you'd gone to the can, Joko. That was Luden. I didn't know...."

"What did he say? Where is he?"

"He left a message."

Flint paused, watching Mulnik hold his breath.

"You should come down to his house immediately."

"Luden said that?"

"Let me finish the message. The police got both Port—I think the name was—and somebody called Semper. Luden is waiting for you at his house, about something important that has to do with a contract."

Mulnik narrowed his eyes. When he talked he hardly moved a muscle. "His house? Why?"

"I don't know. He didn't say." Flint started to sweat under his shirt, not knowing how to handle Mulnik's suspicion. "The only other thing he said was that the cops—he said policemen—were way off the track, so right now was the time for you to get over there. Something about a contract."

"He said that, huh?"

"That's all I remember."

"His house? Why not the studio?"

"Christ, how should I know?" Flint got up, acting angry, to conceal how nervous he was. When he turned back to his desk, he saw Mulnik pick up the phone and start dialing. There was nothing Flint could do, so he went into the next room, looking busy at one of his files.

"Hello," said Mulnik. "Lemme talk to your boss."

"Is this Mr. Mulnik?" said the houseboy. He sounded as smooth and unconcerned as he always did.

"Lemme talk to Luden."

"I'm sorry, Mr. Mulnik. Mr. Luden is on another line."

"Well, tell him...."

"It's studio business, Mr. Mulnik, rather important. Uh— I know Mr. Luden just tried getting in touch with you. Did you get his message?"

"Message?" said Mulnik, and waited.

"Mr. Luden is expecting you, rather anxiously. Can we count on you?"

"He still on that other phone?"

"A conference call, with several parties on the line at the same time. I believe— One moment, Mr. Mulnik. The door."

"Hey, listen—"

"Miss Anders just came in. You will have to excuse me, Mr. Mulnik."

"I'm coming! Tell him to hold everything till—"

The houseboy hung up in the middle of Joko's sentence, and Port hung up at the other phone, after Joko did.

"Satisfactory?" asked the houseboy when Port came back into the hall.

"A beaut. Thank you."

The houseboy nodded and went back to his kitchen.

Now to wait and see who would get here first, the police or Mulnik. Semper was thinking the same thing. He got up from the stairs where he had been sitting and ground his cigarette out on the floor.

"I'm getting out," he said. "Either way you look at it, the cops'll be here some time."

"They got a head start," said Port.

"I'm just fading for this deal, you understand. Don't count me out."

"Bye, Semper."

"You double-crossing son of a bitch," said Semper, and made for the back.

Port let him go the way a hunter sets out a decoy. If Semper could get very far, Port would try it. But Semper ruined that.

The houseboy came out of the kitchen, with his salad bowl—and Port had to wonder why the houseboy kept making salad—when Semper ran into him. The salad spilled down his front, the houseboy apologized, and if it had been anybody but Semper that would have been the end of it. But Semper had to swing. He cursed and swung at the houseboy's head.

With sudden force Semper smacked down on the floor, screaming. The houseboy did know jujitsu.

There was no time for Port to wonder whether Semper could have made it outside. The bell rang, and the house-boy went to answer it. There hadn't been enough time for Mulnik to make it.

Port faded into the next room. They would find him. His own fault. But maybe a little delay would show him a way out.

"Police," came through the open front door. "May we come in?"

"Mr. Luden is not at home."

"We know that," and the footsteps made cracks on the tile floor.

"Who's that back there?" The footsteps crossed the hall, then stopped where Semper would have to be.

"Up on your feet."

"Christ! My arm!"

"What happened here? Hey, you—"

"We quarreled," said the houseboy. "Mr. Semper tried to get away before you arrived."

"What you do, break his back?"

"The shoulder, only a sprain."

"All right, gimme a hand. George, get the others in here. I think we struck pay dirt."

One pair of feet ran to the front door, two pairs of feet, with a third barely moving, came towards the room where Port had been listening. He went past the fireplace, through the archway, and into the next room. It had gun cases and a bar. Port wiped his Magnum and laid it into one of the gun cases. While the men in the next room were sitting down, Port looked around. Nowhere to go. He would wait; no point in heroics. It would be very much nicer if he didn't have to get involved with the police, but one couldn't have everything. There was a couch in the room, in one dark corner, and Port lay down. He would lie there, listen, and wait.

"Go through the house," the voice said. "The other one must be around too."

Port lay there for a long while, listening, very sorry that nothing went on in the next room. Semper was still there and somebody else.

Then they all came back, shuffling in the hall, until somebody said they should go outside and, except for two of them, should cover the landscape.

"How about that room?" it said, and the footsteps crossed where the fireplace would have to be.

Port sighed, and waited.

"I doubt it. Let's ask this joker a few questions."

"I'll ask Frank to take a look. Hey, Frank!"

Frank came in from the hall, and was told to take a look in the next room, and to hurry it, because they wanted to get started with Semper and no interruptions. Frank wore a uniform. He came through the arch, the houseboy with him.

"Where's that door go?"

"Out to the hall," said the houseboy.

Frank looked around for a little, and pretty soon he saw Port. "Who's that?"

"A friend of mine," said the houseboy.

"Friend of yours? What's he doing?"

"Mr. Luden's health coach. He's drunk."

Port took the cue and lay still.

"When Mr. Luden didn't show up for his regular session, my friend sat down in the bar. Here is the bar, you see." The houseboy laughed. "It happens, you know."

They were talking in the next room, and Frank didn't feel right about this.

"Get him outa here. We can't have an interrogation going on with a drunk lying here."

There was grunting and groaning when the houseboy helped Port off the couch, and Frank just stood around long enough to see the two friends start up the stairs. Then he stood in the hall for a while, but the voices in the room with the fireplace were getting excited. Frank went in and stationed himself at the door.

"You got any sense, Semper, you open up and tell us where that buddy of yours went to."

"I been telling you, you thickheaded flatfoot! He was here with me! Right here in this house!"

"Stop yelling."

"He's here!"

"Why should he be? He as stupid as you are?"

"Not as stupid as you, letting him get out of the house with a million dumb dicks in the bushes!"

"I'm gonna bust your other shoulder, friend, if you keep slandering the force like you been doing."

"Leave him be," said the other detective. "He's mad."

"Copper, listen!" It sounded like a pleading.

"My name's George. Lieutenant George. And this is my partner, Sergeant Sherman."

"You dicks make me sick."

Semper got a hard push in the chest, making him sit back in the cushions and gasp.

"Now, Semper." Lieutenant George tried to look confidential. "Where's your buddy?"

"That creep is no buddy of mine, don't you get it? I been trying to tell you that creep is no buddy of mine!"

"You mean Port?"

"Yeah, Port, I never heard of no Port till he started—"

Semper didn't know how to finish.

"Started doing what?" asked the lieutenant. "Muscle in on your blackmail?"

Semper gasped, but said nothing.

"Luden told us. He says you were blackmailing him."

Semper choked with the sheer frustration of it, never having gotten so far as to blackmail Luden.

"Don't bother denying it," said the lieutenant. "One of our defecting brothers spilled the beans. Remember that cop in Palmedo?"

Shot, all shot. A smooth, high-class racket all shot to hell. Semper was exhausted. "Copper, listen to me—"

"George, Lieutenant George."

"Yeah. Please. I was in on it, sure, I didn't know all of it, but I was in on the filming. I'm a darkroom man, see?"

"Lemme see your hands, darkroom man." Sherman grabbed Semper's hand, palm up, then tossed it away. "Smooth and beautiful. Ever see the stains on a darkroom man?"

"I'm trying to tell you!" Semper was screaming again. "You let the top man get away! Right here in this house you let—"

"That's not what our brother in Palmedo kept telling us. He says Port was an outsider."

"Outsider my foot!"

"You kept telling us, Semper, he's no buddy of yours."

"Look. He's got his own outfit. He was selling merchandise to this Luden guy."

"Luden says different. He says Port's in with you."

"I don't know who he is," Semper said in a monotone, "I'm telling you straight. I don't know who he is."

George and Sherman looked at each other, and what Semper had said sounded exactly the way they would have said it. They didn't know who Port was in this picture. Semper and Luden and the cop in Palmedo all had different versions.

"Let's start all over, Semper. What are you doing in town?"

"I just follow orders. The cop in Palmedo sent me down here."

"Why'd you beat up Luden?"

"I didn't. Port did. He said—"

"So Port gives the orders."

"Yeah. He and that cop in—"

"How come Luden says you were muscling in on Port's racket?"

"He's nuts! He even hired Port."

"To stop you from blackmailing Luden?"

"I didn't stop—I never did blackmail Luden."

"Shut up a minute," They all listened to the two footsteps in the hall.

"Mr. Mulnik," said the houseboy and stepped aside to allow Mulnik a ceremonious entrance.

Mulnik saw Semper first and then the uniformed cop inside the door. Mulnik didn't know about the houseboy's jujitsu and when he found himself fly into the room and land hard, he still didn't know how it had happened.

"That's the bastard! That's the bastard behind this whole mess!" Semper kept yelling.

They made Mulnik sit down next to Semper, and then the lieutenant and his partner just sat there listening, while Mulnik and Semper confused everything with their loud accusations. They blamed one another for true and for false things, and when the cops stopped them it was out of sheer desperation.

"You're a gold mine, the both of you. But there'll be plenty of chance for you to say everything over again. Over and over."

"I got nothing to say," Mulnik talked fast. "I been helping Mr. Luden ward off these blackmail attempts."

"How come Luden never mentioned that fact?"

"It's a discreet business."

"Then how come he kept yelling Port was hired by him, and not you?"

"He did? He couldn't have said that. I been fighting Port ever since—"

"You been working for Luden?"

"That's what I trying to tell you."

"Then how come we find a receipt to Port, for services rendered, in Luden's office?"

"How do I know who that guy hires?"

"You should. Semper says you cooked up the whole scheme."

"What scheme, what scheme?"

"Victimizing Luden. Luden, you agree, is the only victim here."

"Victim! That fat jerk was in on the whole deal!"

"Ah!" said Lieutenant George and Sergeant Sherman simultaneously.

"That's right! You didn't know that? Why, he even—"

"He even took you in on the deal, is that it?"

"I'm not talking," said Mulnik.

"Me neither," said Semper.

"You done fine, so far."

The two cops got up, and the two men on the couch did the same. Then they found themselves handcuffed together.

"How come us?" said Mulnik. "How about Luden?"

"We got him," said Sherman.

"And Port?" said Semper.

"All we can figure about Port is he was up against all of you."

"We'll get him," added the lieutenant. "He might even give you guys a clean bill of health. You'd like that, wouldn't you, if we brought in Port?"

Semper and Mulnik kept silent.

The house seemed very quiet after they had gone.

Chapter 23

When it was dark Port came downstairs and had a cup of coffee in the kitchen. The houseboy offered him food, but Port didn't feel much like it. He had some of the salad. It filled the stomach and didn't require an appetite.

He let the houseboy bring him up to date but kept fidgeting all through the story. He wanted to be done with the job. It wasn't done till he had the film.

Just to be sure, Port left his MG where it was and let the houseboy get him a taxi.

"Thanks for your help," he said at the door. "And the salad."

The houseboy shrugged and gave a slight smile.

"Ella Anders is one of my favorites," he said, and closed the door after Port.

At ten in the evening Cadillac Service was as busy as at ten in the morning. Port told the taxi to wait and walked into the place without asking directions. That way, nobody paid any attention to him. He found the paint shop, then he found the car, shiny black now.

Enough people were walking around, or standing around or waiting for cars, that Port walked right up to the trunk of the Cadillac and tried the lid, like an owner. He hadn't realized just how jumpy he was till he tried the lid. It didn't open.

Almost like panic, he thought. A night and a day like hell, and now almost over, and now this. And for the past few seconds he had been staring right at the keys, hanging on a small chain from the shift under the wheel. Easy, he said to himself, easy. The trunk opened, a large empty trunk. Where were the tools?

He found the tools and nothing else. Tools, a tire, an empty trunk.

Easy, he said, easy now, and slowly sat down on the rim of the trunk.

Maybe a cigarette, just sit there with a cigarette for a while. Then look again.

Tools, a tire, an empty trunk.

Port shaped a whistle with his mouth, but at first made no sound. Gradually it became a one-tone beat, then he stopped abruptly.

All right, think of it this way. I'm looking into a trunk because I know something is there. What's there, in detail now, in slow detail.

Tools, a tire—no. In *detail*. Start over.

A jack, a screw driver, a tire wrench, screw driver bits lying loose in the bottom, a hammer, a tire, an empty trunk?

Again. A jack, a screw driver, a screw driver with big metal handle, a tire wrench, screw driver, bits lying loose—a screw driver with a big, fat metal handle and loose bits in the bottom of the trunk. Port found the screw driver slippery in his hand, and trying to open the cap of the handle he was suddenly running with sweat.

Once off, the cap showed a black hole. Black with the rough edge of 16-mm. film.

He had to use one of the bits to pry the tight roll out of the handle. Then another roll, and another, and the last one somewhat smaller than the rest. Mulnik had cut up the film, rolled each part tight, stuffed the tight rolls into the handle on top of each other. All of it? Must be. Why else was the last roll much smaller. He left the trunk open and walked out of the place.

"Miss Anders has retired," said the maid.

"Call her, please. She'll sleep better."

Ella Anders came down the stairs, still putting her robe over the pyjamas. She was too anxious to move slowly, but too afraid to call out to him. Port watched her come down, and for the moment forgot about everything else. It must be being overtired, he thought, the way he registered details. A blue thing like a smock, just down to the hips, and instead of pyjama pants, little shorts of the same material. There were tiny flowers all over, very tiny. Come to think of it, he had never seen her legs. Fine, strong thighs, full calves, ankles like....

"Dan?" she said, and looked up at him.

"Oh. I'm sorry."

"You look tired. Some coffee?"

"Please."

She nodded at the maid and turned to go into the nearest room.

"Elly," he said. "Here. You don't have to wait any longer."

She saw the rolls in his hand, and a soft warmth of gratefulness came over her face. She walked back to Port and leaned against him, her hands on his arms.

"Thank you," she said. "Thank you, Dan."

His face was in her hair and he rubbed his cheek, once, briefly.

"You're welcome."

They went into the room off the hall and after Ella Anders had found the light they sat by the low table. Port put the film there.

"Was it hard?" she asked.

"Yes."

"And you did it."

Port smiled at her.

"I was hoping I'd see you sit there, the way you look now, all rid of it and yourself again."

She smiled back at him.

"You look very beautiful now," he said.

"That's how it feels," she said.

"I'm glad."

The maid came in with the coffee, and Ella Anders pushed the film aside and gave Port his cup.

"I must tell you something," she said.

"First burn it," said Port.

She took the rolls, got up, and put them into the fireplace. Port gave her a match. When the film started to burn she looked up at Port and wrinkled her nose.

"Smells bad," she said.

They laughed and went back to the table.

"I must tell you something, Dan. I think you won't mind."

"Tell me."

"You rushed, and you must have worked very hard, to get this thing finished for me. Because of the contract."

"Believe me. Not just the contract."

She nodded. "I'm not signing it. I'm not signing another one."

"You're not?"

"I've thought about it very much. It was very hard, at first, but then it was very easy. I don't want this any more—" she looked around—"the big empty house, or the house crammed full and crowded."

"Good. You look very happy about it."

"I am. I'm going to get married. Husband and children and everything."

"Ah. Congratulations."

She laughed, shaking her head. "Not yet. I don't have a husband yet."

"Who's it going to be? Do I know him?"

She finished sipping her coffee and put down the cup.

"I don't know him myself yet."

"Oh. You're just starting to look."

"Don't sound so worried, Dan. You don't think I can find one?"

He hadn't known how she could act the coquette, and they both laughed, because she had done it so well.

"I'm not worried," he said. "You'll have your choice."

"I mean to." They laughed again.

Port got up and she got up with him and then she put out her hand.

"Thank you again, Dan. For all of it."

"You'll let me know when you're married?"

"I will. But you may have to watch very closely, in the papers."

"I doubt that."

"And every time I have a baby, I'll let you know."

She opened the door for him and before he turned she pulled down his face, for a kiss.

"Good-by, Dan." She stood watching him walk away.

She closed the door, feeling happy, and she hoped that Port did too....

Port didn't, for a while yet, because Tess Dolphin was clearly not interested when he started explaining. "Who cares?" she kept saying all through his talking. "Who cares?"

"I'm trying to tell you—"

"I know. I was there."

"Those interruptions—"

"I'm sick of interruptions. I'm sick of talking and interrupting."

"I'm trying to explain—"

"I'm sick of explaining," she said. "Understand?"

He understood fast enough when she gave him a sudden hug and a strong kiss. Then they drove out to an empty beach with nothing but surf sounds and night sky where nobody would know where they were.

THE END

Other Stark House books you may enjoy...

Clifton Adams Death's Sweet Song /
Whom Gods Destroy $19.95
Benjamin Appel Brain Guy / Plunder $19.95
Benjamin Appel Sweet Money Girl /
Life and Death of a Tough Guy $21.95
Malcolm Braly Shake Him Till He Rattles /
It's Cold Out There $19.95
Gil Brewer Wild to Possess / A Taste for Sin $19.95
Gil Brewer A Devil for O'Shaugnessy /
The Three-Way Split $14.95
Gil Brewer Nude on Thin Ice /
Memory of Passion $19.95
W. R. Burnett It's Always Four O'Clock /
Iron Man $19.95
W. R. Burnett Little Men, Big World /
Vanity Row $19.95
Catherine Butzen Thief of Midnight $15.95
James Hadley Chase Come Easy—Go Easy /
In a Vain Shadow $19.95
Andrew Coburn Spouses & Other Crimes $15.95
Jada M. Davis One for Hell $19.95
Jada M. Davis Midnight Road $19.95
Bruce Elliott One is a Lonely Number /
Elliott Chaze Black Wings Has My Angel $19.95
Don Elliott/Robert Silverberg
Gang Girl / Sex Bum $19.95
Don Elliott/Robert Silverberg
Lust Queen / Lust Victim $19.95
Feldman & Gartenberg (ed)
The Beat Generation & the Angry Young Men $19.95
A. S. Fleischman Look Behind You Lady /
The Venetian Blonde $19.95
A. S. Fleischman Danger in Paradise /
Malay Woman $19.95
A. S. Fleischman The Sun Worshippers /
Yellowleg $19.95
Ed Gorman The Autumn Dead /
The Night Remembers $19.95
Arnold Hano So I'm a Heel / Flint /
The Big Out $23.95
Orrie Hitt The Cheaters / Dial "M" for Man $19.95
Elisabeth Sanxay Holding Lady Killer /
Miasma $19.95
Elisabeth Sanxay Holding The Death Wish /
Net of Cobwebs $19.95
Elisabeth Sanxay Holding Strange Crime in Bermuda /
Too Many Bottles $19.95
Elisabeth Sanxay Holding The Old Battle-Ax /
Dark Power $19.95
Elisabeth Sanxay Holding The Unfinished Crime /
The Girl Who Had to Die $19.95
Elisabeth Sanxay Holding Speak of the Devil /
The Obstinate Murderer $19.95
Russell James Underground / Collected Stories $14.95
Day Keene Framed in Guilt / My Flesh is Sweet $19.95
Day Keene Dead Men Don't Talk / Hunt the Killer /
Too Hot to Hold $23.95

Mercedes Lambert Dogtown / Soultown $14.95
Dan J. Marlowe/Fletcher Flora/Charles Runyon
Trio of Gold Medals $15.95
Dan J. Marlowe The Name of the Game is Death /
One Endless Hour $19.95
Stephen Marlowe Violence is My Business /
Turn Left for Murder $19.95
McCarthy & Gorman (ed) Invasion of the
Body Snatchers: A Tribute $19.95
Wade Miller The Killer / Devil on Two Sticks $19.95
Wade Miller Kitten With a Whip /
Kiss Her Goodbye $19.95
Rick Ollerman Turnabout / Shallow Secrets $19.95
Vin Packer Something in the Shadows /
Intimate Victims $19.95
Vin Packer The Damnation of Adam Blessing /
Alone at Night $19.95
Vin Packer Whisper His Sin /
The Evil Friendship $19.95
Richard Powell A Shot in the Dark /
Shell Game $14.95
Bill Pronzini Snowbound / Games $14.95
Peter Rabe The Box / Journey Into Terror $19.95
Peter Rabe Murder Me for Nickels /
Benny Muscles In $19.95
Peter Rabe Blood on the Desert /
A House in Naples $19.95
Peter Rabe My Lovely Executioner /
Agreement to Kill $19.95
Peter Rabe Anatomy of a Killer /
A Shroud for Jesso $14.95
Peter Rabe The Silent Wall /
The Return of Marvin Palaver $19.95
Peter Rabe Kill the Boss Good-By /
Mission for Vengeance $19.95
Peter Rabe Dig My Grave Deep / The Out is Death /
It's My Funeral $21.95
Brian Ritt Paperback Confidential:
Crime Writers $19.95
Sax Rohmer Bat Wing / Fire-Tongue $19.95
Douglas Sanderson Pure Sweet Hell /
Catch a Fallen Starlet $19.95
Douglas Sanderson The Deadly Dames /
A Dum-Dum for the President $19.95
Charlie Stella Johnny Porno $15.95
Charlie Stella Rough Riders $15.95
John Trinian North Beach Girl /
Scandal on the Sand $19.95
Harry Whittington A Night for Screaming /
Any Woman He Wanted $19.95
Harry Whittington To Find Cora /
Like Mink Like Murder / Body and Passion $23.95
Harry Whittington Rapture Alley / Winter Girl /
Strictly for the Boys $23.95
Charles Williams Nothing in Her Way /
River Girl $19.95

Stark House Press, 1315 H Street, Eureka, CA 95501
707-498-3135 www.StarkHousePress.com

Retail customers: freight-free, payment accepted by check or paypal via website. Wholesale: 40%, freight-free on 10 mixed copies or more, returns accepted. All books available direct from publisher or Baker & Taylor Books.

Made in the USA
Charleston, SC
14 December 2014